Also by Stephen McCauley

The Object of My Affection

The Easy Way Out

The Man of the House

True Enough

Alternatives to Sex

Insignificant Others

My Ex-Life

You Only Call When

You're in Trouble

You Only Call When

You're in Trouble

A Novel

Stephen McCauley

Henry Holt and Company New York

Henry Holt and Company
Publishers since 1866
120 Broadway
New York, New York 10271
www.henryholt.com

Henry Holt® and 🅗® are registered trademarks of Macmillan Publishing
Group, LLC.

Library of Congress Cataloging-in-Publication Data

Names: McCauley, Stephen, author.
Title: You only call when you're in trouble / Stephen McCauley.
Other titles: You only call when you are in trouble
Description: First edition. | New York : Henry Holt and Company, 2024.
Identifiers: LCCN 2023017122 (print) | LCCN 2023017123 (ebook) |
    ISBN 9781250296795 (hardcover) | ISBN 9781250296801 (ebook)
Subjects: LCGFT: Novels.
Classification: LCC PS3563.C33757 Y68 2024 (print) | LCC PS3563.C33757
    (ebook) | DDC 813/.54—dc23/eng/20230413
LC record available at https://lccn.loc.gov/2023017122
LC ebook record available at https://lccn.loc.gov/2023017123

Our books may be purchased in bulk for promotional, educational,
or business use. Please contact your local bookseller or the Macmillan
Corporate and Premium Sales Department at (800) 221-7945, extension
5442, or by e-mail at MacmillanSpecialMarkets@macmillan.com.

First Edition 2024

Designed by Meryl Sussman Levavi

Printed in the United States of America

10 9 8 7 6 5 4 3 2 1

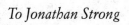

To Jonathan Strong

You Only Call When

You're in Trouble

*T*hus far, Dorothy had written her daughter three versions of the email inviting her to the opening of her retreat center in Woodstock, New York, but she hadn't had the nerve to send any of them. In each message, she'd said that, along with wanting Cecily at the "gala"—the term her business partner had insisted upon using—she needed to talk with her. "There's something important I'm finally ready to tell you," she'd written in the first draft. Direct and honest, but she'd chickened out before sending it. Too ominous in tone. Cecily would think she had a terminal disease.

"There's something you and I need to discuss" had been the second version. After reading it a third time, Dorothy was troubled by the portentous ring. It sounded almost like she was about to scold Cecily. In thirty-four years, she'd never once scolded Cecily. That was for more conventional, disciplinary, and—let's face it—boring mothers. She couldn't stand the suggestion that she was about to start now.

When she composed and rejected the third and most-watered-down version ("I'd love for us to chat"), Dorothy had to admit her main concern wasn't Cecily's reaction but her own misgivings. Bringing up the topic in even the most obtuse way induced a flutter of anxiety that was akin to a heart palpitation, a symptom she now knew too well.

At this hour of morning, the sunlight that poured through the huge new window Dorothy had installed in the building she'd bought almost a year ago was blinding. Everyone who walked into the place praised it and raved about "the light." There was that, but the truth was, she preferred rooms in which the weather and the time of day were easy to avoid or ignore. When she lived outside Boston, she'd sometimes sneaked off to the casino in Connecticut and spent a day or two there. She'd always been drawn to gambling, but more than anything, she loved being in a place where time didn't exist.

She shouldn't have let her designer friends talk her into this expensive addition. Because she had, she'd do what she'd always done: fake loving it in the hope that, eventually, she really would. That hadn't worked with her first boyfriend or her ex-husband, but it had been an effective strategy with sushi and T. S. Eliot.

She repositioned her laptop to face away from the sun and tried the email again.

Finally telling her daughter the truth about her father was the right thing to do. It was time. Cecily had been with the same boyfriend for a few years now, and at some point, they might get married and have a baby. People cared about DNA these days, especially when it revealed interesting roots—that one drop of Egyptian blood that connected you directly to Cleopatra. Cecily had a right to know hers. No royalty in their background that Dorothy knew of, but certainly an element of the unexpected.

The problem was that Dorothy was proud of how honest and blunt she'd always been with Cecily, right from childhood. It had been the guiding principle of her relationship with her. She'd talked with her daughter about her problems with men, her use of drugs, Tom's (her brother and Cecily's uncle) sexuality, even the love affairs of the assorted people who sometimes stayed with them. She'd always treated Cecily like a (much) younger friend. Telling her now that she'd known the identity of her father all along and, obviously, how to contact him would be an admission of her having lied about this crucial piece of information for decades. She hated to paint herself as a liar, especially as a result of telling the truth. She couldn't bear the thought of turning Cecily against her.

She read over the email yet again. She had to send this off. The opening party—the word *gala* had the same cringe factor for her as *town home*—was in two weeks, and she'd promised Fiona, her business partner, she would invite as many people as possible. In fairness, she needed to give Cecily advance warning and time to make plans. The whole point of including these hints was to demolish the option of changing her mind about telling her.

The retreat center was Dorothy's last chance at a business success, a way to redeem herself for past disappointments, to repay Tom what she owed him, and to leave Cecily a small legacy. Fiona had assured her that with her name (made from a bestselling self-help book Dorothy hadn't read yet), they could run a couple of weekend seminars each month and bring in an impressive mid-six figure in the first year alone. "When my next book comes out," she'd said, "we can expand, and things will really take off."

Dorothy had turned on some music when she sat down to write this email. The designer friends had programmed her cell phone and hooked it up to a speaker system, so even she knew how to put on a playlist. She hadn't been paying much attention for the past hour, but now, at just the right moment, she heard the familiar clear soprano of 1970s Joni Mitchell. This had been the background music to most of the important moments in her life. It was Mitchell's iconic song about this town that had given Dorothy the courage to move here. *We are stardust, we are golden* . . . Impossible not to think of the random appearance of Joni, right here, right now, in her too-sunny living room, as a sign. By the end of the song, she'd send the email.

She turned up the volume and started to type.

Chapter One

*L*ater, Cecily would think of her mother's email as the beginning of her own downfall. She was in a café on North Clark, a mere three blocks from the apartment in Chicago she shared with her boyfriend, Santosh, when she received it. The subject line was "Back to the Garden: Upcoming Event." Cecily knew there would be something upsetting in it—the clue was it had come from her mother—so she decided to finish her coffee before opening it. But, of course, the problem wasn't the email. Her downfall had begun earlier and was due to her own behavior and bad decisions. She'd been accused of awful things recently, but no one was going to accuse her of not taking responsibility for her troubles.

Cecily had received a generous and prestigious grant that had allowed her to take this spring semester off from teaching. The plan had been to finish researching and begin writing her next book. It was another step up in what seemed to be the unstoppable ascent of her career.

It was now late April. She'd begun spending big chunks of time in this café only when Deerpath's administration and the Title IX office had contacted her at the end of February, telling her there was a problem and suggesting it would be best for Cecily to avoid campus until their investigation into the allegations against her had been completed and a verdict reached. So much for ascent.

She wouldn't try to pin any of that on Dorothy.

It was hard to accept that the words *allegations* and *investigation* were now part of her life and harder still to believe that, at thirty-four, just as her academic career was taking off, her future depended upon a "verdict." Dorothy's email would provide a distraction, even if a complicated one.

The Daily Grind had a rough-hewn décor somewhere between Wild West barroom and steampunk industrial cafeteria. It was loud and, like so many things with a hipster aesthetic—vintage furniture that was stylish but impractical; overpriced artisanal food whose appeal was more in backstory than flavor; beards—on the edge of unpleasant. Still, half the people surrounding Cecily had become nodding acquaintances over the past month or so. There was the tall woman who appeared to be attempting to organize her tax returns, sometimes with lip-biting frustration; the man surrounded by grubby notebooks who was either insane or writing a novel, not that the two were mutually exclusive; and the wired students of indeterminate age and gender who reminded Cecily, alas, of the young woman who was her accuser.

Then there was Molly, the harried woman with windstorm hair across the table from her now, who was always in residence, often conducting business on her phone at full volume. She and Cecily exchanged the kinds of complaints about weather, international news, and background music that made her feel almost like a friend.

Cecily had begun to appreciate this scrappy community. The world was now too frightening a place in which to go it solo. Everyone—she included herself—in her liberal, academic bubble lived in a state of near-constant outrage and anxiety over the next political atrocity, the rise of fascism, and imminent catastrophe on every front. Who wanted to die alone?

Santosh was an exception. Death wasn't anywhere on his radar. He worked at a small start-up where he and six of his college friends designed computer games. He exuded an aura of good-natured optimism that came from his belief that salvation was always possible, as long as you had excellent hand-eye coordination, knew the right codes, and smoked the right amount of weed. Cecily didn't believe any of this, but it was comforting. It was like listening to people talk about meeting dead loved ones in the afterlife: utterly implausible but sweet. Santosh's cheery optimism was one of the many differences between them that made Cecily love him. As for the rest of his appeal—well, look at the guy.

Once she received word about the investigation, she began withdrawing from friends and had stopped returning calls. Everyone would be sympathetic, of course, but she wasn't up to retelling the events leading up to now, painting herself as blameless, questioning the motives of her student. It was all so much more complicated than that. She certainly wasn't up to hearing about her academic friends' own professional advances. It was easier to exchange pleasantries with the likes of Molly and pretend it was a blossoming friendship. Maybe it was.

Contemplating catastrophe, she opened her mother's email.

Sweetheart!

I have a big announcement. I'm starting a business here in Woodstock with (drum roll) Fiona Snow. Her book was a massive success a few years ago, and she has a huge following. You must have read it. Who hasn't? (Me, but don't tell Fiona. I skimmed.) This investment is going to make your future more secure once I'm gone.

We're having an opening GALA in a couple of weeks. Food, music, the works. You have to come, sweetheart. I'm so proud of your success. Give me the chance to make YOU proud of ME.

I can't get your uncle to respond to emails. Maybe you can talk him into coming with you.

I should have guessed Woodstock was the town I was meant to live in. This will make me a real resident. I've always known that, one way or another, I'd get myself back to the garden.

I'll expect to see you here. Bring Santosh. It's not like I'm going to live forever, my love, and we haven't really _talked_ in so long. There's so much to say. A nice, long *talk*.

Cecily had grown up the only child of a single mother in a chaotic household in which Dorothy's friends and acquaintances were always moving into spare bedrooms temporarily while breaking up with a boyfriend, dissolving a marriage, or taking a course at a nearby college in advance of a career change. It was the kind of household, in other words, in which Joni Mitchell's *Ladies of the Canyon* and *Blue* were constantly playing in the background. Dorothy and her friends knew the albums so well they vacillated between thinking the lyrics had been written about them and believing they'd been written by them. Cecily was pleased her mother had gotten herself "back to the garden," but let's face it, that phrase made a lot more sense with electric piano accompaniment.

Her mother had sold her house near Boston—the one Cecily had grown up in—and moved out to the Catskills almost a year ago. Cecily had thus far managed to put off visiting. She'd seen Tom, her uncle, twice in the same period, but she hadn't told her mother about that: Dorothy counted on Tom to provide for Cecily and then resented him for doing so. Her mother had made a murky reference to a "business idea" on the phone this past winter, but Cecily hadn't pressed for details. Her own life was worth living when she left her mother's life unexamined.

She put the name "Fiona Snow" into Amazon, and up popped *The Nature of Success in Successful Natures*. The book, touted as "the famous international bestseller," had been published fifteen years earlier. Editorial and customer comments made it seem likely it promoted a confusing blend of self-help, bullying capitalism, and a brand of sub-scientific "science"—"the physics of magnetism in thought"; huh?—as a way toward perfect health and pretty much whatever else you wanted. The usual catchphrases were strewn about: "empowerment," "self-care," "living your best life," "following your dreams."

Cecily was disappointed to see she'd finished her coffee, although it was unlikely that more caffeine was what she needed now.

Dorothy had had her issues with drugs, men, and money over the years. They had, in many ways, defined her life. Now it looked as if she was pulling into the end station: a shallow form of self-help, the politically acceptable cousin of religion. Altruism that didn't involve real sacrifice. Self-indulgence made to seem a moral imperative. Meditation pillows. All fine, if only the words *investment* and *business* hadn't been inserted into the email. Upon reading them, Cecily had seen flash before her the parade of unhappiness, regret, and excuses that often came in the wake of her mother's enthusiasms, especially where money was concerned.

Cecily had so much to deal with right now (allegations and investigations) it was exhausting to think that, once again, she'd have to worry about her mother. Who, it was churlish but accurate to note, had never much worried about her. Dorothy's well-meaning idea of "talk" was usually a matter of laying out her grandiose and unrealistic plans. And, by the way, what "talk" was so significant that it merited the use of *italics*?

She wanted to call Tom to commiserate, but she was always calling her uncle with bad news and trouble. He'd been the first person she called—even before Santosh—when she heard about the Title IX investigation into her "misconduct." She hated to drag him into more family drama.

He hadn't said anything—he wouldn't—but she could tell he was trying to distance himself from Dorothy. Unfortunately, that also meant he was distancing himself from her. However much she and Tom agreed upon the frustrations of dealing with Dorothy, they both loved her, and their relationship with each other was dependent upon her.

Cecily checked her school email, as she'd been doing obsessively since being told of the investigation, but of course there was no message. She'd been informed that it could take at least two months to complete the initial phase of the process. It had been going on for seven weeks now. Every day, her fate seemed closer but no clearer.

●

"Bad news?"

She looked up. Molly, the harried woman with the loud voice, was gazing at her with bemused concern from across the table.

"No, not really. Just an email from my mother."

"'Mothers can be the worst'—to quote my daughter. You're a professor, right?"

Given Cecily's newly ambivalent feelings about academia, she didn't know whether to be flattered or insulted by the assumption, especially when it was being broadcast so loudly. It was the first time they'd discussed their careers. "Yes," she said. "Up at Deerpath College. American studies."

"You're on TV."

"I was interviewed once or twice about something I wrote."

It was astonishing to Cecily how many people had seen her few TV interviews, most on local stations with small audiences. Initially, it pleased her, but ever since the allegations and investigation, it had made her feel more vulnerable and exposed.

"Don't undersell yourself," Molly said. "I'm a ghostwriter. All the work, none of the glory. Good money, though."

"I'm not sure how much glory is involved in what I do," Cecily said. "And there's no money in academic books."

Molly pushed at her mass of unruly hair as if adjusting an uncooperative pillow on a sweaty night. "Let's put it this way: Rachel Maddow has never asked *me* for an interview."

She'd never asked Cecily, either, but at the moment, it didn't seem worth getting into, especially given that the misunderstanding was a flattering one. Molly's tangled hair and mismatched clothes—short pants and a nubby woolen sweater, as if she'd dressed for two different seasons—had the odd effect of making her look confident and authoritative, the kind of person who'd know how to plow through legal problems and maternal emails.

Cecily had been drawn to academia for the opposite of glory, whatever that was. Anonymity? She took comfort in hiding out in libraries, immersing herself in research and assembling her findings in an orderly way, creating a small world she could control. Maybe it was what Tom, an architect, felt when designing the compact houses that were now his specialty.

She was genuinely surprised at how much pleasure she took in the publication and unexpected success of her first book, a dumbed-down version of her PhD dissertation on the topic of women on the political right. She'd always been fascinated by people who acted in opposition to their own best interests. Dorothy, for example: her mother was far from right-wing, but she was always making choices that amounted to self-sabotage. Cecily's book had benefited from the number of (white) women who were suddenly happy to support overtly misogynist candidates and party platforms. Hers was one of a host of books to which people had turned to help illuminate what they, in their various pockets of privilege, had missed in their reading of the zeitgeist. It had sold almost eight thousand copies, more than ten times what her university press had expected, and generated sufficient talk to lead to the TV appearances.

She was embarrassed by her love of the small-scale notoriety. She'd always been suspicious of ambition. It was often adjacent to ruthlessness and sociopathy. And yet, the faintest whiff of success had left her wanting more approval and recognition from her colleagues at Deerpath.

Since the end of February, she'd had more recognition than she could handle. Anonymity had never looked so good or so out of reach. Karma, she couldn't help but believe, was coming back to bite her ambitious ass.

Cecily was half listening to Molly discuss her work ghostwriting business books for "horrible people with publicity platforms"—a feat, given her volume—when her phone began to vibrate. She looked down and saw that it was a call from Santosh's mother. It was so shocking that Neeta even had her number, Cecily panicked. Something was wrong with Santosh. No other explanation was possible.

"I'm sorry," she said. "I have to take this call. Would you watch my things?" She rushed out to the sidewalk.

"Cecily, I'm not getting you at a bad moment, am I? It rang so many times."

"No, I was just in a coffee shop. Is everything all right?"

"It is on my end, dear."

Dear?

"I'm calling because I'm coming into the city tomorrow, and I thought it would be nice if we met for lunch."

Nice?

"Are you free?"

As if the invitation weren't worrisome enough, Neeta's rushed speech and tightly cordial tone added to Cecily's suspicion that something must be terribly wrong. Neeta was shrewd enough to avoid open hostility and overt criticism, but she typically treated Cecily with the chilly disregard you'd show your son's prom date if you didn't approve of her dress.

Throughout Cecily's childhood, Dorothy had impressed upon her the importance of dodging bad news. "What you don't know can't hurt you," she'd said. "Like the tree falling in the forest, darling. No one to hear it, no sound."

Even as a child, Cecily had understood that there was something off in that logic. Ignorance is rarely bliss, although it's true that a certain fuzziness about the nutritional details of French pastry makes it easier to enjoy a beignet.

Far back in Cecily's mind was the frail hope that Neeta was ready to accept that, after two and a half years, she and Santosh really were a couple, and she was calling to make a connection. (*Dear. Nice.*) Based on that hope, Cecily agreed to meet Neeta downtown in a restaurant in the upper lobby of one of the city's many grande dame hotels from the late nineteenth century. *I know we haven't been close*, she fantasized hearing, *but I want to change all that*, dear. *I want to make* nice *and give you my blessing.*

"By the way," Neeta said. "I haven't told Santosh I'm coming to town."

Red flag number . . . Well, Cecily had lost count. "I won't mention it, either," she said.

"That's entirely up to you," Neeta granted, now that it was clear her message had been received.

Cecily went back into the Daily Grind, ready to pretend she was working. The book proposal she'd discussed with her editor and had used to secure her impressive grant had become a straw finger trap she couldn't get free of. The more research she did on the topic, the less interested in it she became. She felt like a fraud going out to work on this project, but she could neither give it up nor move forward on it.

"I had to fight off thieves, but your computer is safe," Molly crowed.

"Thank you."

"By the way, I've been meaning to ask about the hair. Not chemo, I hope."

So much for boundaries. The haircut was an anxiety-fueled mistake she'd made with a pair of kitchen scissors three weeks ago. The stylist she'd seen to even it out had recommended a radical start-from-scratch fix. Cecily hoped it came off as a fashion trend. Apparently not. Santosh had assured her that he thought she was beautiful "no matter what," a compliment that left the scent of insult in its wake. *You look good to me, despite what everyone else says about you behind your back.* She could only imagine what Neeta would make of it.

"Not chemo. I just wanted a change." Cecily considered change, like Steven Spielberg, to be overrated, but most people took a desire for it as an acceptable reason for dumping lovers and making egregious choices in the voting booth.

Molly nodded her chin toward the sidewalk. "The mother again?"

"Yes," Cecily said. "But not mine this time. My boyfriend's."

"Even worse. Here's my card." She handed over two. "Write your information on the back of this."

Molly was so aggressively confident, Cecily did as directed. She was surprised to see that her hand was shaking as she wrote. Too much coffee and too many mothers.

Molly noticed and smiled sympathetically. It was becoming apparent there was lots she'd noticed all along. "If it's any consolation," she said, "you'll probably outlive your boyfriend's mother."

"I'll keep that in mind," Cecily said. In truth, it was easy to imagine Neeta outliving her, frogs, and the entire Brazilian rain forest. Cecily would consider it a victory if she survived tomorrow's lunch.

Chapter Two

*T*he following day, at noon, Cecily made her way down-town. She'd spent a more or less sleepless night. She hadn't told Santosh over dinner about the call from his mother, deciding she'd do so "before bed." The resolution shifted to "after sex," "before sleep," and, finally, "during breakfast." It had crumbled entirely when she realized Neeta might call Santosh while he was at work, at which point, her utterly guileless boyfriend would bring it up and add another item to Neeta's mental (and, for all Cecily knew, written) list of reasons she couldn't trust her.

She'd never been inside this hotel before, and upon stepping off the escalator from the street, she felt as if she were walking into a nineteenth-century European train station. The immense vaulted space was encrusted with gilded medallions and paintings of blue sky and pink angels inspired by either the Sistine Chapel or a burlesque house. Here, Cecily was an insignificant traveler unprepared for the journey she was about to take, possibly the reason Neeta had chosen this spot.

She'd put on a gray jumper that was stylish but modest in the right light. Tom, a fanatic about lighting, had instructed her in its importance and shown her the tricks used by von Sternberg and classic Hollywood cinematographers. The older he got, the less light there was in his house. She was convinced that by the time he turned seventy, he'd be living in utter darkness. She didn't know how Alan, his younger partner, put up with it. Now, in the luxurious false daylight of this cathedral, she felt ridiculous. The selling point of this piece of clothing—*I bought it in Amsterdam!*—was meaningless here and, no doubt, meaningless to Neeta in any setting.

As for fashionable dressing, she'd always thought of it as a form of deceit, an attempt to appear interesting and creative by wearing the interesting and creative work of someone else—assuming you had the dough. She'd never been able to pull off fashionable clothes, despite being tall and thin. She always looked like someone who'd been dressed from a friend's closet to attend a party she hadn't been invited to.

Neeta was already at a table in the restaurant, whose seating spilled out into the grand lobby. She commanded her position as if she owned the entire hotel. She was wearing a wool suit in such a tasteful shade of light yellow, she was a pastel rose among gaudy fake flowers.

She was on her phone, but she signaled Cecily over. "I appreciate the call," she was saying, "but we're going to ride it out. Akhil is certain it will come back."

Santosh had told Cecily that his mother managed the family finances. His father, an anesthesiologist, was too busy and didn't have his mother's instincts for money matters. You had to admire Neeta for that. She would have made a brilliant, uncompromising politician, albeit one on the wrong side of every issue.

Although, who was Cecily to have an opinion? Despite their professional accomplishments, Neeta and her husband had to suffer frequent indignities and insults. Santosh wasn't immune, either. Once, when Neeta and Akhil had taken them all out to dinner, the waitress kept looking to Cecily for answers, as if it weren't obvious that she was the least important person at the table.

Cecily sat. Neeta was wearing a cream silk blouse underneath her suit jacket. There were several buttons undone, and although she had a diaphanous orange scarf tucked in around the collar, she was showing a surprising amount of cleavage. She was probably in her midfifties, and was still severely attractive, with a cold, implacable beauty. Santosh had inherited his striking looks from his mother and, fortunately, his tender heart from his father.

Call finished, Neeta put her phone down. She adjusted the orange scarf, gave Cecily a sad, appraising glance, and said, "You look tired. Have you been getting enough sleep, dear?"

Dear!

"I've been spending a lot of time reading," Cecily said. "I probably need glasses."

"Maybe it's the haircut. Very boyish. What is the new topic?"

Cecily felt the trap tighten around her fingers. "I'm researching how cookbooks played a role in the oppression of women in late nineteenth- and early twentieth-century America."

Neeta's face brightened with what was clearly meant to be surprise. "I didn't know you were interested in *cooking*," she said. "At least not from what Santosh has said."

Despite her busy life, Neeta was a spectacularly good cook of complicated, traditional dishes. It was a talent she'd weaponized. She watched as others ate her food without eating any herself. She wasn't looking for validation but was testing you to see if you appreciated her skills.

"Is your mother a good cook?" Neeta asked.

As usual, Cecily wanted to protect her mother from the truth, even though she suspected Neeta wasn't interested in her answer. "I was always well fed," she said.

"Ah, yes. You said she ran a restaurant at some point."

"She was one of the owners. She wasn't cooking." Apparently, most of the time Dorothy had spent in the restaurant's kitchen had involved cocaine, but that was long ago, and the point did not need clarification now.

"All the same," Neeta said, fingering her scarf, "I'm sure it was an interesting childhood, in its way."

"It was. In its way."

When Neeta spoke about Cecily's childhood and family, she always seemed to be speaking about the absence of a father. That was what Cecily heard, anyway.

Whatever loss or occasional anger Cecily had felt about having no idea who her father was, she'd never seen it as a fact of her life that made her lesser in any way. Her mother had had a brief affair—"one-night stand" was probably the accurate description—while traveling out west and hadn't realized she was pregnant until long after she returned home with no way to contact the man. "Not that I would have, even if I could. I wanted you all for myself." Cecily had always had Tom as the steadiest and most reliable male (or female) presence in her life. She'd say he was like a father, but how would she know what that was like?

Her family had seemed normal to her. At her private high school— paid for with major assistance from Tom, of course—the variety of family makeups in terms of race, gender, and size of household had made her situation commonplace, barely worth a disinterested shrug.

Neeta was one of those brilliant, immensely competent women who respected brilliance and competence only in men. Dorothy's efforts at raising Cecily as a single mother counted for nothing.

Last year, when Tom was in Chicago on business, Cecily and Santosh had driven him to Deerpath College and taken him to Cecily's office. As they were leaving campus, Cecily suggested they show him the suburb where Santosh had grown up, twenty minutes away. "Maybe we should see if your parents are home," she had said. "We haven't visited them in a while."

As soon as they arrived at their house, Cecily realized that her motive for coming was to prove to Santosh's parents—to Neeta, in other words, as hers was the opinion that mattered—that she had a legitimate family, even if an unconventional one. She'd always felt proud of Tom, with his good looks (now simultaneously withered and bloated, it was true) and kindness (increasingly frayed, admittedly, though steady when it came to her) and gentle wit (inching these days toward sarcasm with a bitter edge).

"I appreciated your call and this invitation to meet," Cecily now told Neeta. "I know you're busy."

As she was about to say something more, the waiter appeared, an angular and handsome man with tidy sideburns and a look of ironic seriousness that indicated he wouldn't be at this job long and that he was almost certainly gay. Cecily smiled at him, and Neeta cleared her throat, as if interrupting an inappropriately intimate exchange.

"Please, Cecily, go ahead."

Cecily asked for what seemed like the least complicated dish: ravioli in brown butter. Something starchy and comforting and which she could reasonably eat half of without appearing rude.

"I'll have tea," Neeta said. "The Assam, black. They have good teas here, surprisingly enough. And a cup of whatever vegetarian soup you have." When the waiter had left, she said, "You look as if you've lost weight."

Cecily never weighed herself, but since the investigation started, she had found her clothes hanging off her in unflattering ways. She often felt as if anxiety were dripping into her veins, making it difficult for her to eat. She thought the jumper, with its boxy shape and bib, would cover that, but naturally, Neeta had seen through it.

Neeta arranged the silverware in front of her in a precise way. And then, composed, she said, "You have a wrong impression of me, Cecily. You think I don't like you."

"I suspect," Cecily said, "I'm not the type of person you imagined Santosh would end up with." Only after she said it did she realize that the "end up with" might sound presumptuous.

"I respect that you're being honest," Neeta said, a clear indication that she resented her for telling the truth. "At some point in the future, if you're lucky enough to have children, you'll know that you develop a sixth sense about what's best for your child." She smiled wearily. "I'm guessing your mother would say the same thing. It's such a shame we never met her."

"I hope there'll be opportunities in the future."

Neeta shrugged. "Perhaps."

"I'd like to believe Santosh has been happy with me." Cecily's voice, which had suddenly gone high and wispy, was nearly drowned out by the echoes of conversation and distant laughter in the soaring, gilded room, the loud businessmen and -women pretending to be confident and amused.

"I'm not here to put you on the defensive, Cecily. I never said you made him *un*happy." The food arrived, inconveniently, as she was getting to the point. Neeta motioned toward Cecily's plate. "Please," she said, a command Cecily didn't dare ignore.

She sliced into the ravioli as gracefully as she could.

"Akhil, like Santosh, doesn't know we're having this lunch," Neeta continued. "What I'm going to say is just from me." She waited until Cecily had nodded an assent. "An old friend of mine lives in Deerpath. I don't see her that often anymore. Her husband is also a doctor, and they're always busy. They, too, come from near Bangalore. We were very close and important to each other when we were young and first came to the U.S. Such a long time ago."

Nostalgic Neeta was no more convincing than Welcoming Neeta.

"She serves on committees." She turned the little cup of soup. "As a result of this, she has close ties to people in the administration at Deerpath College. She called to arrange dinner with me last week, when she knew Akhil would be at a conference in Toronto." She gave Cecily a knowing look. "She's loved Santosh since he was an infant. She wanted to tell me what she'd heard about you, as any friend would. I'll spare us both the embarrassment of going into the details of our conversation."

"I'd love to tell you my side of the story," Cecily said.

Neeta looked at her with an expression that was somewhere between shock and hurt. "I'm not here to accuse you of anything or to ask you to defend yourself, dear." *Dear.* "I'm here to tell you that I know you are, in fact, *under investigation*. For misconduct. Sexual in nature. That you've been barred from campus. Had to surrender emails and phone records."

It all sounded so tawdry and shameful, no doubt because it was.

Neeta looked genuinely distressed. "It's not a pleasant thing to talk about."

"It might be less so if I told you what really happened."

"Oh? A minute ago, you wanted to tell me 'your side of the story.' Is that the same as 'what really happened'?"

"I'd like to think so."

Neeta took a spoonful of the soup—a slight betrayal of the fact that she was susceptible to something as weak and human as hunger, but she rose above it by swallowing it without appearing to. She put down her spoon. It was safe to assume she wasn't going to pick it up again.

"I've been told this will complicate your tenure case," she said. "It could complicate your entire career, whatever the outcome of the investigation. The extent to which the allegations are deemed true will matter, of course, but unfortunately, the cloud of smoke they produce will persist, however it ends."

"Persist in your mind, you mean?"

Neeta waved away this attempt at self-defense as if it were an insignificant fly.

Cecily speared a corner of a ravioli. "In case you were wondering," she said, chewing, "Santosh knows all about this. I've told him everything."

"I don't doubt it. It must be painful for him to have to lie to us, his parents, by omission. Did Santosh ever tell you that he almost died when he was a child?"

Cecily looked at Neeta to try to understand what she meant by this or at least what her motivation was in saying it. "No, he didn't."

"He wouldn't. He refuses to understand how serious the accident was. He was at the house of a friend, and they crawled out of an attic window and onto the roof. They were seven. It was Santosh's idea." She smiled sadly but fondly at this. "Always the adventurous one." She paused for effect. "He fell off the roof."

Cecily gasped.

"He was in the hospital for over a week. He had a head injury, and one of his lungs collapsed."

Cecily felt a wave of sadness building in her, imagining a tiny Santosh in a hospital, tubes connected to him.

Neeta, who seemed to sense her feelings, gave her a tender look. "You'd think it would have made him more cautious, but, no, it had the opposite effect. It made him more reckless, as if the accident proved he was invincible. You see that in the way he plays sports. He thinks nothing will harm him. He thinks all these injuries of his don't matter, that he will surmount any problem. He probably thinks your situation won't have an impact on him and his life. That the cloud of smoke surrounding you won't envelop him as well."

"I don't see why it would envelop him."

"I know you don't," she snapped. "That's why someone else needs to protect him. Even when it means challenging him on what he wants."

Cecily's appetite abandoned her, something that had been happening more and more often. She put down her fork, not sure what to do with her hands now.

Neeta went on: "I want you to know that this is not a personal matter, that whatever my expectations might be, my preferences—and naturally I have some; how could I not?—they have nothing to do with my plan to protect Santosh."

Plan?

"I've been careful when I talk to Santosh about you. About what you call your family, about your age." Cecily was three years older than Santosh, an apparently shameful gap. "About your book."

"My book was . . ."

"I know all about it. I read some sample pages online." That ended the discussion. "I was willing to sit by and wait until the relationship burned itself out. That's what happened with all of Santosh's many previous girlfriends. He thinks he's in love, and then his attention drifts."

Cecily did her best to show no anger at this provocation. She gripped her thighs and then, unable to keep silent, said, "I'm sorry for you if this one's lasted longer than you hoped. I suppose you'll have to wait a little longer."

"There's no need to get sarcastic, dear. It doesn't suit you. You're an essentially earnest woman. The point is, I'm not willing to sit by and wait while the person Santosh is living with is being investigated for sexual misconduct with a student. A female student. It hurts the whole family. The friend who told me about it was horrified. I'm sure you can appreciate my responsibility as Santosh's mother, no matter what your own family background is."

Cecily felt battered, probably the effect Neeta was aiming for.

"Are you saying you're going to tell him to break up with me?"

"Tell him? No. I was hoping I could help you understand that the decent thing for *you* to do would be to end the relationship yourself."

"I can't do that. I love Santosh."

"Frankly, that's the response I was expecting. In light of it, I have to do what I feel I must. Telling Santosh isn't going to work. We both know that. I'm a patient woman. If I have to stop seeing my son for a while so his life will work out for him in the long run, I will do so."

Cecily took this in and did her best to interpret. "You'll make him choose between me and his parents?"

"I see it as making him choose between you and his own future. He's on the cusp of success. And now this."

"That's cruel," she said softly. "To Santosh."

Neeta sighed. "We gave up everything familiar to come here for our future children, Cecily. Our *only* child, as it turned out. You can't overstate the sacrifices we made with that goal in mind. The indignities we still face daily. The idiotic comments. The subtle insults. The slights. The questions. If my actions seem 'cruel' to you, putting them in that context might help you see them a little differently."

Cecily was struck by a wave of panic. She knew how tormented Santosh would be when he was faced with this choice. It would tear him apart. He was too loyal to her to end things, but it would gnaw at him like physical pain. Then it would eat at their relationship. It wasn't a fight she could win, she knew. Not in the long run. The best she could hope for was to be exonerated at Deerpath. Then, maybe, Neeta would scale back her objections to her previous level of generalized disapproval.

As she was coming in on the train this morning, she'd received a text from Dorothy, asking her if she'd received her email. **Trying to see if I**

can make it, she'd texted back. There was no solution in her mother's gala, but maybe there was a bargaining chip in there somewhere.

"My mother is having an opening for a new business she's starting," Cecily said. "I have to go to it. I was thinking I might stay with my uncle for a bit before attending. I want to do some research in the Radcliffe library."

Neeta was eyeing her with a look clearly intended to say, *How is this relevant to me?*

"If I left soon, in a few days, if I stayed away for a couple of weeks—until the verdict comes in on my case—would you hold off talking with Santosh about this? Would you spare him having to make that choice? For the time being?"

The bill came, and Neeta pulled out a credit card, another triumph over Cecily. "I'm glad you enjoyed at least some of your food," Neeta said. "I told you you needed something to eat."

"Is that a 'yes'?" Cecily asked.

"I'll tell you what, dear." *Dear.* "You let me know when you've made your plans."

"So, you won't . . . ."

"Don't try to hold me to anything, Cecily. I have no desire to discuss something this ugly with Santosh or Akhil. Getting a little distance from the situation might help you see what the right thing to do is. I just told you I'm patient, but not infinitely so."

On the sidewalk, there was a brisk April breeze blowing. Neeta hugged Cecily. It wasn't affectionate so much as consoling, a hug you might give someone at a funeral. *I'm sorry he's dead, but let's face it, it was inevitable.* As if her winning were inevitable. Even her tone had changed to that of the victor. "I'm sure it will be good for you to get away for a while. Tell me when you've booked a flight."

Cecily weighed her options on the train home. If she told Santosh what had happened, her loyal, impulsive boyfriend would go to his parents and defend her. This would, of course, have no effect on them whatsoever. Neeta, with her ability to twist anything to her advantage, wouldn't deny that she'd spoken to Cecily but would make it seem that she, Cecily, had informed him of the lunch as a way to drive a wedge between parent and child. It would complicate things further and with minimal results.

When she was close to home, she checked her email on her phone. Nothing from Deerpath. It had to mean something that the decision was taking so long, but it was impossible to interpret what, based on the limited information she had access to.

The subject line "Back to the Garden—Upcoming Event" leapt out at her. Maybe it was significant that her mother's plea for an appearance at her gala (whatever that was) had arrived yesterday, moments before Neeta's call.

She looked out the train window. Chicago, with its massive buildings and sweeping weather, had always struck her as a city of beautiful shadows. Majestic and mysterious, but lonely. In some ways, she supposed, she always felt a little lonely, even when she was with Santosh; part of her, part of who she was, had always been in shadow.

Tom, she texted. **I'm sorry to say I need your advice and a favor yet again. Forgive me. Call me after work tonight?**

As plans went, it wasn't the ideal one, but at the moment, she didn't see any other option.

Chapter Three

*T*om was at the office, going over the final touches on the schematic designs for a guesthouse, *the* guesthouse, the most important project he'd ever designed. He heard a ping that indicated he'd received a text message from his niece. He glanced at the desk drawer in which he kept his phone but resisted opening it. He'd check when he was heading home later this afternoon. It had been a horrible morning, getting through the next hour required focus, and the last thing he needed was family drama.

His client had called him at dawn to set up a meeting. "I have some exciting new ideas for the guesthouse," she'd said breathlessly. The comment had thrown him into a panic. After more than a year of conversations, changes, tweaks, and battles, they were way past an infusion of "new ideas," especially "exciting" ones. He was ready to submit designs for approval. He'd lined up a project manager. It was late April, and construction was supposed to begin in June.

Anyone who'd ever played with Legos, lived under a roof, or held a pencil was convinced they could design their own house. Part of his job as architect was to praise the client's brilliance while showing them they were delusional. Considering the importance of this project, he might skip brilliance and cut to the chase.

He eyed the desk drawer again.

His resolution about Cecily had lasted thirty seconds. Alan had been right with the accusation that accompanied his departure: when all the receipts were tallied up, Tom's niece *was* the love of his life and, in a peculiar way he couldn't explain, the center of his life. Panic or not, he had to know what she'd said.

> **Tom. I'm sorry to say I need your advice and a favor yet again. Forgive me.**

Just once, he'd like to hear from Cecily when she wasn't in trouble. No, that wasn't fair; she often called to say hello or to catch him up with news about her life and career. Although, come to think of it, usually bad news. At the end of February, when everything in his own life was coming apart, she'd called to tell him about the insulting investigation into her behavior. As if Cecily would ever behave inappropriately with a student.

> **Everything all right?** he texted back.

> **Not exactly. 7 your time good to talk?**
> **Perfect. Are you okay?**
> **Oh, sure. I'll tell you tonight. Xxx**

He should have resisted looking until later. Now he'd worry about this all day, too.

He went back to the designs. Reviewing this project usually made him happy and soothed his nerves, but today it made him anxious. Even Winston Brill, his boss, had referred to the guesthouse as Tom's masterpiece, albeit while emphasizing that this was different from calling it "*a* masterpiece." Whatever. Tom knew it was his *Great Gatsby*, his *Starry Night*, his final opportunity to build something that people might look at in the waning days of human existence and think, *That's beautiful*. It was his last shot at leaving a footprint on the dying planet. He couldn't let it be destroyed by exciting new ideas.

The client for this guesthouse was Charlotte Morley, whom he'd known for much of his adulthood. Charlotte had been friends with his sister, Dorothy, since college, all without approving of Dorothy's impulsive choices. Their friendship seemed to be based on the desire each had to acquire for herself the exact qualities she abhorred in the other. Given that the friendship had endured for decades, you had to assume it was a sound basis.

As a client, Charlotte was precisely as she was in her other roles in Tom's life: smart, opinionated, and impossible. Her passion for this project and the attention she paid to its every detail suggested to him that she fantasized about keeping the guesthouse as a rarely used space that was her private realm, a way to assert her independence from the dashing, difficult husband she adored.

Charlotte's attitude toward halfway retreat from coupledom was the backbone of the business he brought into the firm these days. All these wives—it was always the wife, the husband having already retreated in more nefarious ways—planning for a guesthouse, a reconfigured garage, a six-hundred-square-foot "she shed." Tom referred to it as the Petit Trianon syndrome. Not to his monied clients' faces, of course, as most believed themselves to be far from Marie-Antoinette. They might, on occasion, acknowledge in themselves a slight let-them-eat-cake attitude, but they let you know they at least had the decency to supply the cake.

Charlotte's planned guesthouse was compact and ingeniously symmetrical, modern but not annoyingly self-conscious about it. Glass and steel, but not cold. It would sit, in a dignified way, on the beautiful two acres she and her husband owned and enhance the land and views rather than clutter them. Everything Tom knew and had practiced in architecture over the past thirty years had come together in this project. He couldn't explain its beauty. It had started as an image of a building that had come to him while he was walking Charlotte's land. He saw the structure whole—glimmering, serene, and light—disappearing into the landscape. All the design elements had fallen into place in a way they never had before. If Charlotte did eventually spend time there, he was convinced it would bring her the peace and order she eschewed but desperately needed.

Architecture was destiny. He was doing her a favor, even if she didn't know it.

"Never talk to a client about architecture," Mies van der Rohe had said. "Talk to him about his children."

Tom had no interest in talking with Charlotte about her problematic son, but he might be forced to try if she hauled out too many exciting new ideas.

The past two years had been complicated, a nice way of saying hugely disappointing, which was in itself a nice way of saying disastrous. First, two major projects had fallen apart when both sets of clients, independent of each other, had decided, instead, to have ready-made "tiny houses" wheeled into their backyards and save hundreds of thousands. In January, a third couple had come back from a trip and decided they didn't need a guesthouse after all. "We're getting a divorce," they'd crowed, as if Tom would revel in their decision. Then there had been the gawdy, embarrassing collapse of construction plans with Marek Bachar and his wife, a disaster that came shortly after Alan, Tom's partner of almost ten years, had left him.

Tom had turned sixty-three earlier in the year. He sometimes felt as if he were in a nail-biting race with the planet to see which of them died first. He hoped it would be him. He didn't see himself as a likely candidate for heroism or survivalist ingenuity. One of the benefits of the climate crisis was that it made him relieved rather than anxious that there was no history of longevity in his family. Even so, he wanted career redemption, and Charlotte's guesthouse was his last chance to grab it. *How's that for an exciting new idea, Charlotte?*

•

Charlotte Morley entered the narrow offices of Winston Brill Architects the way she entered most rooms: in mid-sentence.

". . . how much do you know about that email from Dorothy, about the gala? What is she talking about?"

"I have no idea," Tom said. "I ignored it. I'm choosing to assume it's a good thing, and I'm living my own life. I'm pretending the money she made selling the house here is safely invested and that she's living within her means. For once. Beyond that, I'm out."

"You always were an optimist."

Tom wasn't pessimistic by nature, but these days, given global politics, imminent environmental collapse, and the state of his own personal life, optimism, like choosing to make a movie in black and white, was a charming anachronism best saved for special occasions. Charlotte's use of the word to describe him bordered on a slur.

She took off a jacket in a pricey shade of emerald that emphasized her pretty eyes, draped it on the back of a chair beside his desk, and sat. The scent of her furtive cigarette habit and the expensive perfume she used to mask it wafted toward Tom. He could tell she was settling in to make a big announcement. After all these years, he knew her that well. In fact, he knew her intimately. Charlotte was the last woman Tom had slept with. This had been a brief, misguided encounter they'd both used to prove something to themselves or perhaps to each other; Tom no longer remembered. They'd never discussed it, but the fact of it hovered around their interactions like an odor that each silently dared the other to bring up. The smell of violets, perhaps: floral and seductive but slightly unpleasant.

"I've been giving this a lot of thought," she said, "and I've made a few rough sketches."

"Rough sketches," he said, trying to maintain his composure. "Really?"

"Yes, really." She pulled a wad of smudged papers from the pocket of her jacket. "I know myself, and I know I'll walk into the house as soon as it's finished and want more space."

"You brought this up before, and we came to an agreement back then." He could tell his composure was irritating her. "It's larger than many New York apartments as is."

"That's why I don't live in New York. I want to double the square footage."

Tom could feel his breathing grow shallow. He had to get it under control before she noticed.

"Don't worry," she said. "It just means putting a second story on the building."

Tom looked at her to gauge whether she was joking. Naturally, she was not. Charlotte could be acerbic and quick-witted, but when it came to herself, she was always serious. She was spectacularly capable and perpetually aggrieved by the ineptitude of the rest of humanity. This wasn't an appealing quality, but with her brains and organizational skills, both of which she'd used to raise herself out of a miserable child-hood in a shabby town in New Hampshire, Tom felt she'd earned the right to it. Two years ago, she'd gone halftime at her law firm to do pro bono work for immigrants, so there was that to admire as well.

Immigration work or not, he was going to have to take a firm stand on this. "A second story is completely out of the question," he said. "We never discussed it in the past twenty months. Not once. You don't need all that space, and it would throw everything off balance."

"Is that so."

"Yes, it is."

"That wasn't a question. I was dismissing your opinion. Here," she said, smoothing out the drawings. "As you'll see, I've done the heavy lifting for you already."

"You can't randomly stack stories on top of each other like you're mov-ing around shipping containers. It would block all light from the south side of your house and completely interfere with the landscape. You and Oliver live in a trophy house, and I designed you a trophy accompaniment to pay tribute to it. We're way, *way* past the point of a change like this."

"You haven't even looked at my drawings."

"I'm trying to be kind." Summoning up the advice of the masters, he said, "How's Nolan, by the way?"

"It's *my* guesthouse, Tom. You've got your own, and I don't want a shack like that. Nolan hates Switzerland, his job, Oliver, and me, and he's obviously drinking too much again. In other words, he's doing much better. And if I tell you I want a second story, I expect you to make it happen."

Tom decided to play hardball. "Then I recommend you contact another architect and start all over."

Charlotte flung her hair over her shoulder. She was justly proud of her thick, curly hair and was always flinging it around to make a point or challenge a statement or simply let it be known that she wasn't intimidated or impressed. Her coppery hair was her one physical feature that hadn't changed with age—or, at least, hadn't changed in a way that couldn't be altered with something as readily available as coloring. That florid hair was the symbol of her essential self: a tough girl who'd bullied her way to success, much to the dismay of her brutal family.

She no longer wore the clinging outfits she'd worn well into her forties to show off curves above and below a narrow waistline. She no longer had a waistline, an age-appropriate transformation she'd given in to and that fit her remarkably well. Her embrace of her body made her a force to be reckoned with on all fronts. Tom had noted that nothing infuriates or disarms heterosexual men more quickly than a robust woman who carries herself with pride and sexual confidence. In her print dress and low heels, green jacket and rusty hair, Charlotte had the aura of a Scandinavian prime minister who has more important things to worry about than her fucking weight.

As for Tom's own recent weight gain, it had had the opposite effect. He'd noticed a look of suspicious disappointment on the faces of his clients, who seemed to assume that a good architect should have the deprived, streamlined physique of Winston, his boss.

A high school wrestler, Tom had always been short and blocky, with muscular definition that gave him a degree of swagger and an appeal to men who liked to be pushed around. Still, he would never design a house with the inelegant proportions of his body, even at its best. Since his troubles with Alan started—and especially since Alan moved out—he'd had an extra glass of wine each night. The "extra glass" was the public admission he made to distract from the fact that it was usually a bottle. As a result, the edges of his blocky build had begun to blur. Ridiculously, he thought of this as getting back at Alan.

"You'd never talk to one of your other clients like this," Charlotte said.

"Of course I wouldn't. I'd be out of work in a week. And, by the way, you'd never talk to your architect this way if we weren't old friends." He rubbed his hands over his eyes, suddenly exhausted by the exchange and feeling a sense of foreboding and pointlessness. "How can you do this to me, Charlotte?"

"It's not personal, Tom. You know that. This is my project. It has been all along. And don't think you can rope Oliver into an alliance against me." Although she was a self-proclaimed pacificist, Charlotte thought like a military strategist. "I'm not negotiating. I want to see my drawings incorporated into the next set of plans."

"There is no next set," Tom said.

"Then there is no project."

As Charlotte was fuming and trying to get into her jacket, Winston Brill entered from the street, full of louche charm and accompanied by a young man Tom assumed was yet another intern from Harvard's Graduate School of Design. Winston and Charlotte had a special fondness for each other. It had to do with a wary respect they had for ruthlessness. Winston had designed the interiors of a couple of restaurants Charlotte felt compelled to like because it was impossible to get reservations at them. Most important, he'd designed an extremely beautiful house in the Berkshires for an equally beautiful actress who'd won multiple Tony Awards on Broadway (irrelevant) before landing a small role on a popular TV series that involved dragons (hugely relevant). The house was a sprawling piece of opulent austerity that had been featured in design magazines, the *New York Times*, and on a British TV show that looked at "the world's most amazing houses."

Winston kissed Charlotte on both cheeks and said, "I hope Tom is reining in your outrageous demands for enough space to put in a bathroom."

There was value in having a signature trait, even if it was one people liked to disparage.

"No one has ever reined me in, Winston. Certainly not Tom."

"Of course not. You're practically 'siblings.' Almost 'brother and sister.'"

The odor of violets rose up.

"A horrifying thought," Charlotte said.

Winston was incapable of mentioning family relationships without putting a spin on the words that made them sound as if he were bracketing them with quotes.

Tall and meticulous, Winston wore casual clothes that were always so clean and pressed, he appeared to be in a freshly laundered suit even when wearing jeans. Everything on him shone—his narrow, bald head; his Philip Johnson–style eyeglasses; his large, frequently whitened teeth; even his nails. He had small eyes, no lips to speak of, and only the suggestion of a chin, but the shininess of everything created a dazzling aura around him that was more potent and interesting than mere good looks could ever have been. He was allegedly heterosexual, but Tom found it impossible to imagine Winston engaged in anything as messy or spontaneous as sex with a human of any gender.

"We're at an impasse," Charlotte said. "He refuses to give me what I want. I've earned the right to get what I want, Winston."

Ominously, Winston said nothing. He headed to his office with the intern in tow, an awkward smile frozen on the latter's face. Halfway there, Winston stopped. "When you have a minute," he called out to Tom with funereal gravity, "come talk to me."

After he'd disappeared, Charlotte said, "What's that about?"

"If it concerns you in any way," Tom said, "I'll send you a telegram."

"I haven't heard from Cecily in a while. What's going on with her?"

"Charlotte," Tom said. "I'm not going back to casual chitchat. Do you know how much I've put into this project and how important it is to me?"

"If it's that important, Tom, make these changes."

"I'm afraid it's not that simple."

"Only because you're stubborn and inflexible. Give my love to Alan. I haven't seen him in ages."

Tom wasn't lying to anyone about the state of his relationship; he just wasn't advertising it—the favored rationale of many a liar, he was aware. He didn't owe Charlotte anything, especially now. He let her find her own way to the door, feeling as if the meeting had gone much worse than even his worst fears.

Just to pick at his scabs, he looked at his chain of text messages with Cecily.

> **Are you okay?**
> **Oh, sure. I'll tell you tonight.**

"Oh, sure" was basically the equivalent of "absolutely not."

He looked toward Winston's office, a glass box at the end of the open space, and saw his boss gazing at him impatiently. He put the phone away and went to hear more bad news.

Chapter Four

There was something shiny even about the way Winston's semiprivate office smelled: antiseptic and slightly metallic. Winston was drumming his glossy nails on his glass desktop as Tom entered. The new intern was seated in front of his desk.

"Tom," Winston said, "I'd like you meet Lanford Trask. Lanford, Tom Kemp."

Lanford stood and shook hands with the overdone enthusiasm you might produce when introduced to a "famous person" you were assumed to know but had never heard of. "I'm excited to be working with someone who specializes in small spaces," he said, eyeing Tom with implausible reverence.

He bore a striking resemblance to a young Winston, long, narrow head, thin lips, and round eyeglasses included. He was not bald, but because he looked so much like Winston, the mop of dark hair that sat on top of his head looked to Tom like something placed there.

"Is that an interest of yours?" Tom asked.

"Absolutely. Obsession. I did my final project at GSD on creating compact roominess in hyperbolic tiny houses and how it's the emergent form of housing for the climate we'll be facing in the near future. I'm building a house for a friend in Tucson. My final project presentation is online. I'll send you a link."

"I'll look for it."

Like most of the recent graduates who came to Winston Brill Architects, Lanford no doubt had innovative and highly intellectualized plans that combined design, sustainability, and adaptation to the new problems the planet and the species were facing. Tom, by comparison, had guesthouses for suburban couples with money and marital issues. Those were old problems. Lanford was the future as inevitably as Tom was the past.

"Interning?" Tom asked.

"Actually," Winston cut in, "Lanford is joining the team. He'll be working at the desk in front of yours."

"Ah. I see."

In addition to Tom, there had been only three other full-time architects at the firm since Tom joined seventeen years earlier. It couldn't be a good sign that Winston was bringing someone in now. The other desks in the open office were for freelancers who came and went, depending on business. These were always recent graduates who'd grown up on computer games and were so fluent in Revit and SketchUp, there was no need for Tom to have more than rudimentary skills in these architecture programs. His younger colleagues called him "old school" in a respectful, admiring way that indicated they considered him irrelevant.

When Lanford had been dismissed to settle into his work space, Winston indicated the seat the younger man had just vacated and examined his shiny nails.

"What do you think of Lanford? Impressive, isn't he?"

"A little soon to tell," Tom said, a mild attempt at self-preservation.

Winston nodded and moved on. "Interesting person, Charlotte," he said.

"Very. She has brains, looks, and money, and unfortunately, is confident about all of them."

"You think the husband cheats on her?"

How this was relevant to anything was beyond Tom. It was awkward that Winston was even asking him; with his shiny, antiseptic sexlessness, he gave off the air of debauchery common among religious fanatics, celibates, and the excessively well groomed.

Tom shrugged. "He travels internationally for work. He's often alone in hotel rooms with luxury bathrooms and immense amounts of downtime. Since, on top of all that, he rarely drinks, I'd say the odds are high."

True monogamy on the part of men was as rare as true veganism. The rationalizing among most went that sexual flings and roast beef sandwiches don't count if they're indulged in discreetly and you brush your teeth afterward. As for Oliver Fuchs, he was one of those tall, self-centered men who politely disdained lesser mortals. Tom suspected him of being sexually lazy, a problem no doubt magnified by the ample size of his Austrian penis, an appendage Tom had seen while swimming one summer and had found as unattractive as a swollen ankle.

He knew that Winston was circling the field, waiting to land hard on the difficult topic of Oliver and Charlotte's guesthouse, and after a few more minutes of voyeuristic inquiry, he did just that.

"You know what I think about the project you designed for her, don't you?"

"You told me you like it," Tom said.

"I used the word *masterpiece*. I love it." He paused, raised his almost-chin, and said, "Beyond that, if it gets built, it will mean a lot to the firm. Those two have important friends, they have ambition, they throw cocktail parties that get written off on their taxes. They're both show-offs, and in photographs, they're the epitome of the unappealing, well-heeled, aging white couple that Americans claim to loathe while secretly aspiring to become."

"I didn't know you had so much interest in them," Tom said.

"My interest is in you. And your future here."

Shame about recent failures swept over Tom, followed by the familiar financial panic. Old as he was, he was still too young for Social Security.

"Let's face it, the past several years have not been professional high points for you," Winston said.

Several! This was an unfair overstatement, but pointing that out would only draw attention to the professional disappointments of the past two years. They hadn't been personal high points, either, but no need to paint himself as a flop on multiple fronts.

"I'm fond of you, Tom—at least to the extent that I'm capable of 'feelings'—and I'm grateful for the projects you've contributed, the publicity your houses brought, blah, blah. I won't bore you listing them."

If Winston had been capable of "feelings," he'd have known that no one is bored by a recitation, no matter how lengthy, of their professional accomplishments and personal virtues.

"But this is a business, and as difficult as it is to say, your presence here has not been a professional asset to the firm in recent years. You're at a stage of life approaching retirement, but I'm not there yet. I have a whole office and other careers to think of. Lanford's, to name one."

Tom was four years older than Winston, an insignificant age difference unless you were a teenager or, like Tom, were into your sixties. An advantage in the first case, a black eye in the second. They'd always carried on as peers, with the obvious difference of Winston's status as boss left politely unstated. Having it surface now emphasized the urgency of what Winston was telling him.

Winston took off his round, black-framed glasses, and his small eyes became tiny dots in his pale face. His rituals of cleanliness and polishing seemed to be slowly erasing his features, the way surgical cosmetic adjustments and injections sometimes do. He had been left with a pristine mask that most closely resembled a face when he dressed it up with eyeglasses and a scarf around the neck or, in winter, a hat. He put the glasses on his desk with the clatter of plastic against glass. "You need to make this happen, Tom." He gave Tom what was clearly meant to be a significant glance. "If you don't, I'm sure there are other firms that would be interested in looking at your portfolio."

Winston put his glasses back on and suddenly looked more like himself, though, with light glinting off the lenses, decidedly colder.

"That's blunt," Tom said.

"I know, and I'm sorry. I'm not good with awkward situations, so I thought I'd blurt it out."

"I didn't realize it had become this dire," Tom said. "Are you suggesting I add on the second floor she says she wants, if that's what it takes?"

"I'd never suggest stooping so low as to give in to a client. Besides which, it would ruin the building completely and render it meaningless to you and to the firm. You need to convince her that she wants the house as you designed it. And right away. If it doesn't go into construction as is by June, we'll have to assume it's not happening."

Tom considered what he'd just said. "Is this an ultimatum?"

Winston folded his hands on the desk in front of him, a prim, calm gesture. "Let's call it a final opportunity." As Tom was leaving, he added, just to drive the point home, "Try to help Lanford settle in. We need some new ideas around here, and he's got some interesting skills I want to exploit."

Shaken, Tom returned to his desk and looked at the schematics for Charlotte's guesthouse. Having it both his "masterpiece" and his possible downfall was a confusing state of affairs. It was a small, beautiful gem. Perfect. He smoothed out the rumpled paper Charlotte had handed him. It looked like something drawn by an impatient child (a fair description of Charlotte, come to think of it). Despite himself, he was touched that she'd used a ruler to draw the lines.

He took his phone out of the drawer again. He wondered if Cecily's drama was related to Dorothy. A stupid question, since every bit of drama in their minute family seemed to go back to Dorothy. Given her connection to Charlotte, even this disaster with the guesthouse could probably be traced back to his sister.

●

It was Dorothy who'd encouraged Tom to indulge in his love of design by studying architecture. This had happened four years after he graduated college and had been teaching math at a private school in Concord. He'd taught with the commitment and diligence with which he'd done everything since becoming an adult. Adulthood had been assigned to him in a moment—specifically, the moment his father died from an aneurysm during Tom's freshman year of college. Tom had been called home and told by his mother that he was now the head of the family and needed to transfer to a school he could commute to. He'd done as asked, not seeing any alternative, especially not when his mother suggested he bore some guilt for his father's death.

Dorothy was good at encouraging people to take leaps of faith. It was one of her best traits. She usually presented herself as an example of how important it was to worry about consequences only later. At that point, Tom didn't yet know that Dorothy's own leaps would lead to failures, albeit interesting ones: running a restaurant that was locally beloved but that eventually went bankrupt; starting a house-flipping company that was ahead of its time but that ran afoul of building codes to the tune of most of its profits; organizing a team of life coaches who offered innovative advice but ended up buried under a lawsuit after a client's suicide.

"You can't be safe and quietly miserable forever," Dorothy had told Tom. "Just take a chance. It's what I'd do."

Tom's leap into architecture had brought an improvement in his work life, if not exactly instant success. For many years after passing his board exam, he'd worked for large firms. He was a good team player, which is to say he lacked the burdensome ego and bullying confidence of most truly successful architects. His passion had always been for designing small spaces—houses whose interiors came in at under six hundred square feet and tiny apartments modeled on the economy of boats, with every inch given a function and nothing wasted. He'd been poring over designs and floor plans of small dwellings since childhood.

It all went back to his mother.

Incomprehensibly, Tom and Dorothy's mother, the daughter of Italian immigrants, had been plagued by dueling, contradictory afflictions: claustrophobia *and* agoraphobia. It was as if Tom, in his obsessive, highly detailed drawings, was trying to create a place for his mother that had just enough space to stave off her panic on one end of the spectrum without triggering her anxiety on the other. When she died of a rapacious cancer four years after their father's death, Tom and Dorothy, forever bonded by their early orphanhood, had argued about whether their mother would most hate the confinement of burial or the unchecked freedom of scattered ashes.

Tom recognized his fascination with small spaces as neurotic in origin. (As far as he could tell, everything involving an adult male and his living or dead mother was neurotic.) Still, when he was in his mid-forties, he'd gone to Winston Brill, the owner and founder of Winston Brill Architects, a successful boutique firm, and pitched himself by saying he'd like to join him and create a subspecialty in small dwellings.

Winston believed enthusiasm was "the madras shorts of emotions—gaudy and humiliating to witness." His reaction to Tom's proposal—"I don't *hate* this idea"—was uncharacteristically expressive. "It's not going to make either one of us much money," he'd said, "but it will give the firm another angle to pitch and generate local publicity for us. Possibly national as well, if we play it right."

For once, Tom had been ahead of the curve. A few years after he joined the firm, the "tiny house" movement started in earnest. He'd been interviewed by newscasters and vloggers who wanted tours of his compact houses and apartments, complete with explanations of the hidden storage compartments and built-in furniture with shapeshifting capabilities. One of his houses (a modern, largely glass cabin in Vermont with mountain views) had been profiled on HGTV. In a micro-corner of the "tiny" world, Tom was known.

He and Winston made a substantial profit developing a community of a dozen tiny houses on a pretty piece of land in western Massachusetts, a green alternative to the wasteful excesses of suburban living. This had been Tom's great coup professionally.

Then, suddenly, the market was glutted with tiny houses. Worse, the general public started to view them as the cooking shows of architecture: fun to look at on a screen, but do you really want to spend ten hours preparing salt cod? Would you really want to eat it if you did? After a few months of trying to live in two hundred square feet, no matter how cleverly arranged, most owners gave up and listed the dwellings on Airbnb, where the cramped loft beds and never-to-be-used composting toilets were ideal photo ops for social media posts.

He'd pivoted once again to his Petits Trianons, but now, even that seemed to be a declining market. Lanford's "hyperbolic tiny houses," with an emphasis on sustainability and adaptation, were clearly the next logical trend. He was being installed to supplant Tom.

Tom had made the mistake of thinking his early successes with Winston would carry him through any rough patches. What he hadn't accounted for was that while success is potent, it can't compete with the hurricane force of failure.

Chapter Five

*A*t home that night, in the comfortingly dim light of his living room, Tom turned on his record player and sank into his favorite chair, letting the lush, saccharine music wash over him.

After Alan had moved out and, appropriately, around the time he started drinking more than he should, Tom had bought a couple of vinyl Mantovani albums at a thrift shop near his house. He'd bought them for their lurid, campy covers, but as soon as he put one on the turntable and heard the improbably, almost laughably lush orchestral music, he became hooked. If he was going to turn into an old-fashioned suburban drunk—*unemployed* old-fashioned suburban drunk—there was no better soundtrack for his life than this conductor's swooning, cinematic arrangements of waltzes, movie themes, and light classics. This was the music of midcentury, cigarette-and-martini America. Tom had vague memories of his father listening to this music, which transformed any paneled basement "rec room" into an opulent and melancholy hotel lobby. Richard Nixon was said to have listened to Annunzio Mantovani as he surveyed Washington from the Oval Office with the air-conditioning blasting and the White House fireplaces lit. Not a recommendation, but certainly a point of reference.

Tom now found it the perfect music to listen to while he sat in his living room, surveyed the wreckage of his life, wineglass in hand, and telephoned Cecily. Whatever her problem was, he was *not* going to get involved. After all, his inability to tamp down his feelings of responsibility for her was one of the reasons Alan had left him.

It's not that I don't admire you for caring for her so much. Seeing how good you are to her was one of the reasons I fell in love with you. It's just that I now know I'll never come first in your life.

"Where am I getting you?" he asked Cecily. Here was yet another thing you had to adapt to: asking people where they were when they answered their phone—a minor adjustment compared with rising sea levels, but it all added up.

"I'm out walking in my neighborhood," she said.

He flashed on the leafy streets near her apartment: post–Chicago Fire stone two-flats, that descriptive Chicago nomenclature. The apartment was roomy and light filled, albeit depressingly furnished. She'd moved in after Santosh had been renting for a couple of years. Tom had fantasized about helping the two of them purchase it at some point in the future, although he'd suppressed the fantasies—or had tried to—when Alan reminded him that he needed to think about *their* future and let Cecily and Santosh (both professionals) take care of their own.

"Thanks for calling me back, Tom."

"As if there was a possibility I wouldn't?"

"Even so. I'm always calling you with problems."

Tom put down his glass. *Problems.* His resolution about detachment wavered. He wished, suddenly, he'd waited to start drinking. He didn't mind not being fully present for himself—that, after all, was the whole point of drinking—but with Cecily, it was a different story.

From the first moment he picked up newborn Cecily in the hospital where Dorothy had given birth and looked into her pretty, worried face, he'd felt an absolute commitment to be available to her. She seemed to be saying to him, in those first moments of her life, *You're going to help me deal with my mother, aren't you? Please?* And, silently, he had answered, *Yes, of course. Always*, and had kissed her brow. He fell in love with her with an intensity he hadn't experienced before or since. Alan had an entirely valid point about how central she was to him.

There had been other pivotal moments as well.

One morning, when Tom was living in a basement apartment in a house down the street from Dorothy's, a place he'd rented so he could be close enough to help out with his niece, he walked into Dorothy's living room and saw six-year-old Cecily emptying ashtrays and picking up wineglasses from one of Dorothy's dinners from the night before while Dorothy slept on the sofa—she rarely slept in a bed—and a dinner guest snored in an armchair. Tom had ushered Cecily out of the room and taken her to his place to work on designs for her "dream house," a project they'd develop throughout her childhood.

A big part of his life had been spent making up to her for all the overflowing ashtrays and overheard confessions she dealt with as a child—though, on the whole, he was suspicious of people who placed excessive importance on family connections and the disturbing notion of "blood." Like religious beliefs, these ideas were often presented as the source of empathy, love, and generosity, but were more often used as excuses for doling those things out selectively. And yet, what he felt toward Cecily was inseparable from the fact that she was his sister's child, a status that gave him some claim to her.

"Did you learn anything about the investigation?" he asked.

"No, not yet. I got an email from Dorothy about an event she's having in a couple weeks, for a new business. She really wants me to attend."

This again. "Yes," Tom said. "I heard about that, but to be honest, I chose to ignore it."

"I need to get away for a little while, until the committee contacts me. I was hoping I could stay with you for a couple of weeks, if that's all right. Maybe we could go out to Dorothy's grand opening together."

"The guest cottage is all yours," he said. "For as long as you want it."

He went to the window on the north side of the house and looked out across the top of a rhododendron hedge to the cedar-and-glass building nestled in the side yard. If you read his tax returns, it was a professional investment: a testing ground for ideas of economy of space. In truth, though, from the earliest stages, he'd thought of it as a refuge for Cecily, should she ever need one. He built it with the money he'd saved to fix up the main house to make it more livable for him and Alan. He'd been promising Alan the renovation for years. Alan, who adored Cecily, had never forgiven him for putting her needs ahead of their own. The guest cottage had caused irreparable rifts in their relationship.

"As for going out to Woodstock, I'm afraid you're on your own, kiddo," Tom said. "Although, you're welcome to my car. When are you thinking of coming?"

"Tuesday would be ideal. If it's inconvenient, I can find something else for a while."

The timing was disconcerting. Cecily had always planned in advance, no doubt a reaction to her mother's casual relationship to things like time, money, and reality.

"Tuesday is perfect," he said. It wasn't. He should instead be dealing with Charlotte and figuring out the best way to turn around that looming disaster. But, no matter what, he couldn't say no to Cecily.

"Can you check with Alan? I don't want to be in his way, either."

Given the reasons for Alan's departure, Tom had been unable to tell Cecily he'd gone. He picked up the wineglass again to fortify himself. "You won't be in Alan's way, I can promise you that. You're all right, aren't you, Cecily? I'm worried about you."

"I've been better. It'll be good to get a break, and I can tell you more when I get there. Maybe we can go ice-skating."

That had been one their rituals in her childhood. It was touching and concerning that she was thinking about it now. "I'd love that," he said.

"Thanks, Tom. I promise not to make a pest of myself. You know how committed I am to not being needy."

He did know, and that was one of the things that made her so touchingly needy.

He hung up and decided he had to do something about Alan now, before Cecily arrived. Technically, they were still on speaking terms, but Tom was usually the one to initiate the conversations, and much of what Alan had to say was delivered with an edge of disappointment.

He finished his glass of wine and dialed. "Where am I getting you?" Tom asked once again.

"On my phone," Alan said.

Oh, right. Alan had made it clear that he didn't have to tell Tom where he was and what he was doing every time he called.

"Scrap the question. Reflex. I wanted to let you know I just heard from Cecily." Alan's love for Cecily was reciprocated, but Tom had never felt that Alan had replaced him in her affections, and for that, he was grateful. Almost everyone else he knew seemed to like Alan more than they liked him. Tom couldn't blame them; *he* liked Alan more than he liked himself. Alan was good with dogs and children. He played the piano well enough to charm people but not so well as to be intimidating. He teared up at weddings. He was a nurse, and as if that weren't sympathetic enough, he worked with a pediatrician. He was ten years younger than Tom, a fact that had once made people look at Tom as if he must be sexually desirable but that, lately, made them look at him as if he must be sexually predatory. His friends had always resented Tom for having snagged Alan—not exactly a beauty, but unmistakably a catch. Now, confoundingly, the few people he'd told about the split seemed to resent him for not hanging on to him.

"Cecily," Alan sang, suddenly his unfiltered, sentimental self. "How is she?"

"Not great."

"I guess she wouldn't be with the investigation. And could you turn down that depressing music? What the hell is it?"

"Annunzio Mantovani. A largely forgotten musical giant. He sold more albums than any British person before the Beatles surpassed his record. Famous for his cascading strings." Tom was impressed by anyone who was exceptionally good at what they did, even if he didn't care for the thing itself.

"It sounds like music they'd play at a Swiss clinic for assisted suicide," Alan said.

"I'm happy to report, I wouldn't know from experience." Now that Alan had planted the idea in his head, he could hear it: the eerie spaciness of the strings, as if you were being led to another portal. "Cecily is coming to visit next week, probably for ten days or so. She needs a change of venue."

"I'm sure you'll cheer her up. I'm glad the cottage is available for her."

This was a dig Tom chose to ignore. "She wants to see you, too." It was best to dive into this. "The thing is, Alan, I haven't told her you moved out."

There was an annoyed silence on the other end of the phone. "Well, you're going to have to, aren't you?"

Tom steeled himself. "Listen, I know I'm not in a position to ask for favors, but you know how she is. If she finds out we're . . . whatever we are . . ."

"We're no longer living together. For starters."

"Right. She's going to feel bad about having come. And I certainly can't tell her *why* you moved out."

"There was more than one reason."

"One central one, let's be honest. She'll have to deal with her mother on this visit, and that's already a lot. I don't want her worrying about me."

Alan sighed, and Tom heard him drop himself onto the squeaky, used Le Corbusier chaise longue Tom had found for him online to help furnish his otherwise stark bachelor pad. He had a sudden urge to ask Alan what he was wearing. Unfortunately, after years of a lackluster sex life—sustaining an intense erotic attraction for ten years was a challenge; not even refrigerators are expected to last that long anymore—Tom found himself erotically fixated on Alan. His familiarity with every inch of Alan's body, all his freckles and flaws, once the source of fond boredom, now provoked lurid fantasies that were entirely inappropriate for his age.

Come to think of it, all fantasies and aspirations were inappropriate for his age. Upon turning sixty, you were supposed to settle back into the lonely bed you'd made and live with the consequences. To want more personally or professionally, an ardent love life or an architectural legacy project, meant depriving a younger person who hadn't had the opportunities you'd already been presented with and blown—and who, by the way, wasn't responsible for the destruction of the planet. You were expected to cede your career to Lanford, for starters.

"You can't be serious, Tom. You want me to pretend I'm still living there? How's that supposed to make me feel?"

Tom hoped that it would make him feel like he belonged there and wanted to come live with him again, but now that Alan had brought it up, he could see the problem. He was putting Cecily's feelings first, the very issue that had made Alan move out.

"I'll come for dinner when she arrives. Beyond that, we'll play it by ear."

It seemed like a flawed but fair compromise. "Thank you," Tom said. "By the way, Alan, what're you wearing?"

There was a pause, and then Alan ended the call.

Maybe he was setting himself up for more disaster, but at the very least, for one evening, he'd have Alan and Cecily here at the same time—the two people he cared most about in the world.

Chapter Six

*O*n Sunday afternoon, Cecily decided she couldn't put it off any longer. She had to tell Santosh her plans. It was unconscionable that she'd waited so long, but if you wanted to put a favorable spin on it, you could say she'd been hoping she'd change her mind about leaving.

That hadn't happened.

She walked into the apartment after spending the morning at the Daily Grind slightly nauseated by the thought of what she was about to do. Santosh was sitting on a stool at the high table across from the kitchen, under headphones, working on his music. His computer screen was a kaleidoscope of colorful graphs and wave patterns, and he was clicking his way through them, as if playing another of his games. "His music" was a collection of beats and samples he put together to create three- and four-minute songs that throbbed with deep, unexpected trip-hop melancholy and shoe-gaze dreaminess. They were gorgeous, atmospherically and melodically, and the sadness in them revealed a side of Santosh he never otherwise displayed and probably didn't know he had. That he was able to create these complicated, evocative pieces was magic. He played no instrument, couldn't read music, and didn't sing.

A faint smell of weed hovered in the air. Technically, she hated it. Skunky and cloying, like the smell of a dish you'd made with the wrong ingredients, overcooked, and had to throw out. And yet, it always made her feel cozy when she smelled it in the air of the apartment, as if, somehow, it were connected to Santosh's contentment with her and their life together.

He'd told her their start-up was on the cusp of a major breakthrough. There was a tense excitement throbbing in the muscles of his face when he talked about work these days. The project itself remained vague. "I don't want to jinx it," he'd said. "And in case it doesn't happen, it's better not to discuss it. You've had enough disappointments this year." It was a rare acknowledgment of her problems at Deerpath.

She came up behind him swamped with affection and missing him already. He leaned back into her and said, "Give me a couple minutes to finish this?"

She kissed the top of his head. His thick black hair was sweet with the goop he put in it to (unsuccessfully) keep it from falling into his eyes.

She went into the kitchen to make popcorn. In a pot. With oil and a lot of shaking. Tom had insisted they make popcorn this way throughout her childhood. He took a stand against shortcuts like microwave popcorn, frozen waffles, and coffee made from a sealed pod. "The lazy man's version of integrity," as he referred to it.

She looked around the apartment through Tom's eyes. She and Santosh lived like grad students: makeshift furniture and casual sloppiness that she barely noticed anymore. A good portion of the room was devoted to Santosh's sports equipment: skateboards, a net bag of soccer balls, a paddleboard he'd haul to the lake in a couple of months. Sometimes she swooned when she walked into the apartment and saw this messy composite portrait of a man she loved. Santosh had been living here for two years when she moved in. She'd left a small footprint, part of her tendency since childhood to stay in the background and leave her shoes tucked under the bed.

She watched Santosh, lost in his own world, as she shook the heavy pot and the popcorn kernels ricocheted against the sides. He was the most handsome man she'd ever been with: lean, muscular, with dark eyes and the angular features of a young Roman emperor or a Bengali prince. His looks were a sharp contrast to his personality, which was that of a candy- and gaming-obsessed American adolescent.

It was no surprise to Cecily that Neeta thought he was too good for her: he was a truly decent person, a man without malice or cruelty. Now Neeta had incontrovertible proof that she'd been right about Cecily's unworthiness all along. How foolish Cecily had been to think she could keep her shameful situation a secret. These days, privacy was a leaky vessel, and her ship was foundering.

She went to the sofa across the room from his desk and, when he looked up, raised the bowl of popcorn. He made a puppyish dive for her, stuck his hand into the bowl, and sat at the opposite end of the cushion with his feet in her lap, crunching.

"I wish you weren't so good-looking," she said. "Even eating popcorn."

"Wait another ten years. I'll look exactly like my father. Bald, big eyeglasses, many chins."

He never would, but she was suddenly too choked up to say that. He had his mother's beauty, roughed up by testosterone and all those injuries from sports and, as she'd just learned, falling off rooftops.

She started to massage one of his long, frequently wounded feet and told him about the email from her mother with its request for attendance at her event. "I called Tom and asked him what he thought I should do."

"What'd he say?"

"He said I could stay with him, and I could visit her from there in his car."

"That's nice of him."

"I told him I'd be there on Tuesday."

Santosh's eyes flashed, and he became atypically alert. "That soon? The opening's not for a while."

"I can do some research at the Radcliffe library. They have a huge cookbook collection."

His lack of follow-up suggested doubt. "When do you come back?"

"I haven't booked a flight yet."

Santosh wasn't big on confrontation, never started fights, and once, when she provoked him for reasons she couldn't explain, had called her a "bitch" and then wept for having done so. Now she reached for his hand, but he refused to take it. "You should have run your plans past me first."

She shuddered. She wasn't used to his anger.

"I thought it would be easier on both of us if I got away from Deerpath for a while."

"We live twenty-three miles from campus."

He withdrew his feet and sat up facing her with eerie calm and a seriousness she barely recognized as belonging to him. It was as if, in the past few seconds, he'd shed his adolescent playfulness and become the adult male he rarely was except in brief moments when he was looking down at her as they made love. She realized she'd miscalculated. She'd fallen into the trap of treating him like an adolescent, assuming a role with a faintly maternal cast to it.

"My mother . . ."

"It's not about your mother," he said. "If it was, you'd have asked me to go with you, and we'd have spent a weekend for this opening. You'd have booked a return flight."

Now she felt cornered and tried a desperate move: the truth, but only a portion of it. "I'm sitting around waiting for someone to deliver a verdict," she said. "I don't know when it's coming. My whole future depends on it." In so many more ways than Santosh knew. "Maybe a change of scenery will take my mind off it."

He reached down and grabbed the bowl of popcorn. It was an act of domestic normalcy that felt like a small reprieve. She took a few kernels herself, but they were dry in her mouth, and she had trouble swallowing them. Santosh got her a glass of water.

"Thank you," she said.

He took her face in his hands. She loved his long, thin fingers. "Isn't it enough that I know you didn't do anything?"

It's not enough for your mother, she wanted to say.

When she told him about it, Santosh had dismissed the investigation as another example of how ridiculous academia was, how insular and detached from the way people thought and behaved in the real world. It was inconceivable to him that a similar event would have gotten out of hand so quickly where he worked—although, how a video game start-up counted as "the real world" wasn't clear. Every time she'd tried to discuss it in detail, he'd waved it off, telling her he trusted her and didn't need details.

"You're not guilty of anything," he said now, as definite and assertive on the matter as he'd ever been.

"The problem is," she said, "I am. I am guilty of *some*thing. I made mistakes. I am partly responsible. I can't claim I'm not. I should have put my foot down with her months before it happened."

He looked toward his computer. The only annoyance she ever felt toward Santosh was that he—unlike his mother, apparently—was impatient. She couldn't tell if he was frustrated with her insistence on guilt or merely bored with the topic and eager to get back to his music.

"I know I can't change your mind," he said. "About leaving. About any of this."

"No, I don't think you can."

"Then I'm not going to try."

He didn't say it coldly, but she heard the comment as an acceptance of her demand—which, oddly, now felt like a loss for her. He went back to his desk and put on his headphones. The computer screen lit up with its pulsing graphs. In some infinitely small way, he was moving on. She wanted to weep. Not because she felt she'd made a mistake, but because she knew that, in doing this, she was delaying the awful choice his mother had laid out at their miserable lunch days earlier. *I'm doing it for you*, she wanted to shout, but she wasn't the shouting kind. If worse came to worst, he would get over her. She didn't doubt that he loved her, but the awful truth was she was replaceable. A girlfriend, any girlfriend, was. His parents were not; he'd never get over losing them.

She took out her phone and texted Neeta. **You'll be happy to hear I'm leaving town for a while. On Tuesday.**

There was no response. Of course there wasn't. Neeta had never doubted it would come to this.

She waited half an hour and called Dorothy, who, to her credit, had gotten herself back to the garden. As Cecily dialed, it occurred to her that she very possibly had just cast herself out of the garden.

Chapter Seven

*C*onventional wisdom had it you were supposed to hate O'Hare Airport: crowded, noisy, chaotic, unreliable in winter, hell in summer during one of Chicago's oppressive heatwaves. All true, but Cecily had always loved it. Whenever she landed here, she felt she was coming home. To Chicago. To Santosh.

Today, she was leaving.

When Santosh left the house for work this morning, he'd held her face in his hands, once again the assertive man, looked into her eyes, and said, "You'd better come back soon."

"I will," she said, barely able to get the words out. She had no idea if she was making a promise she hoped to keep or was lying.

She went to the window to watch him walk up the street, stooped, wheeling his bike. Then he stopped to talk with one of their landladies, and he seemed his usual animated self. He was adapting. Cecily knew a thing or two about adaptation. It was one skill her upbringing with erratic and unpredictable Dorothy had taught her. She'd never known whether to be angry or grateful for that.

She'd arrived at O'Hare a lot earlier than necessary, so she found herself strolling down the concourse to her gate with more than an hour to kill. She'd checked her suitcase, not because she had to, but because she had a particular animus toward people who tried to walk onto airplanes with ridiculous amounts of luggage and wanted to distance herself from them. If she ever ran for office (ha ha), she'd run on a platform of civic virtues: How to be a good passenger. How to be a helpful neighbor. How to accept that your admiration for Ayn Rand came from your very worst adolescent impulses.

She stopped to consider a sandwich. The food at O'Hare was generally good but ridiculously expensive. She didn't care. She needed the comfort of carbohydrates.

As she was perusing a menu, she glanced up and spotted someone near the window who looked a lot like one of her former students: Lee. Her best student last year. Maybe ever. Her biggest fan. Her accuser.

Cecily had grown so used to a panicked heartbeat when she saw someone who looked like Lee—in the Daily Grind or on the street—that it took her a moment to realize that, this time, it was not an imagined doppelganger but Lee herself, the very person. Small, utterly harmless in appearance, exactly as she'd been when she first walked into Cecily's classroom. With her face buried in a book at the little restaurant table as crowds rushed around her, she looked as isolated as she always had in the lecture hall.

Cecily grew weak under the weight of her backpack, as if her legs were about to give out. She dropped the menu and hurried in what she hoped was the direction of her gate. She'd never felt more grateful for the crowds of people swallowing her up. It was horrifying that she and Lee were in the same building, immense and bustling though it was.

When she'd walked far enough away to be confident she'd escaped—from what, she wasn't sure—she stopped and joined a line at a Starbucks. As she was placing her order, she felt the presence of someone behind her, a little too close. The skin of her neck tingled, but she didn't turn around. She canceled her order.

"God, you saw me back there in the restaurant, and you didn't even come over and say hi? A quick hello?"

Cecily looked right and left before turning to face Lee, irrationally afraid someone from Deerpath might be watching them. "I'm sorry," she said. "It's just that I can't talk to you, Lee. It's not personal, it's just not allowed. It would be bad for both of us."

She tried to walk away, but Lee, small as she was, blocked her path. "Why'd you do that to your hair?"

"That's not relevant here."

"It wasn't 'cause of me, was it?"

In some ways, of course it was—because of her anxiety over the Title IX investigation, because of not knowing what to do or how to respond to the accusation and the request to stay off campus, she'd thought it would be a good idea to cut her hair herself. For the first time in her life. "I had it cut for practical reasons. It makes it easier to get out of the house early in the morning."

"Yeah, I doubt it. Anyway, you're on leave. You can sleep late." She tugged on Cecily's sleeve, the gesture of a small child. It filled Cecily with empathy and regret. "I didn't file a complaint, you know. It's not my fault it all went down. I want you to know that, okay?"

"I'm not supposed to know everything right now, Lee. That's how it works. The one thing I do know is that I'm not supposed to be talking to you." Cecily was swamped with the same horrible feeling she'd had a few months earlier, the afternoon of the incident that had led to all this. Whatever she did or said now would be wrong, would pull her deeper into misunderstanding. Her head was buzzing. She'd never had a panic attack, but she suspected this was the way they started. "I'm not angry, and I'm not blaming you or anyone else," she said. "It's just that we can't talk."

"I have a counselor at school. You probably could have guessed that, since you probably think I'm crazy. I talked about you and how close we got. She asked if you'd ever done anything that made me uncomfortable. Well, what was I supposed to say? No?"

In academia, discomfort of any kind was increasingly equated with trauma. Cecily's instincts were always to make her students as comfortable and at ease as possible, but another part of her thought that some of this was the equivalent of infantilizing twenty-year-olds at the exact moment they should be trained for adulthood.

"I told her how we'd kissed, and she told me she had to report it. After that, I don't even know what happened."

This was a variation on what Cecily had suspected about the events that triggered the investigation. Eventually, she'd get to tell her side of the story, but it was unlikely anyone would ask her if she'd been made to feel uncomfortable. She needed to end this conversation right now. Thanks to the few words they'd exchanged, she would no longer be able to say, with complete honesty, that she'd had no contact with Lee since the complaint was filed.

"Wherever you're going, Lee, I hope you have a good trip."

"Not likely. It's spring break. Not relevant to you, I guess. I'm visiting my mother in Florida. She's freaking out about some man, of course, and I have to talk her off the cliff."

Lee had told Cecily about her childhood in the Florida Panhandle. She'd grown up with a single mother who tended toward erratic behavior and disastrous relationships with men; she'd never met her father. All this had made Cecily feel closer to her, almost as if she were a long-lost cousin. It made Cecily want to give her more attention, to make Lee feel accepted.

"Maybe you'll be surprised and have a nice time," she said.

Lee shrugged, leaving open the possibility, Cecily hoped, that she might. "Where are *you* going?" she asked.

Cecily paused, wondering if she should answer or not. "That's not something I can tell you."

"Oh, come on! Really? Since when did you get so corporate?"

Corporate was hardly the appropriate term, but Lee had artfully chosen one she knew Cecily would find insulting. "Boston," she said.

"Oh, right. You grew up there."

Of course Lee would remember a detail like that. Perhaps Cecily had mentioned it in passing during a lecture. She liked tossing in a few personal details to avoid appearing aloof. On top of that, she'd learned that when attentions drifted, mentioning something about herself brought the students back. Briefly. Despite everything, it touched her that Lee remembered this.

"I have to go, or I'll miss my flight," she said.

"Lame excuse, but your call. And just so you know, I'm probably going to drop out of school."

Cecily paused as she was walking away. It was hard to know if this was just Lee's ploy for attention or something she was really planning. Defeated, she turned. "That would be a mistake," she said. "You're one of the best students I've had at Deerpath. You've got a scholarship. You should seriously rethink that plan."

"Maybe I could call you, and we could talk about it?"

"No," Cecily said. "I'm sorry, but we can't."

"Is that why you blocked me on all your social media?"

"I'm taking a break from social media for a while," Cecily said. "I've deleted some of my accounts." This was the truth. She was terrified she'd accidentally stumble across some angry, inaccurate comments about herself. Responding would be ruinous, and the temptation to respond would be impossible to resist. "I hope you stay in school. Talk it over with your academic adviser. They'll tell you the same thing."

"I'm done with them. They're useless. You're the only one I really respect."

As Cecily was walking away, she felt a pang of satisfaction at Lee's final statement. Was she really so desperate for approval that she took pleasure in what Lee had said? She felt Lee's eyes on her as she hurried down the concourse and was again relieved when she was deep in a crowd.

In the waiting lounge at her gate, she kept looking up from her book, expecting to see Lee or maybe a reproachful colleague glaring at her. When her flight was finally called, she hurried onto the Jetway and into her cramped window seat. She was so relieved to be sealed into the humming little tube with its filtered air, it almost felt roomy.

Chapter Eight

*H*er full name was Lee Anderson.
Lee had enrolled in Cecily's Women and Cults, a 100-level course that was cross-listed under American Studies, Sociology, and Women and Gender Studies. It was a matter of pride to Cecily that although enrollment was capped at fifteen, interest had been high, and, in the end, she'd been asked to change it from a seminar to a lecture. Ultimately, she'd let in fifty-one students. Lee Anderson was the last student enrolled.

Some of her senior colleagues in American Studies had congratulated her. Enrollments were down across the humanities, and her numbers looked good for the whole department. Still, the words of support had been laced with suggestions that her popularity was being attributed to her youth, to the fact that she often showed videos in her lectures, and, most especially, to her appearance as a talking head on a few local newscasts and one five-minute panel she'd participated in on a weekend MSNBC program.

Congrats on the cult class. I guess being on TV really does matter!

Fantastic enrollment numbers, Cecily. Enjoy the accolades before you turn forty!

The department is thrilled with the size of the class. We should make showing movies mandatory.

She often walked around campus telling herself that she had no reason to feel guilty for her popularity, but there was no denying that she did feel as if she'd somehow cheated her way into this small-scale success. Her colleagues would decide her tenure case eventually, so, of course she wanted their approval. More questionable was her desire to be liked and, for once, to feel part of a community of peers. Probably she was destined always to feel like the lone child in a household of adults, exactly as she'd felt throughout her childhood. In her mother's house, she'd always been central but irrelevant. So many of her mother's friends who passed through for parties or dinners or vacations from relationships eyed her as if they couldn't understand where she'd come from or what she was doing there. *Oh, Cecily! I didn't expect to see you here*, she heard. As if they thought a seven-year-old might be off traveling?

The success of Cecily's book had made it seem inevitable that, eventually, she would get tenure at Deerpath College—especially if she followed it up with another academically sound book with crossover appeal. Yes, there were little currents of collegial resentment, but she'd been assured by friends at other institutions that something truly egregious would have to come up to block her path to full professor.

Enter Lee Anderson.

Cecily had conceived of the cult course as an exploration of women's attraction to patronizing male gurus and the way they preyed on women's learned comfort in the role of domestic caretakers. Her central thesis was that women's involvement in cults followed the same patterns as women's relationships with abusive partners and misogynist politicians. Not groundbreaking, but enough of an idea around which to build a syllabus and connect to the topic of her first book.

To her astonishment, many students entered the class with a romanticized view of cults, as if they were nothing more than benign hippie communes. In the discussion groups Cecily held, she found that the "family" aspect of these sects had an unsettling, nostalgic appeal. Her students were only a dozen or so years younger than she, but they all seemed to love wallowing in nostalgia for anything connected to their childhoods: YA novels, theme parks, Disney movies, family road trips in SUVs equipped with televisions and heated seats. It was an unbridge-able gap between their thinking and her own: she never longed for the past. "What do you have against families?" one student had asked. A fair question, but one she wasn't about to answer.

There was immense curiosity about the influence that cults had on fashion, as if Manson's most notable impact had been inspiring Raf Simons.

Right from the outset, Lee Anderson had shown sensitivity and insight into Cecily's frustration with all this. She assumed positions contrary to those of her peers in discussion groups, laying waste to the most facile and offensive opinions. She took the intellectual arguments seriously, but it was clear she was also defending the professor—not so much to seek her approval as to protect her from all the shallow thinking.

Lee often came up to the front of the lecture hall to talk as Cecily was packing up her notes. "Don't let them get you down," she'd say. Or: "That was incredibly interesting and well prepared." Or: "They're just dumb kids. And I hate families, too."

Lee was a sophomore, and despite her confidence and intelligence, she looked barely old enough to be in high school, never mind college. She was small and had the downy blond hair of a duckling. Her clothes were always too big, which had the effect of making her appear even smaller.

The breaking point for Cecily had come when a couple of students appeared in class wearing long "granny" dresses they'd purchased at a thrift store, emulating the garb of the Lingenhoffs, a cult in Appalachia that had entrapped women as unpaid workers in a furniture factory to bring in money for the community. In their off-hours, the women were essentially sex slaves for the men who provided the spiritual enlighten-ment and, if there was time between orgies, the organic vegetables. While the men dressed as they pleased, the woman were required to wear long prairie dresses and bonnets. Obviously, modesty was important for sex slaves. The group had finally been driven out of existence by investiga-tions that had revealed multiple cases of child abuse, surreptitious drug-ging of community members, and, inevitably, sexual molestation.

"Considering the suffering caused by this cult," Cecily had said to the costumed students, "I don't think it's wise to dress up in ways that pay tribute to them. If we were studying the Holocaust, you wouldn't come to class wearing Nazi paraphernalia, would you?"

"You can't find that in thrift stores," one of the granny dresses had called out.

"Try the dark web," Cecily offered, and then had done her best to deliver her planned lecture.

An hour after class, Lee had shown up at Cecily's office. She knocked on her open door with a concerned look, and asked if she could come in.

"Of course," Cecily had said. "Take a seat while I finish this email."

Lee had the appealingly androgynous looks Cecily often saw on female students who identified as queer or somewhere on the gender-nonconforming spectrum. The fact that she projected no particular sexual energy led Cecily to believe she was still negotiating her preferences and priorities and was probably chaste. Cecily was convinced that Lee's interest in her was entirely platonic, and that her crush—if that's what it was—was intellectual in nature. As for pronouns, Lee had bluntly stated that she was fine with anything from *she* to *it*. "I think it's fun," she said, "to find out how people see me from one minute to the next."

She had a uniform that varied little from day to day: oversize work pants and jackets a mechanic might wear. There was something swaggering in her demeanor, a kind of machismo that would have been annoying in a frat boy but had sweetness in someone as gender-fluid, petite, and socially awkward as Lee.

She took a seat on the windowsill in Cecily's office, nervously patting her knees until Cecily sent off her email.

"What's up, Lee?"

"I want to make sure you're all right," Lee said.

"Do you mean about the dresses?" Cecily asked. "I overreacted. They were just having fun."

"It was moronic. As if we were talking about a rock concert instead of a life-threatening situation."

"Well, to be fair," Cecily said, "in some cases, rock concerts have been life threatening. I was in a bad mood. I'm guessing a lot of people haven't caught up on the reading, so they didn't understand the implications."

"If you want, I can take an informal poll of who's done the reading."

This offer was silly but endearing. When Cecily thanked her and said it wasn't necessary, Lee pushed herself off the windowsill and said, "If that's how you feel, just keep me posted," and left abruptly.

Lee was easily offended. Cecily would have to remember that.

As the weeks wearied on, Lee began showing up at Cecily's office more often. She loved talking about the course and batting around ideas. Unlike—Cecily was certain—everyone else enrolled, she did all the required reading and all the suggested additional reading. She watched the videos Cecily posted and sent Cecily links to articles she had uncovered herself online. Her ability to track down primary-source material was impressive, especially for someone so young. Who could possibly resist such diligence and flattering, passionate engagement with the subject? When Cecily sensed that she was losing the attention of students as she was making a point, she'd look to Lee for reassurance that at least one person was taking in every word. Lee never took notes but, later, could repeat back entire phrases from Cecily's lectures.

When she dug into Lee's academic record, Cecily learned she was on a full scholarship, had perfect SAT scores, but was hovering only slightly above where she needed to be grade-wise for her funding. "She's dismissive toward a lot of her professors," her academic adviser told Cecily.

Cecily began to look forward to Lee's office visits, even when they came late in the day, as she was getting ready to go home. She started to think of her as her unofficial teaching assistant. Lee's emails, sent at all hours of the night, sometimes included tidbits of information about other students in the class, something Cecily had no interest in encouraging but did enjoy hearing. "You know Jane and Troy? They always sit on the left in the front row? They started going out after they met in class. He's got one-third her brains, but you knew that"; or "That guy who made the stupid comment about the Mormons today? I heard he's flunking two other classes."

"Best to keep that info to yourself," Cecily had written back. And then, fearing Lee might be offended, prefaced this with "Not that I'm uninterested, but . . ."

When she decided to discourage Lee's too-frequent emails by not responding, more and more arrived, asking if she'd received the previous messages, if she was all right, if there was anything Lee could do to help. It was easiest to type out a quick reply and be done with it.

When Lee talked about her childhood with her erratic single mother, Cecily felt an almost eerie identification, despite many glaring differences. She felt she owed her something, given that she could relate to the disorienting nature of her upbringing. A few times, Lee had forwarded messages her mother had sent her, to which Cecily had responded with a frowning emoji or something equally noncommittal. Lee never talked about friends or romantic interests with her.

Later, when she looked back, Cecily saw that the frequency of Lee's visits increased gradually, so that at first Cecily hadn't noticed. Lee would come in, plop herself down on the deep windowsill, and either debate the finer points of something they'd discussed in class or ask Cecily—brash and faux-confident in a way that was, at least at the time, almost comical—"So, how are you doing, Cecily? Did you get some time to yourself this past weekend?"

Lee behaved a little like a younger sister—in terms of her age, she easily could have been—who was trying to prove her maturity to her older sibling. It had all seemed fine—right up to the moment when it didn't, the moment when it went all wrong.

That moment came on a wet and cold Friday afternoon in November, when Cecily felt a sinus headache coming on and was so exhausted, she wanted to get home and take a nap with Santosh but also so exhausted that she kept putting off leaving her office and facing the sleet on her walk to the commuter train.

Lee appeared in her office doorway, almost silently. She said "Knock, knock" instead of rapping.

"Ah," Cecily said. She was tired enough to be annoyed by the intrusion. "I was getting ready to leave."

"Oh, perfect," Lee said. She sat on the windowsill, her legs spread, her fingers tapping her knees. "I got my paycheck from my job at the library, and I wanted to invite you to dinner. My treat!" She gave a little wink that seemed both pushy and insecure.

The offer and wink made Cecily recalibrate the entire fall. In a flash, she saw the multiple ways in which she was at fault for not correcting course sooner. She felt a sudden chill, even though her office was over-heated and she was wearing a bulky sweater.

"That's the best offer I've had all week," she said, "but I'm afraid I . . ."—and here she paused for a second or two, deciding how much to say—"I have dinner plans already. With my boyfriend."

Lee scrutinized her skeptically. "Sounds kind of like you just made up these plans. '*I, I, I* have plans.' For all I know, you're making up the boyfriend, too, since I've never heard about him before."

The comments started in a jokey tone of voice but ended with anger. Cecily had been careless and selfish in accepting so much attention. The only thing she could do now was get it all out of the way, before she dug herself in deeper.

"The point is, Lee," she said, as gently as she could, "whether I have plans or a boyfriend or not—and I have both—I don't go out to dinner with my students. Especially not at their expense."

"You can treat me, if it would make you feel better."

"It wouldn't." And then, with a reckless, urgent hope that she might bring the conversation to a close, she said, "It looks like the sleet is turning to snow."

"So, now you're 'redirecting'? Now we're supposed to talk about the *weather*? 'Gee, Professor Kemp, I hear it's supposed to be sunny on Tuesday.' I thought we were friends, and now, all of a sudden, I'm just one of your clueless students you talk to about the fucking barometric pressure?"

Cecily was still standing behind her desk but was getting dizzy and was eager to sit down. "You know I think you're the farthest thing possible from clueless. But you are my student. I'm happy we're on friendly terms; you've made the whole semester a lot richer for me and everyone else enrolled."

"So, next semester I won't be your student. We can go out to dinner then. Is that what you're saying?"

"No, it isn't. You'll still be a student at the school."

"Jesus, Cecily," Lee said, "I didn't know you were such a fucking bureaucrat."

It was then that Cecily noticed that instead of the gritty work pants and mechanic's jacket Lee usually wore, she had on navy-blue khakis and a blue-and-white-striped button-down shirt. She looked pretty and carefully put together. She wasn't carrying the oversize backpack she carted to every class. With a combination of horror and sadness, Cecily realized that Lee, almost certainly, had dressed for her, for this dinner date that she had imagined as inevitable. Cecily had done something to make Lee view it as inevitable. At some point, she'd gone from being welcoming and attentive to giving her false hope. She had to accept responsibility for that.

Her office was in one of the old mansions that had been the core of Deerpath's original campus, before the school went coed and started to expand rapidly. It was a beautiful building that, like a lot of beautiful things, did not function especially well. When the heat came on, the pipes in the wall began to bang as if someone were forcefully hammering. Cecily had always found the sound comforting: the radiators in Dorothy's house had banged throughout her childhood. Not that that had been a happy period of her life, but being called back to it at least reminded her of how far she'd come. Today there was something ominous in the sound, as if someone were trapped in the wall and trying to get out.

Cecily continued to cram books into her bag. "I suppose you saw the story in the *Washington Post* about the religious group in Oregon that had its members locked in trailers with no heat or air-conditioning."

"Am I supposed to *care*?" Lee said, too loudly.

The anger seemed like a signal that she was off balance. Cecily was now threading her way through a minefield of possible catastrophes. There was no response to Lee that wasn't going to trigger a game of words that Cecily was destined to lose. There was nothing she could do to cool down what seemed to be mounting fury except agree to go out to dinner with Lee. Given everything that had transpired over the past few minutes, that would be the most perilous course of all.

Maybe a colleague or student would walk into her office and break all this up, but the hallway had been quiet for almost an hour, something Cecily had enjoyed until now. It was highly unlikely anyone would come by this late on a Friday.

It was undoubtedly not the first time Lee had overstepped her bounds with a friend or a teacher or other authority figure. There were probably multiple rejections piled up under this one, making Cecily's words painful and humiliating. Poor, misguided Lee. She'd only had her loopy mother, no Tom in her life to balance out her perspective on the reality of human relations.

"Our meetings have been important to me, Lee. You've got the commitment and enthusiasm that professors always hope they get from their students."

"I don't want to be just another *student*. Why did you lead me on?"

The second comment cut to the heart of Cecily's guilt. She felt as if she'd been spat on. "I think you should leave." She went to her office door and opened it all the way. "It's been a long week, and I need to get going."

Lee leapt off the windowsill and moved as if to dash out the door. As she was passing by Cecily, she flung her arms around her and buried her head against Cecily's chest, almost like a child would. Instinctively, Cecily put her arms around Lee and patted her head, as she would a child. This, too, Lee misinterpreted. She tilted her head back and kissed Cecily's neck. Not wanting to push her away and further insult her, Cecily merely said, "Stop, please." Her voice came out hushed. "This isn't going to go the way you want," she said. "I'm sorry, but that's how it is." She patted Lee's back again and, trying to gently extricate herself, said, "Let's get going. It's late."

Without exactly recognizing the steps that led up to it, Cecily felt Lee's hands on the back of her head, pulling her face down, and then Lee's lips pressed against her own. It shocked Cecily, and when she looked down, she saw that Lee had her eyes closed.

She felt she'd been attacked. All her concern for Lee changed to anger. She pushed herself out of her grasp and backed up until she bumped into the corner of her desk. Two days later, Santosh would ask her where she got the bruise.

"I'm asking you, as nicely as I know how, to leave," she said. "Right *now*. I will never mention this again, to you or anyone, but it would be best if you didn't come to my office hours anymore. It won't affect your grade. We'll forget it and move on. I'll see you in class on Monday."

Lee dashed out, her eyes averted—two things Cecily interpreted as indicators of embarrassment and shame. Regret for what she'd done.

Cecily missed one train back to the city, and by the time she left her office to catch the next one, the walkway was covered in wet, heavy snow. She half expected to see Lee lurking around a corner, but the campus was nearly as empty as it was over breaks. There was very little wind, and considering the snowfall, it was warmer than she'd expected. Peace descended on her. In the distance, she could hear snowblowers and a sidewalk plow, signals that the storm was winding down. She was overreacting to the whole thing, as awkward as it had been.

She was almost off the campus when she saw one of her colleagues hurrying toward her. Melissa Feldman, a small, genial woman who was probably in her sixties.

"You're putting in late hours," Cecily said as their paths were about to cross.

Melissa looked up from under a snow-covered woolen hat. She had on a puffy down coat that came below her knees. Cecily found herself craving something that covered her up that completely. "Ugh. I was at the library when I realized I forgot a stack of papers in my office. Better, I guess, to stumble through the snow than to come in on Sunday. Don't tell me you were being *interviewed* again?"

"I was finishing up some things." And then, thinking she should be specific, she said, "Student meetings."

"At this hour of the night? I'd never dare."

Cecily checked her watch. It was only six thirty. And yet, she was somehow in the wrong for even being on campus. "The meetings were earlier. I've been preparing a lecture for the past couple of hours."

This did seem to appease Melissa. She smiled and said, in her self-deprecating way, "When you've been at it as long as I have, 'preparing a lecture' means trying to find the notes you made twenty years ago. Have a good weekend."

When Cecily got home, Santosh was out. Poker night, which she'd forgotten. They'd had no plans after all. He didn't get in until after one. She woke with a start to him kissing her on the lips. She'd fallen asleep on the sofa with a blanket wrapped around her. She had a moment of not being sure whose lips were on hers, and she shuddered and turned away.

"I wish you'd been home earlier," she said.

"Oh, yeah, how come?" He slid his hands around her, down under the waistband of her pants. He was a little drunk, as he sometimes was when he got home from poker. It wasn't the right moment to tell him what had happened.

The next morning, their bedroom was sunny and comfortably warm. She picked up her phone and checked her school email. Nothing. Maybe it would blow over. She curled against Santosh's warm body and tried to go back to sleep. On Monday, Lee would be in class, and they'd carry on as if nothing had happened. There were only a couple more weeks to the semester.

Except—Lee wasn't in class on Monday. She didn't come back at all and never turned in a final paper. Cecily sent two emails reminding her of the paper and extending the deadline. Still, nothing.

Because Lee had already done so much work for the class, Cecily couldn't bring herself to fail her. She calculated all the extra research she'd done, all the supplemental reading, all the time she'd put into discussion groups. Even if she missed a few classes and had skipped the last paper, she was still, by far, the most hardworking student in the class. It was unthinkable that some of the students who slid by on wry comments and lazily written papers would get a better grade. She gave Lee a B-plus and then, seconds before submitting the grades, changed it to an A-minus. Hadn't William James given Gertrude Stein the highest grade in his class after she wrote on her final that she wasn't in the mood for an exam and walked out of the hall? If Lee's GPA slipped below a certain level, she'd lose her scholarship; Cecily did not want to be responsible for that. It was easy to convince herself Lee had earned a good grade.

She didn't hear from Lee again, and she figured it best not to contact her, in case it led to more misunderstanding. When she was sitting in her office working on a course proposal or attempting to make notes for her new book, she found herself missing Lee's visits. At other moments, she felt anxious and unsettled. The incident in her office came back to her in painful detail unexpectedly. Sometimes, she dreamed about fighting Lee off, pushing her away. More than once, she woke herself up shouting. She told Santosh what had happened, but when she tried to describe the aftershock she was feeling, he insisted it was best to let go and stop thinking about it.

She and Santosh spent Christmas and New Year's Eve at a friend's lake house in Michigan. In the weeks after the end of the semester, Cecily realized she was more shaken by the events than she'd admitted. She was tempted to say she was suffering some form of PTSD, but if you described a kiss from a student as "trauma," what word was left for the suffering of refugees freezing and starving in tents all over the planet? She preferred to think of it as being upset.

Over time, it would fade away and be forgotten.

In the middle of February, she was contacted by the Title IX office. They were investigating her relationship with a former student. They were going to need access to her email account and her records. Until the case was decided, it would be better, since she was on leave anyway, if she avoided campus.

Chapter Nine

*I*n the days before Cecily's arrival, Tom had done his best to find fault with Lanford Trask. Sadly, he'd been unable to come up with much he considered valid.

Lanford had sent, as promised, a link to his final project at the Graduate School of Design. Tom had clicked and fallen down a well of resentful admiration. The hyperbolic tiny house he was designing for his friend in Tucson was one of the most appealing and clever spaces Tom had seen in ages. It had the economy and enfolding curves of an egg. The design was born partly of Lanford's youthful spirit of innovation and partly of the brand of youthful solipsism that allowed him to believe he had license to reinvent the wheel. Narcissism, Tom believed, was an essential component of all dictatorships and of most innovation. In this case, it might be key to saving a few corners of the planet for human habitation. All of it, he had to admit, was out of his own reach.

Even worse than that, Lanford was an appealing young person. He combined some of Winston's glamourous confidence with actual human warmth and hair. It was like seeing a photo of Winston from his college yearbook. When Tom spoke with him about his project and told him how much he admired it, Lanford had reached out and shook Tom's hand and said, in a voice that was choked with emotion, "That means so much to me, Tom. When I was a kid, I saw a video tour of a house you designed for an old couple in Vermont. It was more important to me than I can tell you."

Tom was moved by this comment—leaving aside, of course, the fact that Tom considered the Vermont house a project from his recent past while Lanford saw it as childhood history and that the "old couple" had been in their early forties.

It was complicated and confusing to like someone and be touched by their words when they were on deck, ready to step to the plate once you'd struck out. It was easier to lay his anger on Winston. Tom spent an unconscionable amount of time looking at Winston in his glass office, imagining, every time he picked up the phone, that he was plotting his next step in removing him.

Tom had sent three emails to Charlotte and Oliver, telling them he wanted to arrange a meeting with them as soon as possible. He finally received a short, jovial response from Oliver himself. "In Berlin," he'd written. "All this travel. I'm ready to retire, Tom." Because there was no indication of this in his actions, Tom interpreted it as a hint that it was time for him to hand in his own resignation. "When Charlotte mentioned your impasse, I suggested we check in with Eldridge Johnson. Done some business with him at the firm. We're meeting with him next week. Assuming Lufthansa comes through for me."

Oh, the cloying little attempts at levity, as if Lufthansa weren't the world's most reliable airline. As if Oliver flew commercial these days!

Eldridge Johnson was a nationally known and locally famous architect. He'd designed several buildings on the Harvard campus, a couple of public libraries, several museums, and a vast number of expensive houses. His professional standing and success were indisputable, and Tom believed that those things usually sprang from genuine talent. At the same time, his buildings all looked to Tom like something you'd find on the grounds of a high-end planned community in Florida: lots of pastels and Palladian windows. The appeal escaped him. Tom was certain that whatever Johnson designed would not be half as nice as the house he'd created for Charlotte. And yet, it was true that merely men-

tioning you were putting one of his projects on your property carried
with it a brand-name status that "Tom Kemp" couldn't touch.

Maybe Oliver was behind the whole second-story idea as a way to
drop Tom's building. Charlotte appeared to be in charge of all the
domestic decisions, but Tom had always suspected Oliver was furtively
pulling the strings from behind the curtain. Or from Berlin.

In an act of defeated self-flagellation, Tom began reviewing his financial assets, trying to calculate how long he could live on his holdings if
he couldn't get Charlotte's house into construction and was edged out
of the firm. The short answer was "not long." This was humiliating,
given that he'd been working his entire life and was, among friends,
notoriously frugal. The reason for most of his financial problems was
the amount of money he'd given to Dorothy over the decades. To help
bail her out of legal woes around her failed business deals and, of
course, to help pay for Cecily's education. How could he turn his sister
down and leave her stranded? More to the point, how could he not
support Cecily's needs?

Dorothy had always said she'd pay Tom back as soon as she was able
to make some headway financially, but he'd known all along that that
day would never arrive. When it came to her finances, Dorothy considered her brother a cynic. In matters related to his sister, Tom thought of
the words *cynic* and *realist* as synonyms.

"I thought you told me she'd be here around four," Alan said, an accusation wrapped in annoyance as he eyed Tom's wineglass suspiciously.
Tom hated Alan's new disapproval of everything he did, but he took
perverse pleasure in letting Alan see how low he'd sunk.

"You know how it is with flight delays and traffic," Tom said. "Do
you want me to text her for an update?"

"No, I don't. I hate having to answer messages when I'm trying to
get out of the terminal." This was uttered with irritation, directed not
at Logan Airport but at Tom. What long-past airline transgression of

Tom's was still causing this resentment? Because their relationship had a tenuous present, the past, with all its previously undisclosed disappointments, had become increasingly important to Alan. "Let's hope she gets here soon, before you finish off that wine."

"I offered you a glass," Tom said.

"That's not the point."

Alan Kahale had never been much of a drinker. Not that Tom had been, either—until recently. Like most of the people Tom knew, Alan had come from a family in which alcohol was treated as an essential part of daily hydration, and no small portion of the verbal and sometimes physical abuse Alan suffered growing up in Hawaii had been connected to alcohol. The rest of the abuse had been connected to "love" as defined by his family, adherents of an obscure, angry fundamentalist branch of Christianity. The fact that Alan had emerged from all this as the compassionate and nurturing person he was made him even more admirable and touching. It also seemed to make people—Alan's shrink especially—look at Tom as if he were taking advantage of Alan merely by loving him.

Alan switched to a more typically tender tone to add "Cecily's dealing with enough already, poor thing, without you texting her."

Cecily had said she'd probably arrive at his place before six, but Tom had blurred the hour when making plans so he'd have some time alone with Alan. Thus far, it wasn't going as smoothly as he'd hoped. Alan had used their time together to go through the clothes he'd left behind, to see how much he could fit into a canvas bag he'd brought with him. The fact that he hadn't taken all or even half his belongings when he left a little over four months earlier had given Tom reason to assume the move was temporary.

The irony of Alan's defending Cecily against Tom's impatience was mind-boggling, but at least it was a form of engagement, something Tom craved. Even Alan's criticism of his drinking was reassuring: he still cared.

They were sitting at a table Tom had set up under the little pergola against the side of the house, the pergola being a piece of landscape enhancement that Alan had constructed perhaps six years earlier. Tom could design, but Alan could build—another way in which he was a better person than Tom.

The main house had originally been built as an artist's studio sometime in the 1920s. It was small (though not "tiny," according to the new definition of that term) and shingled. It had a mullioned atelier window that got morning sun. When Tom bought the place, ten years before he met Alan, it had been ignored for decades, was barely heated, and needed major work. It was still a bit of a wreck, something Tom found charming, especially given that he himself was becoming a wreck. He'd never regretted putting the money he saved for renovations into building the guest cottage, even though that move had been the final straw for Alan.

"At least let me put it on Airbnb for when she's not here," Alan had said. Tom couldn't stand the thought of even that. He couldn't handle a stranger living in the space built expressly for Cecily.

In truth, there were lots of final straws. Vacations Tom had canceled at the last minute when he found out Cecily would be in town visiting. Hours he'd spent on Dorothy's paperwork that could have been spent with Alan. His thrill at receiving photographs Cecily sent him of her trips, her book signings, her outings with Santosh, her TV appearances . . . versus his lack of interest in keeping a photographic record of his relationship with Alan.

From where they were sitting, they could see the buildings of Boston in the distance through a break in the trees and shrubs. The city shimmered on the horizon, but something about the scale told you you weren't missing much by not being there. Tom loved the view. *You made the right choice in distancing yourself from me*, it seemed to say.

"What do you think I need to trim back this year?" Tom asked, hoping to enlist Alan in concern for the plants, even if he wasn't exhibiting much concern for him.

Alan looked around the small yard. "For years, you didn't take a role in the gardening. Now, all of a sudden, you're concerned about the thunbergia?"

"I've always been concerned about the thunbergia. There were many nights I lay in bed sleepless, worrying about the thunbergia. I left it to you to take care of the thunbergia because I know you love it and are much less likely to screw it up than I am."

"Interesting how you screwed things up anyway."

"That's fair."

Tom was willing to accept responsibility for having made things difficult in their relationship. Who was perfect? It was undeniable, though, that Wendy Briske, Alan's humorless but jauntily named therapist, deserved at least some blame. Tom was almost certain that if it hadn't been for Wendy's expensive advice and smug dominatrix personality, they could have patched over their problems and moved on. He regretted supporting Alan's decision to go into therapy, especially with a woman who was probably Cecily's age and had (he'd observed the one time he joined Alan in a session) that generation's eagerness to hunt down, unearth, buff, and polish every scrap of experience that could be put on the trophy shelf of Slights, Insults, Microaggressions, and Trauma. Wendy had convinced Alan that he was a Victim, the highest praise she could bestow.

Alan was in his blue nurse's scrubs. He looked kind and professional, a person you'd be comfortable handing your child to at the doctor's office, which is exactly what people did all day long. He was a trim man with shiny dark hair he wore long and pulled back in a ponytail. He did not have the severe, smoldering looks that are generally associated with male beauty; he had instead an indescribable quality of goodness that came through in his brown eyes, which seemed always (even when he was scolding Tom) to be gazing at you sympathetically, as if he were listening to your child's health problems. On public transportation, people often smiled at him for no apparent reason.

Dorothy, who had very few filters, had once said, "You're a good-looking man, Alan, but people don't realize it because you're so nice." This said more about Dorothy than Alan, but in truth, it did say something about Alan, too. Kindness in women is encouraged and then exploited; in men, it's considered the behavioral equivalent of wide hips—feminizing and, if possible, best hidden under baggy clothes.

Tom had rushed to Alan's defense. "*I* realize it," he said.

"Yes, but you don't count," Alan said.

Sadly true. Compliments from a partner of more than five years bear an uncanny resemblance to leftover pizza.

●

"No thoughts on the plants?" Tom asked again.

"You should have cut back the wisteria in late winter. Now you'll have to wait until August. Don't forget it, or it will take over half the house. The forsythia is ready to be trimmed back now. I suppose I'd better do it if there's any hope of its getting done."

This interpretation of their relationship—that Tom did nothing and left all the chores to Alan while he attended exclusively to Dorothy's and Cecily's needs—was one of Wendy's many gifts. It wasn't 100 percent inaccurate, but it was skewed and limited, like describing Frank Lloyd Wright as a minimalist and thinking you'd done your job. Even so, Tom felt calm descend upon him as he watched Alan open the combination lock on the toolshed from memory and begin to hack at the forsythia with the violent ruthlessness enthusiastic gardeners show toward the plants they love.

Because he and Alan clearly hadn't been talking about the garden when they were talking about the garden, Tom took it as a good sign that Alan was giving a little love to the bushes, even if it was with a pair of twenty-three-inch shears. He went to him and put his arm around his shoulder and said, "Don't you feel a little bad about not caring for them after all these years of nurturing them?"

Alan turned slowly and, with his infinite kindness, said, "Don't make things worse than they are, Tom." He gently removed Tom's hand from his shoulder.

Tom was certain Alan still loved him, and his goal was to manage this rift with enough delicacy and patience to win him back. He stepped aside to let Alan do his hacking.

"In addition to ignoring the garden," Alan said, "you don't seem to be taking very good care of yourself."

"I've had a few setbacks at work. Charlotte might be pulling out of our project. She has crazy ideas that would completely compromise the design."

"Luckily, she changes her mind constantly."

"I don't have time to wait around for that. Winston presented me with an ultimatum. My position at the firm hinges on it." Tom decided to leave it there. Even Alan's sympathy lapsed when someone tried too hard to elicit it.

Alan went back to attacking the forsythia with renewed vigor. "I wouldn't worry too much about Charlotte; some friend or neighbor will start building a comparable place, and she'll put the project back on high priority. Competition has always been one of her great motivators."

Entranced, Tom watched Alan's arms and upper back as he clipped. It was ridiculous to want someone only once you knew you couldn't have him. It was a version of not being able to take yes for an answer, an especially grotesque character trait. And really, he'd never stopped finding Alan attractive and had never stopped enjoying sex with him, even if there were occasional others. He and Alan had had an understanding that they were committed but without the pretense of monogamy, a concept both agreed was as unsustainable and unhealthy as a raw food diet and, in the case of male couples, as cloying as matching sweaters. Tom had always enjoyed a certain amount of vulgar, furtive sex to balance out his otherwise always responsible behavior. Look, for example, at the Marek Bachar disaster. Of all the many wonderful things you could have with a long-term partner, furtive vulgarity was perhaps the most difficult to sustain.

Tom was so occupied with these thoughts, it took him a good ten minutes to revisit Alan's comments about Charlotte's competitive streak. Then it struck him: Of course. Why hadn't he considered that at the outset? Alan—dear Alan—had handed Tom a plan of action for getting Charlotte to agree to the guesthouse, no second floor or doubled square footage necessary. All he'd need do was find a plausible competitor, someone who fell in love with the drawings, had money, and could be presented as about to put the house into construction immediately. It would help if it were someone who owed him a favor.

He slipped a little notebook out of his pocket and began making a list of names. As he was doing so, an Uber pulled into the drive.

Chapter Ten

e put down his pen and reminded himself he was offer-ing Cecily a place to stay and his support and encourage-ment—his love—but that he wasn't going to derail his life or put any of his problems on a back burner as he'd done in the past for his sister and his niece.

Then Cecily got out of the Uber.

Throughout Tom's adult life, Cecily had had the same effect on him. It was as if everything dropped away and she became his purpose, as if he were back in the hospital, holding her in his arms for the first time. It was all-consuming, like what happened when he was sketching a structure and looked up to discover he'd forgotten to eat dinner.

His weakening resolution to detach wasn't helped by the fact that Cecily had clearly lost weight and done something unfortunate to her hair.

He tossed the little notebook onto the table and said to Alan, "Come with me to say hello."

They made their way down the sloping lawn to where the Uber driver, a ludicrously beautiful young woman in orange harem pants, was taking Cecily's bag out of the trunk. In grad school, Cecily had driven for Uber, a job that had delighted Dorothy—"I can't wait to hear your stories; I always wanted to drive a cab"—but had given Tom many sleepless nights. Cecily dashed up to Tom, threw her arms around him, and rested her head against his shoulder. He hated how fragile she felt in his embrace.

"You're not crying, are you?" he asked.

"I wish I could," she said. "It's been a long day. Especially if you add in the past three months. Mainly, I'm happy to be here."

Alan dragged her wobbly suitcase up from the drive. Watching the two people he loved most hugging, Tom felt order and normalcy reenter his life. Maybe Cecily felt some of the same, for she said, "As soon as we turned onto the drive and started up the hill, I felt safe. When I saw Alan gardening and you sitting there with your sketch pad, it seemed like everything was in its place."

Tom looked toward Alan, hoping he wasn't going to correct her false assumptions.

Alan and Cecily walked up the sloping lawn to the house with their arms around each other's waists. Cecily had always been tall, a surprise given that, as far as Tom knew, no one on his and Dorothy's side of the family had height. This feature read like a physical connection to Cecily's mysterious father. The weight loss and haircut made her look as gawky as she'd been as a teenager. She had on a pair of chinos that came down to just above her ankles and, on top, a navy sweater with stretched-out sleeves. She'd always worn pants that were a little too short, an indication, as Tom read it, that she was never comfortable with her height.

The guest cottage had less than four hundred square feet of interior space, but all of it was an homage to Cecily's taste. When she was a kid, Tom sometimes sat with her at a drafting table, taught her how to read architectural plans, and made sketches with her in a notebook he labeled "Cecily's Dream House." These included the details that made Cecily happiest: an elevated bed in an alcove inspired by Scandinavian cabinet beds; a window seat inspired by *Jane Eyre*; a desk that faced into the room, inspired by her childhood need to see everyone who was coming and going in Dorothy's chaotic house. Using the notebook to construct this cottage had been the greatest professional pleasure Tom had ever had, even if it hadn't produced his best work. The building had an abundance of flaws and awkward angles, but it was hard to imagine he'd ever have the opportunity to design an homage to anyone else's childhood fantasies of safe harbor.

Cecily went straight for the window seat, with its small built-in bookcase, sat down, and leaned against the glass. "Don't comment on my haircut, okay?" she said.

The last time Tom had seen Cecily, right before the announcement of the Title IX investigation, her hair had been shoulder-length and, coming off a couple of televised interviews, cut with what appeared to be expensive precision. She'd never looked happier or more self-assured, and Tom had felt then that the best part of her life had just begun. Wrong again!

"I love it," Alan said. "Mia Farrow in *Rosemary's Baby*."

Among his many charms was Alan's ability to layer a flattering Hollywood reference onto any physical trait or experience. Tom found compliments like these facile, but everyone else lit up at having their name mentioned in the same sentence as a celebrity's, provided it wasn't Mel Gibson.

"I'm in no position to pass judgment on anyone's appearance," Tom said. Addressing his weight gain put people at ease, as if they were breathing a sigh of relief at not having to ignore the obvious.

"No. You're not," Alan commented.

At a certain point in most long-term relationships, it's expected that public displays of affection will be supplanted by public displays of annoyance. After six or more years, affection in public takes on the flavor of protesting too much and reeks of the uniquely sad kindness an unfaithful spouse showers on the person he's betraying.

"I could easily drop off to sleep," Cecily said. "Thank you both for letting me stay. I promise not to disrupt your life, Alan. Just ignore me."

"I can assure you, you won't disrupt my life in any way at all," he said, his kind brown eyes trained on Tom.

•

At a restaurant down the hill from Tom's house—chosen by Tom for its beautiful lighting, which was to say, utter darkness—they made it

through most of the meal before Cecily described her lunch with Santosh's mother and her decision to buy time by leaving Chicago for a
while. Having come to what Tom assumed was the end of her story, she
put her shorn head in her hands and said, "I made a mistake, didn't I?"
It was almost as if she hadn't been able to see her actions for what they
were until she'd left town.

The audacity of people like Neeta was abhorrent, but how could
you not admire and envy it? She got what she wanted or, at the very
least, knew what she wanted. When he'd visited her with Santosh and
Cecily, Tom was struck by the fact that she seemed both to rule her
quiet, comfortable house in the rich suburbs and, at the same time, be
a prisoner in it. When she stepped outside, she faced the hostile glares
of her wealthy neighbors, who saw, primarily, her differences. She only
wanted what she thought was best for her son, and how could he pre-
sume she didn't know what that was?

Tom reached across the table to take Cecily's hand. "Maybe you
were looking for an excuse to leave town," he said. "Maybe you needed
distance from the investigation."

"Probably true," Cecily said. She indicated her plate. "This is the
first time since January I've been able to eat a decent meal without feeling I was going to get some terrible news in the middle of it."

"I'm glad to hear it," Tom said. "I plan to fatten you up some. Hopefully, on better food than this."

The food was bland and comforting, a culinary category he'd begun
to like more with age. It was becoming increasingly clear that, for him
and most of his peers, attempting to stay "young" amounted to deriding the things they'd grown to enjoy (nostalgic music, dull food, large-
print books) and condemning as "too old" politicians who were more
or less their own age.

"I'm already looking forward to Alan's breakfast," Cecily said.
"Unless that's no longer a thing."

Whenever Cecily came to stay with Alan and Tom, Alan always got
up early and made her an elaborate, fussy breakfast served on dishes
he'd picked up at thrift shops for this purpose.

The comment hung in the air, unanswered for a few seconds too long. Cecily looked at Tom with almost pleading eyes.

Tom sighed. His plan to hide the news from her struck him as ridiculous. Also, as counterproductive. There was nothing of this nature he'd hidden from her, and he found himself relieved as he said, "Alan moved out a few months ago. It wasn't a mutual decision, but as you can see, we're still on friendly terms." He did his best to smile. Remaining on friendly terms after a breakup was a consolation prize of dubious value—akin to winning two dollars from a scratch ticket: no purchasing power, just an inducement to reinvest in a losing game.

It was clear from her face that Cecily wanted to ask more but knew better than to do so. Her childhood had been spent listening to breakup stories, and she was used to hearing half the story and imagining the rest. She thanked Alan for having come to greet her, especially under the circumstances, and said she hoped she'd see him again before she left town.

He smiled at that in an enigmatic way that Tom found unsettling.

●

After dinner, as Tom was helping Alan load his duffel bag of clothes into the trunk of his car, he said, "Thank you for being so nice to Cecily. Thank you for telling her you might come back to see her."

"I'm sorry if I've been cold, Tom. Maybe I've been a little insecure about moving out and have been trying to convince myself I made the right decision."

The yard was surrounded by trees, and the moon- and streetlight that filtered through the leaves and flickered across Alan's face was dappled—it was a windy night—making him look more thoughtful and sympathetic than ever. Also, somehow, more beautiful.

"I think you made an impulsive move," Tom said. "I'm counting on its not being a permanent one."

He could read the displeasure on Alan's face. This was one of the main drawbacks to long-term relationships: you can never make flattering assumptions about what the other person is thinking because you understand their expressions and their dissembling too well. "Won't you consider staying over? Just tonight?"

"I can't. I love how you are with Cecily. You're a good person, Tom. It's what I like best about you."

Tom was touched by this, even though, like every other man on the planet, he'd have preferred to hear Alan say that what he liked best was his cock.

"I assumed you'd be that way with me, but now I know you never will be. You only have room to love one person like that. Most people don't even have that. I'm trying to be realistic about my own future. Just because I'm ten years younger than you doesn't mean I'm young."

It was true that Tom had always seen Alan's problems and complaints as lesser somehow because he would have, from Tom's point of view, an extra decade to address them. He'd never assumed that *he* was one of the problems that needed addressing.

"I've been miserable since you left, Alan. Nothing feels right to me. I sit around here listening to soap opera music and drinking. I want you back. We could start out slowly, a few dates, maybe take a trip somewhere."

"I can't. Not now."

"What does 'can't' mean in this context?"

"I'm sorry," he said. "I've met someone else. We've been seeing each other for a few weeks."

The awful kindness with which Alan delivered the news made Tom realize he was merely telling the truth.

Chapter Eleven

*D*orothy shielded her eyes from the sunlight pouring through the massive new window in the living room and checked her watch. She had an appointment with her cardiologist down in Kingston in an hour. Fiona Snow was driving her and, as usual, was running late. Dorothy had told her she had a routine dermatology checkup. Maybe that had downplayed it too much, but why make things sound worse than they were by telling the truth? Illness— even colds and flu—had always made Dorothy feel like a failure. Now that Cecily had agreed to come to the opening, she needed to feel like a success.

She'd been so pleased when Cecily agreed to come, she nearly wept. Then the anxiety of making sure everything was ready for the "gala" overwhelmed her. As for telling Cecily about her father, Dorothy went into a panic if she thought about it too much. When Cecily called to confirm plans for coming, Dorothy had said, "I can't wait to catch up."

"I agree," Cecily said. "We do need to talk."

It was as if she had a suspicion about what was coming and was resentful that Dorothy hadn't told her sooner. The result had been more than the usual number of sleepless nights and some ensuing symptoms that had convinced Dorothy that, this time, she really did need to keep her appointment with Dr. Min.

Fiona's perpetual tardiness was an odd trait for someone who advised others on, among many things, the importance of time management. She always came up with detailed excuses that were hard to refute and impossible to believe. Dorothy herself was no stranger to dissembling, so she knew how to read between those particular lines.

She'd noticed more inconsistencies in Fiona Snow's behavior lately, but, if viewed in the right light, these hinted at her interesting complexity. Consistency was one of those minor qualities you appreciate in someone only if you can't find something better to praise. It was like praising someone for knowing how to tie a bow tie.

When she thought about Fiona for too long, Dorothy got a specific feeling along the back of her neck that usually meant she was flirting with the possibility of success laced with the risk of disaster. It was a chill and then a spark of warm pleasure that spread through her body. She imagined it was what aerialists felt when they were about to step onto a high wire and attempt a dazzling feat. There was the expectation of triumph (cheers and applause) mixed with the faint, thrilling possibility of death. She'd felt it when starting her businesses and, most spectacularly, when she decided to go through with her pregnancy. And look how beautifully the latter had turned out.

She'd been off drugs for decades—edible marijuana didn't count—rarely drank, and had given up on sex completely, so this feeling was her one high. Fiona's peculiar inconsistencies only added to the thrill. Was she going to show up in time to get Dorothy to her doctor's appointment? The jury was entertainingly out.

Tom claimed that Dorothy ignored warning signals and, thus, courted trouble. An unfair assessment. As soon as it had been pointed out to her that her restaurant had been losing money for five years, she closed it. When it became obvious her house-flipping company was going to lose the lawsuits against it, she was the one who convinced her partners to settle. She'd given up cocaine *cold turkey* a few months after discovering it was the cause of her seizures. Those had been real warnings, and she'd heeded them.

She checked her watch again. If Fiona didn't show up in the next ten minutes, they'd be late for her appointment, and because she already had a history with Dr. Min, that might be a problem.

Dr. Min was another example of how she heeded warnings. Last winter, Dorothy recognized that there was something not quite right about her fatigue and shortness of breath, about the number of times she fell asleep in the middle of the day for no reason. There was something strange in the caged-bird fluttering in her chest that woke her up at four o'clock some mornings. She'd gone to a drop-in health clinic and been referred to Dr. Min. Min's diagnosis had been multisyllabic and upsetting: *myocardial this*, *COPD that*, *arterial stenosis whatever*. She'd left with a handful of prescriptions, contacts for physical therapists, "heart-happy" nutrition plans and recipes. It had all been overwhelming, and with her project for the retreat center underway, she didn't have time for half of it. For any of it, as it turned out. Taking pills made her feel like a failure. PT was exhausting. As for diet, she'd given up a lot in life, but she drew a hard line at salt.

She hadn't had time to attend two follow-up appointments with Dr. Min, but she had had the decency to cancel them, even if at the last minute.

She was going today. She was afraid Min would drop her if she didn't, and because she'd woken up twice in the middle of the night since Cecily had agreed to come—gasping for air, as if she had a pillow over her face—and had felt her heart sputter back to life like the oil burner in her old house after a shutdown, she didn't want that to happen. She wasn't sure if the symptoms had prompted her resolution to tell Cecily about her father or if her resolution had exacerbated her symptoms. Either way, she was going through with all of it.

Her phone buzzed with a text message: **Hey, kiddo, what's cookin??**

Well, so, maybe she hadn't *completely* given up on sex. Not that she cared about it all that much anymore. Harold Berger was a familiar Woodstock type—a wiry man in his early seventies with gray hair, ruined skin, time on his hands, and blue pills in his pocket. These men were surprisingly appreciative of a woman of her age. Like Harold Berger, they were kind, frequently stoned, and invariably married to their hippie sweethearts. (The wives were often women they claimed to have met while on acid at the music festival that still defined the town.) Spending an afternoon with Harold from time to time was a pleasant, private distraction. It was nice to feel the warmth of another body, especially since being diagnosed with whatever it was she'd been diagnosed with. Harold had great handyman skills, too, and god knew she needed those in this glorious white elephant she'd bought. He loved to light a joint and sink into a rewiring project while delivering a political lecture she listened to with the same loose attention she'd always paid to weather and traffic reports.

Sorry, she texted back. **Busy day. Big goings-on with retreat center!** She was fifteen years younger than Harold, and she refused to be the one with health problems. **Call me tomorrow!** she added. **My daughter's coming to the opening next week! You'll love her.**

A car pulled up in front, and a door slammed once, then twice. Dorothy felt that chill and spark at the top of her spine—the arrival of something wonderful with a whisper of possible ruin. Fiona, just in time.

When she'd finally made it up the several staircases to Dorothy's quarters, Fiona was winded. Dorothy was happy to know she wasn't the only one.

"I had a meeting with a potential investor, and it ran a little late," Fiona said. "We had coffee at Bread and Butter, and the service was ridiculous. Plus, she likes to talk. Worst of all, she made no commitment. I wish you'd put in that elevator," she panted. "We have to remember that some of the people who come for workshops won't be able to make the stairs."

"I looked into it," Dorothy said. "A little pricey for right now. Especially since that other investor pulled out last week. That was discouraging."

Fiona went to the kitchen and got a soda and then threw herself onto one of the huge sofas facing each other near the new window, settling in. The sofas, like the window, were a purchase influenced by her interior designer pals Gary and Enji, who, in their professional lingo, had said the two pieces would "tie the entire space together." How nice to have the whole unwieldy living room (and, by extension, her life) tied together. The sofas also provided an extremely comfortable place to sleep. Dorothy had hated sleeping in beds most of her adult life.

"I don't think in terms of being discouraged, dismayed, or disenchanted," Fiona said. "They're all just the double negative of opportunity."

Dorothy didn't understand what this meant, but she'd learned to reach for the strongest noun in Fiona's abstract pronouncements and hang on tight. "What's the opportunity?" she asked.

"I haven't figured it out, but it's there, no doubt. Doubt fertilizes a breeding ground for failure."

Fiona's bestselling message was that you created your own fate with your thoughts. If you imagined good, you drew it to you. "Like a magnet. It's not magic; it's science." (Which branch of science was unclear.) If you reimagine a negative experience (an investor pulling out, for example) as having happened the way you hoped it would, you banish some of the bad effects. Admittedly, it was simplistic and, like so much self-help advice of the past one hundred years, a rehash of *The Power of Positive Thinking* and the more recent *Your Erroneous Zones*. Even the title, *The Nature of Success in Successful Natures*, had derivative overtones. Then again, people were constantly ransacking Shakespeare's plays and Jane Austen's plots.

Dorothy had seen the impact Fiona had on people, the way she gave them hope and encouraged them to believe in their potential. At the weekend seminar they'd held in March—a dry run for the retreat center—eight women and the three reluctant men who'd been dragged along had sat in silence, nodding at Fiona's lectures, laughing at her jokes, and participating in her "yogitation" classes. She had an aura of celebrity that came largely from her "as seen on *Oprah*" advertisements. Technically, this was résumé padding: Oprah had mentioned the book on her show briefly, in a conversation about something else, but it had sparked sales. And when, true to her message, Fiona insisted she'd been on the show, people actually believed they'd tuned in and seen her. They came up to her all the time mentioning how thrilled they were to meet her "after seeing you on *Oprah*."

"I don't want to rush you," Dorothy said, "but I don't want to be late for the appointment."

Fiona waved this off. "Doctors are always late seeing patients. You sit and wait for them. If *you're* a few minutes behind, it's a crisis."

Even so, she hauled herself up from the sofa, and they went out, Fiona clomping down the stairs ahead of her.

●

Fiona Snow was tall and narrow and, for some reason, always wore low boots with boxy heels. They didn't suit her; she had the height already, and they made her walk with a forward pitch, as if she were going to topple over. It was intriguing.

The first time Dorothy saw Fiona lurching down the street in Woodstock, she'd recognized her as someone she wanted to know. More to the point, as someone she wanted to be known *by*. Her walk, with its forward tilt, gave the impression that she had places to go and needed to get there in a hurry. Dorothy had gone up to her and said, "You and I need to meet."

With her head of loose brown curls reminiscent of a flowered shower cap, her piercing blue eyes, and her bulbous nose, Fiona had an "interesting" face. Dorothy's own face, like her name, was neither interesting nor beautiful. Her mother told her she'd been named after the Judy Garland character in *The Wizard of Oz*, as if that made up for the fact that hers was the name of a middle-aged woman. Even "Judy" would have been more interesting.

Fiona had a background in psychology and had worked at college counseling centers throughout her thirties—Vassar and then Yale, schools she disparaged but whose names looked good on a CV and a book jacket. Ultimately, she'd found the profession limiting. "Once I recognized what a good speaker I am, I realized I was wasting my time listening."

In her early forties, she made the kind of bold, risky move Dorothy approved of: she left a secure job and, in a fit of creativity, assembled her notes and notebooks into *The Nature of Success in Successful Natures*. For many years afterward, she'd made a comfortable living giving talks at colleges, luncheon seminars for big corporations, and workshops at well-known spas, self-help institutes, and weekend seminars.

She'd moved to Woodstock to write her next book.

The idea for the retreat center—"a more intimate, more affordable Omega Institute" was their elevator pitch—had grown organically from Dorothy's lunches with Fiona. When Dorothy bought the immense converted barn, she'd imagined making it available to the creative community in town in a way that would form connections for her, make a difference to the residents, and bring in income—a legacy. Finally, after all these years, something her successful daughter could be proud of. Something to wash away earlier mistakes and disappointments.

Dorothy tightened her seat belt as Fiona pulled onto the thruway toward Kingston.

Driving with Fiona was an unnerving but exhilarating experience. Fiona talked so much while driving, she tended to veer out of her lane. Then, when someone honked their horn or cut her off, she became enraged at what she felt was the other person's bad driving. Dorothy knew better than to point out the obvious. She shouldn't have asked Fiona to drive, but in addition to the fact that recurring dizziness made Dorothy reluctant to get behind the wheel unless necessary, she wanted a favor from Fiona.

Now, partly to distract herself from Fiona's swerving and the pending appointment with Dr. Min, she asked her for clarification about how much she'd been expecting from the investor who pulled out the week before.

"Somewhere in the vicinity of a hundred fifty thousand. Gabriela's worth several million from a couple of divorces, and I've helped her enormously. It would have meant nothing to her."

"Why did she pull out?"

"She's eighty-five. Her children got wind of it. They claimed mental incompetence. Some ancient history about her having been institutionalized."

"How long ago was she hospitalized?"

"November. Don't ever let your daughter get control of your money, Dorothy."

"As you'll see next week, Cecily's fiercely independent. She's never been motivated by money." Dorothy was proud of Cecily's intellectual integrity, although, secretly, she felt she was wasting opportunities by not writing something more commercial.

"Take nothing for granted. I'm sure she's a lovely person, but trust no one."

Dorothy had always felt a connection to women like Fiona—women who'd never had children. She viewed her own decision to raise a child as the defining moment of her life, but when people who didn't have children spoke about child rearing, they sounded more credible to her. Possibly because their attitudes were often stripped of sentimentality. She'd defend Cecily with her life, but she did get tired of people like Tom and Charlotte making her feel as if she were a burden on her daughter.

"She never asks for anything," Dorothy said. "She never has." And then, feeling her heart race and that spark of excitement at the back of her neck, she said, "I'm planning to tell her about her father when she's here."

"What about him?"

"Who he is."

"I thought you didn't know."

"That's not exactly true."

"Well, don't let it become a distraction from the gala. That has to be the priority."

"Of course," Dorothy said. "But you must admit, this is major life *stuff*."

"I try not to get attached to *stuff*. And this *stuff* is your past. Our project is your future. And partly your daughter's future, don't forget."

She had a point, albeit one Dorothy was offended by. She didn't offer any more information, and Fiona didn't ask. She was focused on the fuel indicator.

"I don't know why this is almost empty. I filled it recently." Fiona tapped at the glass. "Does the father have money he's looking to invest?"

"That's not part of the deal," Dorothy said. She had an aversion to people who tried to make money off divorces and death. Off children, especially.

"I must have at least another gallon in the tank," Fiona said.

"That should be plenty to get us to my appointment," Dorothy said, hoping it didn't sound too much like a question.

Dr. Min's office was, fortunately, in a nondescript medical building where there probably was a dermatologist or two. They were only ten minutes late, not nearly as bad as Dorothy had feared they'd be. It was true that, in the end, Fiona always delivered on her promises. One way or the other.

"Just text me when you're done," Fiona said. "I'm going uptown to check out some artisanal pizza place that opened last week and will probably close before the end of the month. Remember: Most of what doctors prescribe is unnecessary. They're pressured by Big Pharma. And if you get a good feeling about the practice, find out if they're offering a Groupon for Restylane."

After the standard check-in—her blood pressure was high, and her pulse was "unusual"—and an EKG administered by an exceedingly cheerful technician, Dorothy was ushered into Dr. Min's little exam room. Sitting there waiting, she had a premonition that things were not going to go well. She felt it was her duty—to whom, she didn't know—to put her best foot forward, lest she start feeling like a failure. That lost $150,000 investor rattled her. It was too large a sum to pull out of a hat, but too small to be meaningful to someone with millions. Even *she* had $150,000 in the bank.

When Dr. Min finally entered, Dorothy beamed at her as if she were a friend she hadn't seen in years.

In a surprisingly loud voice, Min said, "Nice to see you again, Dorothy."

"It's wonderful to see you again, too. Did you have a good winter?"

"You missed two follow-up appointments, so I wasn't sure if you'd show today. Especially since you were late." She spoke in the overdone articulation people use with children, the elderly, and the sick.

Dorothy suspected that Dr. Min viewed her as all three. When she first went to see her, she was comforted by the fact that Min was small and looked young. Dorothy assumed she'd be easy to push around. Bad assumption.

"I didn't miss them," Dorothy said. "I canceled. I'm working with Fiona Snow on a retreat center we're hoping to open this summer. I'm sure you've read her book. She was on *Oprah*."

Dr. Min blinked inconclusively and sat down behind her computer. "Tell me how you've been feeling."

"Great," Dorothy said. "I didn't have one cold all winter."

"Have you had any side effects from the medications we put you on?"

"Headaches," Dorothy said. "Pounding ones."

"Those almost always go away after a few days, maybe a week."

Dr. Min wore outsize black-framed eyeglasses. They were either ridiculously nerdy or wildly stylish, depending upon the doctor's intentions when she bought them. She leaned into the computer as if to see better. Nerdy.

"It looks like you haven't called in any refills on your prescriptions."

Dorothy hadn't considered this problem. "I was in Canada," she said, "and the medications are so much cheaper there, I decided to stock up for a while."

In the afternoon sun slanting in through the metal blinds over the room's small window, she could see that Dr. Min was not buying this.

"I went over the EKG we just took, and it looks as if there's been some deterioration since January. That's not consistent with your having been on the drug regimen I prescribed." Dr. Min looked at her in a blunt way that Dorothy couldn't dismiss as disrespectful or condescending. "Based on the data here, I'm guessing you didn't make it through the first week."

"Dr. Min," Dorothy said, "are you accusing me of lying about taking the pills?"

"Yes."

Dorothy was stunned. When asked this question point-blank, most people, even lawyers, hedged. She resented Dr. Min for the accusation but couldn't help but respect her for going at full throttle.

Min looked at her, not bothered. "If you'd like to work with someone else, I can have one of the nurses give you a list of local cardiologists. Whatever you decide, I want to emphasize that your condition is serious, degenerative, and potentially life-threatening. Would you like me to print out the names of some other doctors?"

Dorothy felt panic closing in on her, as if she were being submerged in freezing water. She'd never been dismissed by a doctor, not even back in the nineties, when she was less than truthful about her drug use. She might not be able to salvage her own health, but at least she could salvage this relationship.

"You're right. I did stop taking the pills, shortly after I started getting the headaches."

"Why not just tell me that?"

"I'm a people pleaser," she said. She'd slipped into the tone of a girl trying to win over her third-grade teacher. "I trust you. I want to remain your patient. I'll do whatever you tell me."

Dr. Min looked directly into her eyes, obviously trying to evaluate whether she could believe her. There was something breathtaking about that much authority housed in such a compact, efficient body, and while Dorothy looked back at her, she felt that chill, that exciting tremble, along the back of her spine. She would do what it took to win over Dr. Min. She was not going to lose this battle.

"Please?" she said.

"That was a long checkup," Fiona said as Dorothy got into her car.

Having made a pact with Dr. Min about truthfulness, Dorothy thought it was probably best to be honest with Fiona about her health, but after convincing Min to remain her doctor, she felt as if she'd triumphed, and that triumphant feeling didn't jive with telling Fiona that she had a medical condition that was "potentially life-threatening."

"She removed a couple of small moles from my back," Dorothy said. After agreeing to Dr. Min's terms, Dorothy was still her patient. She appreciated how serious and strict Min was: it made winning her over especially significant. She felt powerful, a feeling she wanted to intensify. "While I was in there," she continued, "I was thinking about the money Gabriela was supposed to invest. We don't need it all right now, but when we have the opening, it would be best to be well funded. It will be obvious if we're not. It would be the wrong signal to send about our project." She felt that chill or tremor—or whatever it was—along the back of her neck: the indicator of excitement laced with the possibility of death.

She could tell she was flushed. If you believed Harold Berger, she was almost pretty. "I can't put up the hundred fifty thousand, but I've got a few investment accounts that are treading water. I've been dying to put them into something more exciting for a while now. Something exactly like this."

Fiona was, as usual, driving with distraction. Dorothy knew better by now than to expect her to react with gratitude. Her whole philosophy was based on the idea that we create our own successes.

"You see what happens, Dorothy, when you stay positive and avoid things like being 'discouraged'? The money, the success—they come flooding in."

"It is amazing," Dorothy said. Given that the money was hers to begin with, it wasn't exactly flooding in to her. Even so, it was an alluring idea. "We should stop at the CVS in Saugerties," she said. "I need some sunscreen." If Fiona didn't follow her into the store, she'd never know that she was getting a heap of prescriptions filled. "And I want you to make sure I don't change my mind about telling Cecily."

"Telling her what?"

Dorothy was both hurt and comforted by the fact that Fiona had already forgotten. "About her *father*."

"Oh, that. Well, if that's what you want, just keep me posted. I'm good at bullying people." She smiled beatifically, as if this were a joke, but like most professionals whose work revolves around self-help, it was true of Fiona.

Once they got off the thruway, Fiona seemed to have forgotten the request for the stop. Dorothy didn't want to raise any doubts or suspicions by bringing it up again and making her change course. She had to head into Saugerties sometime this week anyway. How much difference could a few days make? She needed to prepare her nerves to tell Cecily about her father.

Chapter Twelve

Three days after Cecily arrived at Tom's, she got a call from a Chicago cell number she didn't recognize. Thinking it might be from the Title IX office, she felt her stomach tighten.

"Where've you been? Not sick, I hope."

She knew from the volume that it was Molly, the almost-friend she'd met at the Daily Grind. Was it creepy or flattering that she was checking up on her?

"No, not sick. Just out of town for a couple of weeks."

"A couple of weeks? That long?"

"Yes." She didn't owe her any explanations, but . . . "I—I'm visiting family."

"Oh, the difficult mother! I hope it's fun."

"I'm not sure that's the best word, but the change of scene is a good thing. I'm staying with my uncle right now. He and I are friends."

It surprised her that she was telling her this much. The familiar background sounds of grinding, frothing, and disjointed conversations made her feel closer to Molly than she actually was. They also made her realize how much she missed being at home.

"I see. Sort of a surrogate father?"

The odd thing about intrusive questions was that the more abrasively and unapologetically they were asked, the less inappropriate they seemed. It should have been the other way around. "I suppose he's always played that role in my life," she said.

"Good. I wish I'd had one. Or anyone other than the father I did have. Are you able to work there?"

Although Cecily had been planning to spend most of her time at the Schlesinger Library at Radcliffe, where there was a famous collection of cookbooks dating back to the nineteenth century, she hadn't yet made it there. The cookbook project seemed more unreal and irrelevant every day. If she was going to be bounced out of academia, there was no point in working on another academic book.

When she finished her last book and was waiting for it to be released, she'd been flooded with optimism and conviction. It was as if, having completed this one project, she felt she could accomplish anything. For the first time in her life, she understood her mother's manic, loopy belief in the brilliance of her own ideas. Although, in Dorothy's case, the fuel for a lot of that belief had been drugs.

"I'm taking an unplanned break from writing."

"I approve. One of the main advantages of working on your own project is you don't have to work on it. When I was doing my own stuff, I spent years not writing the book I was writing. That's when I was a professor. Sociology. In my new business, I don't have that luxury. We have some overlapping interests."

"I didn't realize," Cecily said. More accurately, it had never occurred to her to wonder much about Molly's background or current work life, despite seeing her daily.

"I still have a lot of connections in academia. All of them unhappy, by the way. I've done a little of everything—marketing, worked as a paralegal for a while, branding consultant."

"I'm impressed."

"I'm an impressive person, provided you don't dig too deeply. I'll call you in a day or two so I don't worry about you."

Cecily wondered if she should be concerned about Molly's attention. It seemed harmless enough, but she had made that assumption before, to disastrous results.

After texting with Santosh for a few days, she finally called him at ten a.m. at the end of her first week. In Chicago, he'd already be up, showered, and ready to head out to work; they could talk while he was biking.

She was surprised to hear him answer in a groggy voice.

"I'm not waking you up, am I?"

He groaned. "What time is it?"

"Close to nine. Are you sick?"

"Does hungover count as sick? I went out last night after soccer."

She was happy—wasn't she?—that he was enjoying himself, but what if this meant he was now doing what her presence had prevented him from doing? "In a literal sense," she said, "it definitely counts as sick."

He grunted and made noises that indicated he was getting out of bed. Cecily felt such an intense physical longing for him that it hurt.

"How's Tom?" he asked.

"Medium. He has some work problems. On top of that, Alan has moved out."

"Oh, that's too bad," Santosh said. "It can't be easy to find someone at Tom's age."

"I guess not." It struck her that Santosh had moved awfully quickly from the dissolution of Tom's relationship to the next step: replacing Alan. He was a pragmatist after all, despite his romantically melancholy music and fanciful engagement with video games. Since the dinner at which Tom had announced Alan's move, Cecily had been plagued by a concern she now voiced. "I hope I didn't have something to do with him moving out," she said, half in a whisper.

"You? Why would you? That makes no sense."

"I don't know. I've always wondered if Alan resented me. All the money Tom spent building the cottage, using my childhood specifications. Other things, too. All the time he devoted to me." She didn't want to get into the finances of her college education and private school, as doing so seemed disloyal to her mother—and, anyway, the details had always been hidden from her by the relevant adults.

Santosh sighed in what Cecily thought was an especially loud and annoyed way. "Oh, come on, Cecily. Not everything is about *you*, you know."

"I didn't say it was."

"Yes, you literally just did. Alan resented *you*. *You're* the reason he left. You might as well admit it."

Cecily was so stunned, she nearly ended the call. Santosh never spoke to her like this. It would be easy to blame it all on the hangover, but it seemed more likely he was expressing anger over her coming to Boston and a long-simmering resentment he had toward her in general. She didn't think it was true she made everything about herself, but no narcissist ever sees their own flaws.

"I'm sorry," she said. "I'm tired. Plus"—and here she paused, wondering if it was all right to say this—"I miss you."

"See? You shouldn't have left without me." He'd returned to his more gentle and loving tone, as if he'd forgiven her or maybe just regretted his outburst.

She could hear him walking across the creaking floors of their apartment and knew every sound well enough to picture where he was going. Not to make the bed, that was certain; he probably hadn't done that since she left. Suddenly, she was overwhelmed by a physical ache for his touch, his smell, the warmth of his body.

She'd always had a confusing relationship to sex and her own body. She'd been lanky and thin since childhood and was often told by other girls that she was lucky. But she sometimes worried that her boyish figure attracted the men who, however aggressively heterosexual, had a fundamental dislike and distrust of women and their bodies.

Before Santosh, she'd dated men who, for the most part, fit comfortably into her academic life and her humanities-based view of the world. There were several she liked well enough to assume she was in love with them. There was even one, Dreyfus, with whom she talked, in vague and childish ways, about marriage. Then he went abroad on a Fulbright for a year, and the relationship fell apart so quietly, she quickly forgot they ever had one.

While she was growing up, sex had been a source of embarrassment because of her mother's boastful insistence that it was nothing to be embarrassed about. In Dorothy's house, people came and went, often as the result of breakups or affairs. Her mother tried to get Cecily to read the diaries of Anaïs Nin—recitations of confusing erotic adventures passed off as liberation—so she'd feel more relaxed about it all.

When Cecily thought about her childhood and adolescence, she remembered hearing talk and laughter from other rooms and the way it stopped abruptly or changed course if she dared walk in. There was a prevailing atmosphere of adult mischief that had looked to her like childish behavior. She knew Dorothy thought she was teaching her to be a free spirit, but for years, as she was trying to assert herself as an adult, in college and graduate school, Cecily had tried her best to keep her relationships carefully under control.

When she met Santosh, control disappeared. She felt an immediate, almost electric draw to him that was completely new. It had something to do with his beautiful face and battered, athletic body, but she'd been with good-looking men before. She and Santosh had an obsessive attraction for each other for no reason she could identify. Maybe it was the first time she'd felt that someone truly loved and desired her as she was. When they were around each other, for the first year or more, Santosh always wanted to touch her. They had to sit next to each other when they were out, drive holding hands, kiss when they passed each other in the apartment. Sexually, she was in a new world. In their daily life, she felt a degree of responsibility for him and—yes, it was true—an almost maternal desire to take care of him.

Confusingly, but wonderfully, when they were in bed, he became a fierce, dominating presence, and for the first time in her life, she found herself submitting greedily to whatever he wanted to do. There didn't seem to be any limits to either their physical craving for each other or their intimacy, both mitigated by good-humored delight. No man she'd been with before had been as open as Santosh about crying in front of her, and although she'd never have admitted it to anyone, she was always turned on by it.

Santosh's possessiveness had no malice behind it; it had made her feel secure, possibly for the first time in her life. It was hard to believe she could live without it.

"What are you doing for the weekend?" she asked.

"My parents invited me out to dinner with them. Something to do with cousins? I can't remember. I might be spending the night there. Use their washing machine."

There was one in the basement of their own building, but Santosh still sometimes brought his laundry to the suburbs and let his mother wash and fold it. Now that Cecily had removed herself from the picture, Neeta could start reeling him in, one expertly folded towel at a time. No doubt that had been his mother's plan all along. She'd undercut her son's relationship with problematic Cecily incrementally. As she'd told Cecily, she was a patient woman. Cecily had swum right into the trap.

"I should let you get to work. Tom and I are going skating this afternoon."

"Sounds better than having a hangover."

"We'll see about that. . . . Santosh . . . I hate sleeping alone. I keep waking up wondering where you are." *Please*, she thought, *please say something sweet. Tell me you love me.*

"Aww. Well, I'm right here, headache and all. Make sure you tighten the laces on the skates. Best way to avoid twisting your ankle."

It wasn't a declaration of undying love, but given the situation, Cecily would interpret it as close to one.

●

Cecily was seven the first time Tom took her ice-skating. It was during a period of her childhood that had been even more confusing than usual. That year, her mother was exuberant, loving, and generous one moment, wrapping her arms around her and telling her about all the adventures they were going to have together and the places they might move to. An hour later, she was brittle and distant, telling Cecily she should go down the street to visit Tom so Mom could have some time alone.

Dorothy was always losing things in that period. Cecily would walk into a room and find her mother searching through closets or drawers with an intensity that was alarming even to a child. "Don't mind me, sweetheart," she'd say, tossing papers onto the floor. "I'm just looking for a set of keys. I'm just looking for a toothbrush. I'm just looking for my sunglasses." When Cecily came back a minute later with the misplaced item, her mother would say, "Look how smart you are," and then keep searching.

One day, Tom picked Cecily up at school and told her Dorothy was in the hospital but that she was fine. "She tripped and fell, that's all," he explained. "She sprained an ankle. She wants me to tell you she'll be home tomorrow."

"Are we going to visit her?"

"Not now," he said. "She needs to sleep."

"Are we going home?"

"We're going ice-skating."

"I don't have skates."

Tom gestured to the backseat and told her that now she did.

This was in the middle of a cold and dry spell that had lasted a week. It was January. They drove to a pond a few miles from Cecily's school. As they stepped out of the car and into the icy air, she saw that the surface of the pond had been transformed into a sheet of smooth, black glass. Dozens of people were gliding across it, all as if in a dream. The deep blue of the late afternoon and the black of the ice and of the stark, bare trees against the sky were frightening and beautiful. For many years, whenever she felt herself seized by anxiety or overworked, she'd recall the scene that first day Tom took her to the frozen pond.

She fell every time he let go of her hands, but there was something about the sting of the cold, the clacking of blades on ice, and the wonderful strangeness of being on top of the water that tamped down Cecily's worries about her mother. By sunset, when the sky was red, she was able to skate on her own, and Tom had begun to teach her to go backward. They returned to the pond until the weather changed. When her mother left the hospital—not after one night but *five*—she had a bruise around her eye and down the side of her face. The fall had been the start of the seizures that would lead, eventually, to sobriety—or Dorothy's version thereof.

Cecily told her about skating but saw that her mother was disappointed she hadn't been missed more intensely. She sat down in a big chair with Cecily and said, "Do you know what cocaine is, sweetheart?" and proceeded to tell her the truth about what had happened.

Now, all these years later, Cecily and Tom were sitting on a bench putting on their skates in a chilly, echoing municipal building with year-round skating. Probably because it was a balmy day at the end of April, there were only a few other people—a man bent over at the waist with his hands clasped behind him practicing speed skating, a couple of impossibly tiny kids holding on to milk crates to learn balance, and a young woman in the middle of the ice doing spins and perfectly executed jumps. Watching them, Cecily felt an intense, familiar longing to have been born with a physical talent, which, looked at from the outside, seemed more appealing, useful, and healthy in every way than whatever darker intellectual talents she'd been given.

Tom finished lacing up before she did, and he sat looking at her with his elbows on his knees. He was waiting for her to finish, but probably also for her to start speaking. She'd told him she wanted to have a talk.

"I'll meet you out there," she said. "Santosh told me to make sure my laces were tight, so I'm making sure."

She watched as Tom pushed off on one leg and then the other until he was circling the rink. She was touched by the incongruity of his gray hair and new weight and his still-graceful skating. Age was so unkind. It would be to her, assuming she got there, but now she felt a confusing resentment toward Tom. She didn't want his appearance to change, didn't want him to leave her behind as he skated into old age. She'd be left without him. He was the person she could fall back on. One day, he'd be gone.

She hobbled to the edge of the rink with tears in her eyes and then stepped onto the ice unsteadily. Tom skated over to her and made a showy stop, showering her skates with frost. He looked flushed and exhilarated, just as he had when they'd gone skating all those years earlier, when he was her friend and protector and surrogate father. Molly had been right.

He took her hands and, skating backward, pulled her out onto the ice. "Look at you," he said. "You haven't forgotten a thing."

"It's true," she said. "And, believe me, there are a lot of things I'd like to forget."

"No doubt."

Within a few minutes, she was skating steadily, trying to catch up with her uncle on the white, scuffed ice with the arched ceiling of the rink so high above them. This wasn't that frozen pond, that pink twilight, those cold winter afternoons that were becoming so scarce. This was the artificial alternative she had to get used to. Still, it made her happy. As they circled, she felt a blurring of time, of experience, of movement. She'd been here before, done all this countless other times, and yet now it felt new—her age, the ache of the past few months. As she picked up speed, more speed than she realized, she began to lose her balance, her awareness of her body and how she was moving it. It was a strange loss of control that was both unnerving and thrilling. Maybe, more than anything, she just needed to let go. She looked up to the skeleton of the ceiling above, and her feet slid from under her. She slipped and landed on her butt.

By the time Tom skated over to her, she'd rolled onto her side with her head cradled in her arm. She was unexpectedly comforted by the hard coldness beneath her.

"I think I might stay here for a while," she said. "I could use the rest."

Tom held out his hands to her. "I saw you go down. You didn't fall that hard."

As he was pulling her to her feet, she thought, *You have no idea how hard I've fallen.* "Tom," she said, still holding his hands, time still blurred, "I'm sorry for all the trouble I've caused you over the years."

He looked at her as if baffled, even though he had to know what she meant. "What are you talking about?"

"It's such a long litany. It's everything. I'm going to try to make it up to you. I don't know how, but I am going to try."

He put his arms around her, there in the manufactured cold and the strange, filtered daylight. "You have to know you're the best friend I have, Cecily. You're the best thing that ever happened to me. I only wish I could do more."

"I wanted you and Alan to be together forever," she said. "I wanted you to have someone for the rest of your life."

"I did, too, but what can we do. I'm hoping he eventually comes back. No one else would put up with me. Sometimes, even *I* can't."

She put her head on his shoulder. "At some point, if he comes back, or even if he doesn't, you have to start refusing me. You have to stop trying to help."

"That doesn't work out for me," he said. "Even if, sometimes, it complicates things, it's what I have to do. At this point, it's who I am. And it's my greatest pleasure."

She was crying against his jacket, and he had his hand on her hair.

"I hate your hair, dearest," he said. "Please let it grow out. I know it's none of my business, but it doesn't suit you."

"I know. I'm removing all the scissors in my house." The speed skater was still circling the rink, a blur out of the corner of her eye. Although, really, everything was blurred with tears. "I have a funny feeling about this trip to Woodstock. I'm almost sure Dorothy wants to tell me something. She said, in emails and on the phone, we need to 'talk'—in a pointed way."

"Any clue what it could be?"

"No, but I'm not sure I can handle any more news, good or bad."

Tom took her arm, and they slowly circled the rink again. "I've got a big problem at work I need to attend to. It involves our friend Char-

lotte, to give you an idea of how big a problem. But I was thinking it
might do me good to take a break and go out to Woodstock with you."

"You don't have to do that, Tom. I'll be fine."

"I know you will. I'm not going for your sake; I'm going for mine."

She had to laugh at this, it was so obviously not true. And yet, it was
the only good news she'd heard in a long while.

Chapter Thirteen

*T*om had done his best to wrangle information out of Alan about this new person he'd "met." *Who is this person you've met? How did you meet? How long ago was this meeting?*

"Can you ask those questions without the bitter tone?" Alan asked.

"I'm sorry," Tom said. "Let me try again: How long ago did you . . . meet?"

Alan told him they'd met a month earlier and had started dating—another word that caused Tom to clench his jaw—three weeks ago. "The rest," he said, "is not relevant."

Since Tom preferred to think their separation was temporary, it all seemed highly relevant to him. Hearing that Alan was "dating" someone else made Tom desire him with the urgency of a child whose toy truck has been taken from him by another kid in the kindergarten class. "You're *mine*!" he wanted to scream.

He took Cecily to the Harvard Film Archive to see *Nights of Cabiria*, part of a Fellini retrospective. They sat in the dark, side by side, laughing and crying together, each for their own private reasons, Tom imagined, and for one shared reason: Cabiria, the frequently troubled and betrayed character played by Giulietta Masina, reminded them, in her many bad decisions but indomitable spirit, of Dorothy. No matter how many failures Dorothy had, no matter how many brushes with bankruptcy or despair, she always rose—a little more creakily, perhaps; a little less energetically, certainly—still sure the next thing was going to be the big win she longed for. The move to Woodstock, the gala.

He wondered how Dorothy would have handled the professional threat he was now facing. With a lot more conviction and an unrealistic but positive attitude. He tried to summon some of that for himself. He told Winston he was working on Charlotte, that he'd come up with a plan to convince her to put the guesthouse into production, that he was optimistic.

Winston had looked at him through his round, sparkling glasses with languid doubt. "Have you shown the drawings to Lanford?" he asked.

The idea that he might, that Winston thought that was even an appropriate question, was mortifying. "I don't see the point in that," Tom said. And then, trying to imagine himself more confident than he really was, he said, "I'm still on this, Winston. I have a plan, one I think will make Charlotte go ahead with it."

Winston shrugged, and Tom saw that the cordiality of their relationship was disintegrating and that Winston viewed him as having one foot out the door.

Cecily's presence in the guest cottage had the unexpected benefit of making him drink less. Maybe he'd taken to his nightly wine stupors because he was lonely.

In his diligent sobriety, Tom had gone through a list of a dozen people who might be interested in the house he'd designed for Charlotte and Oliver, people with enough money and status to elicit Charlotte's competitive instincts with a credible threat. Unfortunately, working with any of these people would take time and energy. With most, he'd have to develop a new relationship with them, and because Tom had to nail this down in the next few weeks, he needed a shortcut. He needed someone who owed him a favor. The most obvious choice was, alas, the most awkward.

When Alan told him he was moving out, Tom had been working with a married couple named Marek and Eveline Bachar. They were rich and glamourous, the glamour coming largely from the money and a degree of confidence that Tom found compelling and mysterious, especially in people whose physical beauty was mostly related to the perfect tailoring of their clothes. Also, they were affectionate with each other in such an open and spontaneous way, it made Tom happy. It was always easier to be sentimental about someone else's relationship than it was to be sentimental about his own.

At a certain point in the process, Marek took Tom out for lunch and then asked to go back to his place to see, in person, the guest cottage on his property.

"It's very small," Tom said, "and very specific. Designed for my niece based on her childhood drawings. It's not representative of what I'd design for you. Or for anyone else."

"Oh, I know, I know. I'm just curious."

Tom brought Marek back to his house, and halfway into the tour, Marek made a blunt and unambiguous pass. The indiscretion that ensued with Marek was unfortunate from beginning to end: a journey of three brief encounters. Among other things, Tom genuinely liked Marek's wife more than he liked Marek. He wasn't unattractive—those perfectly tailored suits!—but Tom was lured into the mess out of sheer amazement that Marek had come on to him. These days, Tom viewed every sexual opportunity as the erotic equivalent of the last swim of summer, as hard to resist as a sandwich (even an unappetizing one) purchased before one boarded a six-hour flight without meal service.

Tom knew that a lot of his appeal to Marek was his perceived discretion and safety. He wouldn't talk about it with anyone and risk compromising their deal. In the end, the indiscretion had been Marek's. Tom should have been able to predict that. He made the rookie mistake of sending Tom an email detailing what he wanted to do next time they met. Naturally, it was read by Eveline. The whole project, which would have brought a great deal of money into the firm, was canceled.

As Tom saw it, Marek owed him a lot: many of his current professional problems swirled around Marek's decision to leave the browser open on his computer. Like most men, he had no curiosity about what his wife was doing online and therefore thought the lack of interest was mutual.

The Bachars went into counseling, Marek swore off any further exploration of his "curiosity" about bisexuality—*curiosity* being the curious word straight men often used to refer to homosexual activity, no matter how intense or frequent—and they sent him a basket of fruit for his professional help. In other words, Marek's actions cost Marek nothing—they even saved him the expense of the proposed guesthouse—and Tom a great deal.

Tom had emailed Marek to say he wanted to meet with him at a café, to show him some plans and ask a small favor. Marek wrote back almost immediately to say he did not want to risk being seen in public with him "in case word gets back to my wife and there's a misunderstanding." Marek made a counteroffer: "I'll meet you at your house, if you like, but only for conversation. I suppose I owe you an apology. But that's it; nothing else can happen."

Tom was insulted by the last sentence. As if he were the one who'd pursued Marek in the first place. As if, after everything that had happened, he were pining for *him*. As if Marek assumed he had no other options. He did, even if, these days, they were exclusively men who fetishized decrepitude or had a neurotic relationship with father figures. And what was wrong with that? Over the years, he'd discovered that undamaged people with healthy egos tend to be unimaginative lovers.

Insulted or not, Tom arranged a time for Marek to show up.

In the second week of Cecily's stay, three days before the trip to Woodstock, Marek arrived.

Tom was sitting at the table under the pergola with the plans and drawings for Charlotte's guesthouse laid out before him. Cecily had finally used the bicycle he'd bought her and gone to the library. The bike was more money he'd vowed he wouldn't spend, but he hadn't been able to resist, and she'd been delighted by the bike, a green Dutch thing that seemed made for her.

Marek nudged his gray Porsche up the drive. Gray to blend in; Porsche to stand out. There was something furtive even about the way he drove, peering ahead to make sure it was okay to turn the corner. The infuriating thing about closeted men, Tom had noted over the years, was that they seemed to think they were the only ones with anything at stake.

Marek got out of his car and looked around, as if gauging whether there were hidden cameras. He was wearing his work costume: gray pants, a gray dress shirt with the sleeves rolled up, and a pair of aviator sunglasses, even though it was a cloudy day.

Tom had a fleeting moment of guilt. He had tricked Marek into coming here by not mentioning that, in approximately half an hour, Charlotte Morley would be showing up, too. Maybe the trickery was mitigated by the fact that he'd lied to Charlotte as well. She thought she was coming to see Cecily.

Marek shook Tom's hand, precisely as if he and Tom were old but not particularly good friends from college and as if Tom had never pushed his face down into a pillow.

"Been a while since I was here," Marek said, a comment that might have been a reference to the season or, given the way he was looking at Tom, a comment on Tom's appearance. He swept his combed-back hair behind his ears.

"A lot has gone on," Tom said. "Come sit down."

Marek raised his eyebrows lasciviously. "Is this the 'business' part of the conversation?" He had a trying habit of turning everything into a lazily constructed double entendre. He could do this with almost any word, including ones as mundane as *cheeseburger* or *telephone*. His faint Polish accent heightened the effect.

"It's the *only* part of the conversation," Tom said. Once they'd taken their seats, he said, "I'm asking you for a favor, Marek. It's a small favor, in the scheme of things, but it's potentially of great importance to me."

"My life is different now than it was a few months ago," Marek said. "I'm not interested in screwing that up."

"It's a simple matter." Tom slid the sketches and schematics for Charlotte's guesthouse across the table. "I'd like you to look these over."

"We're not doing the building, Tom. I'm sorry."

"I'm aware of that. Still, I'd like you to take a look."

Marek frowned but did as instructed. He studied the drawings with growing interest, asking for clarification about certain dimensions and elevations. Despite his eroticized disdain for Marek, Tom had always been impressed with the man's ability to interpret technical drawings and imagine them in 3-D complexity. He had a fine eye for detail and excellent taste.

"Beautiful place. Why didn't you design something this nice for us?"

"You asked for traditional New England."

"That was Eveline's idea. I could have talked her out of it with a building this special."

"A little late for that now. Getting this particular house into construction quickly is important to me. It might even be vital to my career." And yet, as Tom looked at the plans with Marek's fresh eye, he knew it was more than his job. It was his opportunity, his final opportunity, to do something truly beautiful. "If the client thinks that you plan to build the house I designed for her, or that you have serious interest in it, I'm convinced it will encourage her to move ahead with construction as we originally planned. It would help me out a great deal."

Marek studied the drawings again and said, "Well, if that's all it takes—sure. Tell her you have an interested client."

"It might take a little more than that." Tom looked around the yard, stalling, and then came out with it. "She's showing up here any minute."

Marek was incredulous, as if he were being entrapped—which, in a way, he was. No one is more appalled by being deceived than a deceitful person. "What are you saying?"

"I'm asking you to pretend you and your wife are on the verge of building this house. You have to be convincing. The client's an obstinate person, and we recently had a professional falling-out."

"None of this sounds good."

"Think of it as an acting job."

"I'm a terrible actor."

Marek was both right and utterly wrong in saying this. His presentation of himself to the world, "happily heterosexual man," was, in essence, a performance, and one that was largely successful—provided he scrubbed his browser history more often. He was a physically rugged man, with a compact, solid body. He'd told Tom that he performed an archaic calisthenics routine every morning, counting off his repetitions in Polish as he'd done when in grade school in Kraków. In bed, though, he appeared to take cues from pornography and use stock phrases and a stilted tone that made him sound as if his dialogue had been dubbed by a bored and underpaid voice-over actor. His accent became thicker in bed, especially when he was demanding to be humiliated in a variety of stylized ways, giving a Monty Python quality to the proceedings.

"I'm only asking you to do your best. Just show genuine enthusiasm and be grateful to her for deciding to cancel the project herself. You're planting a seed in her mind. I know this woman quite well."

"You should have told me all this before I came, so I'd have had the option of declining. I don't know her, do I?"

"Unlikely. She's a lawyer and my age. Last I heard, you're in finance. And 'forty.'"

"She doesn't know about our relationship, does she?"

"Of course not. I'm no more interested in broadcasting that than you are. In any case, we have no relationship."

Marek took off the aviator glasses and looked at himself in the lenses, then put them back on. "Lying is easy for me, Tom. Too easy. You know that. I'm trying to stop. I don't want to start down a slope. I'm sorry I caused you problems, but this would be bad for me on too many levels." He stood with impressive resolve and said, "I won't do this, and I'm going to leave now."

At those unpromising words, Charlotte's car crunched up the drive with, Tom noted, some of the same furtive approach as Marek's. She climbed out in what appeared to be mid-stride and mid-conversation. Tom at first thought she was on the phone.

". . . don't know why you don't have the bushes trimmed. You can barely make it around the curve up here without scratching the paint. Alan usually keeps things so tidy. Oh." Upon seeing Marek, who was, in his dark glasses, easy to mistake for handsome and, by their standards, young, Charlotte paused. "I didn't realize you had company."

Tom introduced them and pulled out a chair for Charlotte.

"Where's Cecily?" she asked, dusting off the garden chair as if she suspected it would ruin her skirt.

"She's at the library. She should be showing up any minute. Drink?"

"White wine, if it's decent and chilled." She turned to Marek. "I came to see Tom's niece. She's visiting from Chicago. I've known her since birth. Her mother is an old friend of mine, which is how I know Tom." She paused, but when Marek said nothing, she added: "Your turn."

"I'm working with Marek and his wife on a guesthouse for their property. In Wellesley."

"Really?"

The tone made it clear she found the comment suspicious and would disbelieve any clarifications. Not off to a good start, from Tom's point of view. "You sound as if you don't believe me," Tom said.

"I'm very perceptive, Marek. I can always tell when someone has something to hide. Nice sunglasses, by the way."

Tom went into the house to get Charlotte a glass of wine, lukewarm. When he came outside, the two of them were sitting in awkward silence, looking off at the skyline of Boston with what struck Tom as shared annoyance. Charlotte sipped the wine and put down the glass. Clearly, something had happened in his absence. It was probably safe to assume that Charlotte, with her tendency to resent surprises and her vanity about her own insightfulness, had insulted Marek by asking too many questions about his wife or his connection to Tom. Like a lot of people who are proud of their perspicacity, she assumed her own behavior and motives were impossible to read.

"If you think I'm going to comment on the temperature of the wine, Tom, you're wrong. I see you've been showing Marek your best work."

"Of course. Why wouldn't I? It's the house I'm most proud of. In its present, single-story form."

"You should know, Marek, that Tom is utterly inflexible. If you and your wife want to add anything to the house or change it in some way, you'll have to face his unearned outrage."

Marek turned slowly toward Charlotte and removed his sunglasses. He had a strikingly wide face and clear hazel eyes he now appeared to be using to his advantage. "Tom has been solicitous of the ideas and demands we've brought in. That said, the reason we decided to work with an architect is that neither my wife nor I is an expert in the field. I'm sure you wouldn't claim to be a professional in architectural matters, Charlotte."

Charlotte sat in stillness, a warning sign. "Since we met exactly ten minutes ago, I can't imagine why you'd be sure about anything involving me."

"Like you, I am perceptive."

"Yes, I'm beginning to think we have a lot in common."

"My wife and I came in saying we wanted one thing, but when I saw this, I realized it was exactly what we need. We were imagining a space to put guests, but this will be a trophy on the grounds and increase the value and appeal of the entire property. I'm not especially vain, but I'm also not above imaging the pleasure of seeing this gem in shelter magazines and *AD* and on Kirsten Dirksen's YouTube channel. She'd flip for this place."

Tom was impressed and even touched by the enthusiasm with which Marek was throwing himself into his role. He initially regretted not having had more time to coach him on what to say, but he was a natural.

He wanted to think Marek was doing this as a tattered payback to him for the canceled project, but he could tell from the way he was eyeing Charlotte that it was mainly inspired by the instant dislike the two had taken to each other.

Either way, Charlotte had a look of restless annoyance that indicated that whether or not she was totally buying this enthusiasm for "her" house, she didn't much like it. She was being especially attentive to her hair, sweeping it off her shoulders as a way of letting Marek and, more to the point, Tom know that she wasn't intimidated by this.

Finally, Marek rose, put on his glasses, and said he had to get going. "I'll just use your bathroom before I go," he said and walked into the house.

Charlotte paused in the middle of sipping her wine and put down the glass. It was difficult to put anything past her. Growing up in a family in which dissembling ruled everyone's behavior, she'd learned that survival depended upon noticing the tiniest details and understanding that all of it mattered. She eyed Tom above her round sunglasses and said, "Really, Tom?"

"I have no idea what you're talking about."

"Poor Alan. I mean, whatever arrangement you two have is your own business, but at your age?"

Tom had learned that an important part of aging with dignity was pretending you had no sex life and didn't want one. The public had grown used to open declarations of racism, the details of frequent mass shootings, gruesome images of gastric bypass surgery that played on TV for entertainment value. The one thing no one could stand to hear about was the sexual desire, never mind the sexual activity, of someone in their sixties.

"You're reading an awful lot into a trip to the bathroom," Tom said.

"I'm a good reader."

When Marek had left, taking some of the sketches with him, Charlotte leafed through the remaining plans. "I never said it wasn't a beautiful house. I don't know what point you're trying to prove by having this person and, allegedly, his wife fawn over it, but you're wasting your time."

"It just happened," Tom said. "We were at an impasse, and after you said you didn't want to move forward, I showed them the sketches. They fell in love with them."

"Where did you say they live?"

"Wellesley. Not far from you and Oliver."

Charlotte opened her bag and took out a pack of cigarettes. Her smoking habit was furtive, and the fact that she was being so open about it now suggested to Tom that she was stirred by Marek's interest. She was not the only one taken to reading small details.

She lit a cigarette, took a few drags, and passed it to Tom. He knew very few people who smoked but even fewer who'd turn down the fleeting pleasure of a small dose of nicotine when offered casually.

"To clarify," Charlotte said, "I asked for changes, which you did not deliver. So, please don't make it seem I rejected you outright because I didn't appreciate the design." She held out her fingers in a V, and Tom inserted the cigarette into them.

"I wasn't able to tamper with something I see as perfect," he said.

"So, you decided to try to stir up my jealousy and competitive spirit with this 'friend' of yours." She passed the cigarette back to him. "Finish that off."

As soon as Tom had responsibility for the rest of the cigarette, he lost all interest in smoking it. Still, he felt the conversation was going exactly as he'd hoped. "I'm sure Eldridge Johnson will come up with something interesting for you."

"Considering what it's likely to cost, I hope so. I'm not a huge fan of his work, just so you know."

"In that case, it makes perfect sense you're going to him."

"Oliver has some say in all this."

"I'm sure of that," Tom said, just to challenge her.

"Don't be sure of anything until it's happened."

Chapter Fourteen

ecily was feeling her usual mix of disappointment in how much she hadn't accomplished that day and relief at returning to Tom's property when she pushed her new bike up the steep drive. Charlotte was sitting at the little table between the two houses. She was passing Tom a cigarette, an unexpected bit of intimacy that looked almost postcoital. She'd always had the impression those two shared a secret, like two people who'd been on a rough ocean cruise together or weathered a tornado in a basement—or, perhaps, had as their common denominator a tie to her mother.

Charlotte gave her an enfolding, cigarette-scented embrace. "Our pretty girl gets prettier every year," she said. Most of Dorothy's close friends referred to Cecily as "our girl," as if she belonged to all of them, another way of acknowledging that there was something missing in Dorothy's mothering. "You must be exhausted riding all the way into Cambridge."

"I need the exercise," Cecily said. "My life is too sedentary."

"'Too sedentary,'" Charlotte mused. "It's one of those terms that never made much sense to me. Like 'too delicious' or 'too handsome.' What are you working on?"

Cecily mentioned her cookbook project, but in fact, she'd spent most of the past two days bicycling along the Charles, texting Santosh with diminishing returns, and, much to her surprise, talking to Molly, the ghostwriter who was apparently becoming her new best friend. Molly seemed to be especially good at being nonjudgmental, even when asking difficult questions. Unlike most people who asked provocative questions, she didn't appear to wait impatiently so she could supply the answer herself. Cecily had told Molly things about her childhood, her relationship with her mother, and even hinted at problems at Deerpath.

"Yes," Molly had said, "I know all about that."

This had knocked the wind out of Cecily. Was there anyone who didn't know? "You do? How?"

"I told you; I still have friends in academia. One at Deerpath I worked on a book with. I can't reveal the name."

They spoke more, and Cecily was surprised to find it a relief to talk about this with her. It was so much easier to blurt it all out than it was with close friends, where shame and embarrassment entered quickly. Most of her academic friends would be sympathetic, all the while no doubt shaking their heads in dismay that she hadn't managed the entire situation with Lee more appropriately. Molly's vigorous support of her and self-employment made it easy to feel she could reveal anything.

Now Charlotte said, "I'm completely uninterested in cookbooks, but I'll read every word of anything you write."

She had sent Cecily a long, detailed letter with her reaction to her first book. It had contained a lot of challenges to Cecily's conclusions, but because it was one of the most thoughtful and thorough responses she'd received, Cecily was impressed and grateful. Charlotte had a fine mind, which, despite her professional accomplishments and good works, Cecily had always felt was largely wasted on fighting petty battles with people who were not her equals. It was the plight of most people who needed to be right in every circumstance.

Charlotte ushered them toward the door of Tom's house as if she were the host. "These chairs are unbearable," she said. "Let's move inside."

Cecily had always had a wary fondness for Charlotte. She was driven and outspoken and crazily energetic. She was unabashed about pushing people around and asserting herself—she was a bully—but she had a tender, sentimental side that sometimes poked out around the edges. She was constantly berating Dorothy for being financially irresponsible—comments Dorothy laughed off as if they were mere shtick—but Cecily knew they loved each other.

"How's Oliver?" Cecily asked as they were stepping into Tom's living room. It was pleasantly warmed by the sunlight coming in the atelier window.

Charlotte pursed her lips as if deciding which appetizer to order. "As always, it's hard to know. He got back from Switzerland yesterday. He spent some time with Nolan, trying to talk him into making a commitment to his job."

Cecily nodded but chose not to pursue the subject of Charlotte's son. He was a year younger than Cecily but had always seemed significantly younger than that. She and Nolan had been thrown together throughout their childhoods, even though they'd never had much in common. Like many children forced to play together, each developed a quiet resentment of the other. Cecily felt her time would have been better spent reading or skating or doing almost anything. Nolan, who sensed her lack of interest, was insulting and hostile toward her.

Their relationship had come to a perhaps inevitable head one evening when Cecily was fourteen and Nolan a smirky thirteen-year-old still awaiting puberty. There was an adult dinner thrown by Dorothy, and Cecily and Nolan had been told to play a game in Cecily's bedroom. It was one of those old-fashioned board games with colorful money and hundreds of small pieces that were always getting lost. Dorothy loved these games and spending her play money as lavishly as she spent the real thing. She had no particular interest in winning; she just loved being extravagant.

Naturally, Nolan was losing and in a bad mood about it. He wasn't unintelligent, but he was often arrogant and condescending, attitudes Cecily knew were related to his having two parents with money and professional accomplishments while she had only wacky Dorothy. He accused Cecily of cheating. Then, when she told him she was not—that she wouldn't even know how to cheat at this game of chance, that she saw no point in cheating at something she didn't care about winning—he said, touchingly, despite the hostile tone, "My parents wish I was more like you."

"Why would they wish that?"

"You're never in trouble, you get good grades, you don't cheat. You don't ask Dorothy for anything. My mother says Dorothy didn't deserve you."

"I ask my mother for things," she said. The idea that she didn't sounded pathetic.

"Yeah? Like what?"

"I don't know. Things." Even at that age, she knew that it was best to make her own way or, when she couldn't, go to Tom. "Lunch money. New shoes."

"Those don't count. You need them. You're a better person than me," he spat out. He stood up and knocked over the board, spilling the pieces all over the floor. Then he made an awkward lunge and grabbed Cecily between her legs.

She was so surprised and confused by this, she didn't try to move his hand, just looked at him, waiting to see what was next. Nolan was equally confused about what he was doing, and stood there, unsure how to proceed. Finally, angry at her for what he'd done, he stormed out of the room.

She'd never mentioned it to him or to anyone else. There was something so sad about Nolan that she always felt responsible for what he'd done to her—which, technically, probably counted as molestation. On the plus side, it had prompted her go to Dorothy and say she didn't want to spend time with him anymore. Dorothy studied her face closely and then, without questioning it, had agreed.

"He once told me he wanted to go to culinary school," Cecily said now.

Charlotte frowned. "We heard that, too. Do you really think Oliver would have allowed that?"

"I'm not sure. Would you?"

"Grudgingly. It's probably too late. For the moment, Nolan's following in his father's footsteps."

For all Dorothy's flaws, Cecily had never doubted her mother would support her in whatever she chose to do, even if she didn't understand it (American studies) or approve of it (Barnard). She'd always had freedom in choosing her own path in life, even if it was because her mother was so preoccupied with looking for a new path for herself, she didn't have time to monitor.

They were sitting on a sofa in Tom's living room. Charlotte reached out and brushed the bristly hair on Cecily's head. "Tell me why you're here," she said.

"She came to see me," Tom said.

"She came to stay with you, Tom." She turned back to Cecily. "You're not going to Dorothy's gala opening or whatever it is, are you?"

"I am," she said. "I owe it to her."

"I would never get in the middle of a family matter, but I'm not sure what the debt is. I considered going, but I didn't want to encourage her. I was against the purchase of that ridiculous building from the start. I took the whole move to New York personally."

Cecily mentioned Fiona Snow and her self-help book and the boilerplate version of what she'd gleaned from her internet searches.

Charlotte thrust out her lower teeth and gave an exasperated sigh. "I knew it sounded too good to be true: Dorothy making a few safe, sensible investments and living within her means. This is terrible news. The information I got was vague. I suspect she was waiting to spring it on me. The 'big reveal' once I got there. God! I hate what reality TV has done to America."

Cecily had noted that Americans married to Europeans often became harsh, self-righteous critics of American culture in order to distance themselves from it. The foreign-born spouse usually reveled in all things American. Oliver Fuchs, who was Austrian by birth but had lived the bulk of his life in the States, still took immense pleasure in any inferior thing he could label "so American," from Walmart to weak coffee.

"I'll call you when we get back," Tom said. "I'll let you know what we find out."

Charlotte stood suddenly. Cecily could tell she'd made a decision and was about to take action. It was impossible to talk her out of anything. She suspected that Oliver—who was, in his way, equally definite—found this attractive. There was something about the clash of these two immutable forces that could be surprisingly sexy, even after all these years. Cecily still had vivid memories of admiring them as they screamed at each other across a dinner table throughout her adolescence.

"Oliver is going to New York for a meeting. I'll take the shuttle with him. We can rent a car and drive up to Woodstock on Saturday."

"Oh, please, Charlotte," Tom said. "You and Oliver? It sounds as if it's going to be a circus already."

"If the building has enough room to accommodate a retreat center, it can absorb two more people. Do you want me to leave you a cigarette, Tom?"

"I don't smoke," Tom said.

"Fine," she said. "Take the pack." She tossed it onto the sofa and strode off. "Don't let that man do anything with our plans until we've talked with Johnson."

A few minutes later, there was a long blaring of a car horn from below the house, followed by a chorus of horns. "That's Charlotte," Tom said to a surprised Cecily. "She hates turning out of the drive, so she leans on the horn and proceeds heedlessly. Her style in general."

●

That evening, Santosh told Cecily he was going to spend the weekend at his parents' house.

"More cousins?" she asked, trying to keep her voice neutral.

"A party for a relative I barely remember meeting who's graduating college."

"Has it been nice seeing more of your parents?"

"Mixed bag," he said. "I'm guessing it'll be the same for you when you see your mother."

"I would definitely take a mixed bag."

After they hung up, she opened her email. Three messages from a furniture site she'd made the mistake of buying a rug from, two messages from politicians she didn't support, and, pulling up the rear, one from the Title IX office at Deerpath. "Investigation Update."

She stared at it for a moment in quiet disbelief. She'd been imagining and anticipating receiving this for so long, it was almost as surreal to finally have it in front of her as it had been seeing Lee Anderson at the airport.

> Dear Professor Kemp,
>
>   We're pleased to inform you that we've completed the initial phase of the investigation of your case. We'd like to meet with you to clarify several points. This will be an informal meeting, but you are welcome to have legal representation present.
>
>   Please contact us when you receive this, so we can arrange a convenient time.
>
>   Thank you for your patience throughout this process.

There was so little to react to in the email, in terms of clues about outcome, tone, or attitude toward her, that Cecily was confused. Was "pleased" a hopeful sign? Was "legal representation" worrying?

What she hated most about this case was how intensely lonely it made her feel—she, a person who was used to being alone.

> Dear Mr. Jackson,
>
>   Thank you for your message. I'm currently in Boston, but I'm happy to meet at the earliest available time. As I'm sure you can imagine, I am eager to move the process along in any way possible.

She reread the email, parsed every sentence and comma, and then, with a feeling of resignation, hit Send. Then she texted Molly and asked her if she knew of any good, inexpensive lawyers.

Chapter Fifteen

They left for Woodstock midmorning. The sky was cloud-less, and the sun had an alarming intensity for early May. These days, Tom heard screeching violins from the soundtrack of *Psycho* when he looked out the window and saw unfiltered sunlight. The climate had become a deranged killer about to strike a fatal blow. Worst of all, there was nowhere to hide. When he wore short sleeves, he felt as if the sun were scorching him, even in winter. Was it becoming stronger, or was it that all-purpose explanation for every physical irregularity: age? It felt like a betrayal, as he'd been counting on all the worst of the changes to begin after his death.

Cecily had downloaded a series of podcasts to help pass the time on the three-and-a-half-hour drive. Many of them were about tiny houses and the people who lived in them, ostensibly Tom's interest but, today, a reminder of his troubles. Tom was mystified by the popularity of podcasts. With their ubiquitous ukulele theme music and jokey enthusiasm, they struck him as similar to homemade brownies—frequently delicious but usually made from the same store-bought mix.

None of it mattered. There was something so soothing about being in a small, confined space with Cecily that he wished the drive would go on forever. It had been pointless to think he could back away from his relationship with her just because Alan found him too attached. Life didn't work like that, and even if he wanted Cecily to go off and have a successful life of her own, he now had ample evidence that he could count on her emotional support more than he could count on Alan's.

●

To reach Dorothy's house, they had to drive through the village of Woodstock. On this windy day, with the rustlings of weather changes blowing in, the town was filled with tourists ambling distractedly, as if they were wondering what they were doing there. Almost every storefront along the main street was decorated with wind chimes, prayer flags, colorful pennants, or loose, billowing clothes for sale, whipping back and forth on their sidewalk racks like ghostly figures beckoning shoppers.

There was one specific ghost in evidence, and that was the famous music festival, as distant from the present as Prohibition had been from the date of Tom's birth. Peace symbols and tie-dyed T-shirts and random representations of guitars were everywhere. In the middle of the tiny town green—a vegan restaurant on one side, an upscale wine bar on the other—was a drum circle and a group of gray-haired people in unstructured cotton pants doing what looked like interpretive dance. Like all tourist towns Tom knew, this one seemed both immensely appealing and utterly ridiculous.

Cecily had her window open, taking it all in. "The funny thing is," she said, "this does make sense as the place my mother would end up."

Tom drove off the main street and onto a narrow, winding lane. The road was unpaved and bumpy, and because it must have rained the night before, the potholes were filled with water. Within a few feet, they'd left behind the bustle of the village and entered the countryside. An open field was spread out on one side of the lane, and what appeared to be a farmhouse on the other. Dorothy's building was a two-minute drive from the main street but seemed miles away from everything.

He pulled into one of several parking spaces in front of her building. Cecily hunched down and craned her neck to see the whole of the structure through the windshield.

The converted barn appeared to have grown over the winter, or maybe Tom had reduced its size in his mind to sleep better. He bent over as Cecily was doing, to take it in. Seeing it through her eyes, he recognized again how absurdly large it was, looming up more than four stories. He noticed—it was impossible not to—that an immense square mullioned window had been installed on Dorothy's floor. He thought it was probably best to say nothing to Cecily about it, but it must have cost a small fortune. It was probably bigger than any single wall in his own house. With the change in the climate, Tom had been considering having his atelier window removed and replaced with a solid, insulated wall. The funny thing about Dorothy was that she was so oriented toward people, she rarely spent much time looking at views or appreciating scenic vistas. It was something he admired in her, something they almost shared.

He and Cecily entered through one of several glass doors on the ground floor and found themselves in a sprawling space that had once been an art gallery. It was the size of a small ballroom. On the floor above was a balcony that encircled the room. A little platform had been set up under the balcony, and there were chairs stacked in columns and folded banquet tables scattered around in chaotic fashion. Gala preparations were underway. Tom hoped they wouldn't be asked to do the setup.

He went to a trio of doors at the back of the gallery, opened one, and heard voices drifting down the staircase to the upper floor. The circus was already in full swing. He called out a hello.

"They're here!" he heard Dorothy cry out, giddy with enthusiasm.

Her excitement had an overdone quality that annoyed Tom. It was a like the manic joy a dog exhibits when you enter a room you left only five minutes earlier. *Oh, calm down*, he wanted to say to her.

He gestured for Cecily to go ahead of him. "She'll want to see you first," he said.

They'd made it halfway up the staircase when Dorothy appeared on a landing above them. She let out a shriek of delight and stamped her bare feet.

"Finally!" she said. She rushed down a few more steps to throw her arms around Cecily. There was something so heartfelt and ecstatic about the gesture, Tom felt the decent thing to do was to look away. "You're too skinny," she said. "Have you been feeding her, Tom? Oh my god, you've certainly been feeding yourself! I'm so happy you let yourself go. Finally."

"It was a long winter," Tom said.

"Try living out here in the country!" She pulled Cecily in even closer and said, with a sob and a hushed voice, "I was worried you'd never come."

Cecily, caught for a moment in her mother's spell, was grinning. "That was never an option."

"I told you it was wonderful. I knew you'd love it. We haven't completely set up for the party. When Fiona gets here, be sure to call it a 'gala.' I don't know why it matters, but sometimes it's easiest to go along with what she wants. Anyway, the caterers will be here tomorrow, and some people will be throwing around balloons and streamers."

She released Cecily and hugged Tom. It always surprised him, when he hadn't seen his sister for a while, to discover that she was a good deal shorter than he was. Naturally, in his mind, she took up much more space.

"It sounds like you've got a crowd up there already," he said.

"A small welcoming committee. You didn't think I'd pass up an opportunity to show off my daughter, did you? And please tell me that backpack isn't your only luggage, Cecily."

"I travel light."

"It doesn't matter, I'll buy you some fun things here. I'm going to spoil you rotten." She grew serious for a moment and said, "And we'll talk, too. We do have to *talk*."

Dorothy walked ahead of them. She gripped the railing to help pull herself up and moved like someone carrying a heavy piece of furniture they knew they'd never use. Her body had gone through many changes, from her ragged, skinny days of drugs and sleepless nights to a more voluptuous period when she was flipping houses. Throughout her life, she'd resisted any form of organized exercise or dietary restraint and, instead, had treated her body the way you'd treat a maiden aunt you didn't care for or pay much attention to but whom you counted on for babysitting duties—or, maybe, come to think of it, the way she treated Tom.

Her uniform had always been long sweaters and oversize shirts that came down to her thighs, with colorful tights underneath. The colors and designs had become more elaborate and gaudier as time went on. Today, she had on a billowy red top and a pair of chartreuse tights with—if he was seeing right—ladybugs printed on them. She looked like a dancer in rehearsal—at least until she walked; then she looked like a dancer recovering from rehearsing too vigorously.

At the top of the stairs, she paused and turned, ostensibly to watch them come up, but really, Tom could tell, to catch her breath.

"At least you're getting a lot of exercise going up and down these stairs," Tom said.

"One of the many benefits. Although, to be honest, they're so daunting, I think twice about going out. Fiona insists I should put in a little elevator, and I'm seriously considering it."

An elevator! A fortune no matter how "little."

When they entered the top floor, Cecily reeled back, as if in astonishment. "I wasn't expecting all this!" she said. They were standing in the living room, the former barn's loft, which had been converted into this lovely but unwieldy open space. The size was reminiscent of a boutique hotel lobby. The décor was even more Moorish and opulent than Tom remembered.

"Isn't it a dream?" Dorothy said. "Who'd have guessed I'd end up in a harem?"

Two men who'd been sitting side by side on a large sofa stood in unison and grinned, also in unison. They were physical opposites—one slim, one broad—but given their syncopation, it was impossible to imagine them as anything other than a couple. The monochromatic outfits and the meticulous grooming—unnecessarily artful haircuts and a shiny quality to their skin that suggested they smelled faintly of expensive skin-care products—said to Tom that they lived in Manhattan but came here on weekends. They were introduced as Gary and Enji, and Tom could see from their air of bemused detachment that they were a newish couple still enjoying the illusion that, no matter what, no one would ever interest them more than they interested each other.

A third man came in from the kitchen eating an enormous piece of vanilla cake with his hands. His long, gray hair was so stringy and dry, it appeared in places to be sticking straight out of his head. He had a look of unfocused intellectual acuity that Tom had noticed on a lot of aging professors he'd worked with in Boston. The man's clothes—battered jeans and a sleeveless tie-dyed T-shirt—looked equally untended. For all that, he exuded an air of exhausted sensuality that suggested he'd slept with his share of grad students back in the day and was probably sleeping with Dorothy now. He shoved the last of the cake into his mouth, wiped his hand on his pant leg, and gave Tom a handshake. "Harold Berger. You've got an amazing sister, Tom. She's taken the town by storm."

"Category four or five?" Tom asked.

Harold laughed loudly and clapped Tom on the back. "She warned me about you."

Dorothy, her arm looped through Cecily's, crowed about her "little girl" and her various accomplishments. Tom was happy to see that Cecily was amused by the attention. When Dorothy complimented you, you felt you were receiving a celebrity endorsement—thrilling, even if it didn't sway many voters.

"Your mother serves one hell of a cake," Harold said to Cecily.

"Don't worry," Dorothy said, "I haven't started baking. I just know the best bakeries within a ten-mile radius."

This launched a brief discussion of various local culinary amenities that all three men agreed were superior to anything you could find "anywhere else." Clearly, they meant New York City, given that everywhere else was irrelevant to this crowd.

"I'm going to show Cecily the rest of the house," Dorothy said. "Entertain my guests, would you, Tom?"

"I thought *we* were the guests," he said.

Dorothy laughed at this. "Don't flatter yourself. You're just family. I wish you'd brought Alan. That's Tom's partner. He's a nurse. Tom, but with a heart. Drinks are in the kitchen."

"Follow me," Harold said. "I'm heading back for more cake."

Harold had one of those inexplicable builds that develop in voluptuary men of a certain age—wiry body, ropy arms, and a convex belly with an unsettling resemblance to the curve of pregnancy. Tom had to give him points for his lack of self-consciousness in exposing so much of his ruined skin. At his point in life, vanity is expressed by showing that you don't care what you look like.

"How long have you lived in Woodstock?" Tom asked him.

"My wife and I moved up about fifteen years ago. I used to teach at NYU. Retired early because I couldn't take the bullshit anymore." He knew his way around the kitchen, an open space with endless counters, most of them heaped with boxes of catered food. He cut another huge slab of cake. His appetite, combined with the unkempt appearance, gave off a strong hint of marijuana. "Academia's become a swamp of left-wing fascists."

Tom nodded and poured himself a glass of juice. Academia was the one institution it was always safe to insult, no matter what the political persuasion of the person you were talking to. Like capers, it was universally disliked. Given Cecily's problems, Tom had begun to resent it, too, although her problems resulted from well-meaning people trying to do the right things, always better than people with bad intentions determined to do wrong.

Juice in hand, Tom returned to the living room and took a seat on the sofa facing Gary and Enji. Gary was probably in his early forties, bearish, with a long, sculpted beard that hung down like a bib to the middle of his chest and flapped when he spoke. It was impressive in its way, but the flapping made everything he said slightly ridiculous, even when, as now, he was talking about a serious accident on the thruway the previous week.

Enji had the refined features and spectacular jawline of a Japanese film star. Gary sat with his arm around Enji's shoulders, just in case, Tom felt, it wasn't sufficiently clear they were together. They were partners in an interior designer firm. "We consulted Dorothy on the window," Gary said, nodding toward the new window with the shovel-like beard. "It completely changed this floor. It invites in the view."

Stock phrases always work on certain clients. "It's beautiful," Tom said. "I'm not sure she needed it, but then again, I'm not sure she needed the whole building."

"Maybe it needed her," Enji said.

Tom was impressed by this, as he was by most meaningless statements that sounded profound.

"What this building needs," Harold said, "is a new roof and improved septic."

"Dorothy tells me you're an architect," Gary said to Tom, beard flapping against his chest. His tone was one you might use to tell a six-year-old you heard he plays the piano.

Success or love when it took place in *Boston* was like French fluency with anything other than a Parisian accent—the same language, just not as good.

To get the bad news out of the way himself, Tom said, "My specialty's designing small apartments and guesthouses."

"Naturally, we object," Gary laughed, heartily pulling Enji toward him. "Not enough interior space to design."

"Not a problem in this house," Harold said. "They've been a bad influence on Dorothy. Too many ideas."

"You look a lot like Peter Dorne," Enji said to Tom. "Doesn't he, Gary?"

"I can see that."

Tom sensed that Enji's role was to smooth over uncomfortable situations and, when called for, redirect with non sequiturs. It was soothing to watch couples fall into their allotted roles, like hearing a piece of music return to its tonic key. He was flattered to be compared with someone, even someone he didn't know and who might very well be ugly or a Republican. He felt an immediate attraction to Enji and an overpowering impulse to flirt with him. Fortunately, he caught a brief glimpse of himself in the window, a chilling reminder that he barely resembled the forty-year-old version of himself he imagined others saw when looking at him.

Having once been handsome was probably like having grown up with family money that was then lost: it gave you unearned confidence and filled you with unrealistic expectations.

Tom saw how it must have gone: Dorothy had befriended these two and, in attempting to endear herself to them, had taken them up on their expensive suggestions. It was what she had always done: behave as if she were the kind of person she admired, even if it meant going deeply into debt. This opulent Moorish décor was striking, but there was no way it related to any of Dorothy's taste.

Harold sat down on the sofa next to Tom. "Have you met Fiona Snow yet?" he asked him.

"I haven't. Anything I should know in advance?"

Harold thought this over, scratching his chin while looking at Gary's beard. "She's got an answer for everything," he said. "You have to give her that."

Tom had learned that people who were said to have "an answer for everything" usually had only one answer that they hauled out no matter the question.

"My wife read her book," Harold said. "She underlined every section that she thought would solve my problems."

"Not her own?" Gary asked.

"Her main problem is me. Anyway, no one reads these books to figure out their own problems. They read them so they can tell other people what's wrong with *them*. And let me tell you, you can make a shitload of money selling claims to moral and psychological superiority." This led, inevitably, into a screed against NYU.

"How do you and Dorothy know each other?" Tom asked him.

Harold shrugged and chuckled, probably to drive home the point that they were having sex. He pushed his lopsided wire-rimmed glasses up his nose with the back of his hand. "She needs help around here, so I come over and attend to a few practical matters."

Dorothy had always attracted married men. Tom sometimes wondered if Cecily's father was one of these. Dorothy had had her own husband, but that had lasted only a year and had ended with an amiable divorce that earned Dorothy, at her own insistence, nothing. Tom admired her principled approach to accepting money she felt she hadn't earned while also wishing she would apply it to her own brother.

"Fiona is a genius," Gary said. The flapping beard made this comment seem even less plausible.

Enji's nodding suggested they were in agreement on this point. Without irony, he said, "She looks right through you and can get you to do whatever she wants."

A few minutes later, a car pulled up outside, a door slammed more than once, and a woman cursed.

"There's Fiona now," Harold said. "Horrible driver. Come into the kitchen for a second, Tom."

Tom assumed Harold was ready for yet another piece of cake, but when they got there, he told Tom to sit at a little breakfast table in one corner of the room and then sat down opposite him, suddenly serious. Even the brittle hair jutting out of his head looked less cartoon-like.

"Your sister's a good egg," he said. "A little over-the-top, but who am I to talk?"

For a moment, Tom had the feeling Harold was going to tell him he was in the process of divorcing his wife and wanted his blessing to marry Dorothy. That would solve a multitude of problems.

"Dorothy's too proud to say anything to me about this," Harold continued, "but I think she's getting herself into some financial difficulties."

This was exactly the kind of vague, worrying news Tom did not want to hear. Cecily or not, he should never have come. "Oh?" he said.

"Fiona's one of these people who believes in her own brilliance and believes she's doing you a favor by attaching a vacuum cleaner to your bank account."

"And you think she's doing that to Dorothy?"

Harold shrugged his bony, hairy shoulders. "Keep an eye on it this weekend, that's all I'm saying."

"Your wife doesn't mind you spending time here?"

"We're old free-love types, in case that wasn't obvious. She's got her own distractions. Yoga and yard sales, mainly. She's always happy to get me out of the house. As for the rest, I'm always home by dinnertime."

Why was it that rationalizations about one's own infidelities sounded so reasonable while everyone else's sounded cheap, selfish, and unforgivable? The poor wife.

"You should know that I have almost no influence over Dorothy," Tom said. "I've been knocking at that door for fifty years, and it's never opened."

"You're her older brother."

Harold stood up, opened the refrigerator, and then patted his round stomach and closed the door as if he'd reconsidered. "I want to get out of here before that nut settles in. She can't stand me. Don't tell Dorothy I brought this up. I don't want to get on her bad side."

Aside from Charlotte, who took genuine pleasure in chiding Dorothy for her actions, no one wanted to confront her with their concerns over her health, her bad financial decisions, or her behavior. They all brought their concerns to Tom and expected him to deal with them. His entire life, it seemed, had gone along these lines. For most of it, he'd followed up and done his due diligence. Now he saw it had always made him feel as if his own life, his own health, his own financial stability, somehow counted for less. He wasn't entirely sure if he resented himself for going through with the caretaking or resented others for pushing him in that direction.

Either way, he also saw with new perspective that he'd had almost no impact on what Dorothy did each step along the way. If anything, she seemed to take everything he said as a standard joke and choose the opposite path.

Harold shook Tom's hand. A warm, calloused hand, but with a surprisingly weak grip. "You'll do the right thing," he said, patted Tom on the back, and then opened a door and disappeared down a narrow staircase to avoid Fiona.

What was the right thing? Tom wondered.

Chapter Sixteen

*C*ecily often envied friends' relationships with their mothers. There were the loving bonds, of course—the friends who called their mothers several times a day when apart from them and seemed to miss them as you'd miss a best friend—but those could be slightly mawkish and, for her, were out of reach.

The ones she envied most were the loud, contentious connections, fueled by passion and a competitive anger. Her college friend Sara, for example. Ruth starred in every conversation of Sara's, always as an example of a difficult, unfair, damaging personality, but always presented with an undercurrent of humor and affection that showed how close the two were and how little Sara wanted her mother to change. Once, when Cecily went home with Sara for a weekend, mother and daughter had argued nonstop, sometimes over disputed past experiences, sometimes over facts—the expiration date on a carton of eggs, for example.

"That's the sell-by date, not the expiration date."

"That looks like an eight to me, not a six."

They could bicker about almost anything.

After two days of squabbling that occasionally erupted into shouting, they parted with tearful embraces and declarations of love. Sara sobbed in the train back to the city and said, "I don't really care about her. She just *gets* to me."

In childhood, Cecily accepted Dorothy's inconsistencies and erratic behavior and chose to withdraw. Meaning, she supposed, that she was every bit as responsible for the distance in their relationship as her mother. Maybe more so. She had no hope of ever changing Dorothy, so there had never seemed any point in trying. Cecily loved and respected her mother as you would a difficult piece of music or work of literature—annoyed with her most of the time, but all the while thinking that it was her own inability to fully appreciate or understand her that was at fault.

As they walked around the absurd building and Cecily listened to Dorothy's grandiose plans for furnishing and reconfiguring the spaces and directing "the Center," she couldn't help but feel a weary admiration for her mother's ambition and belief in herself. Dorothy would not have accepted her fate at Deerpath or her situation with Neeta as Cecily had done. She might have lost, but she'd have gone down fighting.

Her mother was beginning to show her age. That was to be expected, but it was still surprising, given her childlike enthusiasm. Her hair, with its odd asymmetrical cut, had roots of gray showing through, and the eyeglasses (round orange things she wore hooked through a ring at the end of a necklace when not peering through them) had the unmistakable look of an accoutrement being used to distract attention from aging skin and what appeared to be a slight limp and hesitation in her gait.

Dorothy opened a door onto a long, narrow room with windows that looked out to the distant mountains. "Oh, good," she said. "Right door. This is going to be yours for this visit. There's a private bath. Don't tell Tom. His room is bigger but has no bath. I might have to add bathrooms for the retreat center, but I don't think that'll be a big deal." She put on her orange glasses and looked around the room as if seeing it for the first time. "I wanted to fix it up more and furnish it better, but I didn't have enough time."

"It's perfect," Cecily said, regarding the bed, the sloping ceiling, and the window. "The view is amazing."

Dorothy hugged her again. It was easy to please her mother: all you had to do was tell her what she wanted to hear.

"Mom," Cecily said. "Sit down for a minute, okay?"

Dorothy looked at her carefully and sat on the edge of the bed. "Is something wrong?" she asked.

Cecily had stopped telling Dorothy her problems long ago. It wasn't that she was afraid her mother would disapprove of her actions or her choices. On the contrary, she'd combine unqualified support with a lack of patience in listening to the details and would refuse to admit that Cecily herself had played any role in her troubles. That wasn't helpful. Dorothy was so resistant to accepting responsibility for her own woes, she thought the highest compliment she could pay someone was to tell them they bore no responsibility for their problems. If Cecily began discussing her current situation at Deerpath, Dorothy would rail against the puritanism of academia and the investigative process and would offer to call Neeta and win her over with charm and reason. Cecily had enough to worry about. She hadn't yet heard back with a firm date for her meeting with the Title IX office, but it would be soon, she was sure. Molly was looking into lawyers.

"I don't have any problems I want to talk about."

Dorothy nodded. "Tell me what you've guessed, then."

What she'd *guessed*? Cecily hated enigmatic comments like this. It was obvious Dorothy wanted to tell her something, but she was going to make Cecily drag it out of her. Maybe she was hinting at the announcement Cecily feared she was planning to make this weekend.

"I want to talk about this," Cecily said. She swept her eyes around the room, but of course, she meant the whole building, the entire crazy plan.

"I knew you'd love it. I knew you'd approve."

"It's amazing, but it's a lot to manage."

Dorothy laughed this off. "You've been spending too much time with Tom, sweetheart. I want you to stay for a week or two. I think it's only fair that you give me a chance to show you what we're building." She paused, as if to say something more, but then stopped herself.

"But at this point in your life? Why not settle down, make some safe investments, live off the money you got from the house in Medford."

Dorothy took her hand and said with tenderness, "Does what you've just described sound in any way, shape, or form like the person you know and love?" She ran her hand over the short hair on Cecily's head. "I love this, by the way. It shows how strong you are. Like me. A big fuck-you to anyone else's opinion. I'm not saying I always succeed, but in the end, I'm always interesting. That counts for something, sweetheart. Did you read Fiona's book, like I asked you?"

Cecily confessed that she hadn't. "I meant to, but I've been busy." She had never bothered to ask Dorothy if she'd read *her* book. It was clear her mother had perused some press and had probably read fragments of what she had posted to her website. Cecily tried not to care. After all, it was widely acknowledged that no one reads academic books. Still, a little more effort at empty praise would have been appreciated.

Dorothy's reading habits were interesting. She'd majored in French literature in college, and their house had been full of classics by Flaubert, Balzac, Zola, many of them in French, some of them dog-eared and underlined. A curious major for someone who showed no interest in visiting France or keeping up with the current political situation there. When Cecily asked her mother why she'd studied French literature, Dorothy said it was because she'd always admired American girls who studied French, the ones who knew how to wear sweaters and make a statement with red lipstick. Cecily was sometimes surprised to find a novel in French half-read on an end table in Dorothy's house, although never one you might expect. Inexplicably, Dorothy had read *Fifty Shades of Grey* and the first of the Twilight series in French translation.

"When you meet Fiona, you'll see: she makes you believe you can do whatever you want to do. Maybe she'll inspire you."

No one can do "whatever they want to do," and probably no one should. When someone starts by telling you you can do "whatever you want," they end up forcing you to do what they tell you.

Her mother went to the window and gazed out at the mountains in the distance. Without turning toward Cecily, she said, "I know you're a scholar, sweetheart. You find the hidden meanings in everything. You interpret small clues and apply then to larger principles. I know you saw I was trying to tell you something in my email. The one with the invitation."

Cecily had been waiting for this, and now she found herself tensing up. *Please*, she thought. *No more bad news. I can't handle it.* "I wondered," she said quietly. "I thought you might be hinting at something."

"You and Santosh are committed to each other. For all I know, you've already discussed marriage."

The word had come up in their conversations, but always in a playful way, as if they were discussing an expensive luxury trip they had no genuine interest in taking.

"It's complicated. We don't have any plans, if that's what you mean."

"But you love him."

Dorothy was a confirmed romantic in almost all aspects of her life. She spoke of love as if it were an immutable quantity one could hold in their hands, as if it didn't change depending on a discussion or a fight or a conversation you'd just had with your loved one's mother. "I do love him," Cecily said.

This seemed to calm Dorothy down, and she sat on the bed again, next to Cecily. She took her hand. "One day, you'll want to have children."

"I don't know." It wouldn't do to mention that the models she had for parenting made her wary.

"Oh, you will. I'm not saying it's necessarily a good thing, but married couples always do. Even Gary and Enji want a baby. When you get there, you'll want to know about your family."

Cecily looked at her mother with a mix of curiosity and disbelief. Was she, after all these years, about to tell her something that would contradict everything she'd told her about her parentage for the past three decades?

"I know a lot about my family already. I know as much as I need to know."

Dorothy brushed this off. "You do see what I'm getting at, don't you?"

Yes, she almost certainly did. But the effects of the long drive and the fact that they hadn't stopped for lunch were beginning to catch up with Cecily. She felt a weariness that made it impossible for her to imagine getting any deeper into this conversation. There was too much going on in her life right now. She'd had to adjust her assumptions about herself so many times over the past few months, she wasn't sure she could face one more shift.

"I think I do," she said. "But not now, Mom. Please. You have a houseful of guests. It's not the right moment." She stood, panicked by the idea of what her mother might tell her.

Dorothy reached out her hands to indicate she wanted an assist in getting up. The gesture made her look old, and Cecily was swamped with sympathy for her. "Let's get through the next couple of days," she said.

"What I learned from having a baby, sweetheart, is that some events demand their own timing. Right now, I hear Fiona's voice out there. She's not someone you want to keep waiting. Maybe we'll talk tonight."

Chapter Seventeen

Fiona was standing in the middle of Dorothy's living room, holding court. She had a plate in one hand with a piece of cake plopped onto it and her fork held aloft as she chewed and swallowed. Cecily was struck by her poise, which seemed equal parts confidence and condescension.

"So, I told him," she was saying, clearing her throat and delivering a punch line, "it just *isn't* that funny."

Gary, his arm wrapped around Enji's shoulder, roared with laughter. *Roar* being the most appropriate verb for someone whose beard was distinctly lion-like. Tom smiled stiffly, as if intending to communicate that he didn't find the anecdote amusing.

It was clear Fiona relished being center stage, probably a good thing for her profession. She took another small forkful of cake and told everyone how delicious it was, as if bestowing a favor upon the cake by giving it her stamp of approval.

She was wearing a shapeless floral top that came down almost to her knees and a pair of wide, white trousers that were so broad and hung so straight, they gave her legs the appearance of mailing tubes. Beneath all this was a pair of black boots with heels that seemed out of place for the outfit, the weather, and the town itself.

"Finally," Dorothy said, "you get to meet my amazing daughter, and she gets to meet amazing you."

Fiona put down the plate and tottered across the room, pitched forward, her arms spread. She took Cecily's hands and looked into her eyes with what struck Cecily as performative empathy. There was something almost shockingly ordinary about her face and grandma curls, but her eyes, which were a clear and stunning blue, had the piercing intensity and hint of insanity that seemed a prerequisite for self-help gurus—if that was the appropriate term for her.

"Forget about me," Fiona said. "Cecily is the guest of honor this weekend."

Maybe she was being genuinely welcoming, but there was a tone in her voice that reminded you the place of honor was hers to temporarily cede.

You'll want to know about your family kept echoing in Cecily's head, making this sideshow seem far less relevant than she'd imagined it would be. After all these years, all these decades, her mother was going to change her story about her father. To what end, she couldn't imagine. It wouldn't matter much to Cecily that she was able to contact some Australian who'd apparently known about her and ignored her for thirty-four years. The pointlessness of it was maddening.

"I'm dying to hear all about your work," Fiona said. "Your mother tells me you had a great success with your first book and are on TV all the time. You'll have to tell me how you did it!" The attitude was that of Meryl Streep feigning interest in an actor in a community theater production of *Fiddler on the Roof*: *How* did *you perfect your Yiddish accent?*

"My mother is known for flattering exaggeration where I'm concerned," Cecily said.

"I don't object to modesty," Fiona said, "as long as you don't believe it. I'm proud of you, and I know you're proud of yourself."

Cecily was proud of herself, and hearing it from this charlatan somehow made her feel as if she deserved to be, as if she were in the early stages of brainwashing. She had a sudden urge to run away from all this: Fiona's ridiculous influence, her mother's upcoming announcement.

"Thank you," she said. "The book had a better reception than I was expecting. I'd rather hear about your work. That's why we're here."

"Fiona's coming to dinner with us later," Dorothy said. "There'll be plenty of time for that then."

"You'd never know Tom and Dorothy were siblings, would you?" Fiona said.

"I was noticing the same thing," Enji said. "What do you think that means?"

"We looked more alike before Tom gained weight and my face fell," Dorothy said. She sat next to Tom and smiled at him.

"We don't inherit traits," Fiona said, "we manifest them."

Gary, nodding and waving his beard, said, "That is so true."

Cecily had a choice between asking in what sense it was true and simply joining the mob in accepting these bland pronouncements as profound without (very likely) having any idea what they meant. Even this use of "manifest" was irritating to her. Given the way her own life was working, it might be best to give in and attempt to "manifest" a good outcome for herself.

Fiona took a seat on the sofa next to Gary and Enji. Her pant legs rose, revealing that the boots were scuffed and the leather cracked. It was like seeing the peeling paint on a prop backstage. "I'd love to do a session with you, Tom," she was saying when Cecily tuned back into the conversation. "I can tell you're under stress about your work."

This was certainly a safe comment. It was such a common practice these days to complain about being stressed by work, along with everything else, that to confess otherwise felt like an admission of laziness or a lack of awareness of current events.

"Harold left?" Dorothy said. "He didn't say goodbye."

"He can't stand me," Fiona said triumphantly. "His wife adores me. I'm speaking to her book group next month. I wish he'd stuck around, though. There's a little problem out behind the house I was going to ask him to look into."

"It's too bad Alan's not here," Dorothy said. "He's handy. You should have dragged him, Tom. I miss him."

"I miss him, too," Tom said with touching melancholy.

"Maybe some of his handiness rubbed off on Tom," Enji said.

"Oh, do you think so?" Fiona asked. It struck Cecily that for someone whose career revolved around performance, she hadn't delivered the line in a convincing way. "I hate to ask you this, Tom, but I noticed a terrible smell on my way in. I went around back, and it seems to be coming from out near the quarry."

"Maybe you need to have the septic system pumped," Tom said.

"No, it's the smell of death." This comment hung in the air ominously. She let it bring down the mood before adding, "Probably a muskrat or something of that size."

Tom frowned. "What do you want me to do with it?" he asked.

"Bury it," Fiona commanded. "I'd do it myself, but I'm squeamish about that sort of thing." She shuddered in such a forced way, it seemed intended to let everyone know she was squeamish about nothing but was choosing not to deal with this specific problem herself.

"You can do it later, Tom," Dorothy said. "We can leave it until Harold comes back. He loves digging graves."

"You've already told me how much Tom likes being helpful," Fiona said. "And I'm here now."

"Are you planning to assist?" Tom asked, standing.

"In the sense that I brought a shovel and some work gloves. It's clear from the smell you'll need gloves. Shall we?"

Chapter Eighteen

*A*t ten that night, Tom was stretched out on his bed, try-ing to prepare what he was going to say to Charlotte and Oli-ver about their guesthouse. He figured it was the last time he'd be in the same place with them and have the chance to manipulate them into putting the building into construction. If he failed, he'd be handing over his desk to Lanford within a couple of months. After that, he could envision any number of catastrophic events leading up to the eventual loss of his own house and, for all he knew, a move into the room he was currently occupying. Surely, Dorothy owed him a roof over his head, even if a leaky one. (Those telltale stains on the ceiling.)

The most peculiar thing about this building was that almost all of the dozens of rooms he'd been in felt as if they'd been ineptly carved out of space that had been intended for storing animals and farm equipment. Yes, it had been built as a barn, but someone with a little skill could have disguised that fact more cleverly. The windows were at odd angles and disconcertingly low or high on the walls, the ceilings sloped awkwardly, the closets were huge but with tiny rods for hanging clothes. There was a DIY quality to everything that led him to suspect the building had structurally unsound elements as well.

It had been an unsettling day all around—the drive, followed by the exhausting welcoming committee, capped off by going to the quarry to bury the fucking muskrat. He assumed that's what it was. His knowledge of small mammals began with mice and ended with raccoons. In the middle were squirrels and rabbits. Everything else was a blur he quietly considered irrelevant.

Fiona had positioned herself on a rock a little way off, supervising with an authority that suggested she'd read up on the subject or had done a few burials herself. "The hole should be at least a foot deeper than that, Tom, so other animals don't dig it up."

"You know a lot about this," he said.

She tilted her head and smiled at him. *I know a lot about everything,* she was silently announcing. *Especially you.*

It infuriated him to think his sister was so easily taken in by people like this: shams with bad haircuts and questionable social skills.

"I suppose you know Dorothy is making a big announcement this weekend," Fiona said.

"I thought that was the point of the party."

"I meant a more personal one. To Cecily."

She wanted to show off her superior knowledge of what was going on. This was 90 percent of her act. *I know more than anyone about everything.* In the end, she'd reveal nothing. His impression was that she was either testing him or trying to drag information out of him.

"Oh, that," he said. "Of course I know."

"Then you know the person in question?"

"It's not my business to discuss this," he said. "We'll leave it there."

As soon as Cecily had returned from her tour of the house with Dorothy, he could tell that something had happened between them. She looked pale and distracted, and she kept eying Dorothy with what appeared to be either concern or muted anger. He'd tried to pull her aside to find out what had gone on, but they'd been surrounded all day, and dreadful Fiona had accompanied them to dinner that night. "The person in question" made Tom wonder if Dorothy was planning to reveal something about Cecily's father. Surely, not even she would do that in a public way.

He could always go look for Cecily, but there were so many rooms and such a confusing array of staircases, he doubted he'd be able to find where she was sleeping. He texted instead: **You seemed a little distracted tonight.**

In reply, she sent a cryptic **Tired.**

He needed to discuss this with someone, but the only person he could think to call right now was Alan, and as he rolled his phone around in his hands, he knew instinctively that was a bad idea. Even so.

"I can't talk for long," Alan said. "I'm going out."

"Oh? At this hour?"

Silence ensued, driving home the point that it was none of Tom's business. "Having fun in Woodstock?"

"Not really. Everything's chaotic and confusing, and this opening tomorrow promises to be no better. Something went on between Dorothy and Cecily, but I don't know what."

"Why don't you ask?"

"I tried. Cecily's avoiding the topic."

"Go ask Dorothy."

Tom heard the unmistakable sounds of Alan closing and locking the door to his apartment. So, he really was going out. At this hour, it could only mean one thing: a visit to the person he was "dating."

Because he couldn't stop himself, Tom said, "It's not like you, going out at this hour."

"A lot of my habits have changed," Alan said. "Go talk to Dorothy. You owe it to Cecily."

"You know," Tom said, "it's confusing to have you coaching me to do more for Cecily while telling me you moved out because I did too much."

"Now that I'm out of the picture, Tom, you can do as much as you like, and your natural impulse is to do a lot. Have a good talk."

The phone went dark in Tom's hand.

●

Tom opened the door of his room and tried to orient himself. He knew he was on a floor below Dorothy's quarters, but more than that, he couldn't say. He roamed a few steps into the hallway and ended up circling the balcony above the gallery, with its tables and chairs waiting to be set up for tomorrow's event. There was moonlight washing through the windows—as far as he could tell, there were no shades or curtains anywhere in the building—making the whole space eerily blue. He could see why Dorothy had been drawn to it: open spaces like this made a subconscious demand on you to fill them with life and public events. It would have made sense as a purchase if only she'd been worth ten million dollars. How much it had cost to heat this place last winter was a question he was not going to pose. The answer was likely to fill him with the same paralyzing anxiety he felt when reading the newspaper or listening to weather reports.

He wandered up one of the staircases and found himself in Dorothy's kitchen, which bled into the living room. He disapproved of "open-concept" living. He viewed it as indicative of an inability to be alone. Everyone wanted to be clustered in one giant room, as long as they could gaze into their individual devices and not interact. As in the gallery below, the furniture and walls in the living room glowed in icy-blue moonlight that seemed to freeze time.

Dorothy was stretched out on one of the immensely long sofas, her head on a throw pillow, her body covered by an afghan. She was sleeping so soundly, he hesitated to wake her, but Alan had told him to do it, and in matters such as this, Alan was usually right. His emotional intelligence surpassed Tom's even if Tom secretly believed he himself probably had the higher IQ.

Dorothy's habit of sleeping on sofas, chairs, chaises longues, and pretty much anywhere other than her bed had started young. She was sleeping in her childhood bedroom when their mother woke her up to tell her their father had died. She'd been in high school at the time and was taking an after-school nap. It was such a sudden death, and Dorothy had loved their father so much, she spiraled into depression. Tom supposed it was the one moment that had shaped her personality and behavior more than any other.

Beginning the very next night, she started sleeping on the sofa in the living room, curled up with blankets and pillows, afraid bad news would come again if she were caught in bed. She usually slept in her clothes, convinced she might need to leap into action. Their mother had allowed this, supposing it was a matter of a few weeks before she went back to her bedroom. Forty-plus years later, that move still hadn't come.

Tom saw in her face, underneath the lines and worry that had been added on over the years, the face of the sister whose care had been handed to him by their mother upon the death of their father. No doubt, that was the moment that had shaped Tom's future as well.

"You're the man of the family now," his mother had said to him. "You need to promise me you'll always look after Dorothy. She and I are your responsibility now." He'd never know if she sensed him balking at this daunting burden, but she had, at that point, broken into sobs. "Oh, Tom, Tom. I wish you hadn't left that journal of yours lying around when you went to college. Why did you? Why didn't you take it with you? Why didn't you burn it?"

His journal? His face was hot with shame. He hadn't left it "lying around." He'd put it in the back of a cluttered drawer in his desk he assumed no one would open.

"He found it and read it a week ago," she'd continued. "Who knows what effect it had on him? He came to me all shook up about what he'd read. Crying, if you can picture that. I tried to reassure him, but it's different between fathers and sons. As far as we knew, he was in perfect health at his last checkup. And now, a week after he read it, *this*."

His mother was actually blaming him for having caused his father's fatal aneurism. By not burning his journal. By having written it to begin with. The journal contained one paragraph, *six artlessly composed sentences*, in which he questioned his real feelings for one of his wrestling teammates. Why had he even written in it? Especially given that he had those feelings for pretty much all his teammates. It was self-indulgent rumination. It hadn't cleared up anything for him. For that matter, why had his father looked in the drawer of his childhood desk? Putting the best interpretation on it, Tom had concluded that his father had missed him and been poking around for tangible reminders. It was miraculous he'd even found the offending sentences amid all the drivel about algebra and the many pages devoted to his admiration for one of the new houses in their Connecticut neighborhood. The house had been constructed along Gropius-inspired lines and had outraged most of their neighbors, who lived in boring, shingled houses in traditional New England style. Everyone, including his father, had been convinced the new house would lower property values across the board. Come to think of it, maybe it was the pages and pages devoted to his love of that house that had killed his father, not the hints at his sexuality.

Tom had hung on to that notebook for years until, one day, in a fit of self-assertion when he was in his forties, he tossed it into a dumpster behind a grocery store, as if it were the body of a murder victim.

How much he believed that what he'd written had killed his father was a mystery to him. It seemed unlikely, but he couldn't be sure. Over time, he'd come to realize that his mother's comments were an expression of her own grief, shock, and panic. Probably of her drunkenness, too. Or maybe it was her premeditated plan to manipulate him. The words, valid or not, haunted him still. His whole life, he'd been paying off his debt to his sister and mother. He'd never mentioned it to anyone, not even Dorothy or Alan.

How absurd to think that six sentences had determined so much of his life, especially since they contained several misspellings.

The sofa Dorothy was sleeping on was so long, he could sit on one end without disturbing her. He watched the rise and fall of her chest beneath the crocheted blanket. He shouldn't have come. Revisiting the past was as ill-advised and unproductive as watching an exercise video while eating ice cream in a recliner. He couldn't afford to let his own current problems fall to the side. As soon as Oliver and Charlotte arrived tomorrow, he'd focus all his energy on trying to get them to agree to build the guesthouse.

There was something waxy about Dorothy's complexion and a staggered quality to her breathing.

As he was looking at her, her eyes opened, and with no transition from asleep to awake, she said, "Tell me the truth, Tom: Didn't you think Fiona was interesting?"

Like anyone who starts off a question with "Tell me the truth," it was apparent that Dorothy had no interest in hearing what Tom actually thought of Fiona.

Tom was so used to being looked up to as a big brother by Dorothy, even if she disregarded pretty much every piece of advice he'd ever given her, that he couldn't help but be touched by her seeking his approval. At this quiet time of night, when the moonlight was painting everything a surreal and restful blue, it was hard not to agree with this leading question, just to please her. That was all Dorothy wanted: to be told she was right, even if she knew you thought she was wrong.

Despite his love of compact spaces, he couldn't deny that there was something reassuring about being perched above so much empty, useless square footage in all the rooms around them. Maybe this was the feeling you got from knowing you had more money in the bank than you'd ever be able to spend.

"You don't really care what I think about Fiona," he said.

"Of course, I do. I might not act on what you say, but I'm interested."

"In that case, I think every self-help guru's job is to make you feel bad about yourself so you'll pay her to make you feel better."

"Yes, exactly," Dorothy said. "It's a highly marketable skill. And, by the way, most people already feel bad about themselves. I'm so glad you showed up here. There's something I need to talk about with you. Something I need your help with."

She was sitting up on the sofa with a pillow to her chest, almost as if she were in pain. In the moonlight, her face looked uncharacteristically troubled.

Tom leapt to the obvious conclusion. "I'm not in a position to loan you any money. If I can't get my project with Charlotte and Oliver back on track, I'm pretty much done for, professionally."

"I hope you're being melodramatic."

"I wish I were. What is it you need?"

"It's about Cecily."

The pieces were beginning to connect. "When I was out burying your muskrat, Fiona told me you're making a big announcement this weekend. From what she said, I gather it has to do with Cecily. I came up here to find out what it's all about."

Dorothy laid her head on Tom's shoulder. Despite everything, he felt comforted by her presence. "You'll think I'm awful, but I hope you'll forgive me. More to the point, I hope Cecily will."

"Please. Just tell me."

"I will. It's hard to get it out, after all this time. I know you think I plow through life, and most times I do. Not this time." She gazed around the vast and opulent room. Like everyone else Tom knew, Dorothy was most sympathetic when she admitted her failings. "The story I told all those years ago, about Cecily's father. Well, it isn't true."

Her words landed with such a ring of inevitability that Tom realized he'd been waiting for this announcement for a long time. Even so, he felt something shift inside him, making room for this change. "Please give me more credit than to think I believed it was true."

"You never confronted me about it."

"I knew it would be a waste of breath."

Dorothy dissembled about most things, and so it seemed likely this was yet another. Tom had been vaguely aware of one man she occasionally saw around the time she announced her pregnancy, but because of his race and distinctive looks, he wasn't a likely candidate. Her story of her vacation adventure was in character and easy enough to accept. At the time, Tom knew Dorothy's life would be changed by her having a baby and that his would be affected, but he had no inkling his own life would be so radically altered. Once Cecily arrived, the question of her father became irrelevant. There was so much else to do. It would have been like endlessly hunting for a lost credit card instead of canceling it and getting a new one.

"I started to tell Cecily this afternoon, right after you arrived, but she cut me off. She said she wants to wait until after the event."

"It's waited this long. I suppose it can wait a little longer."

"No, it can't. I need to get this out of the way." She looked at him with pleading eyes. "I'll confess something you've never heard me say before. I'm afraid. I'm afraid to tell her I've been lying all these years, that I deprived her of knowing her father, of having a relationship with him. I'm terrified, Tom. I can't face her being angry with me. She never has been, not once, her whole life."

"I doubt that's true. She just hasn't expressed it."

"Same thing, in my book. If you tell her, it will give her a chance to absorb it. Then she can come talk with me after she's sorted it out."

He stood up, nearly knocking the cushion off the sofa. "Me? You want me to tell her? Absolutely not. It's out of the question."

"And the thing is, you have to do it tonight."

"Dorothy, I'll try to be reasonable." Tom was not, by nature, a pacer, but he found himself wandering around the sofas, picking up some of the magazines and little glass objects scattered over the end tables. "You invite us out here for this opening, which is a lot already, and now, after thirty years, you're changing your story about Cecily's father. Better late than never, I suppose. But from my point of view, I've done enough. You've got to handle this on your own. Get a good night's sleep, get up early, and talk with her, if that's what you think you have to do."

"Her father will be here tomorrow. She has to know now so she can decide if she wants to be here for their arrival."

"'Their'?" Tom had a moment of confusion before seeing clearly what she was getting at. "Oliver?" he finally said. "You don't mean to say *Oliver* is Cecily's father, do you?"

"Of course he is. It's ridiculous that no one guessed it before. They have the same mouth and a similar look around the nose."

"But how . . . ?"

"Oh, we hooked up once or twice during one of the thousands of times he and Charlotte were broken up. A few years after they were married and Nolan was born, I even told Charlotte I'd slept with him. No one was as prudish back then as they are now. We were all reading those endless Anaïs Nin diaries and thought we were making a statement. What kind of statement, I don't remember. Please, Tom, let's get it over with. Go tell Cecily now. I can tell you how to find her room."

Tom suddenly saw clearly how this would go down. If this was what Charlotte and Oliver were faced with, he'd have absolutely no chance of turning the conversation to his guesthouse. His fate would be sealed. One more sacrifice made to Dorothy's mistakes, right as he was desperately trying to salvage his career.

He sat back on the sofa, his hands cupping his knees. He looked at Dorothy as seriously as he could, to help drive home his point. "The answer is a firm no. I'm going to bed, not that I expect I'll sleep."

Tom and Dorothy heard the sound in the kitchen at the same moment, for they both turned their heads in that direction. They saw Cecily standing in the shadowy recesses of the archway to the kitchen. She was holding half a sandwich in her hand and wearing an expression of sleepy distraction.

"I came to get a snack," she said. "I was having trouble going to sleep. These sandwiches are good."

"Aren't they?" Dorothy said. "Which one is that?"

"I'm not sure. Something with pesto?"

"Oh, yes. Vegetarian. I wanted to cover all the bases. We're serving more tomorrow, too. At the gala. You do know I hate that word, don't you? It's Fiona's idea."

"I'm happy to hear it."

Dorothy patted the sofa. "Come sit, sweetheart. I'm going to my room for a few minutes, but Tom has something he wants to tell you."

Cecily took a bite of her sandwich but didn't budge. "Don't you mean you have something *you* want him to tell me?"

"Well, yes. If we're being precise."

"Precision's probably a good thing at this stage. And if it's about Oliver," she said, chewing, "there's no need."

Tom could see that Dorothy's eyes were beginning to tear up. He couldn't be sure if it was out of relief, sadness, or fear.

"How much did you overhear?" Dorothy asked.

"All the relevant information. I wasn't eavesdropping, not at first.

The acoustics in this place are good. Once I got the gist of what you were saying, I stood there waiting for the details. I told you I didn't want to know, but naturally, I couldn't resist." She took another bite of the sandwich as if it was her entire focus. "I'm happy to know after all this time. And don't worry, Dorothy, I'm not angry at you."

Dorothy got up and started to move toward her.

Cecily raised her hand, a traffic cop preventing a collision at a busy intersection. "Not right now, Mom. I'm tired, and I have a few important emails to answer." She turned at the door and said, "Don't tell Oliver and Charlotte. Will you promise me that?"

Dorothy nodded, like a cowed child.

"I don't want to deal with them this weekend. Besides, Tom needs their attention to talk about his project."

"This is more important," Tom said. "It's a good opportunity to discuss it."

"No," Cecily said. "It's my choice, and I'm choosing to leave it unsaid."

When she'd gone off to whatever corner of the building her room was in, Dorothy looked at Tom with the wide eyes of someone who'd just been told a piece of information they couldn't absorb. "She is angry, isn't she? You see, I knew she would be. God, I've handled things badly."

Tom had been waiting for this admission of mismanagement—over countless decisions and aspects of her behavior—for decades, but now, seeing Dorothy in the moonlight looking so upset, he hauled out his favorite excuse for unfortunate behavior: "You did the best you could."

Sadly, this was probably true.

Chapter Nineteen

*T*om *was unable to sleep. The moonlight in his room, the* lack of curtains, the news about Oliver, his own stupidity at not having guessed—all nagged at him. He wanted to call Alan, but of course, he couldn't. He had to mull it over on his own. Cecily could have a done a lot worse in the lottery of parentage: Oliver Fuchs had money, brains, and a sturdiness that suggested he'd live into his nineties, and that might balance out the Kemp family's tendency to die young. The similar features Dorothy had mentioned were unmistakable now that they'd been pointed out.

Dorothy had announced her pregnancy at one of the dinners she loved to throw in her sprawling, poorly tended house in Medford, back when none of them wore sunscreen and only Oliver and Charlotte had real incomes. *Throw* was the best verb to describe how she put together these events four or five nights out of seven. She would invite a random collection of people, give wide latitude as to the start time—"I never lock my doors, so show up when you want"—and then sweep in carrying bags of food from her restaurant. She claimed she loved to entertain, which was certainly true, at least in the sense that she hated being alone. It was one of the defining characteristics of her life and a trait Tom found irritating but touching.

Charlotte and Oliver were at that dinner. They'd been dating for several volatile on-again, off-again years and had recently reunited after six months apart. During that separation, Charlotte had had a brief affair with a chef from Dorothy's restaurant, an unattractive but sexually profligate man who, Dorothy claimed, had slept with almost everyone who worked there. How did she account for his success? "He started sleeping with the prettiest waitress we ever hired. No one could believe it. The only possible explanation was that he must be an incredible lover. After the beauty quit, the rest of the staff had to find out. It's why men want beautiful women: the endorsement." The staff at Dorothy's restaurant had been prolific in terms of drug use and sexual activity.

Tom attended that dinner with the man he was dating at the time, a skinny kindergarten teacher named Daniel Korbel whom everyone called Danny K. Tom often brought his dates to these events, partly because he knew that his sister's loopy behavior and gossipy dinners balanced out his own rigidity. It was as if he were trying to prove he wasn't as stodgy as he seemed by connecting himself to this good-humored chaos.

Danny K was short and spoke in a high singsong voice, almost as if permanently reading aloud from a picture book. He was extremely bright and unusually perceptive, but most people found it easy to dismiss what he said because of his height and voice. In social situations, he loved playing the *enfant terrible* and making outrageous statements or asking invasive questions in his infantile tones. He got away with it because no one took him seriously, but the price he paid was that no one took him seriously.

Oliver Fuchs was Danny K's opposite. He was in international banking, a tall, fit, imposing man with an Austrian accent that gave extra weight to his pronouncements. Even something as mundane as "It's going to rain" had a portentous, metaphoric heft when delivered by him. Everyone took his comments on financial and political events with reverential seriousness and violent disapproval. It was always useful to have Oliver around. Even if he made you feel intellectually lesser, you always felt morally superior. He also picked up the check.

Oliver was the kind of heterosexual European man who could get away with wearing rings and cologne without raising suspicions. He was spectacularly trilingual and had mastered the unerring command of English grammar that few American native speakers would have bothered to learn. The only time he sounded awkward was when he used slang—"Oh, cool"; "No way, man"—which always registered as slightly out of date and made him seem like a spy making too much of an effort to fit in.

Dorothy had arrived for that dinner later than her guests and accompanied by Florence, a business partner in the restaurant. Florence was strong-featured and fiercely protective of Dorothy in the face of all criticism except her own. She was one of the few people Tom had ever met who could silence Dorothy. She was half Jamaican and half French. She'd direct a look at Dorothy that bore the combined weight and glamour of her international background and say her name with her lovely cross-cultural inflection, and Dorothy would back off. Florence often criticized Dorothy in French, which allowed Tom to believe she was telling his sister exactly what he wanted to say to her himself.

The early part of the evening, when everyone was sober, had been devoted to political outrage, which, in hindsight, had the quaint irrelevance of complaining about the rise in the price of movie tickets from seventy-five cents to one dollar. How cute. Oliver held back in these discussions, claiming that, as a not-yet citizen, he didn't feel he had the right. Everyone assumed he had dark political views he didn't want to share. Surely, dark political views were mandatory for anyone in international banking. There always had been something inscrutable about Oliver, a reserve that you could put down to careful listening or, more likely, a complete lack of interest in anyone else's opinion. For all that, you couldn't help but secretly crave his approval. He'd always been kind to Tom, probably because, back then, Tom still had the fussy, slightly affected musculature of former wrestlers and gymnasts that compensated for his lack of height.

After the many bottles of wine and an hour of mandatory grazing from the takeout containers Dorothy had scattered over the table, Oliver had said to Charlotte, "Well, my dear, are you going to make the big announcement?"

"What's the matter?" Charlotte snapped at him. "Are you too ambivalent about it to make it yourself?"

"I am never ambivalent. I think before I act, in matters both personal and professional."

Oliver was, despite Charlotte's many attempts to take a verbal jab at him, unreachable. Tom thought that her inability to push him around made her feel safe with him and was, possibly, the source of her love for him. As with most bullies, she seemed to have massive respect for anyone who could take her down a peg.

Charlotte frowned at him and said, "Oh yes, he's incredibly steadfast. We all know that. That's why I agreed to . . . well, why I agreed to marry him. Next month, so save the date."

Dorothy leapt up from her seat and rushed around the table to give Charlotte a big hug and kiss. Like a lot of people who claim to resent the strictures and rules of middle-class, heterosexual life, Dorothy and even Charlotte got positively girlish at the mention of engagements, showers, and wedding dresses.

"This is the best news I've heard in ages," Dorothy said. "I'm so happy. For a minute, I was afraid you were going to say you were breaking up. Again."

Tom could see from Danny K's fidgeting that he was about to make one of his provocative *enfant terrible* comments.

Sure enough: "Sounds like someone must be pregnant," he chirped, giving the final word an impressive three syllables. Danny K considered himself an empath who could read the feelings of those around him. Comments such as this expressed what he thought he was picking up on but were passed off as jokes in case he was wrong.

"Well, I'm sure someone *is* pregnant," Charlotte said, turning on him angrily, as she tended to do, "but no one in *this* room."

Florence, with her taciturn glamour, said, "Certainly not me. It is not possible." Florence had a husband, but no one, including Dorothy, had ever met him, and half the people at the restaurant assumed he was a fiction Florence had invented to fend off unwanted attention. Why it was "impossible" she might be pregnant was a question no one dared ask. When she spoke, Florence effectively communicated that she'd told you as much as you needed to know about her, or at least as much as she planned to tell you.

Dorothy had taken her seat again and began to laugh giddily. "You see, Charlotte, it isn't true that you're *never* wrong."

"Meaning?" she asked.

"As a matter of fact, Danny," Dorothy said, turning to him—she'd always had a soft spot for Danny, possibly because he made her look serious—"someone in this room *is* pregnant."

If she had been expecting bubbly congratulations, she must have been disappointed. The comment was met by stunned silence.

"You're not," Charlotte said, eventually.

"As a matter of fact, I am."

Charlotte looked at Tom, but he shrugged. "Please don't tell me it's James," she said, James being the cook at Dorothy's restaurant with whom she'd had her affair.

"Oh, god no. He had a vasectomy years ago. Don't tell me you didn't know that."

Florence gave Dorothy a harsh stare, intended to nudge her onto a different topic.

Tom was submerged in a cloud of confusion, hoping that this was his sister's idea of a joke, while being certain that it was not. His ears had started to ring from a slowly building anger over what he suspected was coming.

"I met someone on the rafting trip in Utah," Dorothy was saying. "It was one of those stupidly romantic things, despite the lack of hot showers. So romantic, I have absolutely no idea how to track him down. Isn't that lucky?"

"How is it lucky?" Florence asked. "And how can you have 'no idea how to track him down'? You don't know his name? You don't have a phone number? You don't know where he's from?"

"He's from Australia, conveniently enough. That's all I know."

Everyone nodded. You never went anywhere without bumping into an Australian on an extended journey.

Charlotte, on the far side of the table, seemed annoyed. Her big announcement had been upstaged. "Well, all I can say is, thank *god* you figured it out in time."

No matter how open-minded everyone in the room was about abortion, the comment cast a pall over the table, and food was passed around in silence. Danny K, ever ready with a quip, said, after a few minutes, "The silence suggests Dorothy has plans for parenthood."

"I don't see how this is any of his business," Charlotte said. Turning to Tom, she added, "Can't you do anything about him?"

Tom's annoyance at Danny and his ridiculous comment (not witty enough to be worth the offense) quickly turned to sympathy for him, especially considering what he took to be the homophobia in Charlotte's scorn. Politically, she was always on the side of fairness, but Tom had long believed that she viewed gay men as essentially silly and irrelevant to the work of the world.

"I don't see how it's any of your business, either, Charlotte," Tom said. "And if you have anything to say to Danny, I suggest you address him directly."

"Thanks, Tom," Danny said. "But I prefer an intermediary."

And then, having been mildly chivalrous toward his paramour, Tom turned to his sister. "You might as well tell us what your plans are. It's not as if we're not going to find out."

Dorothy fell back on her usual stunt of laughing, as if it were all of little consequence. "I've given it a lot of thought," she said. "Danny is right: I am planning to have the baby."

"Oh, come on," Charlotte said. "You don't have the money, the time, the patience, or, as far as I can tell, the desire to raise a child. On top of that, you clearly don't know enough about the father to make a sound decision about having a baby with him."

Dorothy was delighted by the comment. "It's true I didn't do a background check."

"Let's not get off track," Florence said, giving Dorothy one of her penetrating looks. "What in the world are you thinking?"

"I'm not having a baby *with* anyone. It's simpler this way. I won't have to deal with someone else's ideas of child rearing and parenthood."

The most surprising part of this comment was that it suggested Dorothy had ideas, any ideas, about child rearing herself, a subject Tom had never once heard her mention.

"And you think you're ready to be a mother?" Charlotte said. She held up her wineglass toward Oliver, and he obligingly poured.

There was Dorothy's laugh again, robust and confident. "I think I'd make a terrible mother. I'm too selfish and too erratic. As you all know, I make a spectacular *friend*. I'm loving, generous, considerate, and I push my friends to be their best selves. In the end, that's what every child wants: a best friend."

"Children should never be given what they want," Florence said. "That's an American fantasy." Her upbringing and education had been rigidly classical, and it was hard to argue with the striking results.

"I'm big on fantasy," Dorothy said. "I have four bedrooms in this house, and I can easily host an au pair. This town is swarming with au pairs. As for the restaurant, I've always loved women who show up at a job with a baby in a papoose and make it work for them."

So, this was to be yet another venture Dorothy was undertaking because she liked the way single motherhood looked from a safe, childless distance.

"If I've got the dates of that trip to Utah right," Charlotte said, "you still have another few weeks to change your mind."

For the first time, Oliver spoke up. He tended to speak slowly and methodically, a grating habit in that it meant his speech took up a tremendous amount of space. "But, my dear," he said to Charlotte, "I thought you were in favor of a woman being able to *choose*. What did I miss?"

"That doesn't mean that some choices aren't reckless."

"And yet, part of the reason we're getting married is that we plan to have a baby," Oliver said. "Hopefully, soon. That's what we decided."

This produced the loud, gleeful congratulations Dorothy's announcement had not received.

"You see," Dorothy said. "Our kids can be friends and take care of each other!"

Danny K had bounced back from Charlotte's insults and come up with the best idea of the evening: "There's an apartment for rent down the street. I saw the sign when we drove in. You should take it, Tom. You'll be closer to Dorothy and the baby."

Danny had a large and generous heart in his small body. Tom was always surprised by the tiny details he noticed. Their relationship, which had never seemed destined for longevity, had ended a few months after the dinner. Two years later, Tom heard from the man Danny was living with that Danny had died. He'd gone out as everyone expected him to: with humor and a complete lack of self-pity. It was especially sad to Tom that he died at the very end of the period in which his illness was necessarily a death sentence.

Charlotte had turned to look at Danny with uncharacteristic respect. "That's a good idea," she said. "I'm not saying I endorse this decision, if it really has been decided, but it would make me happy to know Tom was next door."

"That's settled," Dorothy had said. And then she leapt up from her chair and said, "I almost forgot. Florence and I arrived with dessert. Where did it end up, Florence?"

Somehow, all the anxiety around that evening, all the disapproval, all the concerns that Tom and Charlotte had had, dissipated as the months went on and a host of friends attempted to prepare things as best they could for the arrival of Dorothy's baby. Tom supposed that the attention came from Dorothy's failure to make the preparations herself, but the collective efforts and the feeling of coming together as a large, loose family were exhilarating.

Dorothy went into labor at the restaurant. Florence offered to drive her to the hospital, but Dorothy insisted she stay and take care of business, as if she were only stepping out for a facial. She took a cab to the hospital alone and gave birth a few hours later, claiming, implausibly, that she'd barely felt it. For all her complexities, Dorothy had never been one to complain about pain or physical discomfort.

Once Cecily was born, everyone politely forgot that Tom and Charlotte had discouraged Dorothy from going through with her pregnancy. Perhaps some of Tom's early devotion to Cecily had been in response to his guilt over his initial attitude.

Had he been curious about who the father of the baby was? Not really. That question was insignificant compared with the reality of Cecily herself. Despite having taught school, Tom had never had any particular interest in children on a personal level. He'd never longed to be a father. He wondered if he was missing a chemical in his brain. When he heard people talk about their longing for children, he suspected them of watching too much daytime TV.

Cecily hadn't been a passive child, but she'd never been demanding. Nolan, Charlotte's son, the only other baby Tom spent a great deal of time with, had been almost demonically needy from the minute he was surgically removed from Charlotte's body after a nightmarish thirty-six hours of labor. Infant Cecily had regarded Nolan during his crying and wailing fits with the cool, curious detachment you sometimes see in cats as they watch dogs demand attention from their humans. She'd look at Nolan and then back at Tom as if to say, *What's* that *all about?*

Tom didn't know what that was all about. Charlotte had taken four months off work to get her house and herself ready for her baby. She read massive books on infant care, took classes in making organic baby food, flooded herself with vitamins, hired a personal trainer to get her into shape for the birth and motherhood, and spent a fortune decorating the nursery. Everything that Dorothy had not done, in other words.

Ironically, Cecily had turned out to be the calmer baby, the happier child, the more productive adult. One time, at Dorothy's house, when Nolan was wailing, Charlotte threw herself into a chair and wept. "What am I doing *wrong*?" she screamed.

It was touching that she blamed herself, but painful to witness. She wanted to be the kind of informed, caring, indulgent parent she'd never had. Despite the long books and expensive accoutrements, she was very like her own volatile mother, albeit with a retirement plan.

Oliver was as stoic and steady in dealing with Nolan as he was in dealing with everything else. He traveled a lot, which helped. Six months after Nolan was born, Oliver hired a live-in nanny to take care of their son while Charlotte went back to work at her law firm. Throughout Cecily's and Nolan's childhoods, Tom would sometimes see Charlotte looking at Cecily or clutching her to her breast with passion and what certainly looked like envy.

It was almost three a.m. before, tossing in the bed in Dorothy's massive building, Tom started to feel sleepy.

It was for the best, on many levels, that Cecily didn't want Dorothy to mention anything when Charlotte and Oliver arrived. There had been enough going on this weekend already. Among other things, he could proceed with his own plans. He felt mercenary even thinking it, but Winston was not a man who changed his mind easily.

Chapter Twenty

*A*fter Tom had gone to bed, Dorothy sat up on the sofa, bathed by the moonlight. Moonlight had always frightened her. It was unearthly. It was cold. Throughout her life, she'd hated being cold more than any other physical sensation. It was one of the reasons she hated swimming or, god forbid, the ice-skating Tom and Cecily enjoyed so much. She wondered sometimes if Tom had gotten Cecily hooked on skating to spite her. Cold equaled death, in her personal lexicon. She'd written poems about it, in French, when she was in college. Thankfully, they'd disappeared into some box or bin ages ago. It was amazing to her how many things disappeared over the years. Her health and vitality were almost expected disappearances. Less so the books and papers and pieces of clothing. The trail of breadcrumbs left behind at the end of a life. Gone.

She hadn't factored the moonlight into her decision to install the window, nor was her aversion to it something she'd ever confess. She preferred to think of herself as someone who found moonlight romantic and dreamy. The way she pretended she liked Chopin, whose mournful études reminded her of moonlight and filled her with anxiety and a fear of death.

The thing she'd been dreading most in life—*most*—had been accomplished. "Tell Cecily about her father" could now be crossed off her to-do list. Not that Dorothy had told her, exactly, but the words had come from her lips, so it amounted to the same thing. Not that she had a to-do list, either. She equated that kind of organization with a complete lack of spontaneity.

Telling Cecily about Oliver had been inevitable, and she was proud of herself for going through with it, even in a roundabout way. Cecily had a right to know, and now she knew. What would follow was impossible to guess, but it was for the best that Cecily didn't want her to bring it up to Oliver and Charlotte this weekend. That would derail any discussion of the retreat center. Fiona was coming over in the early afternoon, a little ahead of the late-afternoon start of the . . . um, gala. She wanted Charlotte and—less plausibly but more importantly—Oliver to be impressed with this latest venture. Even at her age, she was making new friends, finding new business opportunities. And this one would succeed.

She curled up under the blanket and pulled it over her face to block out the moonlight. She felt herself being sucked down into some realm just below consciousness. Then she was gone.

She woke from a profound sleep so abruptly, it was as if cold water had been thrown on her. She checked her watch, some complicated Apple thing Gary and Enji had convinced her to buy. She loved having the latest technology, which made her feel connected to the current moment, even if she rarely figured out how to use any of it. She pulled out her phone with mounting panic. What if no one came? Worse still, what if an embarrassingly small number of people came? She'd be humiliated in front of all the people she wanted to impress and viewed as a failure by the whole town.

It was five thirty a.m. and still dark. The moon was behind clouds.

She got up and stowed the pillows and covers in a nearby closet, then went to the kitchen to get coffee going. When she opened the refrigerator door and the light went on, the suite of rooms bleeding into one another bloomed to life. Looking into the living room from here, she found the space as open and expansive as a bus station. A small bus station, but even so, not a home. All the improvements she'd made under advisement from Gary and Enji had only heightened the impersonal feeling of the place. The huge sofas, the new window, the ornate carved screens—so many places for dust to collect and useless clutter to pile up. And this was just a fraction of the total space. How had she not realized it would overwhelm her and make her feel small and insignificant? The exact opposite of what she'd hoped it would make her feel. Gary had insisted that she hang a large, colorful mobile from the fifteen-foot ceiling. It now looked like a trapped bird, destined to hang there, suspended, forever. That strange sensation began fluttering in her chest. Hummingbird wings batting against her ribs.

She sat down in a chair in the living room until her heartbeat and her breath were under control, then she went off to her bedroom and dug around in the drawer of her bedside table. She should have had those prescriptions filled when she was returning from Dr. Min's. She wasn't good at keeping track of paper scraps, never had been. If it hadn't been for Florence, the bookkeeping at the restaurant would have been a financial disaster. Well, in truth, the restaurant had been a financial disaster, but it wasn't Florence's fault. Probably "the economy," the wonderful, plausible excuse for so many personal failures.

She finally found her prescriptions under a lamp beside a chair. Holding them in her hand made her feel marginally more in control. Next week, she'd head to CVS.

She sat on the edge of her bed, mysterious piece of furniture that it was to her. She shouldn't have let Gary and Enji talk her into a four-thousand-dollar mattress when she knew she'd never use it. She'd just wanted to impress them with her complete acceptance of their advice.

She longed to hear noises that indicated that either Tom or Cecily was up. The problem was, she was always hearing noises from other places in the building: creaking and sighing, and animals scratching in hidden corners of the walls. The wind was up this morning, making the window frames groan. What if Cecily had spent the night mulling over the news and was furious at her? What if, now that she officially had two parents, she utterly rejected Dorothy, rather than merely pulling away, as she'd been doing for the last ten years?

By six a.m., Dorothy could see light in the sky, always a reassuring sight, but not reassuring enough this morning.

Fiona claimed to need very little sleep and said she got up daily by five a.m., at the latest, to write. The voice that answered the phone was unrecognizable, that of a gremlin, a troll under a bridge. Clearly, Dorothy had woken her up. Fiona had such an air of superiority about these matters, it was satisfying to catch her out, especially given that neither one of them would acknowledge what was obvious to both.

"Good morning," Dorothy said, trying to sound cheerful and composed. "I need to tell you what happened last night."

"Isn't it early for you?" Fiona growled.

"My sleep habits are erratic."

"Well, what is it? I'm writing." You had to admire Fiona's ability to respond with a lie, even when it wasn't a plausible one.

"You remember I told you I was planning to tell Cecily about her father? I did. She was fine about it. At least as far as I can tell."

"That's because you've been manifesting positive outcomes, Dorothy. You created her reaction."

Dorothy preferred to think that Cecily, in her emotional generosity, had simply accepted her mother's choices in the matter, but maybe it was true that the way she'd raised Cecily had, in some sense, contributed to her response.

"Is this why you called, at this hour?"

"Not entirely. I'm getting anxious about the event."

"I'm not. I'm meditating on what a huge success it will be. I recommend you do the same."

"A lot of important people will be there. Important to me, I mean. Tom and Cecily and new friends here I want to impress. My old college friend and her husband are coming today."

"Oliver and Charlotte," Fiona said. She had a politician's or a therapist's pride in remembering names. It was an impressive talent, one Dorothy lacked completely. "That's great. We'll have to make sure they're especially impressed with the financial potential of this."

"That won't be easy. On top of all that—well, he's Cecily's father." It was becoming easier to state this fact.

There was a rattling of bottles, as if Fiona were opening the door of the refrigerator. Probably hunting for iced coffee. She kept jars of it in her cluttered fridge until it was cloudy. Dorothy wondered what she wore to bed. What people wear for sleep defines them more than what they wear during the day, as, in most cases, they don't expect to be seen in their sleep. This included people in couples, given that one is invisible to a partner of long standing. Despite Dorothy's admiration for Fiona's public self, thinking of her in any intimate way was disturbing.

"If I'm getting all the biographical information correct," Fiona said, sounding more awake than before, "Oliver is successful. They're a wealthy couple. At least compared with ninety-nine percent of the world's population."

"Oh, definitely. Tens of millions." Like many in their circle of friends, Dorothy felt her status was enhanced by her closeness to Oliver—closer than almost anyone knew—even though she was always deriding his ethics. "He's so private, you can never tell for sure. I doubt Charlotte knows what he's worth. You can bet there are bank accounts hidden all over the world. No doubt, women as well."

"So, it will be especially important to make this a real family reunion of sorts. Unless you're worried about Charlotte's reaction to hearing you slept with her husband."

"She knows. We're long past It. They weren't even together at the time. We told each other everything back then."

"Apparently not," Fiona pointed out.

Close to everything, then. Charlotte had confessed three infidelities, including the one with James, the chef at Dorothy's restaurant, and another that hadn't been consummated. All incidents had been motivated by revenge. She wanted to get back at Oliver for some actual or perceived insult or infidelity of his. The funny thing was, Charlotte was too intimidated by Oliver to tell him what she'd done, so, as acts of revenge, they were impotent.

"You think he'd be angry at you if you told him?" Dorothy had asked Charlotte.

"Much worse," she'd said. "I'm afraid he wouldn't care."

Now Fiona said, "She was gracious to forgive you."

Dorothy said nothing. Graciousness hadn't come into it. Dorothy wasn't the kind of woman Oliver Fuchs would have been genuinely interested in. Charlotte had known that and forgiven her because she knew Dorothy wasn't a threat.

"Cecily does not want it brought up this weekend, so we're not going to be talking about it," she said. "Thank you for pretending we never had this conversation."

"There's a lot of potential gain in discussing it, Dorothy. Haven't you thought of that? You've done the two of them a huge favor. You raised Cecily on your own, you carried the weight of this secret all these years. Apparently, you never asked for a dime of child support."

"Of course not. The choice to have her was mine alone."

"Even so, you certainly could have asked for a hell of a lot more than a dime. Your life would have been simpler, and so would Cecily's. Arguably better."

While Dorothy was proud of not having asked anyone for child support, aside from a few loans from Tom she would almost certainly pay back eventually, she thought it was harsh of Fiona to bring it up so bluntly. "That's not my style. We'll do what Cecily says. Tom is working on a project with them, and I promised I wouldn't do anything to complicate his discussions with them."

Fiona let out a deep breath in what had to be an intentional show of annoyance. "I'm having trouble believing you'd prioritize someone else's project over ours. This isn't just about you, Dorothy. We're business partners. I'm trying to cultivate the base that I have through my book, bring in the clients we'll need to get the center off the ground. Is it too much to ask for you to think about *our* business instead of your brother's? How are we going to create our own destiny here if you're not willing to help? By being honest with these people, you enlist their generosity. Imagine if they put the money for Tom's project into ours. You keep telling me this will benefit you *and* Cecily—who is, don't forget, Oliver's daughter." It was apparent that when Fiona talked about creating her own destiny, it inevitably involved using someone else's money.

"I'll consider it," Dorothy said. "But I'd have to talk it over with Cecily first. It's her decision."

"It's the decision of the person who decides," Fiona said. "Don't forget that. Now, I have to get back to the chapter I was working on when you called. Don't be anxious about the gala. It's going to be a success. I will make sure of that."

Dorothy sat on her bed for a few more minutes, her heart racing. She needed to be alone to think it over and calm down. She closed her bedroom door and stretched out on the mattress, which really was very comfortable. Maybe it had been worth the price. Gary and Enji said they'd gotten her an insider discount.

She could be assured of solitude here; no one would think to look for her in her own bedroom.

She was woken up by a loud banging. Probably the wind. She rolled over in bed. The banging continued. She checked her phone. It was almost noon. How the hell had that happened? Preparations for the party should have started by now. It didn't seem possible she'd overslept like this.

She heard her name, in a panicked tone, and then Tom opened her door. "Didn't you hear me knocking?"

She was sitting on the edge of the bed now, trying to get oriented. "I was taking a nap," she said. "Of course, I heard you."

"For god's sake, Dorothy," he said. "Are you all right? I've been looking for you everywhere. I had no idea where you were in this mausoleum."

"And it turns out, I was in my own bedroom. You should have tried here first."

"Oliver and Charlotte arrived half an hour ago. They're downstairs, arguing."

"That's a good sign." A wave of dizziness passed over her. "They'll be focused on their own drama. That should keep them busy."

Tom sat beside her on the bed and took her hand. "You're sure you're all right?"

"I hate waking up from naps. It's why I never take them." No longer true, but true for most of her life. She must look terrible, if he was making such a fuss.

Tom laced his finger through hers and said, "I don't want to worry you, but Cecily has disappeared."

"Disappeared? What does that mean?"

"She isn't anywhere in the building, and she's not answering calls or texts."

No doubt she was doing as Dorothy had predicted: taking time to figure out what the news about Oliver meant to her, trying to make sense of it. If she was angry at Dorothy, she'd work through it. "Has it ever occurred to you she might be out exploring the town? She's inquisitive and open to everything. She gets it from me."

"She's been gone for hours."

"There's a lot to see, Tom. Let her roam."

Tom had always been overwrought when it came to taking care of Cecily. It wasn't that Dorothy didn't appreciate his concern and love; it was just that, so often, the two were connected to criticism of *her.* Even now. Cecily was a thirty-four-year-old woman who'd been living on her own for more than fifteen years. Dorothy resented his hovering. It made her more relaxed about this "disappearance." Once, on a flight to Hawaii years ago, the plane had run into a storm. She'd never been troubled by flying, even in unsettled weather. (Usually, she was sound asleep, and it took a lot more than turbulence to cut through the trazodone.) This storm was different, though. Bins were opening, luggage was flung around, people where either frozen in fear or screaming. Dorothy was terrified. Then the woman beside her started to moan and cry. She yelped at every jolt, like a terrified puppy. It was so excessive and unattractive to Dorothy that she calmed down instantly.

"It's going to be fine," she told the woman. "These planes are built

for ten times worse than this. Do some breathing with me. You'll see."
Then she'd closed her eyes and fallen back to sleep. When she woke up,
order had been restored to the cabin and the crew was serving lunch.

"Give me a minute to tidy up and change; then we'll go down
together," she told Tom now. "They're in the living room?"

"Yes. And don't forget," he said, "Cecily asked that we don't mention anything to them."

It was enough to make Dorothy want to run down and deliver a huge
announcement. "Did you bring up the guesthouse?"

"Only in passing. Charlotte's in a foul mood. I'll get to it once she
calms down and Cecily returns."

As she and Tom entered the living room, Charlotte strode in from the
kitchen, complaining. "We've been here forty-five minutes. Where
the hell have you been?" She threw her arms around Dorothy and
held her with what Dorothy knew was genuine affection. "Oh, sweetheart," she said, "why did you take all this on? What have you gotten
yourself into?"

"It's beautiful, isn't it?"

"It has elephantine charm. Beyond that, it's way, way too much."

"Where's your husband?"

"He's making a business call from somewhere. I suppose if all else
fails here, you can turn it into a shopping mall. Tom said Cecily is gone."

"She's out having fun. Let's sit down. I should have been attending
to preparations for the opening. I took a longer nap than intended."

"Nap? That's a new practice for you."

"I have a lot of surprises for you."

Dorothy hadn't seen Charlotte in almost a year. In that time, she'd
stepped over a line, as most of her peers had stepped over a line. As
she herself had stepped over a line. The slim, youthful Charlotte from
college had officially died. Dorothy had partly modeled herself on her
friend's audacity and vitality, even though she knew she didn't have the
same level of intellectual rigor as Charlotte. Inevitably, Charlotte would

find out about Cecily, and when she did, there'd be a rough patch, and then they'd smooth it over.

Most of the men who'd been drawn to Charlotte in their youth had the touching passivity of those whose domineering mothers programmed them to connect love with humiliation. Charlotte was baffled as to why she attracted this type. In general, she found them infuriating and pathetic. Naturally, this feeling led her to treat them with the disdain and condescension they craved, making her that much more irresistible.

Oliver Fuchs was the opposite. His confidence in himself was absolute. He wasn't a negotiator. His attitude toward women was like his attitude in business deals: you either accepted his terms or, no hard feelings, he walked. And he never looked back. Dorothy doubted he ever thought about her or what they'd done.

Dorothy had always felt that despite his physical vigor and stolid masculinity, he was not an especially sexual person. The few times they slept together—she was almost certain it had been three; appalling, given the outcome, that she couldn't remember the exact number— he'd fucked with the distracted, purposeful attitude with which you'd eat a meal for the sake of staving off hunger without caring about the taste. She had no illusions that he was attracted to her. What they did was a matter of convenience for him (the meal was served) and hostility toward Charlotte (she was off having her silly fling with James, the cook).

As for why Dorothy had betrayed her friend by sleeping with a man she knew Charlotte loved—well, there was nothing appealing in that, either. She could blame it on youth or Anaïs Nin, but neither was responsible.

There had always been a tone of subtle condescension in Charlotte's attitude toward Dorothy. At times, she treated her the way an older sister might treat her less attractive sibling. This Cinderella treatment had only increased when she landed Oliver, with his European charm, enigmatic politics, and, most important, his money. He wasn't Prince Charming, but he had the grooming and intellectual snobbery of a foreign ambassador whose admiration for America was rooted in the certainty of his own cultural superiority.

In the end, Dorothy had assuaged her guilt about sleeping with him by reminding herself that, eventually, every Cinderella wants to go to the ball at least once. She was convinced that if Oliver hadn't slept with her, he never would have proposed to Charlotte. Once, in the brief intimacy of watching him get dressed, five minutes after he'd finished with her, Dorothy said to him, "You really ought to bite the bullet and marry Charlotte. You'll never find anyone as devoted to you."

"Devoted? The last I heard, she's sleeping with someone else."

"Yes, and so are you. And I'm guessing her infidelity is every bit as meaningless to her as this is to you."

Oliver had no inclination toward dissembling, and no clue of how insulting he could be. "It's possible. I'm leaving on a trip later this week. I'll have plenty of time to think about it on the plane."

Now Dorothy linked her arm through Charlotte's and said, "I didn't get the best night's sleep, but I want to show you everything. You're going to love this building. You're the only one I know who loves excess as much as me."

"What about lunch?"

"There's food everywhere. Let's go find Oliver. Fiona Snow is coming over in bit. You'll hate each other, but only because you're so much alike."

"I'll keep that in mind."

"Cecily will be back before she gets here, and we'll have a lovely afternoon. And then, the party."

"There won't be speeches, will there?"

"Oh, Fiona might say one or two amusing words, that's all."

Naturally, Dorothy had no idea how unamusing Fiona's words would end up being.

Chapter Twenty-One

*A*s Tom had feared, Cecily was not back by the time Fiona was supposed to arrive. Fiona wasn't there, either.

"She's always late," Dorothy said. "It's one of her quirks."

"Delightful," Charlotte said. "I love quirks. So much more appealing than old-fashioned passive aggression."

Charlotte was pacing, while Tom and Dorothy sat in the living room, and Oliver came and went as he took business calls. All their friends had joked that Oliver always looked as if he were awaiting a call from the finance minister of a European ally. They'd had a distracted, rambling lunch, with everyone talking at cross-purposes, avoiding mention of Cecily, the size of the house, and the anticipated arrival of Fiona. Dorothy went downstairs to usher in caterers and musicians setting up a sound system and a woman with a tank of helium to blow up balloons. Eventually, she told Tom she was sick of going up and down and asked him to do the honors.

The gallery below was beginning to look festive, assuming "festive" meant filled up with a lot of colorful junk twenty-four hours from the landfill. Tom began to get nervous about people showing up. No matter how misguided Dorothy had been in keeping Oliver's paternity a secret, he couldn't bear the thought of his sister's disappointment and humiliation if it wasn't a good showing. There was so much space to fill, and she had such high expectations.

"I don't know why you need to do business on the phone on the weekend," Charlotte snapped now as Oliver came back into the living room.

"But I always do," he said. "There's nothing different."

"What's different is we're *here*."

"The world doesn't stop for our road trips, my dear. You forget."

"You forget that the world can run, for one day, without you."

For the past two hours, Tom had stared at Oliver with a fixed, inquisitive gaze, noting facial similarities. He had always been bad at recognizing family resemblances, perhaps because he found them uninteresting—except, of course, in the cases of Prince Harry and Ronan Farrow. Oliver was now in his late sixties, and while he kept himself fit and healthy and, for the sake of business, might even have been getting Botox with some frequency, his jawline was beginning to droop, and his lips were thinning. It was unnerving to think this man was Cecily's father, that his connection to her was so much more solid than Tom's.

Dorothy, eager to change the subject, or perhaps trying to be helpful, brought up Charlotte's guesthouse.

"We got sent preliminary ideas from Eldridge Johnson," Charlotte told her. "Oliver likes them more than I do."

"Pastels and Palladian windows?" Tom asked.

"Some of his signature details," Oliver said. "If you're paying for him, you want to know it's one of his buildings."

What this meant, of course, was that you wanted your neighbors and guests to know. It was the equivalent of a designer label, a fact Charlotte emphasized by saying, "I'd prefer we got something atypical from him and added a plaque."

It was encouraging that there was disagreement between them. Charlotte was coming around, at least a little, and Tom felt certain that, if he cornered them alone at some point before the end of the weekend, he could make progress.

"You have heard that many of his buildings have structural problems, haven't you?" Tom asked.

"Oh, famous architects," Oliver said, waving it off. "They're always having claims filed against them. Look at Gehry. It adds to the conversation."

"Are you planning to sue him already? Even before you start construction?"

"I'm not litigious," Oliver said, a dubious claim. "And to state the obvious, I feel bad that the project with you fell through, Tom." This was said in a perfunctory tone, as if Oliver were making minimal effort to sound credible. Oliver's sympathy, like that of most highly successful men, extended only to the people who didn't need it. He wanted to be associated only with success. Tom had never expected kindness or empathy from Oliver, but he also hadn't expected what was beginning to seem like intentional cruelty. The window of opportunity for turning this around was narrowing.

When two o'clock rolled around with no sign of either Cecily or Fiona, Tom's anxiety spiked. Woodstock was not a big place, and by his count, Cecily had been out of the house for at least five hours. It made no sense to him. He couldn't stand thinking she was wandering the streets depressed and angry. He pushed himself up from the sofa and announced that he was going for a walk. "Maybe I'll bump into Cecily."

"Try the Bread and Butter Bakery," Dorothy said. "People sit there all day and read. I'm sure you'll find her there. If not, try the library. When you meet up with her, don't make it seem as if I sent you out looking. You know how much she loves her independence."

As soon as Tom stepped out of the exasperating building, he breathed easier. There was something benign about the town itself, with its billowing hippie vibe. As he walked down the main street, past all the chocolate shops and cold-pressed juiceries, he wondered why he'd been anxious about Cecily in the first place. What harm could come to her here? Kale overdose?

He stopped an elderly woman draped in colorful scarves and asked for directions to the bakery Dorothy had mentioned. He received a lecture about the business's hiring practices and the virtues of using locally sourced flour. The next person he stopped was more helpful, even though dressed the same.

Cecily wasn't at the bakery. Tom stopped a man he at first thought was Harold—there were a lot of men here who looked eerily like Harold—for directions to the library. He got a lecture on its refusal to add his poetry book to its collection and its unfair policies regarding computer use. Alarmingly, he said, "I'd like to burn it down."

Eventually, Tom found the library on his own, a low-slung clapboard building—shabby and about one-third the size of Dorothy's mausoleum. As he entered, he had a premonition Cecily wouldn't be there. She wasn't.

He went up to the librarian, a small man in a flannel shirt and, for no apparent reason, a yellow headband, and said he was supposed to meet his niece there. He took out his phone and showed the man a picture of Cecily he'd taken the day she arrived, standing beside Alan. They both looked so happy, even Alan. "Have you seen her in here?" he asked.

The librarian looked at Tom as if there were something nefarious about the request, then adjusted the headband and looked at the picture. "Probably not," he said. "I think the man was here."

So much for reliability. "The man was *not* here. I'm looking for her. She would have been in the reading room. She's a professor."

"Good for her," the librarian said. He was looking down, but the eye rolling was apparent from his voice.

"If you do see her, please tell her to call Tom? Do you want me to write it down somewhere?" There was zero likelihood of this helping, but at least he'd done something.

When he approached Dorothy's building again, he saw that Fiona's car was there. Out of morbid curiosity, he peered into the backseat to see what, besides a shovel and gloves, she kept on hand. There was an enormous amount of clutter heaped into the back: plastic bags, shoes, cardboard shipping boxes, lawn tools, newspapers that had gone yellow from the sun, a bag of dried pasta, a six-pack of flavored water, a toaster, some clothes from the cleaner's that looked like they'd been there for months, an open box of Corn Flakes. He distrusted people who kept their cars too clean and spent hours washing and waxing them, but there was a limit.

The gallery on the first floor was a movie set of a party, waiting for the cast and crew to arrive and perform. A spinning orb at the back of the speaker's platform cast disco lighting against the walls, a horribly depressing sight in daylight. "Do you think we should turn this off?" Tom asked one of the caterers.

The man shook his head. That was someone else's problem, apparently.

He'd barely made it up to the living room before he heard Charlotte's voice. "I didn't say your theories are ridiculous, Fiona. Your success speaks for itself. What I said is, I'm offended hearing you refer to this as 'scientific.'"

This was all they needed.

"Offended on behalf of whom?" Fiona's voice was mildly bemused at best, and it was clear she was, once again, eating. The fact that she'd been eating throughout the day yesterday made Tom think she probably ate only at Dorothy's house, not counting a couple handfuls of Corn Flakes while driving.

Tom walked into the living room, and Charlotte jumped up. "Did you find her?"

"Oh, stop it!" Dorothy said. "She's not missing!"

"I didn't bump into her," Tom announced. He had no interest in buying into Charlotte's worries, especially because they mimicked his own. "I suspect I just missed her by minutes somewhere. It's crowded out there. I suppose it always is on weekends."

"Always," said Fiona. "The metrics on that are in our business plan."

Charlotte, pacing, had changed into an outfit that was a cross between pajamas and their opposite, gym clothes. Her hair was pulled back, and she had on no makeup, which, disconcertingly, gave her face the smooth, featureless look of a mask. Eyebrows, it seems, are vastly more important than Tom had given them credit for. He was impressed that Charlotte was allowing herself to be seen this way by Fiona, whom she'd distrusted even before meeting her. One may want to keep one's enemies close, but only if you're looking your best.

"So, that's it? We just wait?" Charlotte asked.

"What is it you want us to do, my dear?" Oliver said, without lifting his eyes from the newspaper he was holding. "She's been gone only a few hours and . . ."

"We don't know that," Charlotte said. "For all anyone here knows, she could have left in the middle of the night."

"A few hours," Oliver continued. He'd mastered the art of always finishing his sentences, especially when he'd been interrupted by Charlotte. He folded back a page of the newspaper, a local rag he couldn't have been interested in, snapped it, and began reading again. "The police would laugh at you if you called them. Here's their log in the paper. A lost pet, a few drug issues, some domestic squabbles, and one break-in. I suggest we all assume she's off having a fun adventure."

"I think Oliver has a good suggestion," Fiona said. "When you panic, you manifest negativity. And no, Charlotte, I am not claiming that's science. Just common sense."

"Cecily will be home in an hour," Dorothy said. "I assure you."

"Let's go with that," Oliver said, putting aside the newspaper.

Fiona asked him a question about his career, which, as was his custom, he sidestepped with insincere humility. "It's terribly uninteresting," he said, the words of a man confident of his own importance on a stage vastly bigger than this one.

Tom doubted Oliver had made eye contact with Fiona the entire time they'd been there. He was bored by women who were sexually irrelevant to him—unless she happened to be Angela Merkel—and men who made less money than he did.

Cecily was not back in an hour, as Dorothy had assured, and Charlotte, pushing the issue, said, "I'm going for a walk. Anyone who'd like to join me is welcome. I've known Cecily her whole life, and this isn't like her."

Fiona gave a wan smile. She reached out and patted Dorothy's thigh. "Since Charlotte is so upset, Dorothy, I think you should let her know there's a reason Cecily might want time to herself, today especially."

Charlotte turned from Fiona to Dorothy. Her annoyance made it look as if the features had returned to her face. "What's she talking about? Cecily isn't pregnant, is she?"

Dorothy laughed. "Not that I know of. If anything, she's losing weight. I'd rather change the subject. Cecily will be home any minute."

"You've been saying that for hours now," Charlotte said. "Are you going to share this information with us, Fiona, or are you just going to dangle your unspecified, superior knowledge of her?"

"I think you've misunderstood my intentions, Charlotte. I've only known Cecily for twenty-four hours." Fiona rose from where she was sitting and adjusted her loose clothes on her tall, narrow frame. "I have to get downstairs and make sure the setup is coming along."

She lurched toward the staircase. Tom was relieved to see her headed toward the exit, but now that she was, he was sad for her. After all, she had thoughtfully supplied gloves for him yesterday, and he always had sympathy for anyone who was an outsider in a group of friends, especially given that that was *his* usual position.

Fiona opened the door and disappeared.

"She's odious," Charlotte said. "If you're not going to tell us what she was alluding to, I'm going for a walk."

"Relax," Dorothy said. "Cecily will be back in an hour."

An hour later, Tom looked out the immense window and saw, far below, Cecily approaching the building. She was walking slowly, gazing up at the bank of dark clouds that was rolling in. She was with a man. He was probably in his forties, had on a green flannel shirt and, from the angle at which Tom was seeing him, appeared to be one of those rugged men who wear carpenter's pants for the purposes they were intended to be worn. At the door, he hugged Cecily and handed her a wrapped parcel he'd been carrying under his arm. It looked like a canvas and was perhaps two or three times the size of a record album. Then he walked off with his hands in his pockets. It was a few minutes before Tom heard Cecily open the door at the rear of the building.

Well, well, well. Tom wasn't in a position to judge, a thought that, he realized, was a judgmental interpretation of what he'd just seen. He wondered if he'd misunderstood Cecily all these years, if her character was completely different from what he'd imagined. After all, close relatives can know children well but also have more hidden from them than any other category of people. It shouldn't have come as much of a shock; he was woefully familiar with people whose public lives were vastly different from their private lives. A certain degree of self-sabotage was probably hardwired into Cecily's DNA.

He felt bad for Santosh, who, for all he knew, might have been off having an adventure of his own.

Dorothy leapt up as soon as Cecily stepped into the living room. "I told you all she'd be back," she said triumphantly. "Did you have a wonderful time? Isn't it a fantastic place, sweetheart? Tell me where you've been."

Tom prided himself on being able to read Cecily's expressions, but he had no clue what she was thinking when she said, "I didn't see that much of it, to be honest. I was at the library most of the day."

Tom glanced at her as she told this lie, then looked away. She wasn't carrying the painting—if that's what it was—so maybe she'd stashed it somewhere below. Another secret.

"We were all worried," Charlotte said.

"I thought I was just going out for coffee, but one thing led to another."

For the past hour, Oliver had been deeply immersed in his computer. Now he unfolded himself from his chair, rose to his full height, and crossed to Cecily. He put his hands on her shoulders and said, "Charlotte told me you have a new haircut, but I still wasn't prepared. You pull it off beautifully." He said this in the jovial, accepting tone he usually used when speaking to Cecily. It was a tone Tom had never heard him use when talking to his son.

"I'm sorry if I had anyone worried," Cecily said. "I decided to leave without my phone, or I would have called." She stepped away from Oliver before he took his hands off her, a bold move. The new knowledge she had had given her power over him.

She had on the khaki pants that were too short for her and the stretched-out sweater she'd been wearing when she flew in from Chicago. As she walked away from Oliver, she looked much less frail than she had then, although it probably had nothing to do with her weight.

"I checked my email when I got up," she said. "I had one from Deerpath. I have to go back for a meeting early next week. I know you wanted me to stay longer, Dorothy, but I can't. I should get back to Boston tomorrow—if that's okay with you, Tom."

"What kind of meeting?" Charlotte asked.

"Oh, academia," Cecily said. "It's all about meetings."

The dismissive tone confirmed what Tom had thought earlier: anything you said about academia was believed as long as it was disparaging. This must mean she was meeting with the team who'd been investigating her. It saddened him to think she was facing it alone.

Music drifted up from the gallery, a guitar being tuned and an electric piano. The show would begin soon.

Chapter Twenty-Two

When Cecily woke up that morning, no one was stir-
ring. She went to the living room, but Dorothy wasn't on
her sofa, and the bedding had been put away. She had no
idea how to read this, but it gave her a sense of peace and control. Perhaps, improbably enough, unburdening herself of that long-held secret
had inspired her mother to sleep in an actual bed.

That was when she checked her messages and found out that, on
Wednesday, she'd be meeting with the Title IX office at three in the
afternoon. Four days from now. It seemed almost perverse that this
meeting, which she'd been awaiting so anxiously, should arrive with
so little fanfare. *I hope this time works for you. We look forward to the
meeting.*

When she shared this information in a text with Molly, asking again
if she had the name of a lawyer, Molly had written back immediately to
say that a lawyer would cost her a fortune and that she might be better
off waiting until the next step in the process, assuming there was one. **I'd
be happy to sit in on this meeting, just for moral support. I was involved
in a couple of harassment suits when I was a paralegal. I won't intervene,
but it'll send a message to them that you're not going to be pushed around.**

After she sent Molly the time of the meeting, she decided to go out
and get coffee. The news about Oliver had given her an intense desire
to get away from everyone she was related to. She suspected she had

been programmed to experience every allegedly big moment in life as an anticlimax. Oliver was her father. Now what? It wasn't something she'd ever consciously suspected, but she'd learned it with a dull lack of surprise. She'd been more stirred by holding her published book in her hand for the first time. She'd created the book; it was an actual accomplishment. This was news of something that had been done to her by those around her, that irritatingly irresponsible circle of friends straddling the values of too many decades and cultural moments to sustain a coherent worldview.

She imagined the importance of her newly discovered paternity was gnawing at her somewhere inside, but now she wanted *out*. She didn't want to be reachable, not even by Santosh. She didn't want to call him, didn't want to answer if he called her, and most of all, didn't want to know if he didn't call her. She left her phone tucked under her pillow and slipped out.

It was warm and almost tropically humid. The temperature caught her by surprise. It had been chilly in her bedroom; it probably took days for weather to penetrate the inner reaches of Dorothy's insane building. The fact that absolutely no one in this town knew her or her connection to Dorothy was an added benefit. Anonymity was a pure, palpable pleasure. Surely, the desire for fame must be related to mental imbalance. It was like longing for an illness or bankruptcy.

And yet, she'd had a mild case of that illness not all that long ago. Sitting down for TV interviews and asking her publisher if they could arrange for more. It was hard to know what she'd been thinking.

In her vague, occasional speculation about the identity of her father, she'd never imagined he'd be so close by. Maybe it made sense that it was Oliver, the exact opposite of Dorothy, someone whose steady, balanced reliability and emotional coolness explained some of her own. He'd always been kind to her, probably because he'd never noticed her or cared enough about her to be disappointed. It should have felt like a gain, this new knowledge, but at the moment, she felt as if she'd lost some fraction of her ability to determine her own destiny. DNA had to pull at you in unseen ways.

The village streets were quiet but full of anticipation. Awnings were being rolled down and tables set up outside shops. The unseasonably heavy, humid air smelled pleasantly of coffee and the buttery scents of baking. The people she passed all had the look of city dwellers who'd made costume-like adjustments to their mostly black wardrobes to fit in with this more casual place—a colorful sash, belt, or scarf they'd bury in a drawer at home once the weekend was over. A woman who was probably in her twenties, gorgeous and stylish, floated past in a strapless dress. There were so many things Cecily ought to regret about herself and her behavior, but at the moment, the one that stung was knowing she wasn't the kind of person who could pull off a strapless dress.

Intuition led her to a bakery with a long line out the door. Following the questionable logic that if a lot of people liked something, it must be good, she took her place in line.

A man a few people ahead of her was bellowing into a cell phone. A show of disrespect for the assembled crowd he desperately wanted to hear him. Why was it, she wondered, we always try to impress the people whose opinions we don't value?

"Tell her we got the script," the man brayed. "Tell her we're sending it out on Monday. But, spoiler alert: It needs another pass, and it's not right for her, anyway. She'll hate it."

Apparently, there was more clout in saying you didn't like something than in claiming you did.

The man directly in front of Cecily turned around and raised an eyebrow. "Who do you think the 'her' is?"

"I don't know," Cecily said. "My guess is, if it were someone impressive, her name would have been mentioned."

"Good point," he said. He had on carpenter pants and a flannel shirt that suggested he might be a local. "Do you think she'll like the script?"

"She'll say she does. Women of her age don't get that many offers."

He smiled and turned back around to talk to the girl standing beside him.

The line was not moving, unless the people constantly piling up at the end of it counted as movement. Maybe the bakery was intentionally letting the line build to create excitement. That's why she was here. Even so, she began to feel restless and wandered off. She could get coffee elsewhere.

She'd gone only a block or two when she felt a pang of tenderness toward Dorothy. She decided to buy her a present. Whatever her mother's motives had been, however unfair of her it had been to cheat Cecily of knowing her father all these years, it couldn't have been easy carrying around the weight of that secret—the only secret, Cecily suspected, Dorothy had ever kept in her life. For an impulsive and unpredictable person, her mother was surprisingly predictable, and Cecily knew she'd be touched by a present, whatever it was, and would give it a place of prominence in her silly house.

She crawled along the street, looking for something acceptable. There was a lot to browse. Most stores were gift shops, although why it was always assumed that the best gifts were the least practical and attractive items manufactured was a mystery to her.

As she was peering into the window of a shop that sold glass items and was called the Bush Tree, someone came up behind her and said, "Couldn't handle the line?"

It was the man she'd exchanged a few words with while waiting at the bakery. He took a bite out of a muffin as if it were an apple. He had the weathered, unevenly tanned skin of someone who works outdoors and is into his forties. He carried himself with an unaffected confidence that made him seem genuinely comfortable in his own skin. Of all the ways in which a person can be attractive, Cecily found this the most underrated.

"I figured I'd go back when the crowd thinned out," she said. "How's the muffin?"

"Extremely mediocre." He held it out to her as if offering her a bite.

She understood they were flirting, but this seemed a step too far. "I'll take your word for it."

She was embarrassed to be caught looking in this window, especially because this man gave off an air of practicality (the work clothes and comfortable sneakers) that seemed anathema to the Bush Tree and its decorative contents. Not to mention the awkward name. Who else but a tourist would ever look in the window of a shop like this, never mind buy something there? She'd always found being a tourist humiliating and infantilizing. You have no real purpose in the place you're visiting, and you're entirely dependent upon others to direct you. You're theoretically helping the economic life of the place but resented for even being there.

"My mother lives in town," she said, a useless piece of information that at least gave her some legitimacy. "I'm visiting. I want to find a present for her."

"Nice daughter," he said.

"If I really were nice, I would have thought to bring something from home."

"Where's that?"

"Chicago," she said.

He nodded. "It's on my bucket list. I don't get out much."

How provincial that someone who lived in New York State had never been to Chicago. Unless it was provincial of her to think that he ought to have been. She'd always associated being well traveled with sophistication, but she also believed there was a sophisticated integrity to being a homebody. She wasn't either.

"I don't think there's anything here she'd like," Cecily said. "Maybe I should look for a painting. A small one. There are a lot of galleries here." Tourist towns were always full of galleries. Apparently, people bought mostly fudge and artwork when they were on vacation.

The man's name was Victor, a good, solid name. There was something practical and solid about his face, too, with its creased skin. His hair had gray in it, although she couldn't tell if this was due to age or a combination of paint and plaster dust.

"I know a little gallery where you can probably find something. Not expensive, not too corny. I guarantee there are no lines."

The fact that it was morning, that this was in service of finding a present for Dorothy, that the town had an air of abandon that was somehow wholesome (the presence of the mountains in the distance, perhaps?), and that, for the first time in years, she didn't have a phone on her and was therefore unaccountable for her whereabouts—all this made it seem acceptable for her to go off with him. She knew there was nothing pure in his motives, but this was balanced out by the fact that there was nothing impure in hers.

He led her down the street, giving a little background and telling her that he'd been in Woodstock most of his life. "That's forty-three years, in case you were wondering. Except for Berkeley, but let's not get into that." This seemed like an invitation to ask more questions, but when Cecily did, he smiled and said, "Dropped out one semester before graduating. Came back here. End of story."

They walked past a bookstore and down a little alleyway crammed with what appeared to be small, untended houses from which, even at this hour of the morning, the unmistakable odor of weed was seeping. They came to a narrow, wooded road with a stream running beside it. Victor pointed to a little cottage that hung out over the water.

"That doesn't look like a gallery," she said.

"It's not. But there are paintings in there. Plus, you still haven't had coffee, and I make great coffee."

"Oh? Why were you at the bakery?"

"I make lousy muffins."

She followed him up onto a deck, unpainted and questionably solid, that was cantilevered out over the stream rushing below. A breeze rose from the water.

"I should tell you . . ." she started to say.

He held up his hand. "No need to. I know. But I do paint, and I do make good coffee. I can't claim I have only good intentions, but I honestly don't have any bad ones."

With the stream running beneath them, it seemed like assurance enough.

The inside of the house was shadowy and cool, and the air smelled faintly of woodstove, cigarettes, and the greasy, delicious odor of oil paints and turpentine. So, he really was a painter. The cottage wasn't too much bigger than the guesthouse at Tom's. There was a ladder on one side of the room that obviously led up to a loft, and the lack of fussiness had a cohesive aesthetic appeal of its own. Two lumpy chairs were draped in material that was no doubt intended to cover wear but was tidily tucked in around the cushions. The place exuded the easy comfort of a dwelling in which someone was living exactly as he wanted to live.

Victor went to the sink—dirty dishes, of course, but nothing that looked as if it had been there too long—and began making coffee in a scorched espresso pot that screamed "garage sale."

He was, as his wardrobe foretold, a carpenter, one of many dozens, he said, in this town. It was the kind of place where men with college degrees could earn a living with their hands without having to explain or feel any sense of defeat about it. Plus, he painted, a pastime that, along with music, washed away all sins here. When she asked him if he showed his work in town, he shrugged. "Sometimes. Mostly, I do it because I enjoy it. Crazy, right? I have zero ulterior motives—for money, recognition, you name it."

Maybe he was making fun of her in saying this, but there was no malice in the way he'd said it.

"But you're going to show me your paintings?"

"I am. I'm even going to let you choose one for your mother, assuming you see something you like. I love giving away my paintings."

"I couldn't take anything unless you let me pay for it."

"Of course you could," he said. "It'll surprise you how easy it is."

She wanted to ask why he was being so generous with her, but she was afraid it would lead to a suggestive response she wasn't in the mood to deal with. She liked the attention and the flirtation, both of which seemed safely far from leading anywhere worrisome.

The coffee was as delicious as promised, made more so, no doubt, by the atmosphere of the house. Victor pulled out a loaf of bread, cut a thick slice, and toasted it; he watched her as she ate, and they talked.

"I'll bet you're a popular teacher," he said, once they'd come to that part of her résumé.

"Reasonably," she said. "I show a lot of videos, so my popularity doesn't exactly count."

"I think it all counts. I'll bet your students get crushes on you and end up taking every course you teach."

"If you only knew," she said. The topic made her suddenly sad, and she found it hard to swallow the toast. "This isn't going to get awkward, is it?" she asked.

"Why would it?"

"Don't make me answer. You know what I mean. You're being awfully nice to me."

He laughed and rolled up his sleeves. "I guess you're not used to people being nice to you."

"I wouldn't have come in if it hadn't been so early. That made it seem okay. That and the fact that the past twelve hours have been incredibly weird."

He sat looking at her with his chin against his fist. She felt an unfamiliar power rise in her under his gaze. She was the younger person and, objectively—let's face it—the better looking of the two of them. In her relationship with Santosh, she was neither of these things. She liked this feeling and the control it gave her. This man knew nothing of her problems or her mistakes, and for the first time in ages, she had the illusion of being on the same upward curve of life she'd been on before everything started to change. She wondered what it would be like having sex with Victor, not because she felt a sexual attraction to him, but because she suspected it might transport her to a realm of pure sensation in which she felt beautiful and strong.

"So, where are all the paintings?" she asked.

"Ah. Those."

He got up from the table and took her by the hand. He led her to the far side of the house and opened a door that she assumed was a closet. He turned on a light, and what she saw hanging from the walls of this attached room, stacked up on the floor, and spilled across furniture was in such glowing abundance, she swooned, leaned against him, and let him put his arm around her. "I'll give you the tour," he said softly.

⬤

Now, back at Dorothy's, she thought about the afternoon as she packed and listened to the band warming up in the gallery below. Victor's painting was tucked into a cabinet on the first floor. In the morning, they'd leave, and she'd hand it to Dorothy. In a few days, she'd be back in Chicago. That was what mattered to her right now. She didn't want her mother to make a show of the painting at the party, which would have been in character. Cecily planned to make it through the party with as little attention on her and as little drama as possible.

Chapter Twenty-Three

A bout an hour before the party was set to begin, the weather got peculiar. It had been uncomfortably humid all day, but at around four-thirty, Tom looked out the huge window in Dorothy's living room and saw that the sky had turned a vivid shade of green. A color you might welcome on a vintage kitchen appliance, a golf outfit, or guacamole, but not in the sky. There was a discernable change in the atmospheric pressure that felt like a thumb pressing on your chest. He checked the weather on his phone, but only "light rain" was forecast. In an area like this, there were probably microclimates all over. He kept gazing out, looking for lightning or something to break up what felt like building tension.

Maybe he was projecting his own tension onto the weather. Shortly after Cecily returned and went off to her room, he'd opened a drawer in the kitchen and found a bill from the caterers, A Child of God Indulgence. The name was either a reference to Joni Mitchell or, perhaps, indication of cult ownership of the business. The bill was for almost ten thousand dollars. He checked it multiple times to make sure he'd read it right, that it was for this event, that it wasn't some piece of paper left by the previous owners. No such luck. It included the wine and food but not the sound system, the jazz trio he could hear playing standards down below, or the balloons someone had been blowing up for the past hour. He hoped there wasn't going to be a balloon drop. What an

insane amount of money! Fiona had chosen the five-thirty start time so
people wouldn't expect to be fed much, but Dorothy, in her unrealistic
generosity, had gone overboard.

He paced the opulent, Moorish room, waiting for someone to
emerge, but everyone had scattered to their various corners. Hopefully,
he'd find Oliver and Charlotte down below.

There was rumbling in the distance, but no sign of lightning. Perhaps
the storm was traveling across from the other side of the mountains.

Dorothy emerged from her room dressed in an unlikely assemblage
of colors and a pair of earrings in the shape of strawberries. "Very nice,"
he said, because either you went all in accepting an outfit like this or
you started talking about Cirque du Soleil.

"I'm glad you approve," she said. "It wasn't until the last year that
I realized all I had to do to stand out was wear loud, clashing clothes.
Think of all the time and energy I could have saved trying to be a
colorful person for decades by words and deeds."

She seemed to have missed the fact that she was still doing that.

"How many people are you expecting?"

"I don't know, but I'm supplying food for two hundred. You can
take some leftovers home. Have you seen anyone arriving? I rented the
field below for parking, so they'll be coming on foot."

"Mostly I've been focused on the sky."

Dorothy gazed out the window as if she hadn't, up to that point,
noticed the weather at all. "Isn't that pretty?" she said. "I've never seen
that color before."

"Don't you find it a little ominous?"

"A storm might add drama, make things memorable. I hope it's not
a flop, Tom. Please don't judge me too harshly if it's a flop. I'll be sufficiently humiliated without any subtle disapproval and I-told-you-so's
from you and Charlotte. I'm a wreck."

It would take so little for him to cross the room and hug her, encourage her, at the very least tell her that everything would be fine and that
he loved her. He'd spent most of the past eighteen hours thinking about
Cecily and how she must be feeling knowing that Oliver was her father.

He hadn't considered how it must feel for Dorothy to have her secret revealed after all this time, to have had Cecily disappear after learning it. For these events to be converging at once.

He moved to take a step toward her but found that he couldn't. He was exhausted from decades of taking care of her, of reassuring her, of encouraging schemes of hers he knew were destined to failure or ones that had already failed. Before he could do any more of it, he needed to tell her how it had felt for him, doing all that caretaking. How much it had cost him—not financially, but emotionally. He didn't need an apology or even an acknowledgment; he'd long ago stopped expecting repayment. He just needed to take a stand for himself, to care for himself for once by telling her.

But, of course, like every other time he'd tried, this was not the right moment.

"It's going to be fine," he said. "You should go greet people as they come in. Enjoy it."

As she was heading downstairs, he heard the storm coming closer; the green of the sky seemed to get brighter.

●

"That sky is unwholesome," Charlotte said upon emerging from her room. "I hope it doesn't hold down attendance. I don't see a single car."

"Dorothy rented a field for parking," Tom said. "People have been arriving."

"I hope they've brought umbrellas. This humidity has me by the throat. I can't breathe." Her robust speech belied this claim.

"I've seen some lightning, but it's far off," Tom said.

Once Cecily and Oliver had joined them in front of the window, the four made their way down the long staircase. Tom was reassured by a rumble of conversation, and when they stood on the balcony surrounding the gallery, he saw at least forty or fifty people below, with more coming in. Not enough to eat ten thousand dollars' worth of food, but at least enough to make a slight dent in it.

"Well, it's not a complete disaster," Charlotte said.

"Cynic," Oliver said. "It looks perfectly respectable. What do you think, Cecily?"

"Dorothy will make the most of it, no matter what."

"The good daughter," Oliver said, an ostensible compliment that sounded very much like an insult.

Tom resented Oliver for his distance, his lack of attention to Cecily. His resentment made no sense. Oliver didn't know about their relationship, but because Tom now did, he wanted him to be more attentive. And while he was at it, why not loving?

He looked to see if Cecily was scanning the crowd for the man in carpenter's pants, but she seemed to be gazing mainly at the platform with the musicians, now playing "Someone to Watch over Me," a song Tom had always found heartbreaking, especially in Cecily's presence.

The four had scattered once they descended to the gallery below. It was an impressively diverse crowd, in all ways. Most surprisingly, in terms of age. There were a good number of people who appeared to be somewhere in their thirties, that nebulous neither/nor decade, the last one in which one's untapped potential counts for anything. He assumed you'd need the desperation and continued disappointments of middle age to seek out someone like Fiona, but maybe he was wrong. Maybe, these days, desperation and disappointment arrived earlier, now that adulthood seemed to be arriving later.

The temperature in the gallery was high, and the humidity suffocating. Everyone was sweating; the crowd looked slippery and aquatic. One disappointed, sweating person was stationed—for the duration, if Tom had to guess—at the food table. Harold. He had a plate heaped with slabs of bloody roast beef and greasy lamb. It had been insane of Dorothy to choose this kind of food, especially in a town that probably included massive numbers of vegetarians. Although, looking around, he saw that the novelty of it was tempting enough to a lot of sweating people. Soon, the room would smell like a barnyard.

Harold was standing with a woman who looked to be about his age. She had his height and slender build. Her white hair was woven into an impressively long, thick braid she had draped over one shoulder, as if it were a shawl that kept sliding down her back. She had the looks of an artisan who worked in heavy, nubby fabrics.

Harold motioned Tom over and said, chewing, "I want you to meet my wife. Peggy, this is Tom, Dorothy's brother."

She smiled at Tom and indicated that her hands were too full—plate, glass—to shake his. "Harold told me how much he enjoyed meeting you," she said.

Tom nodded and smiled, afraid to say anything because exactly how much Peggy knew was unclear. Peggy had a quiet dignity that he'd often noticed in the wives of talkative and boring men. These women asserted their tolerant disapproval by silently communicating a numb lack of engagement that said, *I stopped listening years ago, and I'd advise you to do the same.* And yet, there was a connection between the two, magnified by the similarity in stature, that made him feel sad for Dorothy. His sister was fated always to be the unthreatening other person in relationships, the one who encouraged men to stay with their wives or, in the case of Oliver Fuchs, marry their girlfriends.

"Harold says you're an admirer of Fiona Snow," Tom said, an uncontroversial comment in this setting.

"Very much so. She's engaging and has the ability to make you think she's sincere."

He nodded, impressed that Peggy had made a comment to which there seemed to be no possible response. Fiona was now holding court on the other side of the room with Gary and Enji and a small crowd of youthful male acolytes—not of her, if he had to guess, but of Gary and Enji. Gary's arm was around Enji's shoulder, as if he wanted to display to the assembled multitude that this was what a happy male couple looked like, something they could aspire to.

Tom checked himself. The biggest and most important challenge in growing older was to avoid bitterness toward the people who had what you wanted or, to be more exact, what you once assumed you'd have, personally and professionally. Bitterness meant you were living in the past and were unable to let go and develop a healthy sense of defeat and tolerable depression. Bitterness was as unattractive on someone in his sixties as a crop top. Although, come to think of it, no one looks good in a crop top.

"I'm going to grab some air," Tom said. "The heat in here is getting to me."

Really, he was going to try to get time with Charlotte and Oliver before the presentation, or whatever was coming. They were huddled together in a corner, languidly drinking wine and observing the crowd without speaking. He supposed they were silently communicating their disapproval back and forth. There was something undeniably cozy about snobbish couples, sealed as they were into their bubble of delusional superiority.

He approached them. "How's the wine?" he asked either of them.

Oliver held up his glass and surveyed what was in it. "Surprisingly good. You're not drinking?"

"Not yet. It's a little warm in here."

Charlotte was furiously fanning herself with a plate, but Oliver, who was wearing a sport jacket, didn't seem remotely bothered by or even aware of the temperature. This, Tom supposed, was a key to his success: the ability to remain unfazed by physical discomfort. If he was undeterred by a mere global climate crisis, how likely were you to throw him off his guard?

"I reckon," he said, unconvincingly folksy, "there are at least a hundred people here now."

"He's capable of guessing crowd size through some mysterious calculation that comes to him naturally," Charlotte said.

"One of my many useless talents," Oliver said. His attempts at humility always pointed out his perfection.

"This music reminds me of brunch," Charlotte said. "All those wonderful Sunday afternoons at Dorothy's restaurant."

Tom had always loathed brunch, which he considered a meal of expensive, absurdly rich egg dishes you either left unfinished or wished you had. In the period when it was profitable, Dorothy's restaurant had made most of its money from brunch. Despite himself, Tom felt nostalgic for tables of hungover people who'd never heard of the internet or cell phones reading the Sunday *New York Times*.

"For the record," Charlotte said, "I don't believe Cecily's story about being in the library all day, but I can't think of a reason why it might be my business."

Tom was torn between demonstrating loyalty to Cecily and using Charlotte's comment as an opportunity to align himself with her and push his own agenda. "I'm not sure I believe it, either, but she has a right to her privacy."

"Where is she?" Charlotte asked.

"I saw her on the other side of the room talking to some young woman. And by 'young,' I mean in her forties."

"And what is this meeting at Deerpath?"

Given his new knowledge about Cecily's true relationship to these two people, he read meaning into Charlotte's being so inquisitive about all this, but then again, there was nothing new in her desire to be the most informed person in any room. A quick change of subject was in order, and because the band seemed to be taking a break, he figured now was as good a time as any.

"I'm not going to pressure you," he said. "You know that's not my style, but can you give me some indication of what your time line is with Eldridge Johnson? I mean it strictly out of curiosity."

Oliver bristled visibly at this question. "Everyone in this 'friend group' is in regular contact," he said, "I imagine that, somehow or other, word will get to you."

"We're not committed to him," Charlotte said. "Unless he can come up with something a lot better than what he showed us."

"I was impressed," Oliver said. "He has a compelling voice."

This disagreement between them was what Tom hoped to nurture and exploit. "How visible will it be from your living room, Charlotte?"

"There are some things," Oliver said, "you *want* to see."

"And some you don't," Charlotte said. "Especially if you spend more time at home than you spend flying around the world."

Tom saw that Fiona was coming across the room, headed straight for them. There was determination in her walk; she was pitched forward and taking long, purposeful strides. It set her apart from everyone else in the room, and with the billowing top she was wearing, she did, indeed, look like the star of the show. Fleetingly, Tom was flattered by the mere fact that she was about to pay attention to them. So, this was why Dorothy had sought her out to begin with.

"Are there going to be speeches, Fiona?" Charlotte asked, making sure to get in the first word.

"Only a few brief hellos. I've learned that in settings where people are drinking, less is generally more. I promise I won't bore you."

"You couldn't if you tried. I generally stop listening long before boredom sets in. If you have an imagination, you're never bored."

"I'm going to remember that," Fiona said. She actually laid her hand on Charlotte's arm. "I think that's a wonderful point." She turned to Oliver and said, "I'm sending you our business plan, sir. I think you'll find it quite interesting. The potential here is limitless."

"'Limitless' is an awfully big concept," Oliver said. "But I will be happy to take a look. I leave for Johannesburg on Monday. Send it tomorrow, and I'll read it on the plane. But I warn you, Fiona: unlike my wife, I *am* easily bored."

"I'm not worried. The plan is designed to appeal to the discerning eye. I think yours fits that description."

"Something we can agree upon," Oliver said.

Tom was stunned to see that the two were flirting. It was hard to believe Oliver was so desperate to change the subject of the guesthouse that he'd resort to talking even with the likes of Fiona.

"I'm sorry," Tom said. "We were in the middle of a conversation, Fiona."

"Oh? I wouldn't want to intrude. You were so helpful yesterday, burying that animal." She shuddered.

"Before you go," Charlotte said, "I'm curious what you meant when you said that Cecily had a reason for wanting to disappear earlier today."

"Really," Tom said, "I don't think this is the time to get into it. We should let Fiona prepare for her talk."

"I never prepare," Fiona said. "It comes to me."

Tom wondered if this was supposed to sound like a good thing. "Cecily's situation is a family matter," he said.

Fiona laughed at this, a staggered "uhn, uhn, uhn" at the back of her throat. "Oh, yes, it certainly *is* a family matter."

Fiona was a minor power player whose brief moment of glory was behind her. Tom had seen this in architects who'd fallen out of fashion. The framed photo spreads in *AD* were beginning to fade, and the layouts had an antique aesthetic. It was a horrible position to be in, but from the point of view of someone who'd never really had what could be termed a true moment of glory, it was not an especially sympathetic one. Whether or not Fiona had been on *Oprah*, she'd been applauded on certain stages. Now the backseat of her car was filled with old newspapers and open boxes of Corn Flakes. She was reveling in having the upper hand in this situation. Why Dorothy had entrusted any secret to a woman who was incapable of taking in her own groceries was incomprehensible to Tom. Things rarely ended well for people like Fiona, and they usually dragged those close to them down with them. All those fading movie stars tormenting their daughters for the affront of being younger than them.

The trio was back and the guitarist was playing a languid rendition of Joni Mitchell's song about the famous musical festival, the one that still defined the town and the whole spirit of the place, no matter how much change and gentrification had taken hold. Dorothy came over to them with Cecily in tow. "We should make our announcements soon," she said. "I don't want to wait until everyone is ready to leave and antsy."

The drone of conversation was getting louder, and Tom sensed that, soon, it would quiet down as people signaled all at once, in the way they did, that it was time to get on with it.

"We were discussing family matters," Fiona said. "I made the mistake of bringing myself into the discussion. I suppose we should head to the microphone, Dorothy. Lead on."

Tom was furious that Fiona had effectively shut down his discussion with Charlotte and Oliver. He supposed he should applaud her skill. And her tact in leaving them for the podium.

Although, she wasn't there yet.

Fiona left Dorothy standing by the food tables and began her lurch across the room back toward them. Tom was not flattered by her approach this time. She had an ominously determined look in her eyes.

"I'm sorry," Fiona said. "Sometimes, the right thing to do is the most difficult thing to do. I'm sure you can appreciate that, Cecily."

Cecily shrugged and looked at Tom.

"Sometimes," Tom said, "the right thing to do is to remain silent and let other people sort out their lives themselves. It looks like Dorothy is waiting for you." His sister was nervously eyeing them from the buffet table.

"Oh, please," Charlotte said. She drank the rest of her wine. "If you have something to tell us, Fiona, I suggest you do so, instead of all these coded comments back and forth. Frankly, I've started to take offense."

"I know this isn't your wish, Cecily," Fiona said, "but you should know that secrets are just lies with better press agents."

"Personally, I've never had a problem with either," Charlotte said. "But I'm sure Cecily will want to have that phrase crocheted onto a pillow."

Cecily was staring at Fiona, and later, when Tom asked her about it, she said, "I knew what was coming and knew I couldn't stop her."

The trio wound up their last song, and the crowd began to quiet, clearly in anticipation of someone stepping to the microphone to deliver the speeches that were the reason they were all there and the signal that they were almost able to leave.

"What I was referring to earlier was the fact that Cecily might have wandered off this morning because she was delivered a big piece of news last night." Fiona paused, but not long enough for Tom to intervene. "Dorothy told her that Oliver is her father. I think everyone will be better off for knowing. I believe it clarifies everyone's responsibilities."

"What are you *saying*?" Charlotte asked. She thrust her hand out toward Tom and had him grab her glass out of it.

"You're vile," Cecily said to Fiona and headed off into the crowd.

Oliver had a look of strangely focused contempt—not the reaction, if Tom had to guess, that Fiona had been expecting. Charlotte took Oliver's arm as if to steady herself. She looked at Tom with something akin to panic. "Is she *serious*?"

Tom looked at Fiona, trying to gauge which of the many possible responses he might give, and then, seconds later, recognized that he had only one possible response. "Yes," he said, and then, realizing he was speaking too softly to be heard above the din in the room, he spoke more loudly: "Yes. I'm afraid she is, Charlotte."

Charlotte, always eager to find someone to blame for something, said to him, "Did you *know* about this?"

"I learned about it last night."

Charlotte called out to her old college friend, loud and urgent. There was no way Dorothy could mistake what had happened. She was looking at Charlotte with a pleading, apologetic gaze. She leaned back against the banquet table to steady herself and, in doing so, tugged at the tablecloth. A chafing dish got pulled to the floor. The burner under the chafing dish spilled a thin line of flames across the floor. The clatter and crash evoked gasps and then a disconcerting silence. One of the caterers, earning his ten thousand dollars, quickly put out the fire with a bar towel.

That was all the confirmation Charlotte needed. She let out a cry and stormed to the front of the room, clearing a path through the confused and visibly titillated crowd.

Fiona had made her way to the platform and tapped the microphone. "Can you all hear me? It's quite warm in here," she said, as if she were the only one who'd noticed. "Can someone open the doors back there?"

The doors at the rear of the room were opened, and cool, dry air rolled into the space. Oliver handed Tom his drink and said, "I'd better go talk to my wife."

This was the last Tom, or anyone, saw of Oliver and Charlotte before they drove off the next morning, probably sometime near dawn.

The weather had changed, with no rain, no thunder, no lightning at all. Tom was right to have worried about a storm, but as usual, he'd been worrying about the wrong one.

Chapter Twenty-Four

*A*s soon as she and Tom got back to Boston, Cecily messaged Santosh to say the Title IX office had contacted her about a meeting. **Looks like things have moved to the next stage**, she wrote. **Fingers crossed.**

His response, two hours later, was **Finally! Been playing soccer. xx**

She was so desperate to find something positive in his text that she was thrilled by the exclamation point. Then she worried that it expressed annoyance. He hadn't asked for details or specifics, hadn't asked if she was coming back. She ended up crushed by the text. And now, after her afternoon with Victor in Woodstock, Santosh's response mattered more than ever.

The contrast between her life and her boyfriend's was stark: she was being investigated over sexual allegations made by a student; he was out playing soccer. She tried to muster some resentment toward his carefree life, but all she felt was shame. She'd made her own mess and then dragged him into it. He didn't want more information, and she wasn't going to pull him in deeper by giving him more. As for the identity of her father—a word that stuck in her throat—that was another mess, one she could tell him about only in person.

Fiona had betrayed Dorothy's wishes about mentioning nothing about Oliver, but given Charlotte and Oliver's reaction—they abruptly exited and then left for Boston at dawn—it was clear that the message, and not the messenger, was the problem. Cecily wasn't eager to work it out with them. Compared with everything else she was going through, it seemed minor. One step at a time.

Sitting in the window seat in Tom's guest cottage, she made a plan. She'd fly to Chicago Wednesday morning without telling Santosh, rent a car, and drive straight to Deerpath. Molly had agreed to meet her there for moral support and an unbiased view of the proceedings. Santosh didn't need to know how anxious Cecily was about the lurid process. He didn't want to know. Maybe, if things went well, they could celebrate together that night. It was important to believe that, despite everything, events could go in her favor.

On Wednesday morning, she called an Uber. Tom came to help her drag her luggage to the drive. He sighed when the car pulled up the hill, resigned and sad. After he loaded the suitcase into the trunk, he turned to her and wished her good luck. "Call me as soon as you find out anything," he said. "Will you do that?"

She fell into his arms and said, "Please don't worry. You have too much going on here. I don't know if I could stand it if this news about Oliver screwed things up for your project. One more thing I'd never be able to pay you back for."

"It was complicated long before this came to light," he said. "And you're not responsible for any of it. Tell me you know that, and I'll let you go."

She nodded because she did know it, even if, in her heart, she felt the exact opposite.

●

As her plane ascended over Boston, lifting through the clouds, the cabin suddenly filling with sunlight, Cecily realized that for all her skepticism about institutions and all her doubts about her own behavior, she was quietly counting on something good coming from this meeting. She wasn't blameless—she could have done better dealing with Lee—but there was nothing in what she'd done that couldn't be explained. She hoped there was nothing that couldn't be forgiven by the school, even if she couldn't forgive herself.

She pictured herself telling Santosh all her good news and then telling him about her lunch with his mother. They'd drive out to the suburbs and sit down with Neeta and his father. They'd talk through it together.

When she got into her rental car at O'Hare, she pulled down the visor and looked at herself in the mirror. Her face was pale, but she could see the strained optimism in her eyes. A little forced, a little too hopeful, but surely better than the alternative.

Rain appeared from what seemed like a clear sky as she was exiting the airport. The windshield was lashed by it. She turned on the wipers and tried to see through the downpour, but she had to lean forward against the wheel, and even then, it was simply a matter of following the dim lines on the road. When she pulled off the highway at the Deerpath exit, the rain stopped as suddenly as it had started. The weather was as erratic and extreme as her emotions. Maybe the abrupt end of the storm was a good sign.

Deerpath was the kind of suburb she felt she ought to object to on principle. It was too rich, too green, too white. The display of wealth was too showy, and the downtown, with its string of perfectly coordinated Arts and Crafts buildings, was too tidy and symmetrical. Still, there was something irresistible about it. It was the *Pride and Prejudice* of suburbs—you knew real life wasn't so filled with delight, wit, and reciprocated love, but when you were in the middle of it, you couldn't help but be charmed by it and root for a happy ending.

The campus of Deerpath College comprised rows of mansions that had been bought up by the school over decades and added on to as the school became more popular. The newer buildings mixed in were almost shockingly unimaginative and ordinary. They didn't fit with the opulent antique architecture, but they seemed more appropriate for the student body. Many of them came from wealth and knew that they wouldn't have to work too hard to make a living once they got out. Grades would not secure their future—that had been secured by birth. Lee Anderson was an exception, a student from a troubled background who'd earned her scholarship with outstanding grades and near-perfect SAT scores. Her pursuit of Cecily had been born of her hardships and probably the rejection of other students—not that this excused it or the way Cecily had handled it. Still, Cecily suspected she would have responded differently if one of the more typically privileged students from an intact family had made the same advance.

Cecily wore slacks, a men's button-down shirt, and a tailored sport jacket, modest and professional clothes. Pulling into a parking space on campus, she wondered if the androgyny of the outfit had been a miscalculation. Her every move, she realized, would be evaluated through the lens of the allegations against her.

Molly was there already, leaning against a beat-up Prius. She'd dressed for the occasion in what looked like a business suit, although the cut of the jacket—wide shoulders and a nipped waistline—suggested it was from a different period of her life, probably a decade or two earlier. She was carrying the canvas briefcase she always brought to the Daily Grind, and overall, gave the impression of being a capable but disheveled professional. Disheveled or not, Molly's presence put Cecily at ease: she wasn't alone.

"Have you been waiting long?" Cecily asked.

"I gave myself a lot of time," she brayed. "I have a horrible sense of direction and resent being bossed around by a nonperson in an app. A lose-lose situation. Nervous?"

"Not really."

"Good. Best not to show any emotion. I'll take notes and try to keep my big mouth shut. Every school and business has its own process for this, and I'm guessing these folks will follow the college's to the letter. The main thing is, try to answer with as few words as possible. Otherwise, you open up new problems."

"I can't thank you . . ."

Molly cut her off. "Don't try," she shouted. "I'm just the extra pair of ears hearing what you might miss. Plus, I'm an incredibly nosy person who has a morbid fascination with academia."

Cecily had been waiting so many months for this meeting, had been so tense about it for so long, had brought her life so close to the brink of collapse, that she was shocked to feel, as they walked up the steps of the 1890s mansion that housed the Title IX office, tranquility come over her. She passed through the cool, high-ceilinged entryway with the surreal composure of a sleepwalker.

The administrator in the office was an older woman in a cardigan who eyed Cecily and Molly with the suspicion common among people used to dealing with demanding undergraduates. When Molly took charge and announced Cecily, the woman scowled, pulled her cardigan shut, and, without saying a word, called to another office to tell someone she'd arrived. The woman's disapproval seemed like a bad sign: she knew what was coming; these administrators knew everything. When she got off the call, she told them, apropos of nothing, that she'd phoned maintenance three times that day to report the broken lock on one of the back doors, that no one had shown up, and that, door fixed or not, she intended to leave promptly at four thirty.

"I've done my job. Now they have to do theirs. Period. I'm sick of it."

"I don't blame you," Molly said. Her loud voice was effective here in this high-ceilinged room. "If someone breaks in, you can have a clear conscience."

"I'm half hoping someone does. Don't repeat that."

Cecily was not, after all, the reason for the scowling. She was not the center of anyone's universe except her own. The fact that "Katherine" (according to her desk plaque) was sharing this office drama with them made it seem plausible that she knew Cecily had been exonerated by the investigation.

The woman led them into a conference room at the back of the house with a terra-cotta tile floor and an abundance of windows, a conservatory at some point in the house's domestic past. It was a lovely room, although humid and with a loamy smell, as if still filled with potted plants.

"They'll be right with you," she said. "Have a seat anywhere. It's not that I wouldn't stay until five or even six, but I have an eye doctor appointment."

"Emergency?" Molly asked.

This prompted a discussion of Katherine's ocular history and Molly's recent experience with an optometrist. Cecily wasn't capable of this kind of small talk, a fact that, at the moment, seemed to her like a character flaw.

Cecily chose a seat on one side of an oblong table, and Molly sat next to her. The lawn was shimmering in the sun after that sudden downpour. In the distance, two students were tossing a frisbee back and forth. Cecily stared at them longingly, wishing she was doing anything but this. A door behind her opened, and she turned to see her interlocutors entering, carrying notepads and laptops and looking so bright and cheerful, this might have been a meeting for the passing of papers on the purchase of a condo.

She followed Molly's lead and stood to greet them.

Hands were shaken and introductions made. The woman was Nancy, and the man Brian. They were both disarmingly convivial, asking the two women if they'd been caught in the rain, if they'd like anything to drink, if they'd seen the extraordinary sunset the other night. So normal, even if they mostly looked at Molly when they spoke. Everyone sat, Brian and Nancy side by side, directly opposite them. They opened their laptops and arranged their papers with routine precision, as if they did this ten times a day. Maybe they did, for all Cecily knew.

There was something prim in Nancy's wardrobe: a dark print dress with half sleeves, a high neckline, and a bit of a prairie feel. Probably, it was the recommended attire for someone in her profession. It made her look like a clerk for a conservative judge. She couldn't have been thirty yet and oozed eager ambition to climb this particular ladder. She reminded Cecily of a friend of Dorothy's who'd alienated everyone she knew by becoming involved in Amway, but had made so much money doing it, she was widely envied from afar.

Brian was probably closer to forty, but was so well put together, his age was irrelevant. He took off his sport jacket, draped it carefully over the back of his chair, and folded up the cuffs of his shirt a couple of times with military precision. Something about his trim shape and tight fade screamed ex-Marine. He had the muscular forearms of a man who got up at sunrise to be at the gym before work. His smooth skin gleamed, and, to her horror, she found herself wondering what his chest looked like.

"Are you sure you don't want anything to drink?" he asked. She felt it was less a question than a cue to change her mind.

"Water would be great," Molly said.

Nancy, the junior partner here, got up to get it. "One for me, too," Brian said, all smiles, but still reminding Nancy who was in charge.

"Before we get started," he said, "I want to make sure everything is clear to you about this stage of the process, so, if you have any questions at all, at any point, no matter what, jump right in."

"Don't encourage me," Molly said. "I'm endlessly curious."

"A good person to have on board," he said and then turned to Cecily.

"For the moment," she said, "I think I'm set."

The waters were placed in front of them and then, with a good deal more reverence, in front of Brian.

"As you know, the initial stage of the investigation was just completed," he said. "What we're going to do today is ask some questions, basic facts. If there's anything you disagree with or remember differently, tell us. It's important to us that we have all the facts confirmed by you."

"I understand," Cecily said.

"Great." He peered into the computer and made some complaint about the Wi-Fi connection in the room. He had the kind of bulky, muscular physique that's accentuated by modest clothing rather than masked by it. As for his voice, it had the low tones of an actor who's always cast as the improbably seductive man next door who washes his car shirtless multiple times a week. He looked at Nancy, indicating that she should launch the proceedings.

"We'll be taking notes," Nancy said, "but we're not recording the conversation." She took the top sheets off the stack of paper in front of her, double-checked them, and slid them and a pen across the table. "If you wouldn't mind signing this, attesting to the fact that you're not recording it, either."

Everything had suddenly become much more serious. Molly, pen perched over a legal pad, settled into silence.

Brian and Nancy went over what turned out to be a long list of questions establishing a chronology. Cecily was impressed. They were assembling an immense puzzle and wanted to make sure they first had all the pieces laid out on the table. Professionalism was a beautiful thing, even when it was being used against you.

The course had originally been planned as a seminar. When was the change made to list it as a lecture? How many students had attempted to enroll? Were some turned away? The class had been capped at fifty, and Lee Anderson was the fifty-first student enrolled. Correct?

It was the first time Lee's name had been mentioned, and it felt as if the temperature in the room had been turned up by a degree.

"We need to remember that Cecily, like most professors," Molly said loudly, "is under pressure for large enrollment numbers."

"We are aware of that," Brian said, but without irritation.

How many office hours did she typically hold each week? Did students have to sign up, or could they come unannounced? On average, how many students came per week? Did she require an office visit from all her students?

As they zeroed in on this topic, Cecily realized that all this was the opening shot of the movie with the camera circling Manhattan and then gradually zooming in on a particular borough, neighborhood, street, building, apartment within the building, room within the apartment. All leading to the close-up of Lee. Brian was the director, and almost all the questions came from him in his pleasantly louche drawl. Molly's interjections—clearly, she'd done some homework about the department—were greeted with polite responses that didn't deter Cecily's questioners from their laid-out plan.

"On average, how often did Lee Anderson come to your office?" Brian asked, head tilted benignly.

"Initially, maybe once a week?"

"And then, after the first weeks, she began to come more often?"

It was obvious they had this information, so Cecily decided it was best to state the worst. "At some point, she began coming after every class. Then she also began dropping by on days when we didn't have class."

With their different styles and ages, Brian and Nancy were a surprisingly effective team. They looked at her as she spoke with a practiced lack of reaction. She strongly suspected that if she'd been describing crimes against humanity, their faces would have been equally unreadable. Nancy typed into her laptop as Cecily spoke, and Brian made notes on the printed sheets before him.

Brian commented that, in addition to these visits, Lee had begun sending Cecily text messages and calling her by early October. There was a slight lift at the end of his comment, indicating that it wasn't exactly a question, just a fact he wanted confirmed.

"She did," Cecily said. Unable to stop herself, she added, "I know I should have told her not to, but I was afraid I might hurt her feelings. I thought it was less likely to escalate if I just answered briefly and moved on."

Nancy's face was impassive. Brian nodded and smiled. "I understand," he said. "It's hard to know exactly how to respond sometimes." Cecily desperately wanted his approval. He was not a man who made mistakes.

"Again," Molly said, "the department encourages giving access and individual attention to students. It's part of the evaluation process."

"To be clear," Brian said, "we're not here to judge motives or intentions. We want to establish facts as accurately as possible. That's the purpose of the meeting: to have you confirm or contradict everything on a factual level. What's trickier is that we can't assess things like motives or rationale. That's all subjective." He shrugged his impressive shoulders and tossed her a crumb: "I know it can be frustrating, but in the end, it's fair to everyone. No one wants to judge anyone's thoughts. It's all a matter of actions. Of what actually happened."

Cecily was reminded of a hiking trip in the Sierras she'd gone on with Santosh and another couple. She'd been dreading it for fear she'd be the slowest and weakest hiker, but the first few miles had been so beautiful and easy, she was lulled into thinking it was going to be a breeze. A true walk in the park. Then, suddenly, with one turn in the trail, everything changed, and for the next four hours, the ascent was rocky, steep, and terrifying.

The proceedings had officially rounded that turn.

She had a desperate urge to describe her motives, her intentions, but she immediately saw the merits in the route they were insisting upon, even if it made all her decisions—her mistakes, let's face it—look worse. She gazed at these steady professionals with admiration. They were so exacting and precise—Nancy typing without looking down at the laptop—that Cecily was lulled into submission. Even Molly seemed to see the merit in this process. She continued to scrawl notes but interjected less. Cecily sat back in her chair, almost sleepy, as the questions came more quickly.

Had she met with Lee after five p.m. in her office?

"Yes. There were a few times when she showed up as I was getting ready to leave."

And she'd let her in?

"I did," she said, holding back her concerns about Lee's vulnerability, her single mom, her lack of engagement with her peers; her fears that Lee was a person who'd faced rejection starting at an early age. None of that was relevant to the bare recitation of facts they wanted. The more they asked, the worse her own behavior sounded to her.

Lee had sent Cecily multiple emails weekly, sometimes daily?

"Yes, she did."

There was no record of Cecily's trying to discourage this behavior. Was that right?

"If I didn't respond right away, she sent more, asking why I hadn't written back. It seemed easier just to respond as briefly as possible."

So, she didn't tell Lee her emails were inappropriate?

"Not in so many words, but I tried . . ." It exhausted her to think about all the ridiculously subtle and ultimately ineffectual ways she'd tried to signal Lee not to email so much: "Super busy" and "Working on deadline" and "Rushing to meeting." All of which probably ended up creating even more intimacy in Lee's mind. No point in mentioning any of it here and now. They'd read the emails themselves. "No, no, I didn't tell her that."

Eventually, they got to that late afternoon in November. The knock on her office door, the fact that she was getting ready to leave, the dinner invitation from Lee.

And did she ask her to leave?

"I did. I believe I told her to leave."

Reliving all of this and beginning to approach the moment when Lee had kissed her, the moment when her life started to come undone, Cecily found herself breathing more quickly and was sure her face was flushed.

And then she'd had physical contact with the student?

"Yes. I couldn't prevent it. She approached me as if she were leaving the office. It wasn't something I initiated. It wasn't something I was able to stop. It happened so quickly."

Nancy's typing indicated that she'd taken down only the relevant portion of her answer: *Yes.* She looked at Brian and then at Molly. So appalled at Cecily's answer she couldn't make eye contact? Maybe Cecily was reading too much into the young woman's conservative outfit.

Cecily had talked to a colleague as she was leaving campus that evening?

The thoroughness of their investigation was impressive. She saw Melissa Feldman now, in her snow-covered hat and puffy coat. She'd never liked Cecily; that was apparent. Another irrelevancy.

"Yes, I did."

And she hadn't said anything to Professor Feldman about the incident?

"I was so shook up by it, I wasn't sure what to do."

So, she hadn't mentioned it?

"No. I didn't."

"Probably not something you were comfortable disclosing about a student," Molly suggested.

Cecily tried to agree with her, but really, that hadn't been the reason, so she merely nodded.

For the first time since they'd begun—and Cecily had no idea if that was ten minutes or an hour ago—Nancy interjected. "We have it that you told your colleague your meetings with students had ended hours earlier. Is that right?"

Cecily was genuinely baffled by this question, not because she didn't remember the exchange exactly, but because she couldn't believe Melissa Feldman did. Melissa had always struck her as someone who listened to you while gazing off into the distance, waiting for the moment when she could top you with her own war stories.

"Yes," she said. "I believe that is what I told her." She paused and was about to explain herself, her rationale, but she saw that there was no point. That wasn't the information they wanted from her. She'd lied; that was the fact they were looking for. Nancy smiled faintly as she typed, not with malice, but with the pleasure of having had her information confirmed.

"We didn't find any indication that you reported it to anyone," Brian said.

It now seemed so simple. Why hadn't she? Unable to voice her motives, she began to doubt them herself. She'd been an idiot for not talking to her chair about this, preferably as soon as it happened. Most appropriately, she should have called this very office, spoken with these two professionals, who would have made a report and helped her out. Stupidly, she'd thought she was protecting Lee, but maybe it had been a misguided attempt to protect herself.

"And you gave the student an A for the class." Brian's tone, for the first time, betrayed surprise.

"I did."

"Is Deerpath attempting to do anything about grade inflation?" Molly roared. "Just out of curiosity."

"We're not involved in academic affairs," Brian said. "The student didn't turn in a final paper? Not even at a later date?"

"She did not. Her work up to that point had been so strong, had been so much stronger than any other student in the class, I couldn't justify giving her anything less."

"But it says on your syllabus," Nancy said, flipping through the pages in her folder, finding one, and pulling it out, "it says the final paper counts for . . . forty percent of the grade?"

"Sometimes, I don't stick strictly to the math if there's one disappointment among otherwise outstanding work."

"Fair enough," Brian said. He smiled broadly. "I'd be happy to have some of my disappointments overlooked."

This was such an obvious attempt at congeniality, a desire to lighten the mood, she felt like thanking him.

"Tell me about it," Molly said.

The sun was lower in the sky than it had been when they'd come in. She didn't dare sneak a glance at her watch, but it was probably safe to assume it was well past four thirty and that Katherine in her cardigan was now having her eyes examined. It calmed her to think about this woman, gazing at a chart, still obsessing about the work order, completely uninterested in what was happening to her.

Finally, Brian and Nancy looked at each other, silently conferring, probably making sure there was nothing they'd missed.

"I think that about covers it," Brian said.

What clear, sincere brown eyes. A man of integrity and honesty. He was the kind of person you wanted to see in a pilot's uniform as you boarded an airplane. "We appreciate your openness in speaking with us today," he said. "We know it's been a difficult period. If you have any questions for us or anything you'd like to clarify, please contact Nancy or me. You have the email addresses?"

She would and she did.

"Do you have a sense of when we'll hear about a . . . verdict?" Molly asked. Cecily was touched by the "we."

Brian looked at Nancy again. Maybe she was the designated hitter for questions like this, the one who kept up on scheduling matters.

"It should be within the next few weeks," she said.

As they were packing up and had reverted to the usual inane niceties, Nancy said, "Oh, we do have one other question." She shook her head, berating herself for her mistake. "I'm so sorry we forgot to bring it up before." She opened her laptop again.

Brian nodded, remembering. "She's very good," he told Cecily. "She'll be running the department soon."

"We need to confirm that you've had no contact with the student since the investigation was launched," Nancy said.

Cecily was sorry she'd forgotten about that, too. "I'm afraid I have. I was catching a plane to Boston, and she came up in the airport and started speaking to me."

They nodded and made notes. The sound of Nancy softly clicking the computer keys was satisfying. ASMR heaven.

"And you responded?" Brian asked.

"I didn't see any way not to. I couldn't just walk away. I was afraid I'd upset her and that things would escalate. I saw her sitting in a restaurant when I first got to the airport. I quickly turned to get away, but somehow or other, she saw me. She accused me of ignoring her."

Nancy nodded sympathetically. "So, you're confirming that you have spoken with her."

"Yes," Cecily said. "I am. I have. I did mention a couple of times that I wasn't supposed to speak with her. She told me she was thinking about dropping out, and I told her I thought that would be a mistake, considering her academic excellence."

"You gave her academic advice," Brian said. Not questioning but prompting.

"Only in the sense that . . . Yes, yes, I did."

Nancy closed her laptop with a click, and Brian looked across the table, smiling broadly. "I think, this time, we really are finished. Agreed, Nancy?"

"Agreed," she said.

They were both visibly relieved. Now they could go home. Molly stuffed her messy legal pad into her briefcase. She, too, seemed relieved.

"That storm over the weekend was something, wasn't it?" Brian said. He stood and slipped on his jacket.

"I've been off visiting family," Cecily said. "I missed it. Although, come to think of it, we did have storms where I was, too."

"Anyplace fun?" Brian asked.

"Woodstock, New York. Home of the music festival."

"Oh, I've always wanted to go there," Nancy said. "My grandparents met at the festival."

"I've heard *that* story before," Molly said, a tiny dig that didn't seem to land.

In a crazy and—she knew—pointless desire to humanize herself, to appear a little less monstrous, Cecily said, "My mother moved there. She wanted to get herself back to the garden."

Neither Brian nor Nancy seemed to get the reference.

Chapter Twenty-Five

"*That was a disaster,*" Cecily said.

Molly tossed her briefcase into the back of her Prius and took off her jacket. "You didn't need to tell them at the end about giving the student advice, but otherwise, you handled yourself well. I have to put in another couple of hours on a project. Call me later for a postmortem."

When Molly had driven off, Cecily gazed out the windshield of the rented car, across the lush green of the campus. There was no way to spin the preceding seventy minutes as positive. If she'd been in the place of Brian and Nancy, she'd have brought down the gavel, declared the case closed, and asked to have Professor Kemp escorted off campus. Even Molly had seemed disgusted—unless Cecily was reading too much into her departure. The idea of showing up at home and brightly giving Santosh good news was officially dead.

She didn't have a plan B.

She drove through the campus with an ache, feeling as if she were seeing it for the last time. That was improbable, but self-pity has its place sometimes.

As she approached the cheerful, welcoming Arts and Crafts downtown of Deerpath, she began reliving the interview. It was like looking into a store window and seeing herself reflected as others, Neeta included, saw her. Not a pretty picture. Immature. Inexperienced.

Unprofessional. Underneath the veil of stability, unstable. Her heart began to race, and she was certain she was going to burst into tears.

She pulled onto a side street and parked under some trees that were arched out over the road, creating an allée. She recalled all the times she'd walked through this little suburban downtown on her way to and from the train. She saw the person she'd been for the past couple of years as remarkably naïve and innocent or, to put it another way, stupid. She'd been happy; in love with Santosh; excited about her teaching, the publication of her book, the possibilities for writing another. For the first time, she'd felt truly at home, certain that she was settled into a life she'd created.

Slight miscalculation.

Whatever frail optimism she'd had on the plane this morning disintegrated. It would be comforting to believe that it was all because of a rigged system or the overzealous investigation conducted or overseen by those two earnest officials, but the process had only underscored her own questionable actions. The time line shone a light on every moment when she could have done something differently and produced a better outcome. If not for Lee, at least for herself. As Molly predicted, Brian and Nancy had played their parts impeccably.

She heard the trees above her dripping rain onto the roof of the car from the downpour of almost two hours earlier. A soft, slow drip with the regular beat of a metronome or a healthy heart. She pulled herself together and, in doing so, realized she hadn't eaten since grabbing some fruit at the airport in Boston all those hours earlier.

Deerpath wasn't exactly a hot spot for five-star cuisine (so she'd been told), but it did have a lot of pretty and expensive restaurants where locals went for dress-up dinners. There was one across the street, its front entrance banked by urns overflowing with colorful pansies and potato vines. There was something about the décor and aesthetic of all the local restaurants that seemed designed to appeal to women. Florals and pastels dominated. The commercial life of a suburb like this catered almost exclusively to wives. It was a throwback to the 1950s. The men took the train into the city daily and lived the most vital hours of their lives there. In theory, she risked bumping into someone from school by going in, but the risk was minimal. Few faculty members could afford to live in Deerpath.

The hostess seated her at a pleasant table in front, beside a window thrown open to the sidewalk. Strangely, she had no appetite, so she ordered a glass of wine and a salad. At some point, she was going to have to tell Santosh she was back. When she was warmed by the first sip of wine, she texted, testing the waters: **Hey you. What plans do you have for tonight?**

The waitress set a plate in front of her, rotated it twice until the lettuce was facing the right direction, and then, with the overdone formality that was meant to imply good service and satisfy the expectations of the ladies who lunched, came close to curtseying as she slipped away. Couldn't the waitress tell Cecily was a degenerate who was about to be unemployed?

She told herself it meant nothing that Santosh hadn't responded by the time she finished the salad, nor by the time she finished her glass of wine and had ordered another. She was halfway through her second glass when the room began to spin. She wasn't used to drinking. The forced, phony elegance of the restaurant, which had been soothing at first, had begun to grate. She tossed back the wine, paid the check, and stepped out to the sidewalk, unsure of her next move.

She decided to text Santosh again, this time more bluntly: **I'll be back home soon. Sooner than you think. You'd better make the bed and get rid of anyone in it.**

She sat in her car waiting. Still nothing.

She drove onto the highway, lulled into a trancelike state by the wine and the insistent flow of traffic. Without being fully conscious of what she was doing, she took the exit to Santosh's parents' suburb. *Oh, so this is where I'm going,* she thought, almost as if she were in a driverless car being delivered to a destination someone else had decided to send her.

She pulled up at the curb in front of the house. It was twilight. There was something soft and reassuring about the light, warm and golden at this hour, the most beautiful hour of the day. Whenever she and Santosh came here, she found herself nervously adjusting her hair and straightening her clothes before going into the house. "You look great," Santosh would always tell her. Now she realized she'd been trying to make herself more presentable for Neeta, as if all it would take to earn Neeta's acceptance was a straightened collar and a precise part in her hair. Today, all bets were off. She didn't care how she looked or if Neeta smelled alcohol on her breath.

She strode up the walk, turning on the motion-sensing lights as she went.

Neeta opened the door and, looking neither surprised nor unhappy, said, "Well, Cecily. This is certainly unexpected. I thought you were in Boston."

"I was," Cecily said. "I just got back a few hours ago. There's something I want to tell you. I was hoping I could come in."

Neeta looked behind her, as if afraid someone deeper inside the house was observing them. She had on jeans, tight and flattering to her hips and long legs, sandals, and an embroidered top that hung to her waist. Her hair was pulled back. Cecily had never seen her look so casual or completely at ease. She opened the door wider and stepped aside to let Cecily in. Her toenails were painted an almost shockingly beautiful shade of red, and, for a second, Cecily was tempted to compliment her.

She led Cecily through to the library at the back of the house, the room where she and Akhil watched television, when they did. The house was warm, and there was a particular smell of cooking that Cecily associated with soup.

Neeta closed the door to the library, indicated the sofa, and took a seat in an upright chair opposite. Cecily sank into the cushions. Her slouched posture made her feel like a child slumped into a corner in the presence of a strict teacher.

"What is it that brings you here?" Neeta asked.

This was a reasonable question, and to find out the answer, Cecily was going to have to start talking. "I had a meeting at school today. About my case. They've finished one stage of the investigation."

"I see. You don't look especially happy. I hope that doesn't mean things went badly." She said this with what sounded like detached but genuine empathy. It's always easier to have sympathy for a person once you know they've been defeated.

"It wasn't conclusive, one way or the other," Cecily said. "If I had to guess, I'd say things aren't likely to go in my favor."

Neeta crossed her legs and folded her hands on her lap, very much the pose of a nonjudgmental doctor listening to gruesome symptoms. "I'm sorry to hear that. Perhaps your assumptions will be proven wrong."

"Perhaps. In any case, that isn't what I came to tell you." Up to this moment, Cecily couldn't have said what she had come to discuss with Neeta. Now it was abundantly clear. "I came to tell you that while I was visiting my mother, she told me who my father is."

Neeta seemed no more surprised by this than she'd seemed by Cecily's arrival. "That must have been interesting for you," she said. "So, she has been less than truthful to you all these years?"

"I'm sure she had her reasons for what she did. It turns out I've known him all my life. He's a very successful man. He works in international banking. I've always thought of him as ruthless, but he's never been unkind to me."

"There's usually an element of ruthlessness in highly effective men. Or what's perceived as ruthlessness. Akhil is an exception: he's both effective and principled. No ruthlessness in him."

"That's true. But he has you. You're a good team."

Neeta smiled in a sly, genuine way, not, Cecily was relieved to note, offended. "I'm not really ruthless, just determined. There's a difference."

Cecily realized that, against all odds, she and Neeta were having a reasonable conversation. Neeta had no malice toward her and didn't seem disturbed by the fact that she was back in Chicago and sitting in her library. It was the kind of adult talk Cecily had always wished she could have with her mother. "I have a feeling," she said, "he's someone you might approve of. My biological father, I mean."

Neeta was pointing and flexing her feet and looking at them as if trying to see if she needed another pedicure. (She didn't.) She didn't show any sign that she'd heard Cecily say this, but then she said, "I very well might approve of him. In the unlikely event I ever meet him. I'm touched that you're telling me this, Cecily, but I'm not sure why you think any of it is relevant to me."

"I've always suspected you were baffled by my family, as if you didn't believe what I was telling you about my father. It turns out you had good reason. I wanted to clear it up."

Neeta looked at Cecily with her hands still tightly folded in her lap. "And what is it you imagine, now that you've told me? That I'll see you in a different light?"

"I'm a realist," Cecily said. "I accept that that's too much to ask. Still, it matters to me that you know."

Neeta stood up and went to the window. She adjusted the blinds so that she could look out on the back of the house, or perhaps check to see what was going on in the neighbor's yard. She turned and folded her arms over her chest, secure and, as she'd said, determined. "When we had lunch, I told you my concerns for my son. About the way your professional problems will hurt him. You told me now things didn't go well at your meeting today. So, you think this news of your father's identity will compensate? That suddenly I'll welcome you into my family?"

She was waiting for an answer, but Cecily was unable to give one, aside from a whispered "No, of course not."

"You told me that you'd leave town until a decision was reached in your investigation. If I'm understanding what you've told me, no decision has been reached. And yet, you're here."

Cecily felt as if she were once again being questioned by Brian and Nancy. There was no point in discussing her motivation or her intentions; Neeta wanted the facts. "That's true."

"You've come to reassert your claim on Santosh."

"I never said I had a claim on him. I'm only saying I've been in love with him for over two years. I still am. I've hated being away from him. I feel as if I've lost a crucial part of my life."

Neeta looked at her with a striking lack of emotion that chilled Cecily. And only moments before, she'd felt closer to her than she ever had. "If that's the case, then I feel it's my duty to tell you, for your own good, that Santosh has met someone else. Here. At this house. Over dinner. While you were out of town."

Cecily had a realization, like when you hear a few bars of music and recognize what it's from. This, she saw, was what she'd feared all along: that Neeta had been motivated by a desire to get her out of the way so she could introduce Santosh to someone else. Even so, she didn't know if she believed her. Even if what she was saying was true, she didn't believe Santosh would suddenly throw her over like that. No matter how foolish she'd been. Look at what had happened to her in Woodstock, how meeting Victor had confirmed to her how committed she was to Santosh. Yes, she worried more and more when her texts were unanswered and her calls went to voice mail, but Santosh had never been glued to his phone.

"How could you say that to me?" Her voice was a soft, indistinct murmur.

Neeta frowned and said, with undisguised annoyance, "Please speak up, dear, so I can hear what you're saying."

The "dear" was what cut her the deepest. She was so insignificant to Neeta that she could refer to her with an endearment and have it mean nothing. Thinking this, Cecily found her voice. "I said," she articulated carefully, "'How could you?' You don't care about my case at Deerpath, do you? You used it as an excuse to get me out of the way so you could introduce Santosh to someone you had in mind for him all along."

"You told me what you came to tell me, Cecily. Your tone is rude. I'd like you to leave before you make things worse for yourself."

"How much worse could they get for me, Neeta?" It was the first time Cecily had used her name in that way, as if speaking to an equal. It made her feel stronger and more confident. "I'm on the verge of losing everything. How much worse could it get?"

Neeta shrugged. "If that's how you feel, continue."

"You've never liked me, not from the very beginning. You've always thought I was bad for Santosh, that I was amoral or corrupting him or using him somehow. You knew you couldn't say that to him, so you waited for the right moment, when there was something specific you could point to. You must have been thrilled when your friend told you about my problems at school. The accusations. The investigation. You had something concrete you could point to that I'd done. That, once and for all, disqualified me."

"You look as if you're going to cry. For your own dignity, I suggest you leave before you do. I can't imagine we have a lot more to say to each other." She went to a small glass door beside the sofa that opened onto the patio in the backyard.

Because she was beyond caring about almost everything at this point, she looked at Neeta with her new confidence and chilly feeling of being beaten down. "You know what the saddest part of this is?"

"I think there's a lot to choose from."

"I admire you. I wish I were more like you."

"Then we're parting on a good note." Neeta swept her hand to the patio, in command. And yet, she looked a little pale and shaken. Maybe she had some regrets after all.

As Cecily was leaving, the library door opened. Santosh was standing there, his mouth agape.

"Cecily? What? What are you doing here?"

There was no joy or excitement in his face. It felt almost as if he'd caught her breaking and entering. Maybe he had.

Chapter Twenty-Six

*T*he streets of the suburbs at this time of evening were pleasantly empty. Come to think of it, Cecily had never been here when they weren't empty, give or take the occasional car with darkened windows gliding past. After the rain of the afternoon, the air was fresh, almost like a summer evening when a heat wave has been replaced by a new weather system. Still, summer seemed so far away and completely unimaginable. She couldn't predict what state her career would be in or, after this afternoon, her relationship.

Santosh, like so many people of their generation, had a deep, aching nostalgia for his childhood. It was something Cecily admired without being able to fully understand it. Her goal had always been to move on and forget. He'd once taken her for a long walk around this neighborhood, pointing out houses and streets that had meant something to him as a child. His grade school. The house of his best friend. The place where he'd gotten into a fight with a classmate after being taunted with incoherent slurs about his family. Such was Santosh's optimism that even that last story had been presented as a triumphant experience, despite the racism and the fact that he'd needed two stitches on his lip. That walk had been early in their relationship, six months in. They'd been holding hands and leaning against each other the entire time.

They were not holding hands now.

Back in the library, he'd looked at Neeta and asked her if she was all right, as if his main role were to protect his mother. Cecily couldn't unsee it. She resented him for that and loved him for it equally. She had to admire his instinct to take care of the woman who was such a fierce protector of him. It made her feel she'd been right to go to Boston without telling him what had happened between Neeta and her. It was a horrible burden always to see both sides of every issue, especially because she usually assigned more validity to the side opposing her.

"I just don't understand," he said, his voice tinged with anger. "Why wouldn't you tell me you were coming back?"

"I texted," she said feebly.

"From here. An hour ago."

Something that had seemed perfectly logical twenty-four hours ago was now impossible to explain. Just like her behavior with Lee Anderson. She gave it a try. "Please," she said. "Don't try to make sense of it. I can't explain it logically. Look at it through my eyes. It's the most shameful thing that's ever happened to me, and I can't stand having you see me in the middle of it. I can't stand dragging you into it."

"Instead, you came here to tell my mother about it?"

It was strange how a person's entire appearance and demeanor could change over the course of a couple of weeks. Santosh's face looked leaner, more sharply defined than she remembered. If possible, he looked even more handsome and a bit older, as if he'd matured into this new role of responsible son. As she walked beside him, she felt wary, afraid of him for the first time in their relationship.

"Do you respect me?" he asked. "Even a little?"

"I love you," she said. "I've loved you since the first time I saw you. I felt as if we belonged together. Like we'd always known each other."

Santosh stopped walking. It took her a moment to realize this, and when she did, she was a few feet in front of him. When she looked back, he was raking his hair off his forehead with his fingers, as if in distress. She wanted to run to him, throw her arms around him, but she found she couldn't. His eyes were lit by an anger she'd never seen in him before. He didn't look like his usual adolescent self but, as he'd predicted so many times, had traces of his father's face.

"So, that explains why you treat me like I'm your fucking kid brother."

"I've never done that," she said.

"You have!" he shouted. "What's wrong with me that you thought you couldn't trust me? What is it, Cecily? Is that really how messed up this relationship is?"

"Don't say that," she said.

"Why didn't you tell me?"

"I thought if it went well, if it was all behind us, I could call and surprise you, and we'd go out and celebrate. It was a fantasy, I know. A stupid one."

"I don't mean about today. I mean why didn't you tell me you had lunch with my mother?" A car slowed as it went past them. Anyone would see they were a couple having a fight. "Yes, yes," he said. "She told me. Did you really think she wouldn't? I came out here for dinner a few days ago, and I told them how upset I was about your leaving. She told me. Maybe she thought it would make me feel better, but it didn't. It made me feel like you don't trust me, you don't respect me, you don't think of us as equals."

"When have I not treated you like an equal?"

"When you decided on your own how to deal with my mother. As if I wouldn't have sided with you? As if we wouldn't have talked it out with them. Together."

He was so much more optimistic than she was about negotiating with Neeta. Then again, he knew her so much better. He walked up to Cecily and put his hands on her face. "You see why I'm so upset, don't you?" he said quietly. He hugged her, and she felt herself melting into him.

He was wearing a white T-shirt that, in the golden, early evening light was almost luminescent. She smelled laundry detergent, a highly scented brand Neeta favored, coming off his clothes. How much time had he been spending out here? Maybe what his mother had said about him seeing someone else was true.

He leaned back, putting her at arm's length again. "I know it's been bad for you," he said. "For months. I get it. But if you can't tell me this, something so important, how am I supposed to trust anything you do tell me? Why wouldn't I think there's a lot more you're keeping from me? Explain that to me, will you?"

She wondered where this Santosh had suddenly come from, this man who seemed older and wiser and more mature than she'd ever known him to be. It had happened so quickly, or else she'd never accurately seen him before.

"I wish I had a good answer for you," she said.

"I didn't even believe her at first. About the lunch. And now, the first time I see you, you're pulling some crazy stunt, coming out here to my parents' house. I don't even know you anymore. You see that, don't you?"

"Funny," she said. "Standing here with you, I feel as if I don't know myself, either."

And then it occurred to her that because she'd told Neeta, she had to tell him about Oliver. The story came out in a garbled fashion, mixing the events of the afternoon party and Fiona's announcement. She felt as if Oliver's name was buried by the time she revealed it. She wasn't sure what she'd been expecting Santosh to do in response to hearing this: Throw his arms around her again? Congratulate her? As an indication of how hurt he was about all this, he said only, "Secrecy obviously runs in your family."

"I guess we all have secrets," she said. "Your mother told me you met someone. That you've been seeing someone."

He looked at her with his mouth slightly open and shook his head. It wasn't a denial of what she'd said but apparent disgust that she'd said it.

"My father's getting an award tonight. There's a dinner. I'm staying here for that and sleeping over. Tomorrow, I go to L.A. early for a couple of weeks. It's easier to get to O'Hare from here. We're working on a project with a film studio. A tie-in with an action movie. It's major. It could change everything for the company. Exactly what we've been pushing for all along."

"So, that's the secret project? I'm so happy for you. It's wonderful."

"There are a couple of hurdles still, but it's looking very good. It's a big deal, Cecily."

"Weren't you going to tell me?" She looked at him, pleading, wishing his hands were still on her shoulders.

"This trip was just confirmed today. Anyway, since I thought you were in Boston, I didn't think it would matter. You're not in a great position to complain about someone holding back information."

There was no response to this. Secrets and press agents, or whatever Fiona had said.

"You can stay at the apartment while I'm gone," he said, "but we have to talk when I get back."

She felt as if she'd been punched in the gut. "Santosh, what are you saying?"

"I'm saying we have to talk. I don't know how I feel about anything right now. I have to focus on this project. It's what I've been working toward for years, and I can't let this screw everything up. It's not just my work at stake; it's the whole team's. I'm saying we should take a break for a couple of weeks."

"I thought we just had one."

"That was on your terms," he said. He did her the supreme kindness of kissing her forehead. "This one's on mine."

Having said that, he wandered off. She watched his dazzling T-shirt float down the street and into the darkness, like a pale ghost. Now what? She wasn't even entirely sure how to get back to her rented car except to follow Santosh at a safe, discreet distance.

Chapter Twenty-Seven

*A*bout forty minutes after Cecily had left for the airport, Tom heard a car crunching up the drive. He watched as Charlotte's Mercedes nudged its way to a stop. He was in Cecily's cottage, performing the melancholy ritual of collecting used towels and bedding and emptying the fridge of the few things she'd left. He was so sad about her leaving, facing some portion of her fate, that he was happy for the arrival of anyone, even Charlotte.

No one, including Dorothy, had heard from her or Oliver after Fiona made her announcement. Tom had half expected to hear them squabbling in their room that night, but there was only silence. That was a surprise, even given the size of the house. He hated to think what their three-and-a-half-hour drive home was like early Sunday morning.

Charlotte emerged from her car looking unusually subdued. For once, she wasn't talking. Even from a distance, he could see that her jaw was set, as if she were grinding her teeth.

He went out to greet her. "I'm sorry to say you've just missed Cecily," he said. "She left less than an hour ago."

Charlotte sighed but didn't seem especially surprised. "I suspected as much. I called her a few times, but she never picked up. I behaved badly. Although, let's face it, my bad behavior pales in comparison to Oliver's and Dorothy's. He left for Johannesburg the day after we got back, or I'd have insisted he come over here himself."

How Charlotte maintained the fiction that she had a significant influence over her husband was a mystery to Tom. The closer he observed long-term relationships, the more apparent it became that they were usually based on repeating the exact same patterns and expecting totally different outcomes. Madness, in other words.

"He does want to talk with her," Charlotte said. "The trip couldn't be helped."

"I don't understand how he travels as much as he does."

"The alternative is spending more time with me. Do the math. Can we go into the cottage? I've never looked at it closely before."

"I can claim only partial responsibility for it," Tom said. "It was built in collaboration with Cecily."

"Obviously, that's why I want to see it."

Once inside, she strolled slowly, opening a closet and a dresser drawer, apparently looking for clues to Cecily's tastes and habits, things that might connect her more clearly to Oliver, Tom guessed. She sat in the window seat and pulled out a few of the books, examining the spines and flipping through the pages.

"Are these hers?"

"I bought them for her recently, but they're all books she loved as a teenager."

"Advanced reader," Charlotte said, putting *David Copperfield* back on the shelf.

"Lots of schoolkids read that," Tom said. "Or they did. Who knows now?" He had less and less awareness of current trends as he aged, but as compensation, his ignorance bothered him less.

"I couldn't get Nolan to read anything. Comic books, but even those had to be force-fed."

Nolan had been an impatient, unfocused child and teenager who rarely sat still long enough to open a book, never mind read one. The comparisons between the two, which had been going on since childhood, were clearly ratcheting up in light of the new information.

"When is she coming back?" Charlotte asked.

"I have no idea. I'm wondering if she'll come back at all."

Charlotte got up and did more investigating. She pulled the hinged desktop down from the wall and ran her hands along the surface.

"You're morbid. She loves you," she said. "I hate to think what her life would have been like without you." It was perhaps the nicest and most reassuring thing she'd ever said to him. She clicked the desktop back up under its clasp. He was afraid she was about to cry, something that would have been intolerable to witness. A quick pivot was in order.

"Can we go over to my house and discuss your project?" he said.

Charlotte gave him a look of annoyance that quickly melted to a softer and more sympathetic gaze. She took a seat in the window again and flipped through a copy of *Caddie Woodlawn*, a prop she was using to avoid looking at Tom.

"I was lonely last night after Oliver left," she said. "Cecily wasn't picking up my calls, and I'm not ready to talk to Dorothy. I phoned Alan to tell him we'd missed him over the weekend and to explain that Oliver and I were working it through. I assumed he'd have heard everything, and I didn't want him to think we're as heartless as our actions suggest." She looked up. "He told me he doesn't live here anymore."

"At the moment, no, he doesn't. I'm hopeful that's temporary."

"That's not the impression he gave me. He told me he's dating a dentist."

"Dentist? How did you get that information out of him?"

"I asked. What's more, it's someone I went to once for an emergency." Charlotte was notorious for dental problems, a result of having grown up in a family that couldn't afford routine care. "He has an office in Cambridge. I wasn't impressed, to be honest. Although he's extremely nice. And attractive."

"That's more information than I need," Tom said.

This prompted Charlotte to offer more information, specifically, the dentist's name. "He also told me how consequential the guesthouse project is to you. At any rate, he intimated."

Tom was touched that Alan had done this, an effort at helping him out, even if a humiliating one. "All projects are important," he said.

"You know, once I saw your alleged friend's reaction to the plans, I wanted it badly—despite your refusal to give me a second floor. I nearly talked Oliver into it, especially since the sketches we got from Eldridge Johnson were so disappointing. And so expensive. And, by the way, he, too, balked at the idea of a second story. But once we heard about Cecily—let's just say we have more pressing things to deal with than a stressful construction project."

Tom felt his last, frail hopes for his professional future slip out of his hands. His respect for Johnson's work and integrity ratcheted up a notch, now that the two men had a shared view of Charlotte's aesthetics. Recompense, but only minor.

"It's not happening, Tom. I'm sorry. I'm sure it won't matter as much as you fear it will. Winston Brill could never replace you."

There was no point in explaining to Charlotte that he already had.

●

Tom had a terrible memory for names. Because he assumed everyone else did as well, he always introduced himself to people by name when he bumped into them on the street, even people he'd known for a long time. He considered it a matter of politeness, especially as he aged. He supposed he'd soon be calling Alan and saying, "Hi, this is Thomas Kemp."

He hoped the dentist's name would quickly leave his head, but it didn't. It was still ringing in his ears when he went into the office for the first time since he'd been to Woodstock. Alan had told him that, in nursing, it was always best to get bad news out of the way immediately. Sooner or later, Tom was going to have to tell Winston that his plan to get Charlotte's project into construction was dead, so he might as well do it immediately. Even though he was triggering his own firing.

Tom watched from his desk as Winston, in his glass box, conducted his phone business, a model of composure, confidence, and charm that Tom could aspire to but would never match. So be it. His "masterpiece" was to remain forever unbuilt. This was worse than losing his position at the firm and his income. It made him feel as if his professional life had had no purpose.

Lanford—the new guy, the recent grad, the Winston lookalike, the relevant one—had settled into his desk in the days since Tom had gone away. He leaned back in his chair, relaxed, as if he knew his position was secure. He had greeted Tom with jocularity and had even slapped him on the shoulder, as if they were old colleagues and peers. Most strikingly, he'd gotten a radical haircut that made him look more like Winston than ever.

Tom looked toward Winston's shining glass office. His boss, bathed in a sparkle of light bouncing off the glass and the surface of his desk and his gorgeously polished head, was dazzling. When Tom saw him hang up his phone and smile and nod at him, he knew he had to speak with him.

"Thomas," Winston said as he entered his office. "Thomas" was the name he used for Tom when he wanted to indicate collegiality he didn't feel toward him but also a form of condescension, like referring to someone as "sir" when you don't respect them. "Good few days off?"

"Eventful," Tom said. "Dealing with family usually is."

"So I've heard. I spent most of the weekend working, sadly enough." Winston looked out through the glass wall and nodded toward the desks in the outer office. "I don't know why Lanford did that to his hair. He looks ridiculous. Very unprofessional."

Because Tom was not going to have to make nice with Winston for too much longer, he said, "You have noticed that you and he look surprisingly alike, haven't you?"

Winston appeared genuinely shocked. "God, no. We look nothing alike. I hope not, anyway. I find him singularly unattractive."

No one sees themselves as others see them. That was always true. It gave Tom some hope, given that his opinion of his own appearance was so negative.

"Listen, Winston. I've come to tell you something I suspect you already know." Winston blinked behind his round glasses. "I've run out of options. Charlotte has said that she and Oliver aren't going to build the guesthouse. From what she told me this morning, it's definite."

Winston slapped his palm against his desk and shook his head. "I've lost all respect for her. They could have had something wonderful. Well, it's their loss."

Maybe, Tom thought, but at the moment, he was most concerned about his own loss.

"It would be helpful to me to stay on here for a little while. There are some loose ends to tie up. Early August, perhaps?"

"Oh, of course," Winston said. He flipped through a calendar on his desk, wetting his thumb. "Or would mid-July work?"

It wasn't an honest question, so why give an honest answer?

"Yes," Tom said. "That would be fine. Thank you."

Chapter Twenty-Eight

Cecily drove into the city, numb to the traffic, numb to the lights of other cars, numb to everything that had just happened. If Santosh was truly done with their relationship, what could she do? She'd adapt. It was what she always did, what she'd been taught to do, supposedly her greatest strength. His refusal to tell her if he'd met someone else could mean he had and considered it none of her business or he hadn't and was disgusted that she would question him about it. Neither possibility boded well.

After all, it wasn't unthinkable that he was hooking up with someone. Maybe, given how handsome and friendly he was, it was even inevitable. He was on a career high, too, which always gave an inner glow that worked like pheromones. Even she had been offered a temptation in Woodstock. If Victor had been a different kind of person, maybe she'd have given in to temptation. She couldn't honestly say.

Walking into his studio had been like stepping directly into someone's subconscious. It was the abundance of work that had impressed her, more, perhaps, than the work itself, which she was unable to judge. Hundreds of canvases of every size, hanging, leaning, stacked, fitted into racks he'd built along the back wall. Paint was spattered everywhere—the floor, tables, easels—with such exuberance, it made the room itself look like another painting. Victor had raised the bamboo shades covering the windows, and it all came to life with the sunlight that flooded in.

"If you see anything you'd like for your mother, let me know."

She was rendered speechless by the room and had circled it to take it in. There was a big, overstuffed chair in a corner, and she sat down in it, trying to understand why she was so moved. Victor's work was almost entirely abstract, so there were no direct clues as to what he was drawn to in the world outside this space. In fact, that was probably what had struck her most; this *was* a world, a complete world he'd created entirely on his own terms. He wasn't doing these paintings to please anyone else, to sell, to have his talent reviewed or graded or even appreciated. He'd constructed his life and his job in such a way that he could indulge his passion as he wanted, without ever having to answer to anyone. The freedom and self-confidence implied by this were breathtaking.

When she'd conceived of her new book project, the one she was making no progress on, it had been in the back of her mind that she needed a logical follow-up to her first book. She needed something that would meet with the approval of her colleagues when, eventually, her tenure case came up. She had been thinking about the peer review the academic press would initiate. Neeta had been right when she expressed surprise that Cecily had an interest in cookbooks. She didn't. She wondered how she'd gotten it all so wrong. In the desperate desire to be responsible to the expectations of everyone else—of her colleagues, her mother, her imaginary critics—she'd been irresponsible to the one person whose interests mattered most: herself.

Victor had made no such compromises. It was an attitude she found almost incomprehensible, but one that had produced this dazzling private sanctuary. It felt like a privilege to be let in to see it.

Victor had sat on the arm of the chair, looking at the room with her. "If you tell me something about your mother, it'll help me pick out something you can give her."

Cecily pondered this. It was difficult to sum up Dorothy, who had, as one of her most notable traits, a complete lack of consistency.

"She's afraid of mirrors," she finally said. "I don't think I can remember seeing her look into one. Ever. She prefers to believe she looks the way she wants to look. Is that helpful?"

He went to one of the shelves, pulled out some canvases as if searching for one in particular. It was hard to believe he knew where everything was or had a system. He slid out a painting, dusted it off, and held it up. "She'll like this."

Cecily studied it for a moment and was sure he was right.

"I appreciate it," she said, "but I can't take anything."

"I'd love it if you did. It's the only way my work gets seen. I need the space. And in case you're wondering, I am not expecting anything in return. As in *nothing*."

For a moment, she was disappointed, in addition to being relieved.

"It's not that I don't want to," he continued. "It's not that that wasn't why I hoped I'd bump into you again after I got the muffin and why I started talking to you when I did. It's just that I realized it would be a bad idea."

She still hadn't said anything. To pursue the discussion further seemed to be an admission of interest on her part. But she did wonder what it was she'd said or done that had made him change his mind.

It wasn't until later, after he'd wrapped the painting for Dorothy, that she dared ask him. By that point, he felt to her more like a friend she wouldn't mind making out with but knew she'd never fuck.

He said, "You're in love. You'd have hated yourself afterward."

"How can you possibly know that?"

"Women think they're completely unreadable, but they're more transparent than men. Most men just don't bother looking. I do, which doesn't make me a better person. More intrusive, at best."

That had increased her affection for him and her gratitude—for what they'd done together, what she'd learned about herself, and most important, for what he'd so graciously refused to do.

●

Now, on Lake Shore Drive, someone pulled in front of her car, cutting her off. She snapped out of her daze and leaned on her horn, then sped up until she was right behind the other car. She was enraged. Its brake lights flashed on and off, trying to signal her to slow down. She was out of her mind. She took the next exit and made her way through stoplights and traffic to the street their apartment was on. Santosh's apartment, as he'd made clear. She was more composed, but her anger hadn't abated. Instead, she found herself furious at Santosh, at Neeta, and, for the first time ever, furious at Lee Anderson.

She stomped up the stairs of their building, but as she was fumbling for her keys, all anger went out of her. She crumpled against the door. She couldn't face the apartment with the stuff of their lives in it, the clutter of Santosh's life without her, evidence of the fact that he could get along very well on his own and maybe evidence of other things she didn't want confirmed.

She wandered out toward North Clark Street and the Daily Grind, her refuge for so many months now and, in all likelihood, where Molly had gone to do her work. People inside were furiously packing up, and she saw that it was about to close. Cecily knocked on the window and waved at Molly.

She came up to Cecily and threw her arms around her. "I wanted to do this earlier, at the Title IX office, but thought it best not to." She paused and regarded Cecily. "You look a little rough."

"I couldn't face walking into my apartment. Santosh and I had a fight. It's beginning to sink in how badly that meeting went."

In a complete reversal of her usual, boisterous self, Molly said—this time, at a perfectly normal volume—"I live a couple of blocks from here. Let me make you a decent home-cooked dinner. I have some ideas I want to share with you."

She walked with Molly to a building that was almost identical to the one she and Santosh lived in. It was astonishing to her that she and Molly lived so close and that, aside from the café, they'd never crossed paths on the street. Imagine all the other potential friends she'd never met. They went down a few steps to the door of a basement apartment. "Thank god I cleaned this morning," Molly said. "It was such a mess, I'd have been embarrassed to let you in."

The apartment was dank, and the unmistakable odor of mildew

permeated the air. Molly flipped a switch, and the place was flooded with harsh fluorescent light that would have made Tom shrink away, vampire-like—although, it would have taken Fellini's cinematographer to light this apartment in a flattering way. There was an almost incomprehensible amount of clutter piled everywhere—clothes and stacks of books, magazines, and papers covered nearly every surface. Had Molly been joking about having cleaned up this morning or—hard to imagine—had it looked worse twenty-four hours ago?

Naturally, there were cats. Two obese and sluggish creatures—one black, the other a tabby—emerged from the dark recess of a narrow hall and circled Cecily with bored contempt.

"Ignore them," Molly said, throwing down her computer bag. "They're despicable."

"Oh, they seem . . . nice enough."

"Don't be fooled. I only have them because my husband likes them."

Cecily nodded. Although she'd mentioned having a daughter, Molly was so aggressively independent, it never occurred to Cecily that she might be married. "Will he be back for dinner?"

Molly hung up her jacket in a narrow closet that contained only one hanger, as if, for reasons unknown to anyone, this was the single piece of clothing she didn't drop onto a chair or the floor. "He doesn't live here. We've never lived together. I've always known he'd be easier to love if I knew less about him. For the record, so am I. Take a seat."

Cecily scanned the furniture, looking for a space that was relatively uncluttered. As she went toward an armchair in the corner, Molly shouted, "Not there! The cats will attack if you sit there. They're vicious. Have a seat at the table while I fix us dinner."

The dining table was Formica-topped and surrounded by turquoise chairs that were either vintage or convincing fakes. Cecily was reassured that Molly had made a conscious choice about the style of these items. It suggested a degree of domesticity, even if a small one.

"I have a confession," Molly said. "Although nothing you probably haven't figured out."

Cecily was unnerved by the word *confession* and hoped Molly wasn't about to admit to a lurid sexual secret as a come-on. She was ready for celibacy herself.

"All right. I guess."

Molly laughed. "Don't give me that look; I'm not trying to seduce you. I'm pretty much asexual, which is why I get so much done."

This raised more questions about her marriage, but all of them seemed better left unasked.

Molly opened the refrigerator with a flourish and peered inside as if contemplating the menu. There were a few beers on the shelves, a loaf of white bread, and some jars that appeared to have been opened a long time ago. She handed Cecily a beer.

"The confession is I'm your classic bull in a china shop. I go into everything headfirst. Look at the way I pursued this friendship with you."

"I'm glad you did," Cecily said. "I've put most of my friendships on ice until this gets resolved. It meant a lot to have you at that meeting."

"So, about the meeting. It didn't go well."

After being told by everyone she knew that everything was fine, that she'd done nothing wrong, that she would triumph, it was a relief to hear someone say this out loud.

"I lied to you when I said I planned to keep my mouth shut at the meeting. I went into it angry at the way you were being treated, prepared to steamroll over those two deadly earnest people. But, really, in terms of a process, it was frustrating and infuriating at times, but it wasn't unfair."

"I agree, even though it made all my mistakes so glaring."

"Some decent food will be good for you," Molly said, and drank from her own bottle of beer.

The decent food turned out to be two frozen entrees she dug out of the back of the freezer. Almost every time Cecily had been served packaged or prepared food, the host had added a personal touch that allowed them to claim it as their own—an egg plopped on top of the noodles, a lemon squeezed into canned soup, mustard slathered on precooked salmon. Molly's personal touch was one of the more halfhearted attempts

Cecily had seen. "I turn the microwave on and off a few times while they're cooking. It makes a huge difference."

Cecily didn't know if they were eating ground meat or some plant-based alternative, but she didn't care. She found herself slowing down as she ate, so she wouldn't look like a starving dog.

"The reason I hate academia so much," Molly said, "is because I love it. I love the idealism, the exchange of ideas, the optimistic, the unrealistic students. I love all of it. Look at how loud I am; I was a natural teacher."

"I admire the way you're able to project," Cecily said.

Molly's laugh was as robust as her speech. "Spoken with the diplomacy of a junior faculty member whose future depends upon her not offending her colleagues."

"Where did you teach?"

Molly scraped out the last of her entrée and tossed the container into the sink. "A prestigious university on the East Coast."

Cecily couldn't tell if this was a modest way of saying she'd taught at an Ivy League school or an immodest way of making it seem as if she had. Either way, hearing this, Cecily now saw the disorder of the apartment as the result of intellectual preoccupation rather than pathological hoarding instincts.

Money, as Elizabeth Taylor had said, was the best deodorant, but in Cecily's world, Harvard was a close second.

"I got shoved out because I couldn't finish my own project. I couldn't write. It's not as if I didn't understand the terms or what was expected of me. I just couldn't do it."

"But isn't writing your business?"

"Yes. Writing other people's books. As long as my name isn't attached, I can churn out ten or twenty clear, crisp, comprehensible pages a day. If I'm writing for myself, it turns into sludge. It was all my own fault."

Cecily mulled this over.

"Are you trying to tell me you don't think it will go my way at Deerpath?"

"Are you trying to tell me you think it will?"

Cecily admitted that her mood over the past few hours had been a solid indication that she believed it unlikely. "It's a matter of how bad the decision will be."

Molly scrunched up her face in a peculiar way, almost as if she'd just been hit by a terrible smell. There was something pale and soft about her features that made her look like someone who was rarely outdoors and who got exercise even less frequently. "What do you want to happen to you? That's the relevant question here," she said.

"I want to be exonerated, cleared of the allegations against me."

"Yeah, and then what? Your life goes back to what it was before?"

"Yes."

"And you think that will happen?"

"Of course not." She'd said it so as not to seem naïve to Molly, but she saw clearly that she'd just spoken the thoughts she'd been carrying around inside her. Given everything that had happened over the past few months, her life could never go back to what it was, no matter the outcome. "I just don't have a backup plan."

"That's where I come in. I have one for you. It's partly selfish. I'm a lot more successful at what I do than this place suggests. I could live somewhere better, but I'm not all that interested in my surroundings. That probably sounds strange to you, but as you might suspect, it's the least of my eccentricities. I have more work than I can handle, but I refuse to turn any of it down. Writing for someone else is a specific skill, but I've developed impeccable instincts for people who have the talent."

"Are you offering me a job?"

"I'm presenting you with an opportunity. I'll give you a project, pay you to do it. If it doesn't work out, offer rescinded. I like helping people who've been burned by academia. It's better than rescuing stray cats, although it's related. I'll start you off with something palatable."

Cecily listened to the project Molly was offering her: a reworking of a messy, mean-spirited manuscript about the virtues of kindness and decency in the business world. "It'll sell modestly at best, but I'm paid by the job, and it's an ethically responsible project, if not exactly a good one."

Cecily felt the warmth, once again, of being wanted—now, at the end of a day filled with rejection. She could imagine herself doing this, filling up the time while Santosh was in L.A., while she was waiting to hear more from Deerpath. It wasn't something she wanted for a career, but as work to occupy her for a few months or—worst-case scenario—a few years, she could picture a lot worse. It would buy her time to resurrect her reputation, if that was what was needed.

"Can I do it from Boston?" she asked.

"Of course. You can do it from anywhere. You're not breaking up with your boyfriend, are you?"

"I have a feeling he's breaking up with me. He's in L.A. for a couple of weeks, and I don't want to be in our apartment. Plus, I have to make peace with some new family members of mine in Boston. I won't bore you with the details."

"Thank you. Now that we have a professional relationship, it's better I don't know."

There was no point at which Cecily asked to stay with Molly and no point at which Molly offered. But, somehow, as it got later and Molly described the books she worked on, both of them silently assumed that she would.

Molly went to get Cecily some blankets and a pillow so she could sleep on the sofa. "Push anything you find there onto the floor. I really don't care. It's a convertible, but it's a lot more comfortable to sleep on if you don't pull out the bed."

Cecily resisted the temptation to tell her about her mother's sleeping habits.

Most of what was on the sofa was reading material: books and magazines and newspapers. None of it looked new. Molly's life had probably gotten easier when print media began to lose dominance.

As Cecily was setting a stack of books onto the floor, it toppled over, and the books fanned out onto the rug. And there among them was *The Nature of Success in Successful Natures*. It was an old copy, and the cover—the title in bold red letters against a white background—was stained and torn in places. Cecily turned to the back and saw the glamour shot of Fiona above her bio, captured in a moment of triumph that seemed to have passed. There was a situation Cecily could relate to.

The book fell open at the title page, and Cecily saw that Fiona, in a large and florid script, had signed the book to Molly. Surely, Molly hadn't read this. She seemed less likely to seek out self-help manuals than anyone Cecily could think of.

She was still holding Fiona's book when Molly came back into the living room. "You've read this?" she asked her.

Molly squinted and tossed blankets onto the sofa. She grabbed the book from Cecily and laughed. "Oh, this! Where did you find it?"

"It was on the end of the sofa."

"Well, you never know what you'll find here. That's the beauty of being a slob: constant surprises." She turned the book over in her hands a few times, studying the jacket and reading the copy on the flaps. She wore a half smile that was either fond or mocking, Cecily couldn't be sure.

"All she signed was her name. You'd think she could have done a little better than that."

"Are you saying you know her?" Cecily asked.

"Not really. I never met her. This is one of the first books I worked on. It was a giant slog of a manuscript when I got it." She turned to the acknowledgments page and pointed to her name. "She didn't want to acknowledge my help. 'You're a skillful person.' Talk about a lack of gratitude."

"How much of it did you write?"

Molly scrunched her features together as she had earlier, the bad-smell face. "I'd say all of it. She'd probably tell you I just did some editing. The thing is, if you do a good job, the putative author ends up believing they wrote it. Anyway, I never would have started my own business if it hadn't been for Fiona Snow's unreadable manuscript, which did have useful information. I began believing what I was writing, and it gave me the courage to make it work. It's a weird relationship you develop with the 'author'—mutually dependent and mutually hostile."

Cecily was so astonished by this, she didn't know how to respond. "Maybe I've always underestimated the power of self-help books," she said.

"They're all useless, but only because no one uses them. They read them but don't follow any advice. You can borrow it if you want, give you a sense of my writing style. I have no idea what happened to Fiona Snow. She seems to have dropped off the earth."

Cecily was tempted to tell Molly precisely what had happened to Fiona Snow, but somehow, the idea of leaving her with the fantasy that she had vanished was more appealing.

Chapter Twenty-Nine

*T*om *tried to put the dentist's name out of his mind by* scrambling it, reciting names that sounded like his but weren't, and making lists of all the dentists he'd been to in his lifetime. Still, it stuck with him like an annoying advertising jingle you can't get out of your head.

Two days after Cecily left, he broke down and put the man's name into his browser. He was sitting in his darkened living room with five Mantovani albums stacked up on the stereo. The house was filled with the eerily saccharine music that was both out-of-date and futuristic— assuming the future was similar to a long ride in an elevator with a good sound system. He'd left work early, as there wasn't all that much for him to do. For the past couple of days, he'd felt invisible in the office. Invisibility was one of the nicer benefits of age but not in work situations or restaurants.

His internet search produced a website for a dental practice in Cambridge, not too far from Charlotte's office. Not too far from the HMO where Alan worked, either. The dentist himself was an attractive man, probably in his late forties, with, predictably, a great smile. He wouldn't turn heads on the streets of Manhattan or in South Beach, but he had the undistinguished good looks that would no doubt qualify as handsome at insurance conventions and medical supply shows.

Well, that was Tom's jealousy talking. His bitterness. Best to squelch it. To the extent that you can tell anything from a photograph—and, in some cases, you can tell a lot—he looked like a kind man. This gave Tom pause. If he were a swarthy, arrogant man, it would have been easier to assume the relationship would burn itself out. Kindness was a sustainable threat.

Tom was sufficiently lulled by the music to decide that going to Cambridge and checking out the dental office was a Very Good Idea—to get a closer look, if nothing else. It was cloudy and windy out. He was wearing a light jacket, and as he stepped out of the house, it was blown off his shoulder in a gust. It was hard to say if this was normal for this time of year. He couldn't remember if spring was always this windy and erratic or if he'd become a meteorological hypochondriac.

It was a short drive to Cambridge, and in less than fifteen minutes, he was parking on Mass Ave, close to the dentist's practice. As he was taking off his seat belt, he realized he had no plan. Was he going to walk into the office, pretend he was looking for a new dentist? Complain of a toothache? It saddened him to think that he had never been able to pull off such a stunt. Dorothy would most certainly have done it with aplomb, but he wasn't quite ready to take his cues from her. The most he could imagine doing was going for a walk in the wind. He'd stroll past the office and gaze in the windows, nothing more. After all, he was officially at the invisible stage of life.

He was just stepping out of his car when he spotted Alan and the dentist walking down the sidewalk on the opposite side of the avenue. He retreated inside the car and locked the door. They were talking, bumping up against each other, and although he was a reasonable distance from them, Tom could see on Alan's face a look he recognized from *their* years together (their early years, especially) as that of genuine happiness. Happiness and something else, something elusive. Tom watched the two laugh as they were buffeted by the warm wind, delighting in the inconvenient unusualness of the conditions. They were looking forward to spending the evening together, that was clear. They had plans—dinner, a movie, hours in each other's company. The elusive look on Alan's face was hope: he believed he was in the company of someone who would always put him first. Tom felt sick. Not because he was enraged, not because he felt betrayed. It was purely a matter of seeing how right Alan had been about him all along. How right even Wendy, Alan's unbearable shrink, had been all along. What a gross miscalculation his behavior had been. How sadly misplaced all his annoyance toward the person he'd wronged. Alan deserved better. He deserved a dentist who'd look at him just like that.

Tom's phone was ringing: Cecily. She hadn't called him about her meeting at the school, two days earlier. He had to assume that meant the news was not good. He considered letting the call go to voice mail, but because he was sitting alone in his car, he couldn't pretend, even to himself, that she was interrupting anything. How appropriate that he take the call, with its inevitable bad news, now, as he watched Alan and his lover walk on, turn into a store, and disappear from sight.

"Tom," Cecily said. "Are you all right? You sound a little shook up."

"You got that from a simple hello?"

"I know you pretty well."

There was some comfort in this. "It hasn't been the best few days of my life," he said, "but to put the most positive spin on it, I learned a few things for certain. Now I can attempt to deal with them." He shifted gears and asked her how the meeting had gone at Deerpath.

"It's complicated. I was wondering if I could come back to Boston for a little while."

The weather suddenly seemed less alarming, and sitting in the car, he felt less alone. This was the best thing he'd heard since Cecily had left, and he told her so. "Charlotte and Oliver want to sit down and talk with you."

"Yes, I know. She's been calling me. I want to talk with them, too. It's got to happen eventually, so I might as well deal with it now."

And Santosh? Was he okay about her coming back east so soon?

"That's a long story best told in person."

"None of this sounds very promising, dear."

"No, of course not, Tom. We both know I only call when I'm in trouble."

He had to accept that this was largely true. And yet, he couldn't force himself to resent it, no matter how he tried. He was getting old for this, and soon he'd probably be too old. But for the moment, it was still his job. Her calls were the ones that made him happiest.

Chapter Thirty

A week after everyone had left, Dorothy called Gary and Enji and told them Cecily had given her a painting. She wanted their advice on where to hang it. Gary told her they were in Woodstock for a week, shopping daily in Hudson for a client on the Upper West Side. They'd be happy to drop over later in the day. "Anything we can bring you?"

Basically, she needed everything. The party for the opening—she was officially refusing even to let the G-word enter her thoughts—had been so emotionally and physically draining, she hadn't left the house since. By now, most of the food in her refrigerators had gone bad; Fiona, Harold, and some others had packed up and taken with them most of the leftovers from the party. Gary and Enji didn't need to know any of that. She wasn't at the stage of needing people to bring her groceries. Or maybe she was, which made it less possible for her to ask.

"I'm all set," she said.

Six weeks earlier, long after Dorothy had taken their advice on the sofas, the window, and numerous other expensive design pieces and projects, she'd thought to finally do online research on them and their business. They were not as high-end or as successful as she'd assumed. In retrospect, she should have guessed this, given their own unfashionably located house here and the amount of time they spent out of the city. It was a disappointment to learn that she'd invested so much time and money in trying to impress a middling team. Still, the information had made her like them more as people. She could relax around them, could finally admit to herself that she found Gary pompous and Enji's earnest conversation dull. She could guess that their clothes, which she'd once found intimidatingly stylish, were from second-tier designers and had probably been purchased in outlets. What a relief! She could give them advice and amuse them by playing the batty Auntie Mame figure that a certain type of gay man (not Tom, sadly) found irresistible.

For reasons she was unable to pinpoint, their reduced status made it easier for her to forgive them for the crazy window. It was always easier to be loyal to and forgiving of an underdog. And really, they'd never lied about their professional stature; she'd filled in the blanks herself. It wasn't their fault she'd done so inaccurately.

She was not ready to forgive Fiona. She'd behaved maliciously. Dorothy could forgive stupidity and bad judgment and even insincerity—all of which she was guilty of herself at one time or another—but malicious behavior was not defensible. She couldn't bear the thought of calling her. She'd wait for Fiona to contact her and then, if she still felt this way, confront her. In the meantime, their project was on hold, she had a vast amount of time on her hands, and the fate of all that money she'd invested in their center was unclear. Thankfully, she didn't have records accurate enough to calculate the precise amount.

Assuming she could muster the energy, she at least had enough free time to buy groceries herself and, more important, deal with the prescriptions she *was* going to get filled. Her attacks—or whatever they were—had not abated since the weekend. If anything, her palpitations were getting more frequent and intense. It was comforting to remind herself that that would be true for any healthy person, given the stress of the weekend.

Most of this was reparable. Charlotte would come around. At this stage of life, losing a friend you'd been close to for so many decades was unimaginable. There was something absurd and unseemly about it, like getting a divorce at age eighty-five, after sixty years of marriage. What was the point?

Charlotte loved big gestures, and dashing from the party and then sneaking off the next morning before anyone was awake must have satisfied her need for drama and made her feel she'd snatched the upper hand.

Cecily and Tom had left in the early afternoon. As they were leaving, the car's engine running, Tom waiting below in the driver's seat, Cecily had presented her with the painting, which was wrapped in brown paper and string. "I got it directly from the artist yesterday," she said. "I like how it shines. I thought it would fit in with your colors. Don't try to find any hidden messages, Mom; it's an abstract. And if you don't like it, there are a million places here you can store it. I promise I won't look for it next time I come."

As Dorothy started to unwrap it, Cecily had stopped her. "Wait till I'm gone," she said. "That way, you won't have to pretend, in case you hate it."

"But I can't hate it," Dorothy said. "*You're* giving it to me. Now. Despite everything that happened. I'll cherish it. You know that."

Throughout Cecily's adult life, whenever she had seen her off—leaving for school, going on a trip, returning to Chicago with Santosh—Dorothy had always had a moment of panic and fear clutch at her. *What if I don't see her again?* she'd think. That day, she had no such feelings as she followed her downstairs and waved at her and Tom as they backed out of the parking space in front. The car bumped along her dirt road. There were branches on the ground the wind had blown down in the middle of the night, and Tom had swerved to avoid one. Then they were gone.

Dorothy was so breathless by the time she made it back upstairs— what *had* she been thinking buying this place?—that she'd had to lie down. The fear and panic she'd always felt, she realized as she lay on the sofa and caught her breath, had been that she might die without having told Cecily who she was. That fear was gone. She could relax now. No matter how quickly her health seemed to be slipping.

She unwrapped the painting.

It was an abstract thick with layers of paint. The dominant tones were orange and burnt umber, and it was all covered with a clear acrylic that made it glow. Cecily had been right; it did fit in with the wood-work and the upholstery in the living room. The artwork, which she'd propped up against a wall, seemed to change radically depending on the light. Different colors and tones kept emerging, almost as if the paint were alive and swirling beneath the clear coating.

Despite Cecily's having told her not to try to read any meaning into it, she couldn't help herself. The first night, as she lay on the sofa trying to get to sleep in the distracting moonlight, she looked at the painting and saw emerging from the rich wash of colors what looked to her like a seam, a faint line that led somewhere and called to her. Surely, there was significance in that. Looking at it and trying to imagine everything it could mean had helped her fall asleep. When she woke up, the image had disappeared, and the painting had returned to its usual abstract swirl of color.

"Oh, Victor Soto," Gary had said when she showed him the paint-ing. "Where did she get this?"

"She said she got it from the painter. That's all I know. Is he famous?"

"Not for his painting," Gary had said lasciviously.

Enji smiled at this, and added, "He's a contractor. Weekend painter. Doesn't have a gallery. Women love him. Or he loves women. Probably both."

Well, that explained the long absence. Cecily had been off having an adventure. That was a relief, too. She hadn't been hiding out or wandering the streets to avoid confronting her mother and Oliver and Charlotte; she'd been having fun. Cecily loved Santosh too much to really cheat on him, but if she'd had a romantic afternoon with some notorious lothario, so much the better. There had always been some-thing a little proper about Cecily, and Dorothy had taken that propriety personally—as a rejection of her own laissez-faire attitude toward such things. Maybe the weekend had been more of a triumph than she'd guessed.

She could tell that neither Gary nor Enji liked the painting. They seemed to have twin opinions about everything, although it wasn't clear from which of them the opinions originated. They were snobs, and from a purely monetary point of view, the painting had no value. Maybe there was something amateur about it. She was no authority. She'd always liked looking at art in books more than in galleries and museums. Besides, she hadn't had them over for their approval. She wanted them to see that Cecily had given her a present. Once they'd hung it on the wall directly across from the new window—a process that involved so much measuring, it approached parody—it looked to her like an indication that she'd done something right. It meant she had her daughter's forgiveness, acceptance, and even approval. It mattered less if she couldn't patch things up with Fiona, if the retreat center never got off the ground, if her own health was failing.

She had the painting. She'd never have guessed it was the one thing she'd wanted all along.

Chapter Thirty-One

Charlotte and Oliver lived in a modern house they'd bought in one of Boston's wealthier suburbs fifteen years earlier, shortly after Nolan went off to college. It was spectacular. Its sleek, crisp lines, low profile, glass walls, and sharp angles always made Tom's pulse race. The purchase of it sent the message that they were starting anew now that Nolan was living on his own. It was a house for adults, not a family, certainly not an unruly overgrown teenager. It was nestled on two landscaped acres—lots of pines and rhododendron groves and a small pond—and was attended to on a regular basis by teams of gardeners and arborists for the exterior and assorted cleaners with specialties ranging from upholstery and rugs to windows for the interior. All this upkeep was overseen by Oliver; Charlotte had made it clear that she thought it overdone and would have been happier letting the place go to a more overgrown state. Tom had told her that when you owned a house like this—the architect had designed and built it in the 1960s; having come with a pedigree, it had been written up multiple times and photographed for several books before they owned it—you had a responsibility to maintain it.

He regarded the house with the wary, uncomfortable admiration he had for the architecture of Italian Fascists. His design for the guesthouse had been his attempt to reference it while warming it up with democratic humanity.

The house was so meticulously cared for, he always felt, upon driving up, that he was approaching a public building—a library on a bosky college campus, let's say, or even a small and incredibly discreet bank. The neighborhood had several houses of a similar design, giving the area the look and feel of an exceptionally wealthy boarding school campus.

Tom and Cecily drove out for the family reunion dinner—if that's what it was—a couple of days after Cecily returned to Boston.

There was something touching about her having dressed for the dinner in one of the boxy jumpers she occasionally wore and that made her look like a Dutch schoolteacher. Her hair had started to grow back, a fact that accentuated her bone structure and gave her a wispy prettiness. At the same time, when she met Tom on the lawn in front of his house, he noticed that her face was beginning to age, as if she were settling into herself and her true appearance.

There was a special poignance to looking at this young woman he had loved since her birth and seeing her age. He'd never know the complete story of her life or how it would end. Happily, he hoped—but how often was that true? He'd miss decades of her story, an almost intolerable thought. The only compensation was understanding that, statistically speaking, it was likely she'd be there to witness the end of his.

This feeling gnawed at him as they drove, reminding him that he owed her a confession he wasn't eager to make. He needed to tell her before they arrived at the house: his role as her surrogate father was about to change.

It was a pleasant, mild night in May. The weather had continued its madcap roller-coaster fluctuations, so nights like this were best treasured as a cease-fire that was welcome even if acknowledged to be only temporary.

He turned into Oliver and Charlotte's drive and was dazzled, as he always was, by the professional lighting and the aura of calm it produced. He stopped the car before they got within sight of the house, lowered his window, and turned to face Cecily.

"Are we walking the rest of the way?" she asked.

"No," he said. "I want to tell you something. Something I need to get off my chest."

Cecily's expression didn't change, as if this preamble were not a surprise to her.

"When Dorothy first announced she was pregnant, I didn't support her plan to go through with it. I tried to talk her out of it. Not aggressively and not for long, but I did my best to make a case against her having a baby on her own." He'd presented Dorothy with financial statements, projections about the increasing cost of education, reminders of how she'd been unable to care for two dogs she'd impulsively adopted at different times. He was too ashamed and too sad to get into these details now.

"Why are you telling me this?" Cecily asked.

That was a good question. So many confessions are merely selfish desires to unburden oneself. Tom was always mystified by people who confessed infidelities long after the affair had ended, when the knowledge of it could only be hurtful to their spouse. Unburdening was part of his motivation, but not all.

"I want you to know that however many cleanups in aisle five I did throughout your childhood, however many sketchbooks we filled with drawings for you, however many skating trips we made, Dorothy loved you from the minute she learned she was pregnant. It took me until I held you in my arms to do so."

●

Oliver greeted them at the door. He was wearing a pair of blue jeans that looked as if they'd never been worn before and a V-neck cashmere sweater with a white T-shirt underneath. In casual clothes such as these, he tended to look like an actor in a role he was uniquely unsuited to play. Cary Grant as a coal miner or Audrey Hepburn as . . . well, Eliza Doolittle. He gave Cecily a warm embrace, something considerably more intimate and affectionate than he usually managed. She accepted it with the wary smile of a child who's happy for, but uncomfortable with, the enthusiastic attention of a tipsy aunt.

"I am guessing," Oliver said, still pressing Cecily to him, "that all of this will become less awkward over time. Don't you think, Tom?"

"I'm sure of it," Tom said. "Even flossing gets less awkward over time."

Oliver released Cecily and patted Tom on the back, a gesture clearly meant as an act of acceptance. Oliver was the kind of man whose acceptance carried with it an implicit compliment. It had something to do with his masculinity and his money, a chicken-and-egg duo that was impossible to separate.

The air in the house was museum quality: it had a perfect balance of temperature and humidity levels. This gave it a brisk sterility and an astonishing absence of odors, bad or good. Thanks to silent, industrial exhaust fans and state-of-the-art HVAC systems Oliver had had installed without disrupting the home's appearance, you had to be deep in the kitchen and practically on top of the stove before you smelled cooking.

"Charlotte's making dinner," Oliver said. He led them down a long hallway lined with oversize paintings that it was impossible to imagine Charlotte or Oliver selecting for purchase or, for that matter, looking at. Slashes of color on stark white canvases.

Charlotte bustled over to Cecily when the three entered the kitchen and, nearly weeping, asked for her forgiveness for disappearing in Woodstock. "I was in shock," she said. "I'm trying to make it up to you by preparing an elaborate dish from a new cookbook. I'm sure I'm going to blow it, but please believe the effort is sincere. Thank god your hair is growing in."

"I was probably in shock myself," Cecily said. "Really, it was all between Dorothy and me anyway. We've had some long talks since. I think she's recovering from the weekend."

"She's sent me about six photos of the painting you gave her."

Ah, that, Tom thought. It pleased him to know he was the only one who'd seen Cecily arrive at the house with the painter. Not because it protected her, but because it gave them a shared secret, even if she didn't know it.

The kitchen was one of those marvels of modern design in which every functional appliance or useful piece of equipment was artfully hidden behind a panel or a cabinet or a carefully crafted false front. This created a wonderous Zen austerity so far out of Charlotte's natural element that she might have been cooking underwater. Every item left out—a lemon, a water glass, a half-drunk cup of coffee—screeched at you in an unnerving way, the spirit of the architect scolding you for not sticking to his austere vision. Tonight, the visual cacophony was intense. Spices, exotic vegetables, grains, cookware, butter and oils, two small chickens, and several glass vials with saffron threads were spilled across the counter like an assault on the perfection of the design and Oliver's obsessive maintenance of it.

Appearing to notice where Tom was casting his glance, Charlotte said, "Don't worry, Tom. I started this project hours ago. It just needs to be heated up. " She went on at some length about the cookbook she was using, one put out by the chef of a famous restaurant in Miami.

He could tell that this wasn't a project she'd undertaken to make up for her behavior in Woodstock, but instead, a way to keep herself busy, to keep her hands occupied. It always went like this with Charlotte: just when Tom was feeling his most annoyed and angered by her, he was swamped by a reminder of her vulnerability and essentially sympathetic nature.

She was dressed in the multi-layered style that looked a little like protective armor: a shirt buttoned over a turtleneck that itself was pulled down over the waistband of a pair of linen pants, all of it held in place by a big, open cardigan that came down almost to her knees.

Oliver was in charge of drinks, the male role for social gatherings. "I would like to recommend we all try this wonderful cocktail I discovered in Belgium, of all places, last time I was there." Oliver condescended to Belgium for esoteric European reasons that were beyond Tom's reach. "I can't say I'll be able to re-create it, but I'm going to try. There are several infused ingredients. Is anyone opposed to cilantro?"

Tom was mystified by the craze of infusing alcohol. It seemed intended mainly as a topic of conversation, as it produced negligible flavor. He had to announce that he'd stopped drinking entirely.

"Since when?" Charlotte scolded.

Announcing that you've stopped drinking, Tom was learning, solicited the kind of suspicious disapproval usually reserved for an announcement of a move to Florida. "Oddly enough, since I told everyone that Alan had moved out."

"Well," Oliver scoffed. "I'll serve you one anyway. You don't have to drink it." Oliver had the same discomfort with sobriety that he had with homosexuality. In theory, he supported it; in fact, he just didn't see the point. In the present instance, he was being forced to condescend to both.

When they all had their drinks in hand, and Charlotte had popped her elaborate meal into one of the hidden ovens, they went into the living room with its wall of glass that looked out onto the back of the property and the sweep of land where Tom had expected he'd be building his guesthouse. Work should have begun by now—the land prepared, one or two trees of no particular significance cleared.

From here, Tom could appreciate his plan. None of the view would have been blocked, and looking out, you'd still have seen the field and the woods behind. What would have been visible of the guesthouse would have been like a shadow on the grass that enhanced the beauty of the grass itself. He could see the phantom building sitting there, reminding him in its gentle, seductive way of what would never be.

Eventually, Oliver told Cecily he'd love to have a talk with her alone. They'd come to the inevitable part of the evening, the main reason for this gathering. "You two can entertain each other, can't you?" he said, looking at Charlotte and Tom and grinning, as if there were something amusing in that.

"Oh, we're long past entertaining," Charlotte said. "However, I'm confident we can tolerate each other."

Tom was sitting across from Charlotte in one of the Eames chairs that, necessarily, furnished the room. In their identical chairs, facing each other, the glass wall beside them, Tom felt as if they were in a psychiatrist's office but were both the doctor, equally powerful, filled with judgment, and unlikely to reveal much about themselves. They were at an impasse.

Charlotte was the first to break the silence. "In case you were wondering, the news has made Oliver and me closer. I'm not sure why. Maybe it's simply because, after all these years, there's something new and unexpected in our lives."

"I'm glad to hear it."

"We're too old not to be adult about this. As I see it, there's a lot of wasted time here when we all could have been connecting with each other and with Dorothy and Cecily on a more honest basis. There's no point in wasting even more time."

"You'll be welcoming Cecily into the family."

"Gradually, yes. First, there's Nolan to think of."

Tom had rarely talked with Cecily about Nolan, but he sensed that there was an awkwardness between them. No surprise, really, given that Nolan brought an awkward element to most relationships.

"I wish things had turned out differently for you, Tom," she said.

"In what sense?" There were, after all, many senses in which things might have gone differently or, to be more specific, better.

"Alan, for starters. It can't be easy, at your age."

"Believe it or not, it probably is easier at my age—by which I assume you mean 'our age'—than it would be if I were younger. I've stopped taking things so personally, and I'm marginally less greedy." What he meant was that he'd been trying to make peace with what had happened. He was trying to be happy for Alan. It wasn't the same as being happy for yourself, but like watching a slideshow of someone else's vacation or viewing pornography, it created a secondhand pleasure that was better than none.

"Oliver and I would never want to displace you."

This was going too far. He wanted to see the good in her—there was plenty to see—but she kept pushing it out of the way to highlight her selfishness. "I feel no competition for Cecily's affection or attention.

You couldn't displace me even if you tried." He understood, once and for all, that this was true.

"Good." She rested her hands on the arms of the chair, and Tom felt a slight crack, as if he'd scored a point. Charlotte was looking at him in a fixed, slightly ironic way that—if he didn't know better—he'd have said was bordering on flirtation. The carefully odorless room was suddenly filled with the scent of violets. "I admire you, Tom."

"Once, you did more than admire," he said.

It was the first time, in almost forty years, that either of them had acknowledged aloud that they'd slept together—or, at least, had spent a few hours fitfully tossing in the same bed (Tom's) after fucking. Tom had still been teaching school at the time. He got up early and left for work, while Charlotte unconvincingly feigned sleep so they could pretend the night had never happened.

"That is true," she said. "In a sense."

Tom saw Charlotte as she'd been then: a fierce, forceful, and somewhat manic presence driven by an abundance of ambition. More important, he saw himself as he'd been then: young, slim, more objectively desirable to a host of people. It was only recently that he'd lost his longing to be that age again; youth brought with it the potential for another half century of life, and his interest in that had conveniently faded. Tom had never been the last person to leave a party. He'd never worried that he was missing out on the fun time someone else was having. He liked small spaces and preferred sleeping in narrow beds. He figured he'd do just fine with death.

"Do you think it's strange," Charlotte said, "that in all these years, we've never discussed it?"

"I think it's appropriate."

"Have you ever told anyone about it?" she asked.

He didn't need to run through his memory bank. "No one. Not even Alan."

"Neither have I. Not even Oliver. You came out shortly after our brief encounter, and I didn't want anyone to think it was on account of me. It wasn't, by the way, was it?"

Tom found this idea hilarious. "No, Charlotte. It had nothing to do with you. I was fully gay long before we clashed, even if I wasn't fully ready to admit it."

She narrowed her eyes and looked at him with the gathered vestiges of her seductive instincts. It was always a thrilling surprise to see sexuality emerge in a person his own age, even if it did have an element of a phoenix rising from the ashes. "It was not an unpleasant experience for me," she said.

"I'll cherish that," he said.

Feeble as the praise was, he found that it relieved an anxiety, incredibly faint and largely subconscious, that had resided somewhere within him for decades. "And, for the record, it wasn't for me, either. I wish I could say that this overrides my anger at you for the guesthouse, but I'm not there yet. The consequences are too great."

"I am sorry. Maybe early retirement isn't a bad thing."

"I'm certain it can be a good thing—provided you have the money. I'm afraid I don't."

Chapter Thirty-Two

As Cecily followed Oliver down a hallway, she was almost giddy with disorientation born of the fact that she felt so little for him, despite her new knowledge. It was a relief.

She'd grown up aware of the suspicion with which everyone in her mother's circle regarded Oliver. He was the outsider, by virtue of his background, his personality, his politics, and, most of all, his money. She'd always assumed that some of the disapproval surrounding him had to do with jealousy, but it had influenced her view of him even so. Everyone needed to believe that they might have done as well as Oliver financially if only they hadn't been so highly principled and focused on loftier, although never specified, goals.

Oliver's study was at the far end of the house, detached from the rest of the rooms. That seemed in keeping with Oliver, who so often was literally elsewhere—on airplanes, at conferences, out of the country. Like the rest of the house, the study was dressed with clean, polished furniture, but the desk, a long, imposing teak piece, was covered with neatly organized papers and folders, indicating that he actually worked here. It appeared to be one of the most lived-in rooms of the house. Naturally, Cecily had never been allowed in here on the multiple visits she'd made to the house over the years. She pointed this out to Oliver as he was taking a seat behind his desk.

"Very possibly true," he said, as if he'd never felt compelled to track such things. "Now, of course, the situation is different between us, isn't it?" He surveyed her with a bemused smile.

She knew this was so, and yet everything felt much the same. "Does it feel different to you?"

Oliver was not used to being asked direct questions. He raised his eyebrows and touched his fingertips together and said, with his practiced diplomacy, "I've always been impressed with you, Cecily. In your own way, you're an extraordinary person. Everything you've done, you've done on your own."

Cecily was flattered by this comment, coming from Oliver especially. Everyone wants to believe they've earned everything they have, but scratch the surface and, in her case, it became a politically objectionable belief. She'd grown up white and middle-class in a privileged part of the country during a period of relative stability and economic advantage. She'd always known that her mother loved her and cared about her, no matter how erratic Dorothy's means of expressing it might have been. On top of all that, she'd always had Tom as a guiding figure. What Oliver didn't know was that, despite all that, she'd managed to mess it up and was on the brink of losing everything. She almost wanted to tell him this, to surprise him, but she knew it would give him power over her that she wasn't ready to hand him.

"Dorothy loved me," she said. "I never went hungry. I always had Tom. He was the steadiest person in my life, and I suppose the person I've always thought of as a father."

"Yes, of course. We all knew that. This must be hard for him. I hope he doesn't feel displaced."

"He's been carrying me around on his shoulders for so long, he might be ready to be displaced. Your canceling the guesthouse is going to cost him professionally. In other ways, too, I'd guess. Cost a lot. Maybe it will be a relief to not have to fill that role in my life any longer."

Oliver's gaze steadied, and his face hardened. He didn't like hearing that someone else had taken on the responsibility that should have been his. Maybe he didn't like being reminded that his actions had consequences for others. Cecily wondered if the look he was giving her was related to the ruthlessness that everyone referred to but that she had never witnessed.

"I can see what you mean," he said, although the coldness in his eyes persisted. He dropped his forearms onto the top of his desk and leaned toward her. This must be how he dealt with business associates. There was something about his approach, dressed as he was in officially informal clothes, that communicated a willingness to negotiate, even if exclusively on his own terms. "Obviously, Charlotte and I have had a lot of discussions about this. It's been hard for her, mostly because of Nolan. He's not in the best place, Cecily. A good job, a beautiful apartment, a glorious city, yes. But Nolan has demons. He was in rehab for a couple of months this winter."

"I didn't know."

"We haven't broadcast it. He's doing better, but it's a fragile improvement."

This was news but not surprising. She suspected that Nolan's demons had been born of parental expectations and the way he'd been controlled throughout his life. It was enough to make her sympathize with him—he who, confusingly enough, turned out to be her half brother.

Oliver was looking at her expectantly, and she had a flash of understanding about what he was waiting for. "You'd prefer he not know about this," she said.

"I told Charlotte you'd understand. He's always thought, you see, that we felt he . . ."

"I know," Cecily said. She wasn't used to cutting him off, and she found it was satisfying. "He's always thought you were disappointed he wasn't more like me. He told me that once, when he was thirteen or so."

"I'm glad you understand."

"Understand what, Oliver?"

"He's on shaky ground. That's the only reason we want to wait to tell him. This last time in rehab was for painkillers, perhaps other things, as well. We'll see how he does, make sure the timing is right; then we'll be more public about it."

She had no desire to sit down and have a heart-to-heart sibling talk with Nolan. She suspected that, with or without the drugs, that wouldn't be possible. She had no interest in seeing him, even with this new knowledge. Still, she was being treated like a problem that had to be hidden. It wasn't only that they didn't want her to tell Nolan; Oliver meant that she should tell no one. They hoped to contain the spill.

"What we want to know," Oliver said, "is what we can do for you. We're asking a lot of you, keeping this quiet, and if there's some way we can help, we'd like to do just that. At least give me the opportunity to try." Although his face was sympathetic, his tone was detached.

"I don't want anything. It was Dorothy's decision to tell me, after all these years. In some ways, I wish she'd never brought it up."

"Ah, well, too late now." He said it with annoyed sarcasm. He was angry with her for knowing and, probably more so, for her mere existence. She was an unexpected piece of information thrown into the mix late in life, when he needed it least. Right when he was hoping to stabilize his son and edge himself toward retirement.

He turned on his desk lamp, a sleek, modern piece of equipment that looked like a small UFO that had landed in front of his blotter. It lit up half his face and cast the other half in shadow. How appropriate. The kindness he'd shown her throughout her childhood was still there, but it was now overlaid with something else: she'd become an inconvenient new responsibility he'd been surprised with.

And yet, of all the things he was expressing, surprise wasn't one of them. She hadn't seen a flicker of that, not even at Fiona's badly timed announcement. He'd gone cold, but he hadn't seemed surprised.

Every once in a while, Cecily was struck by an inspiration. One had come when the idea for her dissertation, the work that would become her first book, flashed into her head fully formed; another when she decided to apply for the job at Deerpath, despite not fitting the exact qualifications listed. The best flash had come when she looked at Santosh in a coffee shop in Chicago and chose to go against her nature and introduce herself to him. Now, as she sat in Oliver's study, looking at the shadowy recesses of his aged, still-impressive face—her father's face—she was struck by another inspiration. It came to her so quickly and with such assurance, she was certain she was in touch with the truth.

"You've known, haven't you?" she said.

He tilted his head just a little, the softest of inquiries.

"About me," she continued. "You've known you're my father. Dorothy told you."

He face remained still, his eyes unchanged. "I know this hasn't been an easy time for you. I'm truly sorry for that. But don't you think it's best if we all look ahead, not behind us?"

This, she decided was confirmation of her suspicions. People talk enthusiastically about the virtues of moving forward when looking backward puts them in a bad light. "When were you told?" she asked. And then, as it became apparent that he wasn't going to answer, she said, "Not right away. Dorothy said she wanted me all to herself, and in her own way, she did. It must have been around the time she was having her seizures. I was eight then. They terrified her. Probably she told you in case she died."

Oliver didn't look angry or upset at what she was saying. He looked slightly bored. He took an ornamental pen from its holder on his desk and began tapping it against a folder of papers.

Naturally, Dorothy wouldn't have taken any money from him, even if some had been offered. She hadn't taken alimony from the man she'd been married to. Besides, she'd always had Tom to back her up, to fill in the gaps—of which, Cecily knew for a fact, there were many.

In the shadowy silence, Oliver said, "Dorothy knew that if she needed help, Charlotte and I were always there."

Cecily looked at him closely in the peculiar light to try to read his expression. "Charlotte couldn't have known," she said. The idea was frankly hilarious. Charlotte could never have kept a secret like that, could never have resisted claiming Cecily back then, before it would have been a potentially damaging revelation for Nolan. She was impossible, but she had a generosity of spirit that Oliver lacked. She would be furious if she found out that Oliver had known all along and kept it from her. She'd make Oliver's life messy and use it as a weapon to hold over him. He'd no doubt hoped for decades that she'd never find out about Cecily, but now he'd make damned sure she'd never learn that he'd known for nearly thirty years without telling her.

Once again, as usually happened to her, Cecily began to see the other side of the situation. Oliver's motives probably hadn't been terrible. It had been Dorothy's decision to go through with her pregnancy. She hadn't consulted him and wouldn't have listened to his opinion if he'd offered one. Maybe Dorothy had sworn him to secrecy.

"We should head out in a minute," Oliver said. "Dinner should be ready. And Cecily, do praise the food, however it tastes. Poor Charlotte spent many hours shopping and preparing this meal."

"I'm sure it will be delicious," Cecily said, "but even if it's not, I'll praise it. I would have, even if you hadn't said anything. I've always been polite."

"Yes, you have. Maybe make sure Tom knows, too. I hope they're having a good conversation. I realize the guesthouse was a big blow to him, but what can we do? With this news, it was one item too many to add to our lives. Right now, that is."

Cecily turned her chair so that she was facing the window, looking at the same view Oliver was looking at from behind his desk. The land, very probably the spot where Tom had been planning to put the guesthouse, was changing shape as twilight settled in and the shadows of the trees lengthened.

"Is that where you were going to build it?"

Oliver came and stood next to her chair, gazing out. She rose to stand beside him. The evening light, combined with the shadows from the UFO lamp, made it possible for her to see the landscape with hers and Oliver's blurred reflections in the foreground. He was a tall man, and standing next to him, she saw that she'd inherited her height and long legs from him. She and Santosh were the same height and had similar builds. It was something they liked about each other, even though they both knew better than to say this out loud.

"Yes, more or less. Well, the view is lovely as it is, isn't it? So lovely."

A chill ran through her, and for the first time since Dorothy's revelation, she felt an actual connection to him. What had been, up to this point, abstract now became concrete: He was her father. Her genetic makeup—her limbs, the shape of her head, a few of her features, her propensity for developing (or not) congenital conditions—had been determined partly by him, the man standing beside her. Surely other things as well. Her independence that everyone commented on, her quiet determination, her eagerness to adapt to any situation—why not those, too? What was it that Oliver resented so much about poor, inept Nolan if not that he wasn't more like his bold, ruthless father? For a narcissist like Oliver, offspring could give no greater compliment than to behave as he did. Looking at their reflections in the window, Cecily felt emboldened to do something truly audacious, maybe for the first time in her life. It was her birthright. It was what her father—her *father*—would expect of her and respect.

"You asked me what I wanted from you and Charlotte."

"Yes," he said. He put his arm on her shoulder with what felt like genuine affection. "It would be our pleasure."

All right, then. You asked for it.

"I want you to go through with the plans to build Tom's guesthouse."

Oliver laughed. She was surprised at how high his laugh was. She'd never heard him laugh with such unbridled spontaneity. "That, my dear, is a very large ask."

"Yes, it is."

The hand left her shoulder. "Charlotte and Tom couldn't come to an agreement about the design. I doubt that will change."

"You'll have to convince Charlotte to go with his plan. To trust him. It's a beautiful house that will make this property even more valuable when Nolan eventually inherits it—along with everything else he'll inherit, everything he has a right to expect he'll inherit. I expect only this from you."

Oliver turned to look at her more carefully, to study her face in detail, looking, she imagined, to see the similarities to his own. "I believe you're serious about this."

"I am," she said. "Very." Looking at his reflection, she wondered for the first time since learning about him how different her life might have been if she'd known all along. What boldness might he have imparted to her? He was not a man who'd sit by and wait for a decision about his career from a committee of his peers. He'd make demands. "It's a good deal for you, when you think about it. Maybe focus on what you'll be getting in return." It was easy and satisfying to be so audacious. "If what you said about dinner being ready is right, we should probably go out now."

There was no need to falsely praise Charlotte's cooking: it was exceptional. Cecily ate with a hunger she hadn't felt in months.

Chapter Thirty-Three

Cecily had been back in Boston for ten days when she received the email from Deerpath.

She was sitting at the little desk in Tom's guesthouse, the desk that folded down from the wall. She was putting the final touches on a chapter she was ghostwriting about the Brilliant Business of Being NICE. (The word was always in all caps when it appeared in the manuscript, a stylistic choice Molly described as "infantile but effective.") Molly had been right about the tone of the book: there was an uncomfortable nastiness to describing the value of kindness. "Let the ugly, insensitive, and unsympathetic cling to their revolting management practices. The only way to beat them is to let them stew in their own fetid stench while you rise above it on a cloud of decency. By being NICE, you kick them to the proverbial gutter, where they'll bleed out and rot until someone with a gas mask disposes of their carcasses, maggots and all. Think of NICENESS as a knife to their backs or a bullet through their hate-filled hearts."

She found it a challenge to scrub the prose of its venom and rewrite it in a way the author would approve of or—best-case scenario—not notice. It was like trimming the mold off a block of cheese while leaving the block as close to the same size as possible. She loved playing with words, feeling both pride in her work and that her life and career were not at all at stake.

It was breezy outside—she wondered if it was her imagination or if this really had been an exceptionally windy spring—and the rhododendron hedge, partly in pale mauve bloom, was batting back and forth against the window. She was amazed by how quickly she could work, despite a complete lack of interest in the subject matter. She was able to spend hours at this desk, passionately engaged.

Molly was thrilled with what she was doing—mainly, it seemed, because it proved to her that her instincts had been right. Cecily was a natural, as Molly had predicted.

Cecily heard her phone ping, a notification that she'd received an email. She froze. She hadn't heard from Santosh since their encounter at his parents' house. He was still in L.A., a fact she knew from following the Instagram account of one of his coworkers. Reading between the lines of the jovial poolside and hotel room photos, she knew that their work with the movie studio was going well. The posts were largely hyperbolic about everything—the weather, of course; the excitement of encountering various celebrities on the lot; the food; the fact that their company was working on the kind of project they'd envisioned when they first formed it. Even when you cut the hyperbole in half, it seemed their start-up was on track to score a major success. They were staying on for at least another week, a fact that Santosh's colleague seemed thrilled by, but one that Cecily knew about only from her online stalking.

Maybe Santosh had finally broken down and sent her an email. That had never been his preferred means of communication, but hope rose to the surface.

The email was from Brian, her handsome Deerpath interlocutor from what now seemed a lifetime ago.

Dear Professor Kemp,

A decision has been reached about your case. We'd like to meet with you to discuss the outcome, its implications, and the steps forward. Would you be available to come in at any of the following times? Please let us know.

There were three dates and times, all of them in the next week. It was so difficult to interpret any of what was written, she forced herself to stop trying. She would be able to make any of the times. She composed an email saying as much and stating a slight preference. Not that she had a preference, but it was a matter of pride. As she was about to hit Send, she figured it best to check flights first. There was no need to respond instantly. Maybe it would look better if she didn't bounce back an answer within seconds.

She got up from her desk and went to the window seat where, over the past month, she'd spent so many hours reading with varying degrees of distracted anxiety. Much to her own astonishment, most of the reading she'd been doing in the past couple of days had been in Fiona Snow's book.

The book was written in fast, clipped prose that she found hard to associate with the ponderous, sour woman she'd met in Woodstock. Molly had certainly earned her salary as ghostwriter with this project. Cecily couldn't wait to talk with her about how much had been in Fiona's original draft. She was researching the elements of style that made it so readable, elements she could use in the NICE work she was doing for Molly.

But that wasn't true. She was looking for something much more personal. The good thing about having everything go wrong in your life all at once is that you don't have to pretend to be doing fine.

She picked up the book and opened to a chapter titled "Make Your Tomorrow Today." Well, there was a basic, easy idea that, like so many ideas in the book, seemed ridiculously obvious. The problem was, her Tomorrow had been made by someone else, probably a whole committee of other people. Most likely, it hadn't been made Today but Several Days Ago. Judging from the email she'd just received, other people knew everything about her Tomorrow while she knew nothing.

She had a craving to call Santosh and share this development. Not having heard from him in so long had left her emotionally and physically hollowed out. It had been forever since they'd had sex, too, and even though she thought about it often (more or less constantly, if she was going to be honest), it was beginning to be difficult to imagine they'd ever had such an intense physical relationship. Even before they had this break, it had sometimes been hard to believe.

She wondered how she was able to live without that, and she was almost disappointed in herself for being able to. She moved through her day as if life were generally on course—there was the steady beat of meals and work, calls from Molly about the NICE book, the coming and going of Tom—while, at the same time, feeling as if she had no purpose other than waiting.

An hour had passed since she received Brian's email. She chose the closest available date—two days off—made her plane reservation, and wrote to him. There—she'd take a little initiative: she'd created a small portion of her Tomorrow Today.

She went back to Fiona's book, hoping she'd find some clues as to what she might do about her relationship. The headline "How Easily Do You Adapt?" leapt out at her. She was confident Fiona would approve of her extreme adaptability.

She settled in with a pen in hand. "I'm ready, Fiona," she said aloud. "Make me feel good about myself."

Chapter Thirty-Four

*F*iona was trying to scrape together a sandwich using the contents of her refrigerator—shopping was a complete waste of time, and she'd gone through the leftovers from the gala— when her phone lit up. A call from Dorothy. Well, well, well. It was about time she got in touch.

Fiona knew Dorothy was angry at her for having made the announcement about Cecily's father, but two weeks without communicating was unacceptable. Usually, Dorothy called several times in any twenty-four-hour period. Fiona hadn't expected her to cling to her resentment for quite this long.

Dorothy's anger was misplaced. Ridiculous, in fact. With all those people swarming around that weekend and Dorothy calling her up, desperate, in the middle of the night to spill the beans about Oliver, the information would have come out anyway. Fiona had merely nudged fate in its inevitable direction. She'd done Dorothy and her daughter a huge favor. Oliver had not given them any money, but Fiona was sending him emails daily to elicit an investment, an investment in his *daughter's* future.

If Fiona had it to do over, she'd have done the same thing at the gala. Although, come to think of it, she'd have worn a different outfit.

She let Dorothy's call go to voice mail. Two could play the silence game. She pushed at the back door of her condo, plate in hand. There was a nice little patio out there—*little* being the operative word—where she liked to have coffee and eat lunch. Or would have liked to if the door hadn't become almost impossible to open. By contrast, the front door was almost impossible to close. Warped frames or warped doors. She gave up and ate at the table in the depressing kitchenette.

This was not the kind of place she'd imagined living when she came to Woodstock six years ago. She'd pictured one of the little houses overlooking a stream and within walking distance of everything, including yoga studios and a swimming hole—not that she swam. Such places existed in abundance in this town, and she'd tried to manifest one. Unfortunately, this unit with a kitchenette (what a demeaning concept) in a sprawling development was what she'd been able to afford. It was like living in a motel that had been converted into an assisted-living facility. Everyone here appeared to be well above seventy. Attempting a conversation with them meant enduring a lengthy discussion about inadequate heat, a dripping air-conditioning unit, or hot water that was dangerously hot or insufficient, depending on whom you pretended to listen to. The favorite topic was how much they missed Manhattan, a dead end from Fiona's perspective: she'd never lived there and had a low tolerance for nostalgia.

On the plus side, there was parking right outside the door. Motel-style, but convenient. The less walking, the better. Her feet had been a problem for years.

She finished the sandwich and checked her voice mail. "It's Dorothy. Give me a call when you get this. I need a favor. I need some help."

Fiona tossed down the phone. All of a sudden, Dorothy was getting serious and demanding. Her tone was off-putting, a scolding gasp, as if she were so appalled, she couldn't catch her breath. Fiona wouldn't give in to it. One thing she had learned over the years was that a significant portion of her credibility as a motivational speaker and inspirational author was dependent upon dominance and being difficult to approach, while feigning the opposite. Let that drop, and you earned no respect, little attention, and zero income. She'd been schooled in all that by Desiree Blau, her late editor and the architect of her success.

She'd make Dorothy wait, then call back and pretend she never received her message. People never questioned you directly about such statements, even when they didn't believe you.

As she wandered around the cramped and increasingly cluttered apartment, she began to feel a distinct sense of unease. Dorothy needed her, it was true. She, Fiona, was the closest thing to a product Dorothy had to offer, and without her, Dorothy's whole plan for an educational and inspirational retreat center collapsed. She'd be stuck in that crazy building that had been on the market for untold years before she bought it at a price that was still inflated.

On the other hand, it was becoming clear to Fiona that her options for her own future were narrowing. She'd never admit as much to Dorothy, but in the privacy of her own god-awful condo, she had to accept that they needed each other equally.

She decided to leave immediately and drive around until one or two before heading to Dorothy's. She was sick of the winding scenic roads around here, but driving was better than staying inside, caged and prowling.

She pulled her car onto the road in the opposite direction of Dorothy's.

In retrospect, it had probably been a mistake to leave her job as a counselor at Yale all those years ago. If she'd stayed on, earning a steady salary, she'd have had a safe, secure nest egg by now, could have retired and, if she lived as modestly as she was currently living, never had to worry—or play nice to anyone. She knew there was no point in looking backward, but just as it was becoming less practical to do so, she found herself falling into it more often. Memory was complicated as you aged—too little of it was terrifying, too much of it was depressing. It was best to remind herself that leaving Yale had seemed like the brilliant thing to do back when she did it. And for a good while, it had been.

For ten years, she'd made notes on the intelligent, promising, and motivated students she counseled at Yale. Some went on to staggering levels of success; others drifted into unhappiness and obscurity. What lessons were there to learn from these brilliant young people about outcomes and how to shape them?

Everyone was reading self-help at the time, and she figured she could compile her observations into something interesting. She put together a book proposal and a first chapter and, on a whim, not believing it would go anywhere, had sent it to an editor at William Morrow whose name, "Desiree Blau," she'd seen in the acknowledgments page of a successful and reasonably intelligent book of pop psychology. Six weeks later, to her utter astonishment, she had a contract for a book that paid her more than five times her annual salary.

Goodbye, Yale.

She wrote the book over the course of a year. She'd never been so passionate about anything she'd done. It was easy to stay at her desk for ten hours, avoid socializing—never her strong suit anyway—and get up before dawn to bury herself in the project again. It was the first time in her life she was gleeful about her lack of interest in relationships and her aversion to physical intimacy.

The title of the six-hundred-page manuscript she turned in to Desiree Blau was *The Psychological Components of Efficacious Behavior and Success in the Ivy League*. She heard nothing from her for two months. Not a word. Then Desiree called her and said, "Fiona! Come to New York for lunch. Do you eat sushi?"

The restaurant was so minimal, it had seemed to Fiona like an unfinished room. As she waited for Desiree to show up, she realized that she was surrounded by men and women making deals and buzzing with money. There wasn't a bad outfit or a cheap haircut in the bunch. She certainly didn't fit in with this group, but it would be nice if, one day, she did. Everything hinged on Desiree, who, up to this point, she'd never met.

Desiree arrived twenty minutes late. She entered the restaurant wearing a Chanel suit, high heels, a face-lift, and an invisible cloak of power. The restaurant's staff attended to her as if she were a revered relative they'd been waiting for all day.

"I'm sorry I'm late," she said to Fiona. "We're in the middle of an auction for Paul Nazarian's new novel. It's going much higher than I planned. But I promise you, Fiona, I will get it. Don't have any worries about that."

Fiona nodded as if reassured by the promise. She'd never heard of Paul Nazarian. Desiree ordered for both of them. "Otherwise, you'd be intimidated by the prices. Now you can blame me."

Fiona had to wait for any mention of her own book. Desiree's monologue rolled along throughout most of the lunch, her chopsticks flashing. Advances and sales figures and legendary deals were described. While none of it meant much to Fiona, all of it impressed her. Desiree was famous for having worked with politicians, journalists, and novelists who were icons on both the high and low ends of the culture. This was her world. She wasn't bragging, but before she'd even mentioned Fiona's manuscript, she made it clear that having her behind a book was a stroke of good luck that came only once in a lifetime.

Finally, as the $250 array of sushi was cleared (most of the food still untouched), Desiree held up one of her extraordinarily bony arms, shook a bracelet to her elbow, and said, "There are people in the house who thought I overpaid for your proposal. I'm a controversial, polarizing figure, as many powerful women are. I consider it a badge of honor. They're rolling their eyes behind my back."

Fiona was so tense, she didn't dare say anything.

"What they all forget is that the only two *significant* failures I've had in my career were decades ago. I learn from my mistakes, Fiona. I make my successes happen. That's the spirit I liked in your proposal."

"Thank you."

"I'm going to make your book a success. I'm leaving nothing to chance. It's going to earn back every penny of the advance and then some. It won't make you rich, but your life will change."

Relief flooded Fiona, and her face grew warm. "I'm so relieved you liked the book. I wasn't sure when I didn't hear from you."

"I didn't like it. Nor did anyone else at the house."

Fiona floundered, then managed to say, "I'll revise it in any way you want."

"That won't work. I know what this book needs, and I know you're incapable of delivering it. Please don't look hurt. It's a simple statement of fact. At this point, it's not your problem; it's mine."

Fiona was so confused, she didn't know whether this was good news or bad. A tiny dish of green tea–flavored ice cream was placed before her, and she began eating it.

"I've hired a book doctor," Desiree said, nonchalant at reporting this fait accompli. "She's worked on only one other project, but she has a background in academia, so she's able to understand what you've written before she changes it. I had her do a sample chapter. It. Is. Gorgeous." She said the final word with her eyes closed and with a full-body delight that made Fiona uncomfortable.

"When can I read it?"

"I strongly recommend you don't. It would only confuse you. You have to trust me."

Desiree put on an enormous pair of eyeglasses, ones that covered and magnified half her face, and Fiona saw that she was far older than she'd assumed. She pulled a credit card from her purse and handed it to the waitress.

"I don't know if you're interested in getting into the boring weeds," she said, "but we're giving it a new title, cutting it to one-third the length, adding charts and bullet points, and giving a little overlay of spirituality."

"I've been compiling the research for ten years."

"You mustn't take it personally. Raymond Carver didn't like what Gordon Lish did to his stories, either, but that's what made him a household name—albeit in a small number of households. All Lish did was pull out the essence of what Carver had written." Desiree reached across the table and put her hand on top of Fiona's affectionately. "If you handed me a pile of your old, outdated clothes, and I pulled out a few acceptable pieces and threw out the rest, what remained would still be your clothes."

Fiona excused herself and went to the bathroom. It was all so humiliating, she felt like crying. She'd spent a good chunk of her advance, but she could pay it back over time if she withdrew her manuscript. She'd left Yale on good terms; it wasn't inconceivable they'd rehire her. She had to take control of her own work. Book doctor! Overlay of spirituality! Cutting two-thirds of her work!

Back in the restaurant, a tall, distinguished man was standing at their table. Desiree introduced him to Fiona as the publisher of Simon & Schuster. "Fiona Snow just delivered her first book. Brilliant motivational insights. We're giving it a huge promotion next fall. *The Nature of Success in Successful Natures.*"

"Fantastic title," he said. "First printing?"

"Two-fifty, at least."

"You're working with the best in the business, Fiona," the man said. "Desiree is going to make you a star."

Fiona had gone from being invisible in this room of the power elite to being looked at by this important man as if she mattered. She saw him studying her face, memorizing it.

"I'm incredibly lucky to be working with her," Fiona said.

And that was that.

She was amazed by how much she liked the finished book, with its clean, eye-catching graphics and the bright, intriguing cover. It came in at a crisp 325 pages. Fiona had thanked the book doctor, whom she'd never met or spoken to, ambiguously in the acknowledgments section, the only portion of the book that hadn't been rewritten.

During her first interview about the book, she literally forgot that it was so vastly different from what she'd turned in. The more she talked about it, the more it became her own. After all, the book doctor had just worked with what she'd given her. They were still her clothes! When it began to sell well, her pride in ownership and her accomplishment in having written it became even stronger. The success of the book proved its message about the power of thought and imagining triumph.

The book hadn't made her a "star"—whatever that meant in the world of publishing—and she certainly hadn't become a household name. Despite four long phone calls and preliminary interviews with producers from *The Oprah Winfrey Show*, she was never booked. Desiree told her not to worry. They'd agreed to mention the book in a segment, and anyway, she was confirmed for four minutes on the *Today* show. After the Oprah disappointment, the calls and messages from the publishing house began to dwindle.

Once the book earned back the advance Desiree had paid, Fiona felt her editor's interest wane. Her purchase of the book had been vindicated. The book made it to the bottom of the *Times* bestseller list but then dropped off after two weeks.

Fiona's ideas for a follow-up—*The Force of Nature in the Nature of Force*, *The Joy of Success in the Success of Joy*—were met with cool dismissal. As sales were beginning to fade along with interest in her, she was contacted by a loud, crass woman named Wanda who ran an agency for speakers. She promised Fiona she could get her at least twelve speaking engagements per year at a minimum of five thousand dollars per appearance. Figuring she had nothing to lose, Fiona signed on with her. She spent years traveling to universities, adult education centers, yoga retreats, motivational seminars in Tuscany, even on cruise ships as part of the entertainment.

Naturally, those opportunities eventually ebbed as well. Wanda contacted her less often, Fiona's fee kept dropping, and it became clear she had to do something else. Desiree retired from the business and, shortly thereafter, died. Fiona was shocked to discover from her obituary that she'd been eighty when they first started working together.

Fiona was giving a talk at a yoga studio in Woodstock—$375, negotiated up from the initial offer of $150—when it struck her that this place might be a logical next move. Most of the people she met claimed they loved the mountains, the peaceful atmosphere, the welcoming vibe, but if you dug a little deeper, you struck discontent or disappointment as the reason they were here—a massive rent increase, aging out of the job market, a failed marriage or two. It was a town filled with people who were looking for more in themselves and from life in general, provided the search didn't demand too much. She saw herself having a life here. Writing a new book. Getting a foothold.

It was a tenuous foothold and a decidedly small life, but by the time Dorothy approached her on the street, Fiona had her place. People knew her.

Dorothy had come up to her and introduced herself with the bravura of a Wanda or a Desiree, but with a homey vulnerability that Fiona found touching. "Tell me who you are," she'd said to Fiona. "You and I need to know each other." Later, Dorothy took her to her house (everyone in town knew about it, but Fiona had never been inside), and within a matter of days, they had their plan for the retreat center in place. Dorothy had the ability to inspire people. There was something in her good-humored optimism that gave Fiona hope for a fresh start.

What she'd done at the gala—spilling the beans to Oliver and his insolent wife—had been a betrayal, but she'd had to assert herself. All those years of pushing and promoting her book, all those talks and lectures and seminars, she'd always felt a slight chill under the surface of her confidence, under her confident ownership of the book and its message. When you came right down to it, she hadn't written it. Not really. She sometimes wondered if people could tell, if it showed on her face. Naturally, they wouldn't say anything to her. On top of that, she knew there was something about her lack of family, lack of desire for family, that people looked down upon. Smug Tom with his love of his niece and all the talk of "family matters." It was the convergence of all this that had pushed her to do what she'd done. And no, she wasn't sorry.

She'd even begun writing something new, *The Love of Life in a Life of Love*, and she felt certain she'd finish it. If no one wanted it, she could self-publish and sell it at the seminars.

While driving down endless back roads, Fiona had called Dorothy four times, but she hadn't picked up. Strange, indeed. She was never without her phone. And after all, Dorothy was the one who'd initiated contact this morning.

Fiona parked in front of Dorothy's house. She'd apologize. She'd figure a way to phrase it so it didn't sound too humiliating or demeaning. She'd say she'd been rash and impulsive, plead guilty to manslaughter instead of facing the death penalty.

She supposed she'd better alert Dorothy to the fact that she'd arrived, but once again, no answer. Ah, she was probably with Harold. There was a misguided relationship, almost a grotesque one. She did not want to walk in on *that*. It was sad that Dorothy had needed this kind of validation from men all her life. Almost as sad as the fact that Fiona hadn't.

Harold's car wasn't in front of Dorothy's building nor, she found when she walked around back, in the drive there. The sky, which had been bright and blue all day, had suddenly clouded over. Standing below with the big building looming up in front of her, Fiona felt a clutch of dread.

She tottered toward the door on the uneven paving stones of the walk. Desiree was the one who'd told her she should always wear heels. It gave her even greater height and presence, and it showed people that she was committed to standing out above the crowd. That was what her readers wanted. Fiona had been wearing heels all these years—initially to please Desiree and now to pay tribute to her. The shoes had taken a toll, and in the long run she wasn't sure they'd done her any good anyway.

There was something eerily quiet about the building. That shouldn't have been so strange, given that Dorothy was apparently there alone, but it appeared empty.

"Dorothy?" she called out from the bottom of the staircase. When there was no answer, she went up, finding that she was moving more slowly as she went. She'd been thinking too much about the past all afternoon, always a risk when you were trying to move forward.

At the top of the staircase, she called out again. Nothing. She went into the kitchen and found herself walking as quietly as she could, almost with reverence. She'd known something was wrong with Dorothy for a long time. She'd seen her trouble breathing, her moments of slight panic when, Fiona assumed, she felt palpitations or something of that nature. When she'd driven her to Kingston, she knew it wasn't to have a mole removed. But there had been no reason to bring it up, especially given that Dorothy herself seemed so determined to keep it hidden.

No sign of Dorothy in the kitchen, in the living room, or even in the little sitting room or whatever it was being used for. As a last, unlikely resort, she went to Dorothy's bedroom and knocked on the door lightly. No response. She pushed it open gently. Dorothy was stretched out on the bed on one side, fully clothed, with her back to the door. Fiona was going to call out to her, but she could tell there was no point in doing so.

She sat on the edge of the bed. Dorothy was still breathing. She shook her, lightly at first and then more vigorously. Dorothy stirred but didn't move, and when Fiona went to the other side of the bed, she could see that Dorothy was looking up at her with large, frightened eyes. A stroke, obviously. She was trying to say something to Fiona, but Fiona had to bend down to hear her. Her speech was slurred and thick, but Fiona finally made out what she was saying, which sounded like she was repeating the word *fill* over and over.

When she looked down, she saw that Dorothy had a fistful of prescription slips clutched in her hand.

Chapter Thirty-Five

C ecily was leaving in two hours. Tom looked over at the guest cottage, but the trees were now in full leaf, and he could see only the top half of the windows, with no clue as to what was going on inside. No doubt, she was ready or about to be ready.

He'd spent almost no time with her this visit, largely because he had been so busy putting together a portfolio of his work, contacting architects in the business, trying to line something up for himself. So far, the response was what he'd expected: polite rejection with promises to keep him in mind for any special projects that came into the office. He sensed embarrassment in the people he spoke with. Gray hair and CVs make for an inherently embarrassing combination, like condoms and senior discounts.

Cecily had asked Tom a few times if Oliver or Charlotte had contacted him about the guesthouse. "They haven't called yet? Are you sure there's not a message or an email?" There was something insistent about her questions, as if she were waiting for the arrival of a letter she knew had been sent. It was touching at first but finally began to grate— salt in a wound he wanted to let heal. He had to sit her down and tell her to stop.

"It's over," he said. "They've decided against it. It happens. All the time. In the end, it's their house, their money, their choice. Let's just move on. And please do not let it interfere with your new relationship with them."

He'd offered to go to Chicago with her and accompany her to the meeting or sit in the car for moral support as she learned her fate. She'd declined. She had her new friend on call, a woman with some experience with legal cases, should she need her. It was this admirable independence of Cecily's that tugged at Tom. It was the very thing that should have made him worry about her least—she had survival instincts, after all—but was also the quality that recalled to him the look of the infant he'd held in his arms at her birth. And he had understood then, as now, how essentially alone she was. Learning about her father had mysteriously intensified that.

Although, he had to admit that the changes he'd noticed in her over the past ten days were not insignificant. There was a new confidence in Cecily. Even her posture seemed different. Perhaps he was imagining it, but she seemed, for the first time he could remember, to carry herself with comfort in her stature, her height, her long legs, the very physical traits she'd inherited from Oliver. Whether she was exonerated or found guilty, she'd return to the apartment she shared with Santosh to face the fate of her relationship and wait for him to return, also alone.

Maybe it was a given in their family. Dorothy, surrounded as she was by such a large cast of friends and intermittent lovers, by Cecily and even by Tom, had always seemed alone.

He heard his phone vibrating and got up from his desk to retrieve it. A number he didn't recognize. That was never a good sign, but good news was still possible, bidden or unbidden, even from unknown phone numbers.

"Is this . . . Tom?"

A familiar voice, but so tentative, he wasn't sure whose. "It is. Who's this?"

"Oh, great." The man on the other end sounded so relieved and suddenly jovial that Tom recognized at once that it was Harold Berger,

Dorothy's erstwhile lover or friend in Woodstock. "Listen, Tom, I'm afraid I'm calling you with some bad news."

Tom sat back down. He saw right away that he'd been expecting this call, without knowing it, for a very long time. He began bargaining with a god he didn't believe in that "bad news" did not mean the worst news. "All right," he said softly. "What's happened?"

"I got a call from Fiona Snow a couple hours ago. Dorothy's had a stroke. At least that's what they think. To her credit, Fiona called an ambulance and went to the hospital with her. Left shortly after, but hey."

Tom waited for Harold to say more. When he didn't, he said, "How . . . is she now?"

"It's a little hard to tell. She's about to have more tests run. They won't let me in, but she's tough. And on top of that, she's not that old."

It sounded, touchingly, as if Harold were trying to talk himself into believing everything was going to be all right. "Can I speak to her?" Tom asked.

"No, no. Tubes, ICU, all that."

"Are you there at the hospital?"

"My wife and I, yes."

"I'll leave as soon as I can. If you can get a message to her, let her know I'm on my way."

"Thanks, Tom. What about Cecily? Dorothy told me a few days ago she's in Boston."

"Yes, she's about to head back to Chicago, but I'll tell her."

"Great. It's always best to have family here to help make decisions." *Decisions*, in this context, had an ominous ring.

Tom knocked on the door of Cecily's guest cottage and heard, above the sound of the wind, her running across the floor. She flung the door open with a look of excitement so out of sync with his current mood and with her usual appearance these days, he was completely disoriented and forgot for a moment what he'd come to tell her.

"Tom," she said, "you won't believe what I'm about to do."

She'd told him, in an apologetic and self-deprecating way, that she was enjoying the ghostwriting she was doing, but this giddiness could not be related to that. It certainly couldn't be related to the meeting she was about to attend at Deerpath. She was standing in the doorway, and, newly in possession of her stature, she seemed to fill it.

"Try me," he said. "I'm ready to believe almost anything."

She was holding a book in her hands, her fingers stuck between the pages. She held it up, grinning. It was Fiona's tome, and seeing her name in bold red graphics enraged him. So, this was what it meant to be "triggered." Why wasn't *she* at the hospital with Dorothy, the least she could do?

"I've been reading Fiona's book. I didn't tell you about it because, to be honest, I knew you wouldn't approve."

It saddened him to think she considered him so judgmental, but he was flattered to hear his judgment meant something to her. Given the circumstances of her life right now, he would have understood any crazy behavior, even reading *The Nature of Whatever It Was*.

"I'm glad you're finding it so amusing," he said. And then, in a different tone. "Cecily, I . . ."

"I wouldn't say amusing, although it's written in a breezy, entertaining style—no thanks to Fiona. The thing is, Tom, I've been reading it for the past hour or so, making notes on the pages, hoping to find something I can use. For my life. Don't cringe, please. She, or this book, made me see the way I've been handling things in a new light."

Tom had as much faith in allegedly life-altering flashes of insight inspired by pop psychology weekend seminars as he did in New Year's resolutions and marital vows. But if any of them made you happy in the moment, that couldn't be bad. At this late stage of human evolution, a few brief, shining moments were as much as anyone could reasonably expect.

"Cecily . . ."

"I know it sounds ridiculous, like being moved to tears by a commercial for McDonald's, but, well, if you are, you are. Anyway, given how my life has been going, I couldn't legitimately claim my way of doing things has worked out very well for me. I don't think any harm could come from taking this seriously and acting on her advice."

"Let me know how it works out. I'll order a copy for myself." And now, it really was time to burst this bubble of excitement. He hated to do it. "I know you're almost ready to leave, so . . ."

"I'm not going to the meeting about my case. That's my big decision. I'm taking control of my tomorrow today. Don't ask what that phrase means, all right? If I try to explain it, I'll start to doubt myself."

"What do you mean you're not going?" Given Harold's news about Dorothy, that was convenient but confusing.

"I emailed the Title IX office and told them I can't make the meeting. My whole life, I've been adapting. I've been adapting to whatever was put in my path. To Dorothy's crazy decisions, to my student insisting on my attention, to Neeta's threat, even to Santosh telling me he wants a break. I thought it was my best life strategy. I thought it was my greatest strength. Fiona, of all people—along with her ghostwriter—made me realize it's been a mistake. It's passivity with a better press agent. She likes the press agent metaphor."

"I'm glad you're staying," he said—although, knowing what he had to say next, he didn't feel much joy.

"I'm not staying. I'm going to L.A. I just booked a flight that connects at O'Hare." She looked at him, eyes wide, waiting for a reaction to her impulsive behavior.

"To meet up with Santosh," he said.

"I figured out what hotel he's in from his friend's social media. He doesn't know I'm coming."

"You haven't told him?"

"I know it's ridiculous. I know he might turn me down. I know I'm setting myself up for potential humiliation. But even in that case, I'll have the satisfaction of knowing I tried. For once in my life, I didn't adapt. I shouldn't have gone along when he said he wanted a break, as if I had no say in the matter. Please don't try to talk me out of it. Tom. No matter where it leads, I know I'll be better off for having done it."

Tom was frozen. He'd rarely seen Cecily like this—so enthusiastic about an impulsive move. The right thing to do, he knew, was to tell her what he'd learned about Dorothy. That way, he'd leave it up to her to decide whether to go through with her new plan or not. It wasn't his choice to make.

"I have to tell you something about Dorothy," he said.

She cut him off. "It's what she'd do, Tom. It's what she'd have told me to do long ago, if I'd trusted her enough to tell her everything. I'm too used to dismissing her advice. I tried to call her half an hour ago, but there was no answer."

She was right: it was exactly what Dorothy would want her to do. Letting her go through with this risky, impulsive plan was exactly what she'd want *him* to do. It was amazing how much more important the opinions of the sick and . . . and the dead were than of the boring old alive and healthy.

"I'm excited for you," he said. "Do you need any help packing?"

She pointed to a small suitcase in the corner. She was ready.

Later, after she'd gotten into the Lyft and headed off down the steep drive, he went inside his quiet house and gazed out at the view of Boston in the distance. For once, he wished he were there, surrounded by strangers and tall buildings, buffers against this latest bad news. He lay down on his sofa and closed his eyes. Five minutes of quiet to prepare for the drive and what awaited him at the end of it.

His phone woke him up. *Dorothy!* But no, the call was from Winston.

"Well, well, well, Tom," he said. "I've got some very interesting news for you."

The smug, forced eagerness in his voice grated. Things were bad enough already. He didn't need to hear more details about Lanford's latest triumph. "It's not the best moment, Winston."

"You'll definitely want to hear this."

Tom pulled out a duffel bag and began to stuff clothes into it. Lots of clothes. It was impossible to know how long he'd be in the Hudson Valley, and because he was driving, he might as well overpack. "All right," he said. "Go ahead."

"Your friend Oliver just left the office."

"I'm not sure I'd call him a friend, but go on."

"You might feel differently when I tell you why he was here." He let this tease hang in the air and then said, "Their project is back on."

Tom paused in his packing. "In what sense 'on'?"

"In the sense that he wants to go ahead and build the guesthouse. *Your* guesthouse."

Tom was suspicious of this, but Oliver was not the type to play games; his time was too precious to him. It was shocking enough that he'd even bothered to go to the office. "Why didn't he tell me himself?"

"He was looking for you. I offered to deliver a message."

It was difficult to process this news. He understood the importance of it, but it was hard to know why Oliver, a man who never changed his mind, would suddenly do so. Charlotte had no real influence over him, and the last Tom had heard, she, too, was ambivalent.

"It's good news, Tom. It's very good news. He wants to cut a few corners to lower the costs, but nothing that compromises the design. It sounds as if he's taking the reins from Charlotte in moving this along."

"I'm having a little trouble making sense of this," Tom said.

"Does it have to make sense? Does anything in life make sense? The internet? The electoral college? It's enough to know the project is on. This is your masterpiece, Tom. Try to enjoy it. It's just the beginning for us. Now I can let Lanford go."

"I thought you loved him. You consider him a genius."

"Oh, he's that, but people keep asking me if he's my son. I can't have people thinking that. The idea that I'd have a child is horrible enough, but then thinking that I'd hire him and work with him daily is just too much."

Tom wondered if pride should compel him to hold back from excitement over this. After all, Winston was only a few weeks away from having waved goodbye to him. Now a piece of good news, and Tom was supposed to forget all that. But who was he kidding? Pride was just vanity with a better press agent, as Fiona had probably said at some point in her career, and Tom had always loathed vanity.

"You should keep Lanford on," he said. "He can tweak a few elements of sustainability and get us even more attention. Oliver can brag about how green he is while tearing up the atmosphere in a private jet."

"You have a point . . ."

"I have to leave town for a few days. Maybe longer. I'll be in touch." *Oh, what the hell*, he thought. *If you can't be proud, you can fall back on sincerity*. "And, Winston, thanks for your enthusiasm. It means a lot to me."

It took him longer than expected to leave the house. He ended up packing his schematics for the guesthouse and a few of his original drawings. The backseat of his car was completely full. As a last-minute inspiration, he checked his email. There was a message from Charlotte.

"By now you've heard. It was Oliver's decision, not mine. Although, I'm pleased. I wish there were more space, but let's not go over that again. If you're in the mood to thank someone, start with Cecily and not Oliver. This all began the night you were here. He told me she's a lot like him after all. When I asked how, he said 'tough negotiator.' Make of it what you will."

Chapter Thirty-Six

Somewhere in the middle of the Berkshires, it began to rain. Not the gentle downpours Tom usually associated with spring, but a torrential onslaught that made it almost impossible to see. Traffic slowed, and cars began turning on their emergency flashers and pulling off to the side of the road. At some point soon, auto manufacturers were going to have to factor in routine assaultive storms like this one and, inevitably, worse. Design better windshield wipers and lights and perhaps stronger glass. In a matter of seconds, the road turned from an organized stream of cars to a chaotic tangle of flashing lights and swerving vehicles. This was the world in miniature: the thin crust of order disintegrated at the softest touch. The electricity shuts down for an hour, the water stops running, the faint smell of smoke filters into the auditorium. Pandemonium erupts within seconds. It was what everyone felt approaching these days as they watched the looming storm clouds and the angry, violent mobs.

It hadn't let up by the time he arrived at the Kingston hospital. The weather system had stalled over their heads. Cecily, he hoped, was high above, tucked into her slim seat and her optimistic plans. She'd been alone with Oliver for only thirty or forty minutes. That had been when she talked him into it. She'd never tell Tom how. She'd never admit that she had, finally, fulfilled her goal of paying him back. He didn't know if his weepiness for the past four hours was about that or anxiety over Dorothy and the cloud of pending chaos.

The hospital was a modest brick building with a hodgepodge of additions from different eras, an architectural incoherence that gave it the look of a small, unimportant city. The services and care at a vast hospital in a big city were probably superior, but there was a seductive hominess and ease to small hospitals that was irresistible. He had to believe Dorothy, upon arriving, had been comforted, assuming she'd been aware of her surroundings.

Tom opened a large golf umbrella—his only connection to that sport—and dashed into the emergency room entrance. Umbrella or not, he somehow got soaked from the knees down. Inside: more chaos. Harold was sitting in the outdated waiting room in the company of Peggy, his wife, with the extraordinary braid. It was extraordinary, too, that she was here with him now.

Harold shook Tom's hand and said, "It's good you came." He clapped Tom on the shoulder. He had on a sleeveless T-shirt, but over it, he'd added a white shirt that was yellow around the collar and armpits. This was clearly a remnant from his more staid, academic past. Last vestiges. Almost every aging hippie Tom had met owned an outdated vestigial wardrobe comprising suit jackets and dress pants and leather shoes from weddings and funerals and family occasions past. The clothes were hauled out now only for special events—both the celebratory and the somber. Because this was not celebratory, the sight of it saddened Tom.

"You haven't been here this whole time, have you?" he asked Harold.

"No, no. We had to do some shopping down here and dropped in again. Figured we'd wait for you to show up. You remember Peggy, don't you?"

As if, with that braid, anyone could forget Peggy.

"The strain of the party with Fiona was too much for her," Peggy said. "I told Harold to try to talk her out of it." She looked at Tom as if seeing him for the first time and rearranged the braid. "You'll catch a cold in those wet clothes."

"I almost never get colds," he said.

Harold laughed. "That's what Dorothy claims, too."

If Peggy had any response to this suggestion of intimacy, she didn't show it. "Now that you're here," she said, "we should probably get going, Harold."

She'd been clutching a magazine, and when she set it down, Tom saw that it was an outdated copy of *Good Housekeeping.* The incongruity of her reading it delighted him.

"Thank you for staying. Any updates?" he asked.

Harold took him by the arm and led him a little bit away from where his wife was sitting, a pointless bit of discretion with Peggy observing it so closely. "Tell Dorothy I'm counting on her to pull through. Tell her I'm going over to the house to install some new electrical outlets in the kitchen. Call me with any news, okay? You have my phone?"

With that, Harold went over to his wife and had a quiet conversation. She looped her arm through his, and he led her out of the waiting room. *Her* husband, after all—not that there had been any question of that. Dorothy was the mistress, a lesser role, but if you wanted to put a positive spin on it, still a role.

The idiotic clatter of a television suspended from the ceiling made it impossible for Tom to think. Maddeningly, no one was watching it. Phones were much more irresistible now. Even the sleekest television sets had begun to have the clunky look of dial phones and electric typewriters.

Eventually, a nurse appeared in the ominous doorway leading to the bowels of the hospital and called his name. He followed her down a long corridor lined with cubicles in which people in various stages of distress were sprawled, attended to by clusters of family or friends, leaning into their loved one's body, clutching at limbs. He was introduced to Dorothy's doctor, a stern woman whose humorlessness inspired confidence, if not joy. She shook his hand and told him she was happy to meet him. Her explanation of her history with Dorothy over the past several months was thorough and tipped toward reminding him that Dorothy's current problems had largely been brought on by her refusal to follow protocol. A lawsuit, in other words, would be futile. Don't even consider it.

"It was a stroke?" Tom asked.

"That's the immediate crisis we're attending to now. There's significant collateral deterioration that complicates everything."

Dr. Min's tone was steady but with a lack of sentimentality that bordered on accusation. Not of Dorothy, but of him for not having overseen his sister's well-being—making sure she had her prescriptions filled, that she was taking her medications.

"What's her condition now?"

She regarded him with what looked like mild surprise over his even asking. "Critical," she said, the "of course" implied.

The word was alarming, but in so many ways—physical, financial, psychological—Dorothy's condition always had been critical.

"And the prognosis?"

"The next twenty-four hours will tell us more. The fact that she's currently stabilized gives me hope she's going to pull through."

He remembered the time he'd spent in hospitals, sitting at the bedsides of friends who were so sick and frail, it was almost impossible to imagine their living more than a few minutes. Incomprehensibly, many lingered on for weeks and months, no doubt from sheer force of will. Others, those who seemed almost robust, slipped away quietly overnight when no one was looking. Yes, life was unpredictable, but it was nothing compared with death.

"I'm relieved to hear that," Tom said.

"Yes, but don't expect that she's going to be herself. She'll need care. Certainly, in the short term. This won't be easy."

"It never has been," he said. "Can I see her?"

"Once we get her settled, I can have the nurse take you up to intensive care." She checked her watch. "It will probably be a while. I'd recommend getting something to eat now."

Tom wanted to ask Dr. Min if she thought they should try to get Dorothy to a bigger hospital. In New York City or even Albany. And yet, even in this dire situation, he worried first about offending her.

"Will you be on duty for a while?"

Like almost every doctor he'd ever dealt with, she laughed at this and nodded. "Oh yes," she said, "I'll be on duty for a while," in a tone that suggested she was always on duty. The laugh alone made him see her as a person rather than a doctor, probably with a husband, possibly with children, a person whose existence was not centered on taking care of Dorothy. That was *his* job. "I'm sorry that Dorothy didn't follow your advice, didn't take the prescriptions. She's always done things her own way."

Dr. Min looked at him through her big black-framed glasses. She was grateful for the apology; she was about to toss him a treat. "Pretty much everyone does things their own way in life. Sometimes that means being compliant; sometimes it means ignoring advice. We'll focus on the fact that she got here today. And that you did. There aren't any good places to eat nearby. Drive uptown and come back in an hour or so."

Chapter Thirty-Seven

Cecily's flight from Boston to Chicago had been delayed, and she almost missed her connection to L.A. She ran down the concourse at O'Hare and was one of the last people to board. She received the stares of derision reserved for late arrivals as she rushed down the aisle to the last row on the plane. Well, someone has to be the last to board, don't they? In the air, en route to L.A., a man refused to stay seated until they reached cruising altitude, and one of those loud altercations she'd seen in viral videos erupted. Half the people on the plane took off their own seat belts, grabbed their phones, and started to record. In seconds, the crew lost control of what had seemed like an orderly gathering of polite people. It's so much easier to follow bad behavior than good. Next on the list of travel miseries was flying into turbulence. It broke up the brawl but lasted almost an hour.

Cecily was numb to all of it. She had a mission, and the discomforts associated with achieving it were insignificant. As long as the plane was moving forward in its westward direction, she was content.

It was early evening by the time she arrived in L.A., and the warm, dry air wrapped around her like a seductive scent. She'd rented a car online and felt an almost giddy happiness as she collected the key and got behind the wheel. She'd loved L.A. the couple of times she'd visited. Its improbable architecture, appalling sprawl, and terrible traffic gave it a faded, edgy glamour that was unlike anything in the East or the

Midwest. The extremes of climate and apocalyptic fires were horrifying but felt of a piece with the unstable ground. It was a city, more than any other, in which you could be whoever you wanted to be—assuming you knew who that was. Cecily had never desired to live here—she was more of an indoor person, for one thing—but while she was visiting, she sensed it was one of a small handful of American cities where she might end up.

The hotel Santosh's team was staying at was in Santa Monica, not far from the ocean. She saw the lights of the pier shimmering in the distance as she drove down Colorado Avenue. There's something relaxing about iconic views and landmarks: you have such a strong impression of them before even seeing them in person, you don't have to observe them too closely to feel the full impact of their beauty and history. It was like seeing a movie for the third time and enjoying the acting and cinematography without the anxiety of worrying over the resolution of the plot.

She pulled up to the hotel, and a uniformed valet seamlessly removed her luggage, took her place behind the wheel, and drove off to a mysterious parking garage she knew she'd never see the inside of. This left her standing in front of the hotel with her bag, listening to the palm fronds clattering in the breeze high above her. She went into the lobby, as different from the hotel lobby in which she'd had lunch with Neeta as Chicago was from L.A. As different as her life was from Santosh's at this moment. The lobby was all glass and steel and cool, light furniture that appeared to be floating. She, too, felt as if she were floating.

She picked up a house phone and asked to be connected to Santosh's room. No answer. It was still early enough that he and his colleagues probably hadn't returned from dinner. She took a seat on a sofa with a wall of cascading water behind it. The décor was a distant relative of the interior of Charlotte and Oliver's house, and something about that gave her confidence in what she was doing. She was the daughter of audacious, obstinate Oliver. This behavior was her birthright.

She had a clear view of the entrance. If Santosh came in, she couldn't miss him. She was so reassured by this thought, she fell asleep.

She was woken up by the sound of laughter, loud and roguish. On the other side of the lobby, she saw three of Santosh's colleagues entering the enormous glass doors while tossing a bean bag. They looked drunk, but whether on alcohol or the sheer joy of their success here, it was hard to know. They were celebrating with the rowdy pleasure of adolescents on the last day of school before summer break. They'd earned this celebration.

Santosh was not among them.

The bean bag got tossed and landed near her feet. Ryan Kwan, the colleague whose Instagram account she'd been following, came over to retrieve it. His double take upon seeing her had the exaggerated perfection of a cartoon character's. "Cecily?"

He was Santosh's age, tall and athletic, someone Santosh played soccer with on weekends. The previous January, before all the bad news had come her way, Ryan and Santosh had gone snowboarding in Wyoming. He was engaged to be married to his college sweetheart, but Cecily had always felt he was in love with Santosh. She didn't resent it a bit; Santosh deserved all the love that came his way.

"What the heck are you doing here?" he asked.

"Hi, Ryan. Big surprise, eh?"

"Yeah, I'll say. Does Santosh know you're here?"

"I thought I'd surprise him."

She could tell from the way he was looking at her—his eyes and open mouth saying more than he intended—that he was shocked she'd pull off such a stunt. She supposed all Santosh's friends viewed her as "serious" and maybe a little stuffy—her academic job and probably her age. "I tracked him down through your Instagram account."

"Nice," he said noncommittally. "Yeah, well, he'll be surprised, all right." He looked at her a little quizzically. "I had the feeling you guys were having a rough time."

He wasn't being coy in the way he phrased it, she knew. He wouldn't know any specifics. Santosh would never have discussed her with Ryan in any detail. Still, he was watchful of Santosh's moods and could read between the lines. Or maybe he knew something about someone else in Santosh's life. Men were more comfortable divulging their conquests than they were discussing their failures.

"We've been better," she said. "I was dealing with a lot of professional stuff, and I wasn't handling it very well. I came to talk it over with him."

Ryan tossed the bean bag and snatched it out of the air. Her problems, naturally, were not his.

"Tell me the truth, Ryan: Is he going to be upset I came?" Stupid question, she knew. These guys were loyal to each other. And now, because they were flush with the success they'd all created together, they were closer than ever. "Never mind," she said. "I'll find out soon enough."

Relieved, he tossed the bean bag back to his coworkers who were joking with the desk clerk. "The pool is great," he said and indicated it with his chin.

She could see it, blue and shimmering in the evening breeze, just outside the doors behind the reception desk. She wandered out. The air was sweet, cooling down now, the way it does at night in the desert. Maybe, if this job they were working on led to other things, Santosh would want to move here. She could imagine him in Southern California, with a climate that allowed for sports all year long. A move like that would make sense for him. He'd get away from his parents for a while, become successful in his field. She didn't know how much sense it made to her, or even if it was relevant to ask. She couldn't know the outcome of her case yet, but Neeta had been right: the smoke created by the Title IX investigation would trail behind her for a long time. It would be years before she'd have an appointment in academia untainted by this, and even if she were asked to stay at Deerpath, she knew she'd feel an uneasiness entering any meeting or classroom, much as she'd felt when entering a room with gossiping adults when she was a child.

What could she do? She'd trained her whole life for teaching; it was what made her happiest. And despite the mistakes she'd made with Lee, she knew she was a good teacher. Working for Molly was a fun diversion that paid better than she'd expected, but it wasn't her calling. If things didn't go her way in the case, she was ready to fight for her career, just as she'd fought for Tom. Just as she was now ready to fight for Santosh. The outcome was unknowable; the effort was what mattered.

She felt the breeze stir the air and went back inside to sit by her suitcase. As she was reentering the lobby, she saw Santosh walk in the front door. He was disheveled and beautiful, dressed in casual clothes she'd never seen before but that suited him perfectly, especially in this warm, balmy climate. His hair was longer and unkempt, perhaps from swims in the evening. He was with a lanky man and a small, dark-haired woman wearing a polo shirt that looked a lot like his. She had the flushed prettiness and spectacular calves of an athlete. Cecily felt something inside her sink and then, a moment later, a touch of happiness for Santosh.

But, no—that was adapting again. She was here to make her Tomorrow Tonight, or whatever murky advice Fiona had given in that book.

The lanky man put his arm around the pretty woman's waist, and the two of them left.

Cecily looked at Santosh until he sensed her eyes on him and glanced up. His face, as he walked toward her, was dark and serious, as angry as when they'd said goodbye on the street.

"Santosh," she said, "I just got off the plane. I came here from Boston. I was supposed to go to Deerpath for a meeting, but I canceled it. I'm not really sure what I'm going to do professionally, but I . . ."

"You came?" he asked, stern eyes piercing. "You tracked me down and you came here without even telling me? Is that what you're saying?"

"Yes," she said. "That's what I'm saying." For, what else could she say? The evidence was right in front of him.

His face changed, and he was smiling at her. "You came," he said, his voice full of tenderness, as if he'd been waiting for her to arrive the entire time he'd been there. "You came." He threw his arms around her and buried his face in her neck.

When she looked at him again, she saw that this wasn't going to be easy. It wasn't going to be clean, solved by a plane ticket and a night in a hotel. Everything worth having took a long time to get right, and you had to go into the effort knowing there were no guarantees of success.

"Can we go somewhere to talk?" she asked.

He looked around, down at the key card in his hand, at the elevators, and then nodded toward the pool. She picked up the handle of her bag. When they were halfway across the lobby, he reached out and took it from her. His hand brushed against hers and then lingered there for a few seconds before he pulled away. Such a small thing, but as she looked to the shimmering pool and listened to the suitcase wheels clattering on the tiles, she felt hope swelling within her.

Chapter Thirty-Eight

Dorothy was hooked up to a roomful of machines, each of them gasping, beeping, or sighing at different intervals. The fact that they were performing functions that her body should have been performing on its own meant she was being both kept alive and stripped of her humanity.

Once upon a time, Tom had felt foolish talking to people in this condition. It had the worst qualities of both hogging a conversation across a table and talking to yourself in public. Everyone said that hearing was the last thing to go, but how could you be sure? He imagined that, when he was in this state, he'd appreciate a little silence or perhaps some soft Mantovani playing in the background.

He sat at her bedside and took her hand. "It's Tom, Dorothy. Believe it or not, you don't look too bad. I mean, you look terrible, but honestly, I was expecting worse."

He felt a slight pressure on his hand, which he chose to interpret as her affirming to him that she'd heard.

"I suppose now would be a good time to give you a lecture on your finances," he said, one of the pointlessly lame jokes hospital visits invariably inspired. The bar for humor in these situations was low. "I saw the bill from your caterers. What the hell were you thinking?"

He felt her fingers lightly squeeze his hand. It put him at ease. This was a conversation, after all. He'd have to remember this for when he was in the position Dorothy was in now. Whose hand he'd be squeezing was another matter. It seemed increasingly likely to him that he was destined to be single for the rest of his life. If you had the right attitude, there was nothing sad in this. We're all destined to die alone, so why not live out one's old age alone and not have to deal with the inconvenience of a shared bathroom?

He realized, as he was making small talk, that he knew his sister's probable responses so well, he could easily fill in the blanks, guided by the pressure of her hand. Eventually, he got around to what he assumed was the information she most wanted to know.

"I'm sorry Cecily's not here," he said. "She's in L.A."

There was no response, probably an indication of disappointment.

"She doesn't know you're here. I found out before she left, but I didn't tell her. I hope you can forgive me for that. She and Santosh have been having serious problems. I suppose she told you that."

She'd tipped her head away from him, maybe in anger.

"The thing is, she got inspired to go out there to try to fix things, to confront him and tell him she wants to make their relationship work. You won't believe what inspired her. I barely believed it myself." He raised his voice enough to make sure she heard, whatever her state. "Fiona Snow's book! I'm not kidding you. That's ridiculous, isn't it? Fiona made a mess of things with Oliver and Charlotte, but maybe that's for the best, too. You were right about her after all. She's the one who got Cecily to fight for herself. Maybe knowing about Oliver, too. So, you see, the plans you had with Fiona, the whole weekend, even the gala itself—they were a triumph. You changed her life."

Tom gazed off out the window. It gave onto the windows in another wing of the hospital, all lit by hideous fluorescent light. This was a design flaw, but probably the best they could have done with the limited space and the years between the many additions. When he looked back to the bed, Dorothy had moved her head a fraction, turned back toward him. She was, indisputably, smiling. He took her hand and kissed it.

It was impossible to know if she'd make it through the next twenty-four hours, but the smile was encouraging. And what if she did pull through? At best, she'd need time in rehab. There would be endless trips to doctors and physical therapists. Driving would be out of the question, at least initially. She couldn't live on her own. That building of hers was completely inaccessible to a person with any of the challenges she'd face, and the elevator was now a fantasy. Depending on how far she came back, there were nursing homes, but he couldn't have her out here with no one to oversee her care.

His future was clear. He had to tell Dorothy what he was going to do for her, but he couldn't do it yet. He first had to take a stand for himself.

"When you get out of here," he said, "we'll talk about next steps. I don't want you to worry. I'll arrange it. You know I'll figure it out." He had to force himself to say what came next. "But, Jesus, Dorothy, it's been an awful lot for me all these years. Ever since Dad died. It's been my job. My life, when you come down to it. It's not that I regret it, but I do need to tell you. The time, the money, the way it's made my own choices secondary—you know how I feel about Cecily, so I'd do it again in a minute, but it's cost me everything. Even Alan. I don't want any thanks, I just want you to acknowledge it, even if it's painful for you to do it."

He saw that she had tears in her eyes and was looking directly at him. He was going to interpret this as her having understood. She was trying to say something, but she was too hoarse for him to hear. She squeezed his hand so tightly it nearly hurt and pulled him toward her. He told her more. About his journal, their mother's accusation—all of it coming out in a rush. It was easier to do than he'd imagined it would be for so many decades and was not shameful at all.

"You'll come back to Boston," he said. "You can move into the cottage. I know it's small, but it's accessible and has amazing climate control. You can pretend the outside world doesn't exist. We'll see how much we can get for your monstrosity out here. We'll make it work somehow. I'll make it work."

Here he was, once again, volunteering to shoulder the burden, take on more weight, disrupt his whole life. But at a certain point, you have to accept that your life is the choices you've made, and you'd better learn to be happy with them.

The rain was still lashing against the window with demented intensity. And yet there was something dazzling about the way the light from the surrounding buildings was hitting it and making it into rivers of orange and red. There was music in the sound of it washing down the glass and over the sill. So maybe—even in the catastrophic—it was possible to find something beautiful. Maybe Charlotte's guesthouse was only part of his legacy. It was best to believe his real masterpiece was the care he'd given Cecily and Dorothy all these years. That was the one true, loving project he'd been working on his whole life. Steel and glass and concrete would all endure, but in the end they couldn't compare with that.

Acknowledgments

Immense thanks to everyone at the Provincetown Public Library; the Athenaeum in St. Johnsbury, Vermont; the Woburn Public Library; the Forbes Library in Northampton, Massachusetts; and the Space on Main Street in Bradford, Vermont.

Thanks also to Christopher Castellani and Justin Smotherman. Also, for sharing their time and expertise, to Paul Brouillette, Paul Rovinelli, and several others who wish to remain anonymous.

Thanks to Amy Einhorn, Denise Roy, and Denise Shannon. Also, belatedly, to Amelia Possanza and Nancy Trypuc. Also to Conor Mintzer. Also to Amy Hoffman and Anita Diamant. Also to Lisa Pannella and Barbara Strauss.

Much love to Patti, Chuck, Robbie, Danielle, Matt, Brooke, Jack, and Alice.

Also to Sebastian Stuart.

About the Author

Stephen McCauley is the author of seven previous novels, including the national bestsellers *My Ex-Life*, *The Object of My Affection*, and *Alternatives to Sex*. Three of his books have been made into feature films. The *New York Times Book Review* dubbed him "the secret love child of Edith Wharton and Woody Allen," and the French Ministry of Culture named him a Chevalier of the Order of Arts and Letters. He currently codirects the creative writing program at Brandeis University.